The Hand In The Dark

By Arthur J. Rees

Originally published in 1920

The Hand In The Dark

© 2010 Resurrected Press

Published by Intrepid Ink, LLC

Intrepid Ink, LLC provides full publishing services to authors of fiction and non-fiction books, eBooks and websites. From editing to formatting, to publishing, to marketing, Intrepid Ink gets your creative works into the hands of the people who want to read them.
Find out more at www.IntrepidInk.com.

ISBN 13: 978-1-935774-00-6

Printed in the United States of America

FOREWORD

Though born in Australia, Arthur J. Rees (Arthur John), came to know his adopted land of England and its people quite well. His writings are full of descriptions of the different classes and regions of the country, from the West End of London to the remote coasts of Norfolk and Cornwall. Of particular interest are his observations of the inner workings of the police and the interactions of the various levels within the force from the local constable to the chief superintendent. At least one source makes the claim that Rees worked for a time at Scotland Yard. Whether it was from this or from his experiences as a newspaperman he gives a realistic picture of the tensions between subordinate detectives and their superiors. Yet his characterizations of the police are carefully nuanced. The upper echelons are depicted not as bumblers, but as drawing from experiences with common criminals rather than those driven by passion, and perhaps being more concerned with politics both internal and external, than justice. Rees's police are not the clichéd buffoons often found in mysteries, but instead are overworked civil servants looking for the path of least resistance. Yet, when confronted with the truth, they are accepting, if sometimes reluctantly, of outcomes contrary to their own initial prejudices.

His portraits of the English upper class are also less than flattering. Many are portrayed as rather shallow individuals, spendthrift in their ways and more interested in golf and shooting than anything else. The life of the country gentry is also shown to be less glamorous than it would appear on the surface, rigid and routine, and rife with prejudice against the lower classes. For all this, Rees seems to have a fascination with the old families of Britain, those who can trace their roots to the Norman Conquest or beyond.

While an interesting mystery, *The Hand in the Dark* also provides a glimpse into a life and time that has now vanished.

About the Author

Arthur J. Rees (Arthur John 1872-1942) was born in Australia and worked as a newspaperman before moving to England in his twenties. He wrote numerous mystery novels starting with the Merry Marauders in 1913. He collaborated with John R. Watson on two books, *The Hampstead Mystery* (1916) and *The Mystery of the Downs* (1928). Other works include *The Shrieking Pit* (1919), *The Hand in the Dark* (1920) and *The Moon Rock* (1922). His last book, *The Single Clue* was published shortly before his death in 1940. At least one advertisement for *The Hampstead Mystery* makes a claim that he worked for Scotland Yard at one point, but we have been unable to confirm this fact.

Greg Fowlkes
Editor-In-Chief
Resurrected Press

1

Seen in the sad glamour of an English twilight, the old moat-house, emerging from the thin mists which veiled the green flats in which it stood, conveyed the impression of a habitation falling into senility, tired with centuries of existence. Houses grow old like the race of men; the process is not less inevitable, though slower; in both, decay is hastened by events as well as by the passage of Time.

The moat-house was not so old as English country-houses go, but it had aged quickly because of its past. There was a weird and bloody history attached to the place: an historical record of murders and stabbings and quarrels dating back to Saxon days, when a castle had stood on the spot, and every inch of the flat land had been drenched in the blood of serfs fighting under a Saxon tyrant against a Norman tyrant for the sacred catchword of Liberty.

The victorious Norman tyrant had killed the Saxon, taken his castle, and tyrannized over the serfs during his little day, until the greater tyrant, Death, had taught him his first—and last—lesson of humility. After his death some fresh usurper had pulled down his stolen castle, and built a moat-house on the site. During the next few hundred years there had been more fighting for restless ambition, invariably connected with the making and unmaking of tyrants, until an English king lost his head in the cause of Liberty, and the moat-house was destroyed by fire for the same glorious principle.

It was rebuilt by the freebooter who had burnt it down; one Philip Heredith, a descendant of Philip Here-Deith, whose name is inscribed in the Domesday Book as one of the knights of the army of Duke William which had assembled at Dives for the conquest of England. Philip Heredith, who was as great a fighter as his Norman ancestor, established his claim to his new estate, and avoided litigation concerning it, by confining the Royalist owner and his family within the walls of the moat-house before setting it on fire. He afterwards married and settled down in the new house with his young wife. But the honeymoon was disturbed by the ghost of the cavalier he had incinerated, who warned him that as he had founded his line in horror it would end in horror, and the house he had built would fall to the ground.

Philip Heredith, like many other great fighters, was an exceedingly pious man, with a profound belief in the efficacy of prayer. He endeavoured to thwart the ghost's curse by building a church in the moat-house grounds, where he spent his Sundays praying for the eternal welfare of the gentleman he had cut off in the flower of his manhood. Perhaps the prayers were heard, for, when Philip Heredith in the course of time became the first occupant of the brand-new vault he had built for himself and his successors, he left behind him much wealth, and a catalogue of his virtues in his own handwriting. The wealth he left to his heirs, but he expressly stipulated that the record of his virtues was to be carved in stone and placed as an enduring tablet, for the edification of future generations, inside the church he had built.

It was a wise precaution on his part. The dead are dumb as to their own merits, and the living think only of themselves. Time sped away, until the first of the Herediths was forgotten as completely as though he had never existed; even his dust had been crowded off the shelf of his own vault to make room for the numerous descendants of the prolific and prosperous line he had founded. But the tablet remained, and the old moat-house he had built still stood.

It was a wonderful old place and a delight to the eye, this mediæval moat-house of mellow brick, stone facings, high-pitched roof, with terraced gardens and encircling moat. It had defied Time better than its builder, albeit a little shakily, with signs of decrepitude here and there apparent in the crow's-feet cracks of the brickwork, and decay only too plainly visible in the crazy angles of the tiled roof. But the ivy which covered portions of the brickwork hid some of the ravages of age, and helped the moat-house to show a brave front to the world, a well-preserved survivor of an ornamental period in a commonplace and ugly generation.

The place looked as though it belonged to the past and the ghosts of the past. To cross the moat bridge was to step backward from the twentieth century into the seventeenth. The moss-grown moat walls enclosed an old-world garden, most jealously guarded by high yew hedges trimmed into fantastic shapes of birds and animals; a garden of parterres and lawns, where tritons blew stone horns, and naked nymphs bathed in marble fountains; with an ancient sundial on which the gay scapegrace Suckling had once scribbled a sonnet to a pair of blue eyes–a garden full of sequestered walks and hidden nooks where courtly cavaliers and bewitching dames in brocades and silks, patches and powder, had played at the great game of love in their day. That day was long since dead. The tritons and nymphs remained, to remind humanity that stone and marble are more durable than flesh and blood, but the lords and ladies had gone, never to return, unless, indeed, their spirits walked the garden in the white stillness of moonlit nights. They may well have done so. It was easy to imagine such light-hearted beauties visiting again the old garden to revive dead memories of love and laughter: shadowy forms stealing forth to assignations on the blanched, dew-laden lawn, their roguish faces and bright eyes–if ghosts have eyes–peeping out of ghostly hoods at gay ghostly cavaliers; coquetting and languishing behind ghostly fans; perhaps even feeding, with ghostly little hands, the peacocks which still kept the terrace walk above the moat.

The spectacle of a group of modern ladies laughing and chatting at tea in the cloistered recesses of the terrace garden struck a note as sharply incongruous as a flock of parrots chattering in a cathedral.

It was the autumn of 1918, and with one exception the ladies seated at the tea-tables on the lawn represented the new and independent type of womanhood called into existence by the national exigencies of war. The elder of them looked useful rather than beautiful, as befitted patriotic Englishwomen in war-time; the younger ones were pretty and charming, but they were all workers, or pretended workers, in the task of helping England win the war, and several of them wore the khaki or blue of active service abroad. They were all very much at ease, laughing and talking as they drank their tea and threw cake to the peacocks perched on the high terrace walk above their heads.

The ladies were the guests of Sir Philip Heredith. Some months before, his only son Philip, then holding a post in the War Office, had fallen in love with the pretty face of a girl employed in one of the departments of Whitehall. He married her soon afterwards, and brought her home to the moat-house. It was the young husband who had suggested that they should liven up the old moat-house by inviting some of their former London friends down to stay with them. Violet Heredith, who found herself bored with country life after the excitement of London war work, caught eagerly at the idea, and the majority of the ladies at tea were the former Whitehall acquaintances of the young wife, with whom she had shared matinée tickets and afternoon teas in London during the last winter of the war.

The hostess of the party, Miss Alethea Heredith, sister of the present baronet, Sir Philip Heredith, and mistress of the moat-house since the death of Lady Heredith, belonged to a bygone and almost extinct type of Englishwoman, the provincial great lady, local society leader, village patroness, sportswoman, and churchwoman in one, a type exclusively English, taking several centuries to produce in its finished form. Miss Heredith was an excellent, if somewhat terrific, specimen of the class. She was tall and massive, with a large-boned face, tanned red with country air, shrewd grey eyes looking out beneath thick eyebrows which met across her forehead in a straight line (the Heredith eyebrows) and a strong, hooked nose (the Heredith falcon nose). But in spite of her massive frame, red face, hooked nose, and countrified attire, she looked more in place with the surroundings than the frailer and paler specimens of womanhood to whom she was dispensing tea. There was a stiff and stately grace in her movements, a slow ceremoniousness, in her politeness to her guests, which seemed to harmonize with the seventeenth-century setting of the moat-house garden.

At the moment the ladies were discussing an event which had been arranged for that night: a country drive, to be followed by a musical evening and dance. The invitations had been issued by the Weynes, a young couple who had recently made their home in the county. The husband was a popular novelist, who had left the distractions of London in order to win fame in peace and quietness in the country. Mrs. Weyne, who had been slightly acquainted with Mrs. Heredith before her marriage, was delighted to learn she was to have her for a neighbour. She had arranged the evening on her behalf, and had asked Miss Heredith to bring all her guests. The event was to mark the close of the house party, which was to break up on the following day. Unfortunately, Mrs. Heredith had fallen ill a few hours previously, and it was doubtful whether she would be able to join in the festivity.

"I hope you will all remember that dinner is to be a quarter of an hour earlier to-night," said Miss Heredith, as she handed a cup of tea to one of her guests. "It is a long drive to the Weynes' place, so I shall order the cars for half-past seven."

The guests glanced at their hostess and murmured polite assent. "I am looking forward to the visit so much," said the lady to whom Miss Heredith had handed the cup. "It will be so romantic–a country dance in a lonely house on a hill. What an adorable cup, dear Miss Heredith! I love Chinese egg-shell porcelain, but this is simply beyond anything! It's—"

"Whatever induced Dolly Weyne to bury herself in the country?" abruptly exclaimed a young woman with cropped hair and khaki uniform. "She loathed the country before she was married."

"Mrs. Weyne is a wife, and it is her duty to like her husband's home," said Miss Heredith a little primly. She disapproved of the speaker, whose khaki uniform, close-cropped hair, crossed legs, and arms a-kimbo struck her as everything that was modern and unwomanly.

"Then what induced Teddy Weyne to bury himself alive in the wilds? I'm sure it must be terrible living up there alone, with nothing but earwigs and owls for company."

"Mr. Weyne is a writer," rejoined Miss Heredith. "He needs seclusion."

"My husband doesn't," said a little fair-haired woman. "He says newspaper men can write anywhere. And we know another writer, a Mr. Harland, I think his name is, who writes long articles in the Sunday newspapers—"

"I don't think his name is Harland, dear," interrupted another lady. "Something like it, but not Harland. Dear me, what is it?"

"Oh, the name doesn't matter," retorted her friend. "The point is that he writes long articles in his London office. Why can't Mr. Weyne do the same?"

"Mr. Weyne is a novelist–not a journalist. It's quite a different thing."

"Is it?" responded the other doubtfully. "All writing is the same, isn't it? Harry says Mr. Harland's articles are dreadfully clever. He sometimes reads bits of them to me."

"Mrs. Weyne feels a little lonely sometimes," said Miss Heredith. "She has been looking forward to meeting Violet again. It will be pleasant for both of them to renew their acquaintance."

"I should think she and Violet would get on well together," remarked the young lady with the short hair. "They both have a good many tastes in common. Neither likes the country, for one thing." The other ladies looked at one another, and the speaker, realizing that she had been tactless, stopped abruptly. "How is Violet?" she added lamely. "Do you think she will be well enough to go to-night?"

"I still hope she may be well enough to go," replied Miss Heredith. "I will ask her presently. Will anyone have another cup of tea?"

Nobody wanted any more tea. The meal was finished; but the groups of ladies at the little tables sat placidly talking, enjoying the peaceful surroundings and the afternoon sun. Some of the girls produced cigarette-cases, and lit cigarettes.

There was a sound of footsteps on the gravel walk. A tall, good-looking young officer was seen walking across the garden from the house. As he neared the tea-tables he smilingly raised a finger to his forehead in salute.

"I've come to say good-bye," he announced.

The ladies clustered around him. It was evident from their manner that he was a popular figure among them. Several of the younger girls addressed him as "Dick," and asked him to send them trophies from the front. The young officer held his own amongst them with laughing self-possession. When he had taken his farewell of them he approached Miss Heredith, and held out his hand with a deferential politeness which contrasted rather noticeably with the easy familiarity of his previous leave-taking.

"I am sorry you are compelled to leave us, Captain Nepcote," said Miss Heredith, rising with dignity to accept his outstretched hand. "Do you return immediately to the front?"

"To-night, I expect."

"I trust you will return safely to your native land before long, crowned with victory and glory."

Captain Nepcote bowed in some embarrassment. Like the rest of his generation, he was easily discomposed by fine words or any display of the finer feelings. He was about twenty-eight, of medium height, clean-shaven, with clear-cut features, brown hair, and blue eyes. At the first glance he conveyed nothing more than an impression of a handsome young English officer of the familiar type turned out in thousands during the war; but as he stood there talking, a sudden ray of sunlight falling on his bared head revealed vague lines in the face and a suspicion of silver in the closely cropped hair, suggesting something not altogether in keeping with his debonair appearance—secret trouble or dissipation, it was impossible to say which.

"Will you say good-bye to Mrs. Heredith for me?" he said, after a slight pause. "I hope she will soon be better. I have said good-bye to Sir Philip and Phil. Sir Philip wanted to drive me to the station, but I know something of the difficulties of getting petrol just now, and I wouldn't allow him. Awfully kind of him! Phil suggested walking down with me, but I thought it would be too much for him."

They had walked away from the tea-tables towards the bridge which spanned the entrance to the moat-house. Miss Heredith paused by two brass cannon, which stood on the lawn in a clump of ornamental foliage, with an inscription stating that they had been taken from the *Passe-partout*, a French vessel captured by Admiral Heredith in the Indian Seas in 1804.

"It is hard for Phil, a Heredith, to remain behind when all young Englishmen are fighting for their beloved land," she said softly, her eyes fixed upon these obsolete pieces of ordnance. "He comes of a line of great warriors. However," she went on, in a more resolute tone, "Phil has his duties to fulfil, in spite of his infirmity. We all have our duties, thank God. Good-bye, Captain Nepcote. I am keeping you, and you may miss your train."

"Good-bye, Miss Heredith. Thank you so much for your kindness during a very pleasant visit. I've enjoyed myself awfully."

"I am glad that you have enjoyed your stay. I hope you will come and see us again when your military duties permit."

"Er–yes. Thank you awfully. Thank you once more for your kindness."

The young officer uttered these polite platitudes of a guest's farewell with some abruptness, bowed once more, and turned away across the old stone bridge which spanned the moat.

2

Miss Heredith turned her steps towards the house. The guests had dispersed while she was saying farewell to Captain Nepcote, and nothing further was expected of her as a hostess until dinner-time. It was her daily custom to devote a portion of the time between tea and dinner to superintending the arrangements for the latter meal. The moat-house possessed a competent housekeeper and an excellent staff of servants, but Miss Heredith believed in seeing to things herself.

On her way to the house she caught sight of an under gardener clipping one of the ornamental terrace hedges on the south side of the house, and she crossed over to him. The man suspended his work as the great lady approached, and respectfully waited for her to speak.

"Thomas," said Miss Heredith, "go and tell Linton to have both motors and the carriage at the door by half-past seven this evening. And tell him, Thomas, that Platt had better drive the carriage."

The under gardener touched his cap and hastened away on his errand. Miss Heredith leisurely resumed her walk to the house, stopping occasionally to pluck up any weed which had the temerity to show its head in the trim flower-beds which dotted the wide expanse of lawn between the moat and the house. She entered the house through the porch door, and proceeded to the housekeeper's apartments.

Her knock at the door was answered by a very pretty girl, tall and dark, who flushed at the sight of Miss Heredith, and stood aside for her to enter. A middle-aged woman, with a careworn face and large grey eyes, dressed in black silk, was seated by the window sewing. She rose and came forward when she saw her visitor. She was

Mrs. Rath, the housekeeper, and the pretty girl was her daughter.

"How are you, Hazel?" said Miss Heredith, offering her hand to the girl. "It is a long time since I saw you. Why have you not been to see us lately?"

The girl appeared embarrassed by the question. She hesitated, and then, as if reassured by Miss Heredith's gracious smile, murmured that she had been so busy that she had very little time to herself.

"I thought they gave you an afternoon off every week at your place of employment," pursued Miss Heredith, seating herself in a chair which the housekeeper placed for her.

"Not always," replied Hazel. "At least, not lately. We have had such a lot of orders in."

"Do you like the millinery business, Hazel?"

"Very much indeed, Miss Heredith."

"Hazel is getting on nicely now," said her mother.

"I am very glad to hear it," responded Miss Heredith, in the same gracious manner. "You must come and see us oftener. I take a great interest in your welfare, Hazel. Now, Mrs. Rath."

There are faces which attract attention by the expression of the eyes, and the housekeeper's was one of them. Her face was thin, almost meagre, with sunken temples on which her greying hair was braided, but her large eyes were unnaturally bright, and had a strange look, at once timid and watchful. She now turned them on Miss Heredith as though she feared a rebuke.

"Mrs. Rath," said Miss Heredith, "I hope dinner will be served punctually at a quarter to seven this evening, as I arranged. And did you speak to cook about the poultry? She certainly should get more variety into her cooking."

"It is rather difficult for her just now, with the food controller allowing such a small quantity of butcher's meat," observed Mrs. Rath. "She really does her best."

"She manages very well on the whole, but she has many resources, such as poultry and game, which are denied to most households."

When Miss Heredith emerged from the housekeeper's room a little later she was quite satisfied that the dinner was likely to be as good as an arbitrary food controller would permit, and she ascended to her room to dress. In less than half an hour she reappeared, a rustling and dignified figure in black silk. She walked slowly along the passage from her room, and knocked at Mrs. Heredith's door.

"Come in!" cried a faint feminine voice within.

Miss Heredith opened the door gently, and entered the room. It was a spacious and ancient bedroom, with panelled walls and moulded ceiling. The Jacobean furniture, antique mirrors, and bedstead with silken drapings were in keeping with the room.

A girl of delicate outline and slender frame was lying on the bed. She was wearing a fashionable rest gown of soft silk trimmed with gold embroidery, her fair hair partly covered by a silk boudoir cap. By her side stood a small table, on which were bottles of eau-de-Cologne and lavender water, smelling salts in cut glass and silver, a gold cigarette case, and an open novel.

The girl sat up as Miss Heredith entered, and put her hands mechanically to her hair. Her fingers were loaded with jewels, too numerous for good taste, and amongst the masses of rings on her left hand the dull gold of the wedding ring gleamed in sober contrast. Her face was pretty, but too insignificant to be beautiful. She had large blue eyes under arching dark brows, small, regular features, and a small mouth with a petulant droop of the under lip. Her face was of the type which instantly attracts masculine attention. There was the lure of sex in the depths of the blue eyes, and provocativeness in the drooping lines of the petulant, slightly parted lips. There was a suggestion of meretriciousness in the tinted lips and the pretence of colour on the charming face. The close air of the room was drenched with the heavy atmosphere of perfumes, mingled with the pungent smell of cigarette smoke.

Miss Heredith took a seat by the bedside. The two women formed a striking contrast in types: the strong, rugged, practical country lady, and the fragile feminine devotee of beauty and personal adornment, who, in the course of time, was to succeed the other as the mistress of the moat-house. The difference went far beyond externals; there was a wide psychological gulf between them—the difference between a woman of healthy mind and calm, equable temperament, who had probably never bothered her head about the opposite sex, and a woman who was the neurotic product of a modern, nerve-ridden city; sexual in type, a prey to morbid introspection and restless desires.

The younger woman regarded Miss Heredith with a rather peevish glance of her large eyes. It was plain from the expression of her face that she disliked Miss Heredith and resented her intrusion, but it would have needed a shrewd observer to have deduced from Miss Heredith's face that her feeling towards her nephew's wife was one of dislike. There was nothing but constrained politeness in her voice as she spoke.

"How is your head now, Violet? Are you feeling any better?"

"No. My head is perfectly rotten." As she spoke, the girl pushed off her boudoir cap, and smoothed back the thick, fair hair from her forehead, with an impatient gesture, as though she found the weight intolerable.

"I am sorry you are still suffering. Will you be well enough to go to the Weynes' to-night?"

"I wouldn't dream of it. I wonder you can suggest it. It would only make me worse."

"Of course I shall explain to Mrs. Weyne. That is, unless you would like me to stay and sit with you. I do not like you to be left alone."

"There is not the slightest necessity for that," said Mrs. Heredith decisively. "Do go. I can ring for Lisette to sit with me if I feel lonely."

"Perhaps you would like Phil to remain with you?" suggested Miss Heredith.

"Oh, no! It would be foolish of him to stay away on my account. I want you all to go and enjoy yourselves, and not to fuss about me. At present I desire nothing so much as to be left alone."

"Very well, then." Miss Heredith rose at this hint. "Shall I send you up some dinner?"

"No, thank you. The housekeeper has just sent me some strong tea and dry toast. If I feel hungry later on I'll ring. But I shall try and sleep now."

"Then I will leave you. I have ordered dinner a little earlier than usual."

"What time is it now?" Violet listlessly looked at her jewelled wrist-watch as she spoke. "A quarter-past six—is that the right time?"

Miss Heredith consulted her own watch, suspended round her neck by a long thin chain.

"Yes, that is right."

"What time are you having dinner?"

"A quarter to seven."

"What's the idea of having it earlier?" asked the girl, propping herself up on her pillow with a bare white arm, and looking curiously at Miss Heredith.

"I have arranged for us to leave for the Weynes' at half-past seven. It is a long drive."

"I see." The girl nodded indifferently, as though her curiosity on the subject had subsided as quickly as it had arisen. "Well, I hope you will all have a good time." She yawned, and let her fair head fall back on the pillow. "Now I shall try and have a sleep. Please tell Phil not to disturb me. Tell him I've got one of my worst headaches. You are sure to be back late, and I don't want to be awakened."

She closed her eyes, and Miss Heredith turned to leave the room. As she passed the dressing-table her eyes fell upon a handsome jewel-case. As if struck by a sudden thought, she turned back to the bedside again.

"Violet," she said.

The girl half opened her eyes, and looked up at the elder woman from veiled lids. "Yes?" she murmured.

"Your necklace—I had almost forgotten. Mr. Musard goes back to town early in the morning, and he wishes to take it with him."

"Oh, it will have to wait until the morning. I don't know where the keys are, and I can't be bothered looking for them now." The girl turned her face determinedly away, and buried her head in the pillow, like a spoilt child.

Miss Heredith flushed slightly at the deliberate rudeness of the action, but did not press the request. She left the room, softly closing the door behind her. She walked slowly along the wide passage, hung with bugle tapestry, and paused for a while at a narrow window at the end of the gallery, looking out on the terrace gardens and soft green landscape beyond. The interview with her nephew's wife had tried her, and her reflections were rather bitter. For the twentieth time she asked herself why her nephew had fallen in love with this unknown girl from London, who loathed the country. From Miss Heredith's point of view, a girl who smoked and talked slang lacked all sense of the dignity of the high position to which she had been called, and was in every way unfitted to become the mother of the next male Heredith, if, indeed, she consented to bear an heir at all. It was Miss Heredith's constant regret that Phil had not married some nice girl of the county, in his own station of life, instead of a London girl.

Miss Heredith terminated her reflections with a sigh, and turned away from the window. She was above all things practical, and fully realized the folly of brooding over the inevitable, but the marriage of her nephew was a sore point with her. She proceeded in her stately way down the broad and shallow steps of the old staircase, hung with armour and trophies and family portraits. At the bottom of the stairs she encountered a manservant bearing a tray with sherry decanters and biscuits across the hall.

"Where is Mr. Philip?" she asked.

"I think he is in the billiard room, ma'am," the man replied.

Miss Heredith proceeded with rustling dignity to the billiard room. The click of billiard balls was audible before she reached it. The door was open, and inside the room several young men, mostly in khaki, were watching a game between a dark-haired man of middle age and a young officer. One or two of the men looked up as Miss Heredith entered, but the young officer went on stringing his break together with the mechanical skill of a billiard marker. Miss Heredith mentally characterized his action as another instance of the modern decay of manners. In her young days gentlemen always ceased playing when a lady entered the billiard room. The middle-aged player came forward, cue in hand, and asked her if she wanted anything.

"I am looking for Phil," she said. "I thought he was here."

"He was, but he has just gone to the library. He said he had some letters to write before dinner."

"Thank you." Miss Heredith turned away and walked to the library which, like the billiard room, was on the ground floor. She opened the door, and stepped into a large room with an interior which belonged to the middle ages. There was no intrusion of the twentieth-century in the great gloomy apartment with its faded arabesques and friezes, bronze candelabras, mediæval fittings, and heavy time-worn furniture.

The young man who sat writing at an ancient writing-table in the room was not out of harmony with the ancient setting. His face was of antique type–long, and narrow, and his long straight dark hair, brushed back from his brow, was in curious contrast to the close crop of a military generation of young men. His eyes were dark, and set rather deeply beneath a narrow high white forehead. He had the Heredith eyebrows and high-bridged nose; but, apart from those traditional features of his line, his rather intellectual face and slight frame had little in common with the portraits of the massive war-like Herediths which hung on the walls around him. He ceased writing and looked up as his aunt entered.

"I have just been to see Violet," Miss Heredith explained. "She says she is no better, and will not be able to accompany us to the Weynes' to-night. I suggested remaining with her, but she would not hear of it. She says she prefers to be alone. Do you think it is right to leave her? I should like to have your opinion. You understand her best, of course."

"I think if Violet desires to be alone we cannot do better than study her wishes," replied Phil. "I know she likes to be left quite to herself when she has a nervous headache."

"In that case we will go," responded Miss Heredith. "I have decided to have dinner a quarter of an hour earlier to enable us to leave here at half-past seven."

"I see," said the young man. "Is Violet having any dinner?"

"No. She has just had some tea and toast, and now she is trying to sleep. She does not wish to be disturbed– she asked me to tell you so." Miss Heredith glanced at her watch. "Dear me, it is nearly half-past six! I must go. Tufnell is *so* dilatory when quickness is requisite."

"Did you remind Violet about the necklace?" asked Phil, as his aunt turned to leave the library.

"Yes. She said she would send it down in the morning, before Vincent leaves."

Phil nodded, and returned to his letters. Miss Heredith left the room, and proceeded along the corridor to the big dining-room. An elderly man servant, grey and clean-shaven, permitted a faint deferential smile to appear on his features as she entered.

"Is everything quite right, Tufnell?" she asked.

Tufnell, the staid old butler, who had inherited his place from his father, bowed gravely, and answered decorously:

"Everything is quite right, ma'am."

Miss Heredith walked slowly round the spacious table, adjusting a knife here, a fork there, and giving an added touch to the table decorations. There was not the slightest necessity for her to do so, because the appointments were as perfect as they could be made by the hands of old servants who knew their mistress and her ways thoroughly. But it was Miss Heredith's nightly custom, and Tufnell, standing by the carved buffet, watched her with an indulgent smile, as he had done every evening during the last ten years.

While Miss Heredith was thus engaged, the door opened and Sir Philip Heredith entered the room in company with an old family friend, Vincent Musard.

3

Sir Philip Heredith was a dignified figure of an English country gentleman of the old type. He was tall and thin, aristocratic of mien, with white hair and faded blue eyes. His face was not impressive. At first sight it seemed merely that of a tired old man, weary of the paltry exactions of life, and longing for rest; but, at odd moments, one caught a passing resemblance to a caged eagle in a swift turn of the falcon profile, or in a sudden flash of the old eyes beneath the straight Heredith brows. At such times the Heredith face–the warrior face of a long line of fierce fighters and freebooting ancestors–leaped alive in the ageing features of the last but one of the race.

His companion was a man of about fifty-five. His face was brown, as though from hot suns, his close-cropped hair was silver-grey, and he had the bold, clear-cut features of a man quick to make up his mind and accustomed to command. His eyes were the strangest feature of his dominating personality. They were small and black, and appeared almost lidless, with something in their dark direct gaze like the unwinking glare of a snake. His apparel was unconventional, even for war-time, consisting of a worn brown suit with big pockets in the jacket, and a soft collar, with a carelessly arranged tie. On the little finger of his left hand he wore a ruby ring of noticeable size and lustre.

Vincent Musard was a remarkable personality. He came of a good county family, which had settled in Sussex about the same time that the first Philip Heredith had burnt down the moat-house, but his family tree extended considerably beyond that period. If the name of Here-Deith was inscribed in the various versions of the Roll of Battle Abbey to be seen in the British Museum, the name of Musard was to be found in the French roll of "Les Compagnons de Guillaume à la Conquête de l'Angleterre en 1066," the one genuine and authentic list, which has received the stamp of the French Archeological Society, and is carved in stone and erected in the Church of Dives on the coast of Normandy. Vincent Musard was the last survivor of an illustrious line, a bachelor, explorer, man of science, and connoisseur in jewels. He had been intended for the Church in his youth, but had quarrelled with it on a question of doctrine. Since then he had led a roving existence in the four corners of the earth, exploring, botanizing, shooting big game, and searching for big diamonds and rubies. He had written books on all sorts of out-of-the-way subjects, such as "The Flora of Chatham Islands," "Poisonous Spiders (genus Latrodectua) of Sardinia," "Fossil Reptilia and Moa Remains of New Zealand," and "Seals of the Antarctic." But his chief and greatest hobby was precious stones, of which he was a recognized expert.

His father had left him a comfortable fortune, but he had made another on his own account by his dealings in gems, which he collected in remote corners of the world and sold with great advantage to London dealers. He was intimately acquainted with all the known mines and pearl fisheries of the world, but his success as a dealer in jewels was largely due to the fact that he searched for them off the beaten track. He had explored Cooper's Creek for white sapphires, the Northern Territory for opals, and had once led an expedition into German New Guinea in search of diamonds, where he had narrowly escaped being eaten by cannibals.

The passage of time had not tamed the fierce restlessness of his disposition. Although he was not quite such a rover as of yore, the discovery of a new diamond field in Brazil, or the news of a new pearl bed in southern seas, was sufficient to set him packing for another jaunt half round the world. He was the oldest friend of the Herediths, and Miss Heredith, in particular, had a high opinion of his qualities. Musard, on his part, made no secret of the fact that he regarded Miss Heredith as the best of living women. It had, indeed, been rumoured in the county a quarter of a century before that Vincent Musard and Alethea Heredith were "going to make a match of it."

It was, perhaps, well for both that the match was never made. Musard had departed for one of his tours into the wilds of the world, not to return to England until five years had elapsed. Their mutual attraction was the attraction of opposites. There was nothing in common except mutual esteem between a wild, tempestuous being like Musard, who rushed through life like a whirlwind, forever seeking new scenes in primitive parts of the earth, and the tranquil mistress of the moat-house, who had rarely been outside her native county, and revolved in the same little circle year after year, happy in her artless country pursuits and simple pleasures.

Of late years, Musard had spent most of his brief stays in England with the Herediths. He had his own home, which was not far from the moat-house, but he was a companionable man, and preferred the warm welcome and kindly society of his old friends to the solitary existence of a bachelor at Brandreth Hall, as his own place was named.

He had recently returned to England after a year's wanderings in the southern hemisphere, and had arrived at the moat-house on the previous day, bringing with him a dried alligator's head with gaping jaws, a collection of rare stuffed birds and snakeskins for Phil, who had a taste in that direction, and a carved tiki god for Miss Heredith. He had also brought with him his Chinese servant, two kea parrots, and a mat of white feathers from the Solomon Islands, which he used on his bed instead of an eiderdown quilt when the nights were cold. He had left in his London banker's strong room his latest collection of precious stones, after forwarding anonymously to Christie's a particularly fine pearl as a donation towards the British Red Cross necklace.

Musard's present stay at the moat-house was to be a brief one. The British Government, on learning of his return to his native land, had asked him to go over to the front to adjust some trouble which had arisen between the head-men of a Kaffir labour compound. As Musard's wide knowledge of African tribes rendered him peculiarly fitted for such a task, he had willingly complied with the request, and was to go to France on the following day.

Miss Heredith had taken advantage of his brief visit to consult him about the Heredith pearl necklace—a piece of jewellery which was perhaps more famous than valuable, as some of the pearls were nearly three hundred years old. Sir Philip had given it to Violet when she married Phil. But Violet had locked it away in her jewel-case and never worn it. She had said, only the night before, that the setting of the clasp was old-fashioned, and the pearls dull with age. Miss Heredith, although much hurt, had realized that there was some truth in the complaint, and she had asked Musard for his advice. Musard had expressed the opinion that perhaps the pearls were in need of the delicate operation known as "skinning," and had offered to take the necklace to London and obtain the opinion of a Hatton Garden expert of his acquaintance.

Vincent Musard smiled at Miss Heredith in friendly fashion as he entered the dining-room, and Sir Philip greeted his sister with polite, but somewhat vague courtesy. Sir Philip's manner to everybody was distinguished by perfect urbanity, which was so impersonal and unvarying as to suggest that it was not so much a compliment to those upon whom it was bestowed as a duty which he felt he owed to himself to perform with uniform exactitude.

Musard began to talk about the arrangements for his departure the following day, and asked Tufnell about the trains. On learning that the first train to London was at eight o'clock, he expressed his intention of catching it.

"Is it necessary for you to go so early, Vincent?" inquired Miss Heredith. "Could you not take a later train?"

"I daresay I could. Why do you ask?"

"I was thinking about the necklace. Violet was too unwell to give it to me to-night, and she may not be awake so early in the morning. I should like you to take it with you, if it could be managed."

"I can take a later train. It will suit me as well."

"Is Violet unable to go with us to the Weynes' to-night?" said Sir Philip, glancing at his sister.

"Yes; her head is too bad."

"It is a pity we have to go without her, as the party is given in her honour. Of course, we must go."

"Where is her necklace?" asked Musard. "Is it in the safe?"

"No," replied Miss Heredith. "It is in Violet's room, in her jewel-case."

"Well, as Mrs. Heredith will be alone in the house to-night, I think it would be wise if you locked it in the safe," said Musard. "There are many servants in the house."

"I think that is quite unnecessary, Vincent. Our servants are all trustworthy."

"Quite so, but several of your guests have brought their own servants—maids and valets."

"Very well. If you think so, Vincent, I will see to it after dinner."

The conversation was terminated by the sound of the dinner-gong. The guests came down to dinner in ones and twos, and assembled in the drawing-room before proceeding to the dining-room. The men who were not in khaki were dressed for dinner. The gathering formed a curious mixture of modern London and ancient England. The London guests, who were in the majority, consisted of young officers, some young men from the War Office and

the Foreign Office, a journalist or two, and the ladies
Miss Heredith had entertained at tea on the lawn. These
people had been invited because they were friends of the
young couple, and not because they were anybody
particular in the London social or political world, though
one or two of the young men had claims in that direction.
Mingled with this very modern group were half a dozen
representatives of old county families, who had been
invited by Miss Heredith.

The party sat down to dinner. There were one or two
murmurs of conventional regret when Miss Heredith
explained the reason of Mrs. Heredith's vacant place, but
the majority of the London guests–particularly the female
portion–recognized the illness as a subterfuge and
accepted it with indifference. If Mrs. Heredith was bored
with her guests they, on their part, were tired of their
visit. The house party had not been a success. The
London visitors found the fixed routine of life in a country
house monotonous and colourless, and were looking
forward to the termination of their visit. The life they had
led for the past fortnight was not their way of life. They
met each morning for breakfast at nine o'clock–Miss
Heredith was a stickler for the mid-Victorian etiquette of
everybody sitting down together at the breakfast table.
After breakfast the men wandered off to their own
devices for killing time: some to play a round of golf,
others to go shooting or fishing, generally not reappearing
until dinner-time. After dinner they played billiards or
auction bridge, and the ladies knitted war socks or
sustained themselves till bedtime with copious draughts
of the mild stimulant supplied by their favourite lady
novelists. At half-past ten o'clock Tufnell entered with a
tray of glasses, and the guests partook of a little
refreshment. At eleven Miss Heredith bade her visitors a
stately good-night, and they retired to their bedrooms.
The great lady of the moat-house was a firm believer in
the axiom that a woman should be mistress in her own
household, and she saw no reason why her guests should

not adopt her way of life while under her roof. She was a country woman born and bred, believing in the virtues of an early bed and early rising, and she was not to be put out of her decorous regular way of living by Londoners who turned night into day with theatres, late suppers, night clubs, and other pernicious forms of amusement which Miss Heredith had read about in the London papers.

Dinner at the moat-house was a solemn and ceremonious function. In accordance with the time-honoured tradition of the family, it was served at the early hour of seven o'clock in the big dining-room, an ancient chamber panelled with oak to the ceiling, with a carved buffet, an open fireplace, Jacobean mantelpiece, and old family portraits on the walls. There were sconces on the walls, and a crystal chandelier for wax candles was suspended from the centre of the ceiling above the table. The chandelier was never lit, as the moat-house was illuminated by electric light, but it looked very pretty, and was the apple of Miss Heredith's eye—as the maidservants were aware, to their cost.

The dinner that night was, as usual, very simple, as befitted a patriotic English household in war-time, but the wines made up for the lack of elaborate cooking. Sir Philip Heredith and his sister followed their King's example of abstaining from wine during the duration of war, but it was not in accordance with Sir Philip's idea of hospitality to enforce abstinence on their guests, and the men, at all events, sipped the rare old products of the Heredith cellars with unqualified approval, enhanced by painful recollections of the thin war claret and sugared ports of London clubs. Such wine, they felt, was not to be passed by. Of the young men, Phil Heredith alone drank water, not for the same reason as his father, but because he had always been a water drinker.

Under the influence of the good wine the guests brightened up considerably as the meal proceeded. Sir

Philip, in his old-fashioned way, raised his glass of aerated water to one and another of the young men. He was an ideal host, and his unfailing polished courtesy hid the fact that he was looking forward to the break up of the party with a relief akin to that felt by the majority of his guests. Conversation had been confined to monosyllables at first, but became quite flourishing and animated as the dinner went on. Miss Heredith smiled and looked pleased. As a hostess, she liked to see her guests happy and comfortable, even if she did not like her guests.

The conversation was mainly about the war: the Allies' plans and hopes and fears. Several of the young men from London gave their views with great authority, criticising campaigns and condemning generals. Phil Heredith listened to this group without speaking. Two country gentlemen in the vicinity also listened in silence. They were amazed to hear such famous military names, whom they had been led by their favourite newspapers to regard as the hope of the country's salvation, criticised so unmercifully by youngsters.

"And do you think the war will soon be over, Mr. Brimley?" said a feminine voice, rather loudly, during a lull in the conversation. The speaker was a near neighbour and friend of Miss Heredith's, Mrs. Spicer, who was not a member of the house party, but had been invited to dinner that night and was going to the Weynes' afterwards. She was stout and fresh-faced, and looked thoroughly good-natured and kind-hearted.

She addressed her question to a tall young man with prematurely grey hair, prominent eyes, and a crooked nose. His name was Brimley, and he was well-known in London journalism. His portrait occasionally appeared in the picture papers as "one of the young lions of Fleet Street," but his enemies preferred to describe him as one of Lord Butterworth's jackals—Lord Butterworth being the millionaire proprietor of an influential group of newspapers which, during the war, had stood for "the last drop of blood and the last shilling" rallying cry. As one of the foremost of this group of patriots, Mr. Brimley had let his ink flow so freely in the Allies' cause that it was whispered amongst those "in the know" that he was certain for a knighthood, or at least an Empire Order, in the next list of honours.

Mr. Brimley looked at the speaker haughtily, and made an inaudible reply. Although he was a lion of Fleet Street, he did not relish being called upon to roar in the wilds of Sussex.

"Won't the poor German people be delighted when our troops march across the Rhine to deliver them from militarism," continued the old lady innocently.

There was a subdued titter from the younger girls at this, and a young officer sitting near the bottom of the table laughed aloud, then flushed suddenly at his breach of manners.

"Have I said something foolish?" asked the old lady placidly. "Please tell me if I have–I don't mind."

"Not at all," said another young officer, with a beardless sunburnt face. "Personally, I quite agree with you. The Germans ought to be jolly well pleased to be saved from their beastly selves."

"What a number of land girls you have in this part of the world, Miss Heredith," remarked the young officer who had laughed, as though anxious to turn the conversation. "I saw several while I was out shooting to-day, and very charming they looked. I had no idea that sunburn was so becoming to a girl's complexion. I saw one girl who had been riding a horse through the woods, and she looked like what's-her-name–Diana. She had bits of green stuff sticking all over her, and cobwebs in her hair."

"That reminds me of a good story," exclaimed a chubby-faced youth in the uniform of the Flying Corps. "You'll appreciate it, Denison. Old Graham, of the Commissariat, was out golfing the other day, and he turned up at the club all covered with cobwebs. Captain

Harding, of our lot, who was just back in Blighty from eighteen months over there, said to him, 'Hullo, Graham, I see you've been down at the War Office.' Ha, ha!"

The other young men in khaki joined in the laugh, but a tall gaunt man with an authoritative glance, the Denison referred to, looked rather angry. Miss Heredith, with a hostess's watchful tact for the suspectibilities of her guests, started to talk about a show for allotment holders which had been held in the moat-house grounds a few weeks before. It seemed that most of the villagers were allotment holders, and the show had been held to stimulate their patriotic war efforts to increase the national food supply. The village had entered into it with great spirit, and some wonderful specimens of fruit, vegetables, poultry and rabbits had been exhibited.

"The best part of it was that Rusher, my own gardener, was beaten badly in every class," put in Sir Philip, with a smile.

"Not in every class," corrected Miss Heredith. "The peaches and nectarines from the walled garden were awarded first prize."

"Rusher was beaten in the vegetable classes—in giant vegetable marrows and cabbages," retorted Sir Philip, with a chuckle. "He hasn't got over it yet. He suspects the vicar of favouritism in awarding the prizes. The fact that his daughter won first prize for rabbits with a giant Belgian did little to console him."

"And we raised quite a respectable sum for the Red Cross by charging threepence admission to see a stuffed menagerie of Phil's," added Miss Heredith.

"A stuffed menagerie! What a curious thing," remarked a young lady.

"Not quite a menagerie," said Sir Philip. "Merely the stuffed remains of some animals Phil used to keep as a youngster. When they died—as they invariably did—he used to skin them and stuff them. He was quite an expert taxidermist."

"Tell them about your museum exhibit, Philip," said Miss Heredith, with quite an animated air.

"We also arranged a little exhibition of–er–old things," continued Sir Philip diffidently. "Armour, miniatures, some old jewels, and things like that. That also brought in quite a respectable sum for the Red Cross."

"From the Heredith collection, I presume?" said Mr. Brimley.

"What wonderful old treasures you must have in this wonderful old house of yours," gushed the young lady who had spoken before. "I am so disappointed in not seeing the Heredith pearl necklace. What a pity dear Mrs. Heredith is ill. She was going to wear the pearls to-night, and now I shall have to go away without seeing them."

Sir Philip bowed. He did not quite relish the trend of the conversation, but he was too well-bred to show it.

"You shall see the pearls in the morning," said Miss Heredith courteously.

"I adore pearls," sighed the guest.

"If you admire pearls, you should see the collection which is being made for the British Red Cross," remarked Vincent Musard. "I had a private view the other day. It is a truly magnificent collection."

All eyes were turned on the speaker. The topic interested every lady present, and they were aware that Musard was one of the foremost living authorities on jewels. The men had all heard of the famous traveller by repute, and they wanted to listen to what he had to say. Musard seemed rather embarrassed to find himself the object of general attention, and went on with his dinner in silence. But some of the ladies were determined not to lose the opportunity of learning something from such a well-known expert on a subject so dear to their hearts, and they plied him with eager questions.

"It must be a wonderful collection," said a slight and slender girl named Garton, with blue eyes and red hair. She was a lady journalist attached to Mr. Brimley's paper. Twenty years ago she would have been called an advanced woman. She believed in equality for the sexes in all things, and wrote articles on war immorality, the "social evil" and kindred topics in a frank unabashed way which caused elderly old-fashioned newspaper readers much embarrassment. Miss Garton was just as eager as the more frivolous members of her sex to hear about the Red Cross pearls, and begged Mr. Musard to give her some details. She would have to do a "write up" about the necklace when she returned to London, she said, and any information from Mr. Musard would be so helpful.

"It is not a single necklace," said Musard. "There are about thirty necklaces. The Red Cross committee have already received nearly 4,000 pearls, and more are coming in every day."

"Four thousand pearls!"

"How perfectly lovely!"

"How I should love to see them!" These feminine exclamations sounded from different parts of the table.

"I suppose the collection is a very fine and varied one?" observed Sir Philip.

"Undoubtedly. The committee have had the advice of the best experts in London, who have given much time to grading the pearls for the different necklaces. In an ordinary way it takes a long while–sometimes years–to match the pearls for a faultless necklace, but in this case the experts have had such a variety brought to their hands that their task has been comparatively easy. But in spite of the skilful manner in which the necklaces have been graded, it is even now a simple matter for the trained eye to identify a number of the individual pearls. The largest, a white pearl of pear shape, weighing 72 grains, would be recognized by any expert anywhere. There are several other pearls over thirty grains which the trained eye would recognize with equal ease in any setting. The few pink and black pearls are all known to collectors, and it is the same with the clasps. One diamond and ruby clasp is as well-known in jewel history as the State Crown. The diamonds are in the form of a Maltese Cross, set in a circle of rubies."

"That must have been the gift of the Duchess of Welburton," remarked Sir Philip. "She inherited it from her great aunt, Adelina, wife of the third duke. There was a famous pearl necklace attached to the clasp once, but it disappeared about ten years ago at a ball given by the German Ambassador, Prince Litzovny. I remember there was a lot of talk about it at the time, but the necklace was never recovered. The clasp, too, has a remarkable history."

"All great jewels have," said Musard. "In fact, all noteworthy stones have dual histories. Their career as cut and polished gems is only the second part. Infinitely more interesting is the hidden history of each great jewel, from the discovery of the rough stone to the period when it reaches the hands of the lapidary, to be polished and cut for a drawing-room existence. What a record of intrigue and knavery, stabbings and poisonings, connected with some of the greatest jewels in the British Crown—the Black Prince's ruby, for example!"

Musard gazed thoughtfully at the great ruby on his own finger as he ceased speaking. The guests had finished dinner, and Miss Heredith, with a watchful eye on the big carved clock which swung a sedate pendulum by the fireplace, beckoned Tufnell to her and directed him to serve coffee and liqueurs at table.

"What is your favourite stone, Mr. Musard?" said a bright-eyed girl sitting near him, after coffee had been served.

"Personally I have a weakness for the ruby," replied Musard. "Its intrinsic value has been greatly discounted in these days of synthetic stones, but it is still my favourite, largely, I suppose, because a perfect natural ruby is so difficult to find. I remember once journeying three thousand miles up the Amazon in search of a ruby reputed to be as large as a pigeon's egg. But it did not exist–it was a myth."

"What a life yours has been!" said the girl. "How different from the humdrum existence of us stay-at-homes! How I should like to hear some of your adventures. They must be thrilling."

"If you want to hear a real thrilling adventure, Miss Finch, you should get Mr. Musard to tell you how he came by that ruby he is wearing," said Phil Heredith, joining in the conversation.

The eyes of all the guests were directed to the ring which Musard was wearing on the little finger of his left hand. The stone in the plain gold setting was an unusually large one, nearly an inch in length. The stone had been polished, not cut, and glowed rather than sparkled with a deep rich red–the true "pigeon's-blood" tint so admired by connoisseurs.

"Nonsense, Phil"–Musard flushed under his brown skin–"your guests do not want to hear me talk any more about myself. I've monopolized the conversation too long already."

"Oh, please do tell us!" exclaimed several of the guests.

"Really, you know, I'd rather not," responded Musard, in some embarrassment. "It's a long story, for one thing, and it's not quite–how shall I express it–it's a bit on the horrible side to relate in the presence of ladies."

"I do not think that need deter you," remarked one of the young officers drily. "We are all pretty strong-minded nowadays–since the War."

"Oh, we should love to hear it," said the lady journalist, who scented good "copy."

"Shouldn't we?" she added, turning to some of the ladies near her.

"Yes, indeed!" chorused the other ladies. "Do tell us."

"Go ahead, Musard–you see you can't get out of it," said Phil.

"Perhaps, Phil, as Mr. Musard does not think it a suitable story–" commenced Miss Heredith tentatively. Her eye was fixed anxiously on the clock, which was verging on twenty minutes past seven, and she feared the relation of her old friend's experience might make them late at the Weynes. But at that moment Tufnell approached his mistress and caught her eye. A slight shade of annoyance crossed her brow as she listened to something he communicated in a low voice, and she turned to her guests.

"I must ask you to excuse me for a few moments," she said.

She rose from her place and left the room. As the door closed behind her the ladies turned eagerly to Musard.

"Now, please, tell us about the ruby," said several in unison.

The explorer glanced at the eager faces looking towards him.

"Very well, I will tell you the story," he said quietly, but with visible reluctance.

4

"It was before the war. Many strange things have happened in the world before the Boche broke loose with his dream of 'Deutschland über Alles.' I had been to Melville Island trying to match a pearl for the Devonshire necklace, and I went from the pearl fisheries to New Zealand, led there by rumours of the discovery of some wonderful black pearls. It was, however, a wild-goose chase. These rumours generally are. One of the experts of the New Zealand Fishery Department had been exploring the Haurakai Gulf, and returned to Auckland with a number of black pearls, which he had found in an oyster-bed on one of the Barrier Islands. He thought his fortune was made, though, being a fishery expert, he ought to have known better. They were black pearls right enough, but they came from edible oysters, and were valueless as jewels—not worth a shilling each.

"I put up at the Royal hotel, Auckland, waiting for a ship to take me back to England. I had arranged to return round the Cape, to look at a parcel of diamonds which were expected to arrive at Capetown from the fields in about six weeks' time. The day before I was due to sail, a rough-looking man named Moynglass, a miner, came to the hotel to see me. He had heard of me as a mining expert, and he had a business proposition which he wanted to place before me.

"He told me he and four others had just returned to Auckland after putting in six weeks among the volcanic beaches of the North Island, searching—'fossicking,' he called it—for fine gold. These black sand volcanic beaches are common in parts of New Zealand. The black sand is derived from the crystals of magnetic iron, and there is frequently a fair amount of fine gold mingled with them.

By the continued action of the surf the heavier materials, gold, and ironstone sand, are mingled together between high and low water mark, and what appears as a stratum of black sand is found on the surface or buried under the ordinary sand. The gold is usually very fine, and the trouble of sifting and collecting it is great. A man works for wages, and hard-earned wages at that, who goes in for this kind of mining. But your true miner is ever an adventurer and a gambler, and gold thus won is dearer to his heart than gold which might be earned with less effort and more regularity in the form of sovereigns. You see, there is always the chance of a big find.

"Moynglass and his party had met with fair success along the beaches, but they wanted more than that. Moynglass was anxious to trace the fine gold to its source, and find a fortune. He believed, like most miners, that this fine gold is carried along the beds of the larger rivers and distributed by the action of the sea along the different beaches where it is found. His theory was that if the drift of the gold sands could be traced to their source, a great quartz reef would be found which would make the discoverers wealthy men. But he and his mates knew nothing about geology, and they wanted somebody to go with them who could chart the course, and lead them to the launching point of the gold.

"I had heard this theory before, and was not impressed by it. I should probably have turned down Moynglass's proposition if, in the course of his conversation, he had not produced a sample of ruby quartz from his pocket and showed it to me. He said he had found it while exploring one of the rivers of the Urewera country. I examined the quartz attentively. It was emery rock, and imbedded in the pale green mass were ruby crystals, and true Oriental rubies at that. I realized the valuable nature of the discovery, and questioned the man closely as to where he had obtained the ruby rock, but he became instantly suspicious, and guarded in his replies. If I joined his party—well and good:

he would show me the spot, and we would share and share alike, but he would tell me nothing otherwise.

"I decided to go, and the terms were agreed upon. We set out from Auckland, the five of us, a week later. We went by coastal steamer to a little port in the Bay of Plenty, and there we plunged into the Urewera Mountains. My companions thought of nothing but the search for the source of the golden sands, but I was interested only in the ruby rock. There lay the fortune, if I could find it. I carried the specimen of corundum in my waistcoat pocket.

"The river we were ascending to its source was called the Araheoa. It was a rushing, noisy torrent, winding along a deep and narrow gorge, which in places almost met overhead. Some patches of olivine and serpentine encouraged me to think that we should find a heavy belt of the rock somewhere along the upper part of the valley, but my hopes were not realized. Day after day passed, and I found no more of it. When my companions washed the sands of likely stretches of river beach for fine gold, I examined the waste for corundum crystals, but I found no signs of them.

"We followed the river until we reached an inaccessible mountain gorge which seemed to bar our further progress. But, by diverting our course some miles to the northward, we were able to ascend to the upper reaches of the river, and, here, to my delight, I found the banks and rapids studded with great green masses of olivine rocks.

"I was anxious to examine these rocks, which extended up the mountain side, and my companions agreed with me that it was advisable to leave the bed of the river for the spur of the mountains where the river apparently took its rise. We crossed the stream, and commenced a gradual but oblique ascent of the spur. But after climbing for some hours we found our further progress stopped by a wide and deep gully, a sinister place, full of masses of dark green rocks. At the foot of one of the largest of these rocks we came across a large hole descending almost perpendicularly into the earth.

"We lit our lamps and descended. After some scrambling we found ourselves on a landing-place, from which another low passage of an easier gradient led into a large cave in the solid rock.

"The surface underneath our feet was covered with a dust so fine that it slipped from beneath us like sand, and rose in thick clouds about us. The cave was high enough to walk upright in, and seemed to run a great distance, with many lateral passages and smaller recesses off the principal chamber. Moynglass entered one of these passages and disappeared from view. A few moments afterwards we heard him, in a very excited voice, calling us to follow him.

"We proceeded stooping, in Indian file, down the passage, and found Moynglass in a smaller cave at the end of it, staring intently at something which was at first difficult to see in the gloom. Then, by the light of our lamps, we made out a sapling sticking up between two rocks, with a withered human hand impaled on it by a rusty sheath knife.

"As I was examining it, one of my companions, who had been exploring the cave, gave a cry of astonishment which caused me to look round. In a corner of the cave, revealed by his lamp, lay two skeletons side by side. The hand of one skeleton was missing, and in the eye of the other there gleamed a large uncut ruby. We examined the skeletons and searched the cave, but found nothing to throw any light on the mystery or reveal any clue of identity. There was not a vestige of food or clothing around the remains, and not a scrap of writing—only the two crumbling skeletons, the sapling, the sheath knife, and the ruby.

"What had brought about such a tragedy in the dim recesses of that prehistoric cave? Who could say? Perhaps the men had been prospecting together, and one had found the ruby and hidden in the cave, where his companion had found him and cut off his right hand with some primitive idea of making his vengeance fit the crime. Then, perhaps, they had been unable to escape from the cave, and had died together of thirst and hunger. But what is the use of speculating? The secret must ever remain hidden in the cave where the skeletons still lie."

Musard stopped abruptly, and sat staring straight in front of him. His strange eyes had a fixed look, as if gazing into the distance. His brown hand rested lightly on the white tablecloth, and the great ruby on his little finger gleamed fitfully in the light.

"You haven't told us all the story yet," said Phil Heredith quietly.

The other looked doubtfully at the ring of intent faces regarding him. "I left that part untold for a good reason," he admitted. "It is—well, I thought it a little bit too horrible to relate."

"Oh, do tell us," said the lady journalist enthusiastically. "We are all dying to hear it. It is such an unusual and exciting story that it would be cruel to leave us in suspense about the end."

"Very well, then," said Musard, as the other ladies chorused their approval. "We left the cave, and Moynglass, who considered himself the leader of the expedition, put the ruby in his pocket. That night we camped at a wild desolate spot, not far from the edge of a cliff about two hundred feet high, at the foot of which the bitter sulphurous waters of the river flowed into a chasm. In the morning we found Moynglass lying dead in his blanket, with the rusty sheath knife he had brought away from the cave sticking in his breast. The ruby was gone, and, so, also, was the eldest member of our party—an elderly dark-faced Irishman named Doyne, who, the previous day, had angrily disputed Moynglass's right to carry the ruby.

"We searched for Doyne all that day, but could find no trace of him. The next day we tracked across a glacier-like expanse littered with large blocks of sandstone. It was a grim spot. A horrible, stony, treeless waste which might have been the birthplace of the earth and the scene of Creation–a tableland between great mountains, full of masses of rhodonite contorted into grotesque shapes of stone images; a place where our lightest whispers came shouting back out of the profound stillness from the huge castellated black rocks bristling on the edge of a precipice which slit the valley from end to end.

"It was there we found Doyne, staggering along the lip of the gorge. He had gone mad in the solitude, and was wandering along bareheaded, tossing his arms in the air as he walked. When I saw him I thought of Cain trying to escape from the wrath of God after killing Abel. He saw us as soon as we saw him, and started to run. We set out in pursuit, but he fled with great speed, leaping from rock to rock like a mountain goat. He was getting away from us when he slipped and fell into the chasm with a loud cry. We found a path down the precipice and descended, and discovered him at the foot, battered to death, with the ruby clutched in his hand. That ended the expedition. The others insisted on returning to the coast without delay, and when we arrived there they gladly sold their shares in the ruby to me."

There was rather a long silence when the explorer had finished his narration. The long hand of the clock on the mantelpiece was creeping past the half-hour, but the circle round the dining-room table had been so enthralled by the story that nobody had noted the passage of time.

"What a ghastly adventure, Mr. Musard!" began one of the ladies, with a mirthless little laugh. "Did you never discover anything more about the two dead men in the cave?"

"No," replied Musard. "As I said, there were no papers or any clue to throw light on their identity. The skeletons must have lain there for many years, for the bones were crumbling into decay."

"You have never revisited the spot?" asked Sir Philip.

"I was in the Ureweras two years later with a Maori guide, investigating copper deposits for the New Zealand Government, but I did not go back to the valley."

"Would it not have been possible to give the poor things–the skeletons, I mean–Christian burial?" Mrs. Spicer asked timidly.

"It was impossible to dig a grave in the solid rock. Besides, they have a sepulchre of Nature's which will outlast any human grave," replied Musard.

"The thing that puzzles me is how the ruby got into the skeleton's eye," remarked the lady journalist musingly. "If that was the skeleton of the man who killed the other for stealing the ruby, who placed the ruby where you found it? Obviously, he could not have done it himself, for it must have been put there after death. Who, then, could it have been?"

"I have no idea," said Musard, in a tone which suggested that he did not care to discuss the subject further.

"May I look at the ring?" Miss Garton asked.

Musard drew it off his finger and handed it to her in silence. The others wanted to see it, so it was passed from hand to hand round the table, to the accompaniment of many admiring comments on the size and beauty of the stone. One of the young officers, with an air of much interest, asked Musard whether he thought there were other rubies like it to be found near the spot.

"Hardly in that form," replied Musard. "It is a puzzle to me how the men who found the ruby managed to get it out of the ruby rock and partially polish it. They had no tools or instruments of any kind–at least, we found none in the cave. Undoubtedly there are rubies in that part of the world. It was near the valley that Moynglass found his sample of corundum, with a ruby crystal in it. On our way back, at the head of the valley, I came across a belt of magnesian rocks charged with ores of copper and iron, and probably containing the matrix of ruby crystals."

"I wonder you wear the thing," said the chubby-faced youth of the Flying Corps, handing the ring across the table to the explorer.

"Why not?" asked Musard.

"Well, I wouldn't care to wear a ring found in a skeleton's head. I should expect the old bus to flop to the ground while I was doing a stunt, if I had a thing like that on my finger. Aren't you frightened of being haunted by the original owner?"

"Oh, I don't know," replied Musard indifferently. "There's a horrible history attached to most jewels, if it comes to that. I am not superstitious." He replaced the ring on his finger, and added thoughtfully: "I suppose many people would regard it in that light—as a grim sort of relic. Certainly, I shall never forget the valley of rocks where we found it. It was the strangest place I have ever seen—a 'waste howling wilderness.' And sometimes I fancy I can still hear the cry Doyne gave as he slipped or jumped from one of the black rocks into space. I remember how it came ringing back from the cliffs a hundred times repeated. It was—"

He broke off suddenly, as a scream pealed through the moat-house—a wild shrill cry, which, coming from somewhere overhead, seemed to fill the dining-room with the shuddering, despairing intensity of its appeal. It was the shriek of a woman in terror.

The ladies at the dinner table regarded one another with frightened eyes and blanched faces.

"What was that?" several of them whispered together.

"It came from Violet's room! My God, what has happened?" exclaimed Phil. He sprang to his feet in agitation and pushed back his chair. His face was white, his mouth drawn, and he fumbled at his throat with a shaking hand, as though the pressure of his collar impeded his breathing. Musard rose from the table and walked to where the young man was standing.

"Don't get upset needlessly, Phil," he said soothingly, placing a hand on his shoulder.

Sir Philip had also risen from his seat, and for the briefest possible space the three men stood thus, facing each other, as if uncertain how to act. Then the tense silence of the dining-room was broken by the loud report of a fire-arm.

"Let me go!" cried Phil shrilly, shaking off Musard's arm. He turned and limped rapidly towards the door, and as he did so his infirmity of body was apparent. One of his legs was several inches shorter than the other, and he wore a high boot.

Musard reached the door before him in a few rapid strides, and Sir Philip came hurrying after his son. The rest of the male guests followed, flocking towards the door in a body.

The first sight that Musard's eye fell upon as he passed through the doorway was the figure of Miss Heredith, rapidly descending the staircase. By the hall light he could see that her face was pale and agitated. She walked swiftly up to her old friend, and laid a trembling hand on his arm.

"Oh, Vincent, I was just coming for you–something terrible must have happened!" she began, in a broken, sobbing voice. "I was going upstairs to my room, when I heard the scream, and then the shot. They must have come from Violet's room. Will you go up and see, Vincent?"

Musard did not wait for her concluding words. He was already mounting the staircase, taking two or three of the broad shallow stairs in his stride. Phil hobbled after him, and Sir Philip and some of the guests straggled up in their wake.

5

A shaded light in an alcove at the head of the stairs threw a dim light down the passage which led off the first-floor landing, but Musard felt for the electric switch and pressed it. The light flooded an empty corridor, with the door of the room nearest to him gaping into a dark interior.

Musard stepped inside the open door, struck a match to find the switch, and walked over and turned on the light. As he did so, Phil and his father reached the door and followed him into the room, where, less than two hours before, Miss Heredith had been with Phil's young wife, and left her to sleep. The room seemed as it had been then; there was no sign of any intruder. The cut-glass and silver bottles stood on the small table by the head of the bed; the gold cigarette case was open alongside them; a novel, flung face downward on the pillows, revealed a garish cover and the bold lettering of the title—"What Shall it Profit?"—as though the book had dropped from the hand of some one overcome by sleep. But the white rays of the electric globe, hanging in a shade of rose colour directly overhead, fell with sinister distinctness on the slender figure of the young wife, lying in a huddled heap on the bed, her fashionable rest gown stained with blood, which oozed from her breast in a sluggish stream on the satin quilt. A sharp, pungent odour was mingled with the heavy atmosphere of the room—the smell of a burning fabric. There was no disorder, no weapon, no indication of a struggle. Only the motionless, bleeding figure on the bed revealed to the guests clustering outside the room that somebody had entered and departed as silently as a tiger.

Musard went swiftly to the bedside and bent over the girl. "She has been shot," he said, in a tone which was little more than a whisper.

"She has been murdered!" It was Phil, pressing close behind Musard, who uttered these words. "Murdered!" he cried, in an unnatural voice, which was dreadful to hear. He made a few steps in the direction of the bed with his arms outstretched, then stopped, and, swinging round, faced the guests who were thronging the corridor outside. "Murdered, I say!" he repeated. "Where is the murderer?"

He stood for a moment, fixing a wild eye on the group of frightened faces in the doorway, as though seeking the murderer among them. Then his face became distorted, and he fell to the ground. His limbs seemed to grow rigid as he lay; his legs were extended stiffly, the upper part of his arms were pressed against his breast, but the forearms inclined forward, with the palms of the hand thrown back, and the fingers wide apart. Even in his unconsciousness he looked as though he were warding off the horror of the sight which had stricken him to the ground.

In the presence of domestic calamity human nature betrays its inherent weakness. At such times the artificial outer covering of civilization falls away, and the soul stands forth, stark, primitive, forlorn, and cries aloud. The strain of the tremendous tragedy which had entered his house, swift-footed and silent, was too much for Sir Philip. He sank on his knees by the side of his unconscious son, whimpering like a child—a weak and helpless old man. There was no trace of the dignity of the Herediths or pride of race in the wrinkled face, now distorted with the pitiful grin of senility, as Sir Philip crouched over his son, stroking his face with feeble fingers.

One or two of the women in the passage became hysterical. The young men looked on awkwardly, with grave faces, not knowing what to do. There was something very English in their shy aloofness; in their dislike of intruding in the room unasked.

Musard, looking round from the bedside, glanced briefly at the prostrate figure of Phil, and then his gleaming eyes travelled to the group at the doorway. He, at all events, was calm, and master of himself.

"The ladies had better go downstairs," he said, speaking in a subdued voice, but with decision. "They can do no good here. And will you two"—he singled out two of the young men with his eye—"carry Phil downstairs? He has only fainted. Please take Sir Philip away also. Telephone for Dr. Holmes immediately, and send for Sergeant Lumbe. And some of you young men search the house thoroughly—at once. No, not this room. Search the house from top to bottom, and the grounds outside. Be quick! There is no time to be lost."

The group in the doorway melted away. The ladies, pale-faced and weeping, went downstairs together like a flock of frightened birds, and the young men, only too glad to obey somebody who showed nerve and resolution at such a moment, dispersed at once to search the house.

Musard was left in the room alone, but not for long. Miss Heredith entered from the corridor almost immediately. Tufnell accompanied her to the door, but stopped there, with staring eyes directed towards the bed. Miss Heredith's face was drawn, but she had recovered her self-control. She walked quickly towards Musard, who was still bending over the bed.

"Vincent!" she cried. "In pity's name tell me what dreadful thing has happened? They have carried Phil downstairs, and they tried to detain me, but I broke away from them and came straight to you. Is Violet—"

Musard sprang to his feet at the first sound of her voice, and wheeled round swiftly, as if trying to impose his body between her and the figure on the bed.

"Go back, Alethea!" he sternly commanded. "Go back, I say! This is no sight for you, and you can do no good."

He still sought to intercept her as she approached, but she gently put aside his detaining hand, and, walking to the bedside, looked down. Then, at that sight, her fingers sought for his with an impulsive feminine movement, and held them tight.

"Do not be afraid for me," she whispered. "See! I am calm—I may be able to help. Is she—dead?"

"Dying," said Musard sadly.

"Is it...?" her voice dropped to nothingness, but her frightened eyes, travelling fearfully into the shadowy corners of the big bedroom, completed the unspoken sentence.

Musard understood her, and bowed his head silently. Then, turning his face to the door, he beckoned Tufnell to approach. The old servant advanced tremblingly into the room, vainly endeavouring to compose his horror-stricken face into a semblance of the impassive mask of the well-trained English servant.

"Go downstairs and get me some hot water," said Musard quietly. "Look sharp—and bring it yourself. I do not want any maidservants here to go into hysterics."

Tufnell hastened away. Musard resumed his place at the bedside, silently watching the figure on the bed. There was blood on his hands and clothes.

"Is there no hope? Can nothing be done to save her?" whispered Miss Heredith.

"Nothing. The lung is penetrated. She is bleeding to death."

His quick eye noticed a change in the figure on the bed. The face quivered ever so slightly, and the blue eyes half opened. Then the stricken girl made an effort as though she wanted to sit up, but a sudden convulsion seized her, and she fell back on her pillow, with one little white hand, glittering with rings, flung above her head, as if she died in the act of invoking the retribution of a God of justice on the assassin who had blotted out her young life in agony and horror.

"She is dead," said Musard gently. "This is a terrible business, and our first duty is to try and capture the monster who committed this foul crime." They stood there in silence for a moment, looking earnestly at one another. Outside, somewhere in the woodland, there sounded the haunting gush of a night-bird's song, shivering through the quietness like a silver bell. The sweet note finished in a frightened squawk, and was followed by the cry of an owl. The song had betrayed the singer.

Musard turned away from Miss Heredith, and walked restlessly around the bedroom, scanning the heavy pieces of furniture and the faded hangings, and peering into every nook and corner, as if seeking for the murderer's place of concealment. A roomy old wardrobe near the window attracted his eye, and he stopped in front of it and flung its doors open. It contained some articles of the dead girl's apparel—costumes and frocks—hanging on hooks.

His eye wandered to the window, shrouded in the heavy folds of the damask curtains. He walked over to it, and drew the curtains aside. The bottom half of the window was wide open.

Miss Heredith, who was following his movements closely, gave vent to a faint cry of surprise.

"The window!" she exclaimed.

Musard looked round inquiringly.

"The window—what of it?" he asked.

"It was closed when I came in here before dinner to see Violet."

"You are quite sure of that?"

"Oh, yes! At least, I think so."

"I do not understand you."

"I mean that the atmosphere of the room was heavy and thick, as if the window had not been opened all day."

"It has been a still, close day."

"But Violet never had a window open if she could help it. She disliked fresh air. She was always afraid of catching cold."

Musard looked out of the window into the velvet darkness of the night. "If the window was closed before, the murderer has opened it and escaped through it," he said.

"It is hardly possible."

"Why not?" He turned round and faced her.

"The ground falls on that side. The window is nearly twenty feet from the ground. And—there is the moat to be crossed. There is no bridge on that side of the house, and this window opens on the garden. Don't you remember?"

"I remember now."

"I thought you would."

"Still—" Musard broke off abruptly, and walked away from the window.

Near the window stood the dressing-table. The swing oval mirror reflected its contents—ivory brushes, silver hand mirrors, all the costly bijoutry of a refined woman's toilet. Among them stood Violet's silver jewel-case. Musard strode over and examined the case. It was locked.

"This ought to be put away," he said.

"I was coming up to get it when I heard the scream," whispered his companion.

"Perhaps you will take charge of it now," he said, placing it in her hands. As he did so there flashed across his mind the cynical appropriateness of the old proverb about locking doors after stolen steeds.

There was a restraint and lack of spontaneity about their conversation of which both were acutely conscious. The note was forced, as though from too great an effort to strike the right key. A curious psychological change had swept over both since they stood together by the bedside of the dying woman. It had come with the entry of death. They conversed hurriedly and guardedly, as if they mistrusted each other. In each of them two entities were now apparent—a surface consciousness, which talked and acted mechanically, and a secondary inner consciousness, watchful, and fearful of misinterpretation of the spoken word. The faculties which make up the human mind are different and complex, and mysteriously blended. It may be that when tragedy upsets the frail structure of human life the brute instincts of watchfulness and self-preservation come uppermost, guarding against chance suspicion, or the loud word of accusation. Perhaps through Musard's mind was passing the thought of the strange manner in which the murder had been committed, and how he, by detaining everybody downstairs at the dinner table while he told his story had been an instrument in its accomplishment.

The situation was terminated by the arrival of Tufnell with some hot water. Almost on his heels came the young men who had been searching the house. Musard was relieved by their return, though his impassive face did not reveal his feelings. Miss Heredith left the room with Tufnell, taking the jewel-case with her. Musard met the young men at the threshold.

The tall young officer with the sunburnt face, Major Gardner, informed Musard that they had completed a search of the house from top to bottom, but had found nothing. They had also searched the grounds, without result.

"Mrs. Heredith is dead," Musard gravely informed them. "She died while you have been searching for the miscreant who fired the shot we heard at the dinner table. Gentlemen, he must be found. It seems hardly possible that he has succeeded in getting clear away in so short a time."

"We have searched the place from top to bottom," remarked one of the young men.

"It is a strange, rambling old place, and difficult to explore unless you know it thoroughly," said Musard.

"We have done the best we could."

"I do not doubt it, but there are many old nooks and corners in which a man might hide."

"His first thought, after such a dreadful crime, would be to get away as quickly as possible," said Major Gardner.

"But how did he escape? Certainly not by the staircase, because we rushed out from the dining-room directly we heard the shot, and we should have caught him on his way down."

"Is there not a window in the bedroom? Could he not have escaped that way?"

"The window is nearly twenty feet from the ground."

"An athletic man might jump that distance," remarked Major Gardner thoughtfully.

"I still think it possible he may be concealed about the premises," replied Musard. "There is an old unused staircase at the end of this passage, which opens on the south side of the moat-house. Did you find it? It shuts with a door at the top, and might easily have escaped your notice."

"I opened the door and went down the staircase," said the young flying officer. "Nobody could have escaped that way. The door at the bottom is locked, and there is no key."

The scared face of a maidservant at that moment appeared at the head of the stairs.

"If you please, sir," she said, addressing Musard, "one of the gentlemen downstairs sent me up to tell you that he has been trying for the last ten minutes to ring up the police, but he can't get an answer."

"Send the butler to me at once."

The maid disappeared, and in another moment the butler came hurriedly up the stairs.

"Tufnell," said Musard quickly, "you must go at once to the village and get Sergeant Lumbe and Dr. Holmes. Hurry off, and be as quick as you can. And now, gentlemen," he added, turning to the others, "let us go downstairs. While we are waiting for the police I will help you make another search of the house and grounds. The murderer may escape while we stand here talking. We have wasted too much valuable time already."

6

The butler left the moat-house at a brisk pace which became almost a run after he crossed the moat bridge. His way across the park lay along the carriage drive, bordered by an avenue of tall trees, between an ornamental lake and some thick game covers, and then through the outer fields to the village.

It was a soft and mellow September night, with a violet sky overhead sprinkled with silver. But a touch of autumn decay was in the air, which was heavy and still, and a white mist was rising in thick, sluggish clouds from the green, stagnant surface of the lake. The wood was veiled in blackness, in which the trunks of the trees were just visible, standing in straight, regular rows, like soldiers at attention.

Tufnell hurried along this lonely spot, casting timid glances around him. He was not a nervous man at ordinary times, but like many country people, he had a vein of superstition running through his phlegmatic temperament, and the events of the night had swept away his calmness. The croaking of the frogs and the whispering of the trees filled him with uneasiness, and he kept glancing backwards and forwards from the lake to the wood, as though he feared the murderer might suddenly appear from the misty surface of the one or the dim recesses of the other.

He had almost reached the confines of the wood when he was startled by a loud whirr, which he recognized as the flight of a covey of partridges from a cover close at hand. What had startled them? Glancing fearfully around him he saw, or thought he saw, the crouching figure of a man in one of the bypaths of the wood, partly hidden by the thick branches which stretched across the path a short distance from the drive.

Tufnell's first impulse was to take to his heels, but he was saved from this ignominious act by the timely recollection that he was an Englishman, whose glorious privilege it is to be born without fear. So he stood still, and in a voice which had something of a quaver in it, called out:

"Who is there?"

In the wood a bird gave a single call like the note of a flute, the wind murmured in the tall avenue of trees, a frog splashed in the still waters of the lake, but there was no sound of human life. Glancing cautiously into the wood, the butler could no longer see anything crouching in the path. The man—if it had been a man—had vanished.

"It may have been my fancy," muttered the butler, speaking aloud as though to reassure himself by hearing his own voice.

He walked quickly onward, and was relieved when he had left the wood behind him, and could see the faint lights of the village twinkling beyond the fields. Crossing a footbridge which spanned a narrow stream at the bottom of the meadows, Tufnell climbed over a stile, and walked along the road on the other side until he reached a cottage standing some distance back from the road at the summit of a gentle slope. Tufnell ascended the slope and knocked loudly at the cottage door.

After the lapse of a few moments the door was opened by a woman with a candle in her hand—a stout countrywoman of forty, with a curved nose, prominent teeth, and hair screwed up in a tight knob at the back of her head. Her small grey eyes, scanning the visitor at the door, showed both surprise and deference. The butler of the moat-house was not in the habit of mixing with the villagers, and by them he was accounted something of a personage. He not only shone with the reflected glory of the big house, but was respected on his own merit as a "snug" man, who had saved money, and had a little property of his own.

"Is your husband at home, Mrs. Lumbe?" he asked, in response to her mute glance of inquiry. He spoke condescendingly, like a man who recognized the social gulf between them, but believed in being polite to the lower orders.

"Yes, he is in, Mr. Tufnell. Will you come inside?"

The butler rubbed his boots carefully on the doormat, and followed the woman down a narrow passage to a small sitting-room at the end of it, where a man was sitting, reading a newspaper and smoking a pipe. "Robert," said the woman, "here is Mr. Tufnell to see you."

The man looked up from his newspaper in some surprise, and got up to greet his visitor. He was not in uniform, and his rough, ungainly figure and round red face revealed the countryman, but from the crown of his close-cropped bullet head to his thick-soled boots he looked like a rural policeman. There was an awkward pose about him as he stood up—a clumsy effort to maintain the semblance of an official dignity. The questioning look his ferret eyes cast at the butler through the haze of tobacco smoke which filled the room indicated his impression that the visit was not merely a neighbourly call. Tufnell did not leave him in doubt on the point.

"You are wanted at the moat-house at once, Sergeant Lumbe," he said gravely. "A terrible crime has been committed. Mrs. Heredith has been murdered."

"Murdered!" ejaculated the sergeant, looking vacantly across the table at his wife, who had given vent to a cry of horror. "Murdered!" he repeated, as though seeking to assure himself of the truth of the butler's statement by a repetition of the word.

"Yes. She was shot in her bedroom a little while ago while the other guests were at dinner. You must come at once."

Sergeant Lumbe laid his pipe on the table with a trembling hand. He was overwhelmed by the magnitude of the catastrophe, and hardly knew what to do. His previous experience of crime was confined to an occasional arrest of the village drunkard, who invariably went with him confidingly. His eye wandered to a bookcase in the corner of the room, as if he would have liked to consult a "Police Code" which was prominently displayed on one of the shelves. Apparently he realized the indignity of such a course in the presence of a member of the public, so he turned to Tufnell and said:

"I'll go with you, but I must first put on my tunic."

"Be as quick as you can," said the butler, taking a chair.

Sergeant Lumbe went into an inner room, where his wife followed him. Tufnell heard them whispering as they moved about. Then Sergeant Lumbe hastily emerged buttoning his tunic. There was an eager look on his face.

"The wife has been saying that we ought to take her brother along," he said. "He belongs to Scotland Yard. He's spending his holidays with us."

"Where is he?" asked Tufnell, impressed by the magic of the name of Scotland Yard.

"He's just stepped over to the *Fox and Knot* to have a game of billiards, finding it a bit lonesome here, after London. Do you think we might send for him and take him with us?"

"I think it would be a very good idea," said Tufnell. "But can he be got at once?" he added, with a glance at the little clock on the mantelpiece. "The sooner we return the better."

"The wife can bring him while I am changing my boots. Hurry down to the *Fox*, Maggie, and tell Tom he's wanted at once."

"Don't tell him what it's for until you get him outside," hastily counselled the butler as the policeman's wife was departing on her errand. "Sir Philip won't like it if he hears that what happened to-night was discussed in the *Fox* tap-room." The little clock on the mantelpiece had barely ticked off five additional minutes when Mrs. Lumbe returned in a breathless state, accompanied by a young man with billiard chalk on his coat and hands.

"This is my brother, Detective Caldew," said Mrs. Lumbe, between pants, to the butler. "I told him about the murder, and we hurried back as fast as we could."

"It's a horrible crime, and we must lose no time while there is still a chance of catching the murderer," said the young man, regaining his breath more easily than his stout sister. He brushed the billiard chalk off his clothes as he spoke. "Let us go at once."

Tufnell cast a curious glance at the new-comer. He saw a man of about thirty-five, tall, well-built and dark, with a clean-shaven face and rather intelligent eyes under thick dark brows. He had some difficulty in recognizing Detective Caldew as the village urchin of a score of years before who had touched his cap to the moat-house butler as a great personage, second only in importance to Sir Philip Heredith himself.

Tufnell was not aware that in the former village boy who had become a London detective he was in the presence of a young man of soaring ambition. Caldew had gone to London fifteen years before with the idea of bettering himself. After tramping the streets of the metropolis for some months in a vain quest for work, he had enlisted in the metropolitan police force rather than return to his native village and report himself a failure. At the end of two years' service as a policeman he had been given the choice of transfer to the Criminal Investigation Department of Scotland Yard. He had gladly accepted the opportunity, and had shown so much aptitude for plain-clothes work that by the end of another two years he had risen to the rank of detective. Caldew thought he was on the rapid road to further promotion, and had married on the strength of that belief. But another ten years had passed since then, and he still occupied a subordinate position, with not much hope of promotion unless luck came his way. And there seemed very little chance of that. Caldew's professional experience had imbued him with the belief that the junior officers of Scotland Yard existed for no other purpose than to shoulder the blame for the mistakes of their official superiors, who divided amongst themselves the plums of promotion, rewards, and newspaper publicity. That, of course, was the recognized thing in all public departments. Caldew found no fault with the system. His great ambition was to obtain some opening which would bring him advancement and his share of the plums.

He believed his opportunity had arrived that night. It had always been his dream to have the chance to unravel single-handed some great crime–a murder for choice–in which he alone should have all the glory and praise and newspaper paragraphs. He determined to make the most of the lucky chance which had fallen into his hands, before anybody else could arrive on the scene. He had confidence in his own abilities, and thought he had all the qualifications necessary to make a great detective. He was, at all events, sufficiently acute to realize that opportunity seldom knocks twice at any man's door.

The three men set out for the moat-house. At the butler's request Sergeant Lumbe went ahead to summon the doctor, who lived on the other side of the village green, and while he was gone Caldew drew the details of the crime from his companion. Lumbe rejoined them at the footbridge which led across the meadows into the Heredith estate, and they proceeded on their way in silence. Sergeant Lumbe's brain–such as it was–was in too much of a whirl to permit him to talk coherently; Tufnell, habitually a taciturn individual, had been rendered more so than usual by the events of the night;

and Caldew was plunged into such a reverie of pleasurable expectation, regarding the outcome of his investigations of the moat-house murder, that the stages of his promotion through the grades of detective, sub-superintendent, and superintendent, flashed through his mind as rapidly as telegraph poles flit past a traveller in a railway carriage. The crime which had struck down one human being in the dawn of youth and beauty, turned another into a murderer, and plunged an old English family into horror and misery, afforded Detective Caldew's optimistic temperament such extreme gratification that he could scarcely forbear from whistling aloud. But that is human nature.

They passed through the wood, and crossed the moat bridge. The mist was creeping out of the darkness on both sides of the moat-house, casting a film across the faint light which gleamed from one or two of the heavily shuttered windows. Caldew, pausing midway on the bridge to glance at the mist-spirals stealing up like a troop of ghosts, asked his brother-in-law if the moat was still kept full of water. He received an affirmative reply, and walked on again.

A maidservant answered Tufnell's ring at the front door, and informed him in a whisper that Sir Philip and Miss Heredith were in the drawing-room. Thither they bent their steps, and found Musard awaiting them near the door. He nodded to Sergeant Lumbe, whom he knew, and glanced interrogatively at Caldew. Lumbe announced the latter's identity.

"You had better come in here first," said Musard, opening the door of the drawing-room and revealing the baronet and Miss Heredith sitting within. Brother and sister glanced at the group entering the room.

"This is Detective Caldew, of Scotland Yard," Musard explained to them, indicating the young man. "He is staying with Lumbe, who thought it advisable to bring him."

"Have you told them everything?" Miss Heredith spoke to Tufnell. Her dry lips formed the words rather than uttered them, but the old retainer understood her, and bowed without speaking. "What do you wish to do first, Detective Caldew?" she added, turning to him, and speaking with more composure. She was quick to realize that he would take the lead in the police investigations. A glance at Sergeant Lumbe's flustered face revealed only too clearly that the position in which he found himself was beyond his official capabilities.

Caldew stepped briskly forward. He was in no way embarrassed by his unaccustomed surroundings or by the commanding appearance of the great lady who was addressing him. He was a man who believed in himself, and such men are too much in earnest to be diffident.

"I should like to ask a few questions first, madam," he said. "So far, I have heard only your butler's version of what happened." Without waiting for a reply he launched a number of questions, and made a note of the replies in a pocket-book.

Musard, who assisted Miss Heredith to answer the questions, was rather impressed by the quick intelligence the detective displayed in eliciting all the known facts of the murder, but Sergeant Lumbe, who remained standing near the door, was shocked to hear Caldew cross-questioning the great folk of the moat-house with such little ceremony. He thought his brother-in-law a very forward young fellow, and hoped that Miss Heredith would not hold him responsible for his free-and-easy manner.

"Now I should like to commence my investigations," said Caldew, replacing his pocket-book. "There has been too much time lost already. I will start with examining the room where the body is, if you please."

"Certainly." Miss Heredith rose from her seat as she uttered the word.

"My dear Alethea!"–Musard's tone was expostulatory–
"I will take the detective upstairs. There is no need for
you to come."

"I prefer to do so." Miss Heredith's tone admitted of no
further argument. She was about to lead the way from
the room when she paused and glanced at Tufnell. "When
will Dr. Holmes be here?" she asked.

"Almost immediately, ma'am."

"You had better stay here and receive him, Philip."
Miss Heredith placed her hand affectionately on her
brother's shoulder. He had not spoken during the time
the police were in the room, but had sat quietly on his
chair, with bent head and clasped hands, looking very old
and frail. "It will be as well for him to see Phil before
going upstairs," she added.

Sir Philip looked up at the mention of his son's name.
"Poor Phil," he muttered dully.

"I think the doctor should examine Phil the moment
he comes," continued Miss Heredith, aside, to Musard.
"His look alarms me. I fear the shock has affected his
brain. Tufnell, be sure and show Dr. Holmes to Mr.
Philip's room directly Sir Philip has received him."

"You can rely upon me to do so, ma'am," said Tufnell
earnestly.

"Very well. We will now go upstairs."

She left the drawing-room and proceeded towards the
broad oak staircase, with Musard close behind her.
Detective Caldew followed more slowly, noting his
surroundings. When they reached the head of the
staircase Miss Heredith switched on the electric current,
and the bedroom corridor sprang into light. Detective
Caldew was surprised at its length.

"Where does this passage lead to?" he asked abruptly.

"To the south side of the moat-house," replied Musard.

"Has it any outlet?"

"Yes; a door at the end communicates with a narrow staircase, leading to another door at the bottom. The second door was a former back

entrance—it opens somewhere near the servants' quarters, I think?" He glanced inquiringly at Miss Heredith.

"Those stairs are never used now," she replied. "The entrance door at the bottom of the staircase is kept locked."

"There are such things as skeleton keys," commented the detective.

Musard opened the door of the death-chamber and switched on the light. Caldew walked at once to the bedside. He drew away the covering which had been placed over the face of the young wife, and stood looking at her.

Death had invested her with pathos, but not with dignity. On the pallor of the death mask the tinted lips, the spots of rouge, the pencilled eyebrows of the dead face, were as clearly revealed as print on a white page. The lips were parted; the small white teeth were showing beneath the upper lip. The little nose rose in the sharp outline of death; between the half-closed eyelids the darkened blue eyes looked out vacantly. The thick, fair hair, spotted with blood, flowed in disordered waves over the white pillow; the numerous rings on the dead hands blazed and glittered with hard brilliance in the electric light.

It was these costly jewels on the murdered girl's hands which prompted the question which sprang to the detective's lips:

"Did the murderer take anything?" he asked. "Has anything been missed?"

"No," said Miss Heredith. "Nothing has been taken."

"Mrs. Heredith had more jewellery than this, I suppose?" pursued the detective. "Brooches and necklaces, and that kind of thing. Where were they kept?"

"Mrs. Heredith's jewel-case is downstairs, in the safe in the library," replied Miss Heredith. She did not feel called upon to add the additional information that she had taken it there herself, and locked it up, not half an hour before.

Detective Caldew made a mental note of the fact that the motive for the crime was not robbery, unless, indeed, the murderer had become flurried, and fled. His eye, glancing round the room, was attracted by the window curtains, which were stirring faintly. He flung them back, and saw the open window.

"How long has this window been open?" he asked.

Miss Heredith gave her reasons for believing that the window was closed when she left Violet to go downstairs to the dining-room. Caldew listened thoughtfully, and nodded his head in quick comprehension when she added the information that the bedroom window was nearly twenty feet from the ground.

"You think the murderer did not jump out of the window," he said. "The more important point is, did he get in that way? It is not a difficult matter to scale a wall to reach a window if there is any sort of a foothold. It is a point I will look into afterwards."

He tried the window catch, and then walked about the room, examining it closely. His quick, eager eyes, looking about in every direction, were caught by something glittering on the carpet, close to the bed. He glanced at his companions. As a detective, he had long learnt the wisdom of caution in the presence of friends and relatives.

"I should like to be left alone in the room in order to examine it more thoroughly," he briefly announced.

When Miss Heredith and Musard had left the room he locked the door behind them, and, kneeling down by the bedside, disentangled a small shining object almost concealed in the thick green texture of the carpet. It was a trinket like a bar brooch, with gold clasps. The bar was of transparent stone, clear as glass, with a faint sea-green tinge, and speckled in the interior with small black spots. Caldew had never seen a stone like it. The frail gold of the setting suggested that it was not of much intrinsic value, but it was a pretty little trinket, such as ladies sometimes wear as a mascot. Caldew reflected that if it were a mascot it was by no means certain that the owner was a woman. Many young officers took mascots to the front for luck.

As he turned it over in his hand he observed some lettering on the underside. He examined it curiously, and saw that an inscription had been scratched into the stone in round, irregular handwriting–obviously an unskilled, almost childish effort. Holding the brooch closer to the light, he was able to decipher the inscription. It consisted of two words–"Semper Fidelis."

It seemed to Caldew that the inscription rather weakened the correctness of his first impression that the trinket had been worn as a feminine mascot. He doubted very much whether any modern woman would cherish a mid-Victorian sentiment like "Always Faithful." On the other hand, many men might. His experience as a detective had led him to the belief that men were more prone to such sentiments than the other sex, though their conduct rarely accorded with their protestations and temporary intentions.

Struck by a sudden thought, he dropped the trinket back on the carpet. It was just visible in the thick pile.

"A good idea!" he murmured, as he rose to his feet. "I'll watch this room to-night."

As he stood there, speculating on the possibility of the owner of the trinket returning to the room to search for it, he was interrupted by a low tap at the door. He walked across and opened it. Tufnell stood outside, grave and composed.

"Mr. Musard would like to see you in the library," he said.

His tone was even and almost deferential, but the detective's watchful eyes intercepted a fleeting glance cast by the butler over his shoulder in the direction of the still figure on the bed.

"Very well, I will see him," said the detective.

"I will take you to him, if you will come with me." The butler preceded him along the passage with noiseless step, and Caldew followed him, deep in thought.

The butler escorted him to the library, and entered after him. Musard was in the room alone, standing by the fireplace, smoking a cigar. He looked up as Caldew entered.

"I have just learnt something which I think you ought to know," he said. "The information comes from Tufnell. He tells me that while he was going around the house this afternoon he found the outside door of the back staircase unlocked."

"Do you mean the door at the bottom of the staircase in the left wing?" asked Caldew.

"Precisely."

"I understood from Miss Heredith that this door was always kept locked."

"So it is, as a rule. It was only by chance that the butler discovered this evening that it had been unlocked. You had better explain to the detective, Tufnell, how you came to find it unfastened."

"I was going round by the back of the house this evening," said the butler, coming forward. "As I passed the door I tried the handle. To my surprise it yielded. I opened the door, and found that the key was in the keyhole, on the other side. I locked the door, and took the key away."

"What time was this?" inquired Caldew.

"A little before six—perhaps a quarter of an hour."

"Is it your custom to try this door every night?"

"Oh, no, it is not necessary. The door is always kept locked, and the key hangs with a bunch of other unused keys in a small room near the housekeeper's apartments, where a number of odds and ends are kept."

"When was the last time you tried the door?"

The butler considered for a moment.

"I cannot rightly say," he said at length. "The door is never used, and I rarely think of it."

"Then, for all you know to the contrary, the key may have been in the door for days, or weeks past."

"Why, yes, it is possible, now that you come to mention it," said the butler, with an air of surprise, as though he had not previously considered such a contingency.

"The key had been taken off the bunch?"

"Yes."

"Do the servants know where the key is kept?"

"Some of the maidservants do. The back staircase is occasionally opened for ventilation and dusting, and the maid who does this work gets the key from the housekeeper."

"Who has charge of the room where the keys are kept?"

"Nobody in particular. It is really a sort of a lumber-room. The housekeeper has charge of the keys."

"Thank you; that is all I wish to know."

The butler left the room, and Caldew looked up, to encounter Musard's eyes regarding him.

"Do you think this has anything to do with the murder?" Musard asked.

Caldew hesitated for a moment. It was on the tip of his tongue to reply that he attached no importance to the butler's statement, but professional habits of caution checked his natural impulsiveness.

"I want to know more about the circumstances before advancing an opinion," he replied. "Tufnell's story was rather vague."

"In what respect?"

"In regard to time. The door may have been left unlocked for days."

"Who would unlock it?" replied Musard. "The inference, in view of what has happened, seems rather that the door was unlocked to-day, and Tufnell stumbled upon the fact by a lucky chance—by Fate, if you like. At least it looks like that to me."

"And the murderer entered by the door?"

"Yes."

"I think that is assuming too much," said Caldew. He had no intention of pointing out to his companion that such an assumption overlooked the fact that Tufnell's discovery, and the locking of the door, had not prevented the crime and the subsequent escape of the murderer.

He turned to leave the room, but Musard was in a talkative mood. He offered the detective a cigar, and kept him for a while, chatting discursively. Caldew was in no humour to listen. His mind was full of the problems of this strange case, and he was anxious to return upstairs. He took the first opportunity of terminating the conversation and leaving the room.

It was his intention to conceal himself in one of the wardrobes of the bedroom in the hope that the owner of the trinket he had found would return in search of it. As he reached the landing he was surprised to see that the door of the murdered woman's bedroom was wide open, although he remembered distinctly that he had closed it when he left the room to accompany the butler downstairs. With a quickly beating heart he hurried across the room to the spot where he had left the trinket. But it was gone.

7

It was the morning after the murder, and five men were seated in the moat-house library. One of them attracted instant attention by reason of his overpowering personality. He was a giant in stature and build, with a massive head, a large red face from which a pair of little bloodshot eyes stared out truculently, and a bull neck which was several shades deeper in colour than his face. He was Superintendent Merrington, a noted executive officer of New Scotland Yard, whose handling of the most important spy case tried in London during the war had brought forth from a gracious sovereign the inevitable Order of the British Empire. Merrington was known as a detective in every capital in Europe, and because of his wide knowledge of European criminals had more than once acted as the bodyguard of Royalty on continental tours, and had received from Royal hands the diamond pin which now adorned the spotted silk tie encircling his fat purple neck.

The famous detective's outlook on life was cynical and coarse. The cynicism was the natural outcome of his profession; the coarseness was his heritage by birth, as his sensual mouth, blubber lips, thick nose, and bull-neck attested. It was a strange freak of Fate which had made him the guardian of the morals of society and the upholder of law and order in a modern civilized community. By temperament and disposition he belonged to the full-blooded type of humanity which found its best exemplars in the early Muscovite Czars, and, if Fate had so willed it, would have revelled in similar pursuits of vice, oppression, and torture. As Fate had ironically made a police official of him, he had to content himself with letting off the superfluous steam of his tremendous temperament by oppressing the criminal classes, and he had performed that duty so thoroughly that before he became the travelling companion of kings his name had been a terror to the underworld of London, who feared and detested his ferocity, his unscrupulous methods of dealing with them, and his wide knowledge of their class.

He was a recognized hero of the British public, which on one occasion had presented him with a testimonial for his capture of a desperado who had been terrorizing the East End of London. But Merrington disdained such tokens of popular approval. He regarded the public, which he was paid to protect, as a pack of fools. For him, there were only two classes of humanity—fools and rogues. The respectable portion of the population constituted the former, and criminals the latter. He had the lowest possible opinion of humanity as a whole, and his favourite expression, in professional conversation, was: "human nature being what it is...." He was still a mighty force in Scotland Yard, although he had passed his usefulness and reached the ornamental stage of his career, rarely condescending to investigate a case personally.

His present visit to the moat-house was one of those rare occasions, and was due to the action of Captain Stanhill, the Chief Constable of Sussex, who was seated near him. Captain Stanhill was a short stout man, with a round, fresh-coloured face, and short sturdy legs and arms. He wore a tweed coat of the kind known to tailors as "a sporting lounge," and his little legs were encased in knickerbockers and leather gaiters, which were spattered with mud, as though he had ridden some distance that morning. He was a very different type from Superintendent Merrington—a gentleman by birth and education, a churchman, and a county magnate. He never did anything so dangerous as to think, but accepted the traditions and rules of his race and class as his safe guide through life. Like most Englishmen of his station of life, he was endowed with just sufficient intelligence to permit him to slide along his little groove of life with some measure of satisfaction to himself and pleasure to his neighbours. He was a sound judge of cattle and horses, but of human nature he knew nothing whatever, and his first act, on being informed of the murder at the moat-house, was to ring up Scotland Yard and request it to send down one of its most trusted officials to investigate the circumstances. In reply to this call for assistance, Superintendent Merrington, not unmindful of the county standing and influence of the Herediths, had decided to investigate the case himself, and had brought with him two satellites—a finger-print expert who was at that moment paring his own finger-nails with a pocket-knife as he stared vacantly out of the library window, and an official photographer, who was upstairs taking photographs in the death chamber.

Seated near the finger-print expert was a police official of middle-age, Inspector Weyling, of the Sussex County Police. He was a saturnine sort of man, with a hooked nose, a skin like parchment, and a perfectly bald sugar-loaf head, surmounted at the top by a wen as large as a duck-egg. His deferential attitude and obsequious tone whenever Superintendent Merrington chose to address a remark to him indicated that he had a proper official respect for the rank and standing of that gentleman. Inspector Weyling was merely a police official. He had no personal characteristics whatever, unless a hobby for breeding Belgian rabbits, and a profound belief that Mr. Lloyd George was the greatest statesman the world had ever seen, could be said to constitute a temperament.

The fifth man was Detective Caldew, who had just completed a narrative of the events of the previous night for the benefit of his colleagues, but more especially for Superintendent Merrington, in whose hands lay the power of directing the investigations of the crime. It was by no wish of Detective Caldew that Superintendent Merrington had been brought into the case. Caldew

thought when the county inspector arrived and found a
Scotland Yard man at work he would be only too glad to
allow him to go on with the case, and he anticipated no
difficulty in obtaining the consent of his official superiors
at Scotland Yard to continuing the investigations he had
commenced. But Inspector Weyling, when notified of the
crime by Sergeant Lumbe, had telephoned to the Chief
Constable for instructions. The latter, distrustful of the
ability of the county police to bring such an atrocious
murderer to Justice, had begged the help of Scotland
Yard, with the result that Superintendent Merrington
and his assistants appeared at the moat-house in the
early morning before the astonished eyes of Caldew, who
was taking a walk in the moat-house garden after a night
of fruitless investigations.

In the arrival of Merrington, Caldew saw all his fine
hopes of promotion dashed to the ground. He was by no
means confident that Merrington would permit him to
take any further share in the investigations, but he was
quite certain that if he did, and the murderer was
captured through their joint efforts, very little of the
credit would fall to his share when such a famous
detective as Merrington was connected with the case.
Merrington would see to that.

Caldew, in his narration of the facts of the murder,
laid emphasis on the mysterious nature of the crime, in
the hope that Merrington might deem it wiser to return
to London and leave him in charge of the case, rather
than risk a failure which would greatly damage his own
reputation. Merrington listened to him gloomily. He fully
realized the difficult task ahead of the police, and his
temper was not improved in consequence.

"Apparently the murderer has got clean away without
leaving a trace behind him?" he said.

"Yes."

"No sign of any weapon?"

"No."

"Anything taken?"

"No. Miss Heredith says nothing was taken from the room, and nothing is missing from the house."

"The motive was not robbery then," remarked Captain Stanhill.

"It may have been," responded Merrington. "Caldew says the first intimation of the crime was the murdered woman screaming. The scream was followed in a few seconds by the revolver shot. If she screamed when she saw the murderer enter her room, he may well have feared interruption and capture, and bolted without stealing anything."

"Why did he murder her, then, in that case?" asked Captain Stanhill.

"To prevent subsequent identification. Many burglars proceed to murder for that reason. I know plenty of old hands who would commit half a dozen murders rather than face the prospect of five years' imprisonment. I do not say that burglary was the motive in this case, but we must not lose sight of the possibility."

"It seems a strange case," murmured Inspector Weyling absently. He was thinking, as he spoke, of his rabbits, and wondering whether his wife would remember to give the lop-eared doe with the litter a little milk in the course of the morning.

"It's a very sad case," said Captain Stanhill. "Poor young thing!" The Chief Constable was a human being before he was a police official, and his face showed plainly that he was stricken with horror by the story of the crime.

"It's a damned remarkable case," exclaimed Merrington, in his booming voice. "I do not remember its parallel. An English lady is murdered in her home, with a crowd of people sitting at dinner in the room underneath, and the murderer gets clean away, without leaving a trace. No weapon, no finger-prints or footprints, and no clue of any kind."

Caldew had been hoping to get an opportunity of telling Merrington privately about the missing trinket, but he realized that he was not doing his duty by delaying the explanation.

"There was something which might have helped us as a clue," he said. "Last night, while I was examining Mrs. Heredith's bedroom, I saw a small trinket lying on the floor near the bedside."

"What sort of a trinket?" asked Merrington.

"A small bar brooch."

"Where is it?"

"I do not know," replied Caldew awkwardly. "I left it where I saw it, hidden in the carpet, thinking it possible that the person who had lost it might return in search of it, but while I was downstairs it disappeared."

"It is rather strange," said Merrington thoughtfully. "I am not inclined to think there is anything in it to help us," he added, after a moment's consideration. "Still, I will look into it later. Why did you leave the trinket in the room, Caldew?"

"I thought it possible that if the owner had anything to do with the crime he—or she—might return for it," said Caldew. "So I left it where I found it, and watched the room from the end of the passage."

"A murderer doesn't go about wearing a cheap trinket, and, if he did, he wouldn't risk his neck coming back to look for it. The brooch was more likely dropped by one of the maidservants, who picked it up again."

"Would a girl go into a room where there was a dead body?"

"A country wench would. English countrywomen have pretty strong nerves. You ought to know that. But why did you leave the room if you expected the owner of the trinket to return in search of it?"

"I was called downstairs to see Mr. Musard. An unused outside door which is generally kept locked was discovered unlocked by the butler before the murder was committed. As the door opens on a staircase leading to the left wing, Mr. Musard thought the butler's discovery had some bearing on the crime."

"He thought the murderer may have entered the house that way? Such a theory would suggest that one of the servants is implicated."

"Yes; but I do not agree with Mr. Musard."

"What is your own opinion?"

"I think the key must have been left in the door by one of the servants–perhaps some days ago. The fact that the butler locked the door when he found it unfastened did not prevent the murder being committed, or the murderer escaping afterwards."

"The murderer may have entered by the door before the butler discovered that it had been unlocked, and then concealed himself inside the house awaiting an opportunity to commit the crime."

"In that case, he would have tried to escape the same way, but it is quite certain that he did not do so. Mr. Musard says that the staircase was the first place to be searched when the guests rushed upstairs. If the murderer had gone that way he would have found the door at the bottom locked, and the key removed, and he must have been caught before he could get back upstairs."

"There's something in that," said Merrington. "But how do you account for the door being unlocked in the first instance?"

"The servants know where the key is kept. One of the maids may have taken it to steal out of the house that way to keep an appointment with a sweetheart, and forgotten all about it when she returned. The back staircase and entrance are never used by the members of the household, and the key, which was inside the door, may have been there for days without being noticed. Tufnell admits that it was only by chance he tried the door yesterday. He had not tried it for weeks before."

"I'll have a look at this door later. And now, we had better get to work. We have got to catch this murderer pretty quickly, or the press and the public will be up in arms. He's had too long a start already. You must make

up your mind for considerable public indignation about
that, Caldew."

"I do not see how I can be held responsible for the
murderer getting away," said Caldew, in an aggrieved
tone. "He had his start before I arrived. I did everything
that I could. I searched the house inside and out, and
Sergeant Lumbe has been scouring the country-side since
daybreak looking for suspicious characters."

"I am not blaming you, Caldew," responded
Merrington, but his voice suggested the reverse of his
words. "I am merely pointing out to you the way the
British public will look at it. They will say, 'Here is a
young wife murdered in the bosom of her home and
family, and the murderer gets right away. What do we
pay the detective force for? To let murderers escape?'
Mark my words, if we don't lay our hands on this chap
quickly, we'll have the whole of the London press howling
at our heels like a pack of wolves. Half a dozen special
reporters travelled down in the train with me and
pestered me with questions all the way. They are coming
along here later for a statement for the evening editions.
But never mind the journalists—let us get to work without
further loss of time. Have you made a list of all the guests
who have been stopping in the house?"

"Not yet. Here is a sketch plan of the moat-house
interior and the grounds which you may find useful."

"Thanks. You had better prepare a list of the guests
before they leave. They are sure to get away as fast as
possible, and we may want to interview some of them
later on. Now we had better have a look at the body."

They went upstairs to the bedroom. There they found
a young man, with a freckled face and a snub nose,
packing up a photographic apparatus. He was the
photographer, and he had been taking photographs of the
dead body.

"Finished?" inquired Merrington. "That's right. Then
you and Freeling had better return to London by the next
train—you'll be wanted in that Putney case."

The photographer and the finger-print expert left the room together, and Merrington walked across to the bed. He drew away the sheet which covered the dead girl, and bent over the body, examining it closely, but without touching it.

"The corpse has not been moved, I suppose?" he remarked to Caldew, who was standing beside him.

"Not since I arrived. But she may not have been shot in that position. She lived some minutes afterwards, and may have moved slightly—not much, I should say, for there are no marks of bloodstains on any other part of the bed."

Merrington nodded. He was looking at the bullet wound, which was plainly visible through a burnt orifice in the rest-gown which the dead girl was wearing. The wound was a circular punctured hole in the left breast, less than the size of a sixpenny piece.

"The wound has been washed," he observed. "Was that done by the police surgeon?"

"The police surgeon has not been here. The corpse was examined by the village medical man, Dr. Holmes."

"I should like to see him. Where is he to be found?"

"He will be here in the course of the morning. He is attending young Heredith, who is suffering from the shock. The doctor fears brain fever."

"When he comes I want to see him. It is idle speculating about the cause of death in the absence of a doctor. Death in this case appears to have been due to hæmorrhage. Apparently the murderer aimed at the heart and missed it, and the shot went through the lungs. The shot was fired at very close range too—look how the wrapper is burnt! Any sign of the bullet, Caldew?"

"I found none."

"Well, we shall have to wait for the doctor to clear up these points."

His trained eyes swept round the bedroom, taking stock of every article in it. He next carefully examined the door, and the lock on it.

"The door was open when the others came upstairs, you said, Caldew?"

"Yes—about half open."

"That accounts for the scream and the shot being heard so plainly downstairs. It also suggests that the murderer fled very hurriedly, leaving the door open behind him."

"It seems to me more likely that he escaped by the window, even if he did not enter that way. Miss Heredith, who was the last inmate of the household to see Mrs. Heredith alive, thinks that the window was closed when she was in the room before dinner."

Merrington walked over to the window and examined it, testing the lock and looking at the sill.

"Does Miss Heredith say that the window was locked, or merely closed, when she was in the room?" he asked.

"She cannot say definitely. She thinks it was closed because the air was heavy, and she knew that Mrs. Heredith disliked having her bedroom window open."

Merrington shrugged his shoulders contemptuously.

"A woman's fancies are not much to build a theory upon," he said. "Have you any other reason for thinking that the murderer may have escaped by this window?"

"Yes. After the shot was fired the guests rushed upstairs immediately, and the murderer would have run into them if he had attempted to escape downstairs."

"Is there no other means of escape from the wing except by the staircase?"

"There is the back staircase I told you of, at the end of the corridor. That staircase is never used. The door is kept locked, and the key hangs in a room downstairs. It was the door at the bottom of this staircase which was found unlocked by the butler yesterday evening."

"I'll have a look at it, and then we'll go downstairs. I want to see this bedroom window from outside."

They left the bedroom and proceeded to the end of the corridor, where Caldew pointed out the door at the top of the staircase. Merrington opened it, and went down the stairs. He reappeared after the lapse of a few minutes with dusty hands and cobwebs on his clothes.

"The murderer didn't get in that way," he said. "On the face of it, it seems a plausible theory to suggest that he entered by the locked door and hid himself somewhere in this wing, and escaped after committing the murder by jumping through the bedroom window. But it is impossible to get over your point that if he had entered by the door he would have tried to escape by the same means, not knowing that the door had been locked in the meantime. To do that he must have traversed the corridor twice and gone down and up these back stairs while the guests were coming up the other stairs. He couldn't have done it in the time. He would have been caught—cut off before he could get back. Look at this steep flight of stairs and the length of the corridor! That disposes of the incident of the door. Whoever unlocked it was not the murderer."

Merrington retraced his steps along the corridor. As he walked, his eyes roved restlessly over the tapestry hangings and velvet curtains, and took in the dark nooks and corners which abound in old English country-houses.

"Plenty of places here where a man might hide," he muttered, in a dissatisfied voice.

At the head of the front staircase he paused, and looked over the balusters, as though calculating the distance to the hall beneath. Then he descended the stairs.

It still wanted half an hour to breakfast time. There was no sign of anybody stirring downstairs except a fresh-faced maidservant, who was dusting the furniture in the great hall. She glanced nervously at the groups of police officials, and then resumed her dusting. Merrington strode across to her.

"What is your name, my dear?" he asked, in his great voice.

"Milly Saker, sir."

"Very well, Milly. I'll come and have a talk with you presently—just our two selves."

The girl, far from looking delighted at this prospect, backed away with a frightened face. Merrington strode on through the open front door, and turned towards the left wing.

It was a crisp autumn morning. The early sunshine fell on the hectic flush of decay in the foliage of the woods, but a thin wisp of vapour still lingered across the moat-house garden and the quiet fields beyond. Merrington kept on until he reached the large windows of the dining-room, which opened on to the terraced garden.

"That's Mrs. Heredith's window," he said, pointing up to it. "Her bedroom is directly over the dining-room. If the murderer escaped by the window he must have dropped on to this gravel path."

"It is a pretty stiff drop," said Captain Stanhill, measuring the distance with his eye.

"Oh, I don't know," replied Merrington. "He'd let himself down eight feet with extended arms, and that would leave a drop of only ten feet or thereabouts—not much for an athletic man. But if he dropped he must have left footprints."

"There are none. I have looked," said Caldew.

The information did not deter Merrington from examining the path anew. He got down on his hands and knees to scrutinize the gravel and the grass plot more thoroughly.

"Nothing doing here either," he said as he scrambled to his feet. "There are neither footprints nor marks such as one would expect to find if a man had dropped out of the window. What are you looking at, Weyling?"

In reply Inspector Weyling made his first and only contribution towards the elucidation of the crime.

"Could not the murderer have climbed up to the bedroom by that creeper?" he asked, pointing to a thin trail of Virginia creeper which stretched up the wall almost as high as the window.

Merrington tested the frail creeper with his great hand. His sharp tug detached a mass of the plant from the brickwork.

"Not likely," he replied. "It might bear the weight of a boy or a slender girl, but not of a man. What do you think, Caldew?"

Caldew nodded without speaking. Weyling's remark had started a train of thought in his mind, but he had no intention of revealing it to a man who plainly did not intend to confer with him on equal terms, or disclose his own theory of the murder–if he had formed one.

"Let us get inside again," said Merrington, in his masterful way.

He turned back towards the house, and the others followed.

8

As they reached the library again a small silver clock on the mantelpiece gave a single chime. Merrington looked at it, and then glanced at his watch.

"Half-past eight!" he said. "That clock is five minutes slow–by me. The people who have been staying here will go off after breakfast. Visitors always leave a house of trouble as soon as possible–like rats deserting a sinking ship. The thing is to question as many as we can get hold of before they go. As some of them knew Mrs. Heredith before her marriage, we may elicit something about her or her antecedents which will throw some light on the motive for the crime."

"I do not think Sir Philip will care to have his guests questioned," remarked Captain Stanhill doubtfully. "They must be all well-connected and very respectable people, or they would not have been invited here."

"There have been very respectable and highly connected murderers before to-day, Captain Stanhill, as no doubt you are aware," rejoined Merrington caustically.

"The guests were all downstairs in the dining-room at the time the murder was committed," said Caldew. "Miss Heredith told me so herself."

"I am aware of that fact also," retorted Merrington sharply. "Nevertheless, they must be seen. We cannot afford to throw away a chance."

"It is a delicate and awkward business," murmured the Chief Constable.

"It will be a delicate and awkward business for us if we don't lay our hands on this criminal," responded Merrington. "Sir Philip Heredith, with his influence and connections, will be able to make it pretty hot for Scotland Yard and the County Police if the murderer of his son's wife is allowed to escape. You'd better take the job in hand at once, Caldew. Weyling can go with you and help. See as many of the guests as you can–especially the ladies–and get what you can out of them. But I'd be glad if you'd first ask Miss Heredith to grant me an interview before breakfast. Don't send a servant, but see her yourself."

Caldew left the room to undertake the investigations allotted to him, and Weyling followed him with a startled expression of face. He felt overweighted by the magnitude of the task which had been thrust upon him, and doubted his ability to discharge it properly.

"Miss Heredith will be able to give us more information than Sir Philip," remarked Merrington in a friendly tone to Captain Stanhill, as the door closed behind the subordinate officials. "A woman is generally more observant than a man–particularly if anything underhand has been going on."

Captain Stanhill cast a puzzled glance at his companion. As a simple-minded English gentleman he was quite unable to penetrate the obscurity of expression which masked the meaning of the last remark. Merrington caught the look, but had formed too poor an opinion of his companion's understanding to explain himself further. Besides, he liked mystifying people.

"I'm going to put the servants through their facings straight away," he continued. "If there is anything to be learnt we are more likely to find it out from them than the guests. Trust the backstairs for knowing what's going on upstairs! Servants want skilful handling, though. You've got to know when to bully and when to coax. Half measures are no good with them."

Captain Stanhill did not reply. He wandered round the spacious library, glancing at the rows of books in their oaken shelves. Superintendent Merrington, while awaiting the arrival of Miss Heredith, drew forth the plan of the moat-house which Caldew had sketched, and studied it closely.

The moat-house had only two stories, but it was a rambling old place and covered a considerable area of ground, facing three sides of the county. The principal portion, consisting of the old house which had been burnt down and rebuilt, faced the north. The two wings had been added later. The front door opened into a spacious entrance hall which in former times had been the dining-room. At the end of the hall was the grand staircase, adorned by statues, armour, and the Heredith arms carved in panels. The principal rooms, with the exception of the dining-room, were all on the ground floor of the main building, but corridors led off the entrance hall to the newer wings at each side, extending on the right side to the billiard room, conservatory, greenhouses, and orangery, and on the left side to the dining-room, Miss Heredith's private sitting-room, and Sir Philip's study.

Merrington carefully studied the arrangements of this wing, as depicted on Caldew's sketch plan. The upper portion was reached by a staircase which opened off the corridor almost opposite the dining-room door, and ran, with one turning, to a landing which was only a few feet away from the door of the bedroom in which Mrs. Heredith was murdered. Next to this room was a dressing-room, and a spare bedroom. The remainder of the wing consisted of two bathrooms, a linen room, and Miss Heredith's bedroom, which was at the south end of the wing. The rooms all faced the west side of the house, and were lit by windows opening on the terraced gardens. They were entered by a corridor which ran the whole length of the wing, terminating in the door which opened on the unused back staircase.

Before Merrington had finished his scrutiny of the plan, the door opened, and Miss Heredith entered the library. She looked pale and worn, and there were dark rings under her eyes which suggested a sleepless night. But her face was composed, though grave.

Captain Stanhill advanced and shook hands with her, uttering a few words of well-bred sympathy as he did so, and then introduced Superintendent Merrington.

"Superintendent Merrington has been kind enough to come down from Scotland Yard at my request to give us the benefit of his skill in investigating this terrible crime," he said simply.

"I desired an interview with you in order to ask a few questions," said Merrington, coming to the point at once.

Miss Heredith bowed.

"Were all the blinds down in the dining-room last night during dinner?" asked Merrington.

Captain Stanhill looked quickly at his colleague. He failed to see the purpose of the question.

"I think so," replied Miss Heredith, after a moment's reflection. "I cannot say for certain, as I was out of the room during the latter portion of the dinner, but I can easily ascertain." She touched a bell, which was answered by a maidservant. "Tell Mr. Tufnell I wish to speak to him," she said.

The girl went away, and Tufnell appeared a moment afterwards.

"Were the blinds all drawn in the dining-room during dinner last night, Tufnell?"

"Yes, ma'am. I pulled them down myself before sounding the gong."

"Thank you, Tufnell."

"I understand that you were not present at the dinner table when the shot was fired?" said Merrington when the butler had left the room.

"No, I was not."

"May I ask why you left the table?"

The question was put suavely enough, but a half-uttered protest from Captain Stanhill indicated that he, at least, realized the sting contained within it. But Miss Heredith, looking at Merrington with her clear grey eyes, replied calmly:

"I was called out of the room to speak to our chauffeur. He had been ordered to have an extra vehicle in readiness to convey our guests to an evening entertainment, and he wished to consult me about it."

"Why did you not return to the dining-room?"

"Because dinner was nearly finished when I left the room."

"Where were you when the shot was fired?"

"I was on the stairs, on the way to my room when I heard the scream. I was hastening back to the dining-room as quickly as possible, but before I reached it the shot rang out."

"Surely these questions are unnecessary, Merrington," exclaimed Captain Stanhill. "Anyone would think–I mean that there is not the slightest idea in our minds that Miss Heredith–at least, I meant to say–" Captain Stanhill floundered badly as he realized that his remarks were capable of a terrible interpretation which he did not intend, and broke off abruptly.

"I am very glad that Superintendent Merrington has asked these questions," said Miss Heredith coldly.

Merrington bowed a grim acknowledgment. He had still many questions he wanted to ask Miss Heredith, and he proceeded to put them in his own masterful way, very much as though he were examining a witness in the police court, Captain Stanhill thought, but in reality with a courtesy and consideration quite unusual for him. It was his best manner; his worst, Captain Stanhill was to see later. As a matter of fact, it was impossible for Merrington to be gentle with anybody. He had spent so many years of his life probing into strange stories and sinister mysteries that he had insensibly come to regard the world as a larger criminal court, made up of tainted and adverse witnesses, whom it was his privilege to cross-question.

He questioned Miss Heredith searchingly about the young bride. According to an eminent expert in jurisprudence, the tendency to believe the testimony of others is an inherent instinct implanted in the human breast by the Almighty. If that be so, it is to be feared that the seed had failed to germinate in Merrington's bosom, for his natural tendency was to look upon his fellow creatures as liars, particularly when they were of good social standing, with that hatred of notoriety which is characteristic of their class. Merrington had this fact in his mind as he interrogated Miss Heredith closely about the circumstances of her nephew's marriage. He hoped to extract from her something which her English pride might lead her to conceal, something which might throw a light on the motive for the murder.

Miss Heredith answered him with a frankness which even Merrington grudgingly realized left nothing to be desired. She was, apparently, only too anxious to help the police investigations to the best of her ability. But what she had to tell amounted to very little. Her first knowledge of her nephew's intention to marry was contained in a letter written home some four months before, in which he announced his engagement to a young lady engaged in war work in a London Government office. A month later came the news that he was married, and was bringing his young bride to the moat-house. The young couple arrived a week after the receipt of the second letter. They were welcomed home, and settled down to country life in the old place. Phil left his post in the War Office, and busied himself in looking after the estate. He was very fond of his young wife, but it was obvious from the first that Violet found the quiet country existence rather dull after her London life. She knew nobody in Sussex except Mrs. Weyne, the author's wife, who had been an acquaintance of hers in London years before, and she did not seem to care much for the county people who visited the moat-house. She received letters from girl friends in London, and sometimes read extracts from them at the breakfast table, but her life, on the whole, was a secluded one. It was in order to brighten it that Phil suggested a house party. The guests consisted principally of Violet's and Phil's London friends and acquaintances.

"Do you know the names of these girl friends who used to write to her?" asked Merrington.

Miss Heredith replied that she did not.

"I suppose her husband would know them?"

"It is quite impossible to question my nephew," said Miss Heredith decisively. "He is dreadfully ill."

Merrington nodded in a dissatisfied sort of way. He was aware of Phil's illness, and his suspicious mind wondered whether it had been assumed for the occasion in order to keep back something which the police ought to know. His thick lip curled savagely at the idea. If these people tried to hide anything from him in order to save a scandal, so much the worse for them. But that was something he would go into later.

The next questions he put to Miss Heredith were designed to ascertain what she thought of the murder, whether she had any suspicions of her own, and whether there was any reason for suspecting Miss Heredith herself. At that stage of the inquiry it was Merrington's business to suspect everybody. He could not afford to allow the slightest chance to slip. His object was to get at the truth; to weigh each particle of supposition or evidence without regard to the feelings or social position of the witness.

The case so far puzzled him, and Miss Heredith's answers to his questions revealed little about the murder that he had not previously known. The only additional facts he gleaned related to the murdered girl's brief existence at the moat-house; of her earlier history and her London life Miss Heredith knew nothing whatever. Merrington made some notes of the replies in an imposing pocket-book, but he was plainly dissatisfied as he turned to another phase of the investigation.

"Were all your guests in the dining-room at the time the scream and the shot were heard?" he asked.

"They were all there when I left the room. The butler can tell you if any left afterwards."

"I will question Tufnell on that point later. No, on second thoughts, it will be better to settle it now. I attach importance to it."

Tufnell was recalled to the room, and, in reply to Superintendent Merrington's question, stated that none of the guests left the dining-room before the shot was fired. Tufnell added they were all interested in listening to a story that Mr. Musard was telling. Having imparted this information the butler returned to the breakfast room, overweighted with the responsibility of superintending the morning meal in his mistress's absence.

"Is this Musard the jewel expert of that name?" asked Merrington.

"Our guest is Mr. Vincent Musard, the explorer," replied Miss Heredith coldly.

"The same man." Merrington made another minute note in his pocket-book, and continued, "May I take it, then, that all your guests who were staying here were assembled in the dining-room at the time the murder was committed?"

"Yes; except one who left during the afternoon."

"Who was that?"

"Captain Nepcote, a friend of my nephew's. He received a telegram recalling him to the front, and returned to London by the afternoon train."

Merrington made a note of this in his pocket-book with an air of finality, and asked Miss Heredith to see that the servants were sent to the library one by one, to be questioned. Miss Heredith said she would arrange it with the housekeeper, and was then politely escorted to the door by Captain Stanhill.

The next few hours were educative for Captain Stanhill. Although he was Chief Constable of Sussex, he took no part in the proceedings, but sat at the table like a man in a dream, living in a world of Superintendent Merrington's creation–a world of sinister imaginings and vile motives, through which stealthy suspicion prowled craftily with padded feet, seeking a victim among the procession of weeping maids, stolid under-gardeners, stable hands, and anxious upper servants who presented themselves in the library to be questioned. But it seemed to Captain Stanhill that though the women were flustered and the men nervous, they knew nothing whatever about the atrocious murder which had been committed a few hours before in the room above their heads. Merrington also seemed to be aware that he was getting no nearer the truth with his traps, his questions, and his bullying, and he grew so angry and savage as the day wore on that he reminded Captain Stanhill of a bull he had once seen trying to rend a way through a mesh. As the morning advanced, Merrington's face took on a deeper tint of purple, his fierce little eyes grew more bloodshot, and between the intervals of examining the servants he mopped his perspiring head with a large handkerchief.

The significance of one fact he did not realize until afterwards. The last of the inmates of the moat-house to come to the library was the housekeeper, Mrs. Rath, who presented herself at his request in order to acquaint him with the details of the domestic management of the household. Mrs. Rath entered the room with a nervous air. Her white face contrasted oddly with her black dress, and her hands shook slightly, in spite of her effort to appear composed. Merrington stared at her careworn face and hollow grey eyes with the perplexed sensation of a man who is confronted with a face familiar to him, but is unable to recall its identity.

"Where have I seen you before?" he blurted out.

The housekeeper raised frightened eyes, ringed with black, to his truculent face, but dropped them again without speaking. Merrington did not repeat his question.

He did not imagine the housekeeper knew anything about the murder, but it was a mistake to put a witness on her guard. It was in quite a different tone that he thanked Mrs. Rath for sending the servants to the library, and asked her to describe the household arrangements of the previous night. Mrs. Rath, who had been palpably nervous after his first question, became reassured and more at her ease, and answered him intelligently.

"And where were you at the time of the murder, Mrs. Rath?" pursued Merrington, when he had drawn forth these details.

"I was in my sitting-room."

"Did you hear the scream and the shot?"

"I heard the scream, but not the shot."

"How was that?"

"My sitting-room is a long way from Mrs. Heredith's room. Perhaps that is the reason."

Merrington looked at the position of the housekeeper's room on the plan of the moat-house which Caldew had drawn. As she said, it was a considerable distance to her room, which was in the old portion of the house, near the rear, and on the ground floor.

"Were you alone in your room?" he asked.

"No. My daughter was sitting with me."

To a quick ear it may have seemed that the answer was a trifle long in coming.

Merrington shook his head irritably. Really, it seemed impossible to reach the end of the people who were in this infernal moat-house at the time of the murder.

"Does your daughter live with you here?" he asked.

"Oh, no. She came to see me yesterday afternoon, and stayed all night because she missed her train back after—after the tragedy."

"Is she here now?"

"No. She went away by an early train. She is employed as a milliner at Stading, the market town, which is ten miles away."

"She lives there, I suppose?"

"Yes. She lives in."

"Who is her employer?"

"Mr. Closeby, the draper. Daniel Closeby and Son is the name of the firm."

Merrington made another note in his pocket-book. It sounded plausible enough, but the girl must be added to the lengthening list of people in the case who would have to be seen.

"I think that is all I need detain you for, Mrs. Rath," he said.

The housekeeper lingered to inquire when the gentlemen would like their lunch. Merrington, who had breakfasted early and passed an arduous morning, replied bluntly that it could not be too soon to please him.

"I'll have it served in the small breakfast-room in a quarter of an hour," said Mrs. Rath, hurrying away.

Her whole bearing, as she departed, indicated such an air of irrepressible relief at having passed through a trying ordeal that all Merrington's former doubts of her revived.

"I'd give something to remember where I've seen that infernal woman before," he ejaculated, slapping his thigh emphatically.

"What infernal woman?" asked Captain Stanhill, who had come to the conclusion that he did not like Superintendent Merrington or his style of conversation.

"Why, that woman who has just left the room—that housekeeper. I've seen her before somewhere, in very different circumstances, but I cannot recall where. I recollect her face distinctly—particularly her eyes. I flatter myself I never forget a pair of eyes. Confound it, where the devil have I seen her?"

Captain Stanhill turned away indifferently, and the conversation was terminated by the appearance of Detective Caldew, who appeared in the doorway as Mrs. Rath left the room.

"Dr. Holmes is waiting in the drawing-room if you wish to see him," he announced.

"Bring him here," commanded Merrington curtly. He had a great notion of his self-importance, and had no intention of dancing attendance on a mere country practitioner.

Caldew went away, and shortly reappeared with a little man whom he introduced as Dr. Holmes. The doctor was a meagre shrimp of humanity, with a peevish expression on his withered little face, as though he were bored with his own nonentity. He was dressed in faded clothes and carried a small black bag in one hand and a worn hat in the other. If he had any idea of airing a professional protest at being compelled to wait upon the police, the thought vanished as his eye took in the stupendous stature of Superintendent Merrington, who towered above him like a mastiff standing over a toy terrier.

"Sit down, doctor," he curtly commanded. "I want to ask you a few questions about the death of Mrs. Heredith. You examined the body, I understand?"

Dr. Holmes bowed, put on a pair of gold-rimmed spectacles in order to see Superintendent Merrington better, and waited to be questioned.

"I understand you were summoned to the moat-house last night, doctor, after Mrs. Heredith was murdered, and examined the body. What was the cause of death?"

"The cause of death was a bullet wound," pronounced the doctor oracularly.

"I am aware of that much," answered Merrington irritably. "But a bullet wound is not necessarily fatal. Mrs. Heredith lived some time after her death, so it is certain that the bullet which killed her did not penetrate the heart. What is the nature of the injuries it inflicted?"

"Death in Mrs. Heredith's case was the result of a bullet passing through the left lung. It passed between the second and third ribs in entering the body, traversed the lung, causing a great flow of blood, which filled the air passages."

"Then the cause of death was hæmorrhage?"

"Yes. There was very severe internal hæmorrhage. The face and the left-hand side of the neck were covered with blood. There had also been bleeding from the mouth and nose. Mr. Musard, who accompanied me to the room, told me he had washed it away while Mrs. Heredith was dying, in an endeavour to staunch the flow."

"She was quite dead when you saw her?"

"Oh, yes. Judging by the warmth of the body, and by the fact that blood had ceased to flow, I should say that death had taken place about forty minutes before."

"What time did you reach the moat-house?"

"It would be about twenty minutes past eight. Sergeant Lumbe called at my house at ten minutes past the hour–I made a note of the time–and I went immediately. It is about ten minutes' walk to the moat-house from the village."

"Was the main blood vessel of the lung broken?" asked Captain Stanhill, who had been following the doctor's remarks with close attention.

"The aorta? It is difficult to say from an external examination. Mr. Musard tells me that Mrs. Heredith died about five minutes after he reached the room. The aorta is a very large vessel, and if it were burst bleeding to death would be very rapid."

"Could the wound have been self-inflicted?" asked Merrington.

Dr. Holmes pursed his lips.

"I can form no definite opinion on that point," he said. "By the direction of the bullet, I should say not."

"Have you found the bullet?"

"No, it is in the body. As apparently it took a course towards the right after entering the body, and there is no corresponding wound in the back, I should say that it is lodged somewhere in the vertical column. Of course, I cannot be sure."

"The Government pathologist will clear up these points when he makes the post-mortem examination," said Merrington. "I do not think we have any more questions to ask you, doctor."

"How is your patient, the young husband?" asked Captain Stanhill, as Dr. Holmes rose.

"The symptoms point to brain fever. The family, on my advice, have sent to London for Sir Ralph Horton, the eminent brain doctor."

"I do not wonder his mind has given way under the shock," remarked Captain Stanhill. "To lose his wife in such terrible circumstances after three months' marriage must have been a cruel blow."

"It was the worse in his case because he has always been nervous and highly strung from childhood–partly, I think, as the result of his infirmity. He has a deformed foot. His present illness seems to be a complete overthrow of the nervous system. I have been with him the greater part of the night. He has been highly delirious, but he is a little quieter now."

Merrington pricked up his ears at this last remark. After his fruitless investigations of the morning he was inclined to think that the clue to the murder lay in the past–it might be in some former folly or secret intrigue of the young wife's single days. The question was, in that case, whether the husband was likely to have any knowledge of his wife's secret. If he had, he might, in his delirium, babble something which would provide a clue to trace the murderer. It was a poor chance, but the poorest chance was worth trying in such a baffling case.

"I should like to have a look at your patient," he said to Dr. Holmes.

"It would be impossible to question him in his present state," replied the doctor stiffly.

"I do not wish to question him. I merely wish to look at him."

"In that case you may see him. He is quite unconscious, and recognizes nobody. I will take you to his room, if you wish."

The little doctor bustled along the corridor, and turned into a passage traversing the right wing of the moat-house. About half way down it he paused before a door, which he opened softly, and motioned to the other two to enter.

It was a single bedroom, panelled in oak, which was dark with age, with one small window; but it had the advantage of being as far away as possible from the upstairs bedroom in the left wing where Phil's wife lay murdered. A small fire burnt in the grate, a china bowl of autumn flowers bloomed on a table near the bedside, and a capable looking nurse was preparing a draught by the window. She glanced at the three men as they entered, but went on with her occupation.

The sick man lay on his back, breathing heavily. His black hair framed a face which was ghastly in its whiteness, and his upturned eyes, barely visible beneath the half-closed lids, seemed fixed and motionless.

"Any change, nurse?" the doctor asked.

"No change, sir."

But even as she spoke Phil's face changed in a manner which was wonderful in its suddenness. His features became contorted, as though a sword had been thrust through his vitals, and he struggled upright in his bed, with one shaking hand outstretched. His eyes, glaring with delirium, roved restlessly over the faces of the men at the foot of the bed.

"She's dead, I tell you! Violet's dead.... Have they found him? Ah, who's that?"

Once again he uttered his young wife's name, and fell back on the pillow, motionless as before, but with one arm athwart his face, as though to cover his eyes.

"I shall be glad if you will leave the room," said the little doctor gravely. "Your presence excites him." He hurried round to the bedside and bent over his patient.

9

"Have you formed any theory of the murder yet?"

It was the evening of the same day, and Superintendent Merrington and Captain Stanhill were once more in the moat-house library. It was Captain Stanhill who asked the question, as he stood warming his little legs in front of a crackling fire of oak logs which had just been lighted in the gloomy depths of the big fireplace. Although it was early in autumn, the evening air was chill.

Superintendent Merrington was walking up and down the room with rapid strides, occasionally glancing with some impatience at the clock which ticked with cheerful indifference on the mantelpiece. He was about to return to London, but was waiting for the return of Detective Caldew and Sergeant Lumbe. Caldew had cycled to Chidelham to see the Weynes, and Lumbe had been sent to investigate a telephoned report of a suspicious stranger seen at a hamlet called Tibblestone, some miles away.

Merrington's face wore a gloomy and dissatisfied expression. He had spent the afternoon in a whirlwind of energy in which he had done many things. He had explored the moat-house from top to bottom, squeezing his vast bulk into every obscure corner of the rambling old place. He had rowed round the moat in a small boat, scrutinizing the outside wall for footmarks. He had mustered the male servants, and superintended an organized beat of the grounds, the woods, and the neighbouring heights. He had interviewed the village station-master to ascertain if any stranger had arrived at Heredith the previous day, and had made similar inquiries by telephone at the adjoining stations. He had inspected the horses and vehicles at the village inn to see if they showed marks of recent usage, and he had peremptorily interrogated everybody he came across to find out whether any one unknown in the district had been seen skulking about the neighbourhood.

Merrington lacked the subtle and penetrative brain of a really great detective, but he possessed energy, initiative, and observation. These qualities had stood him in good stead before, but in this case they had brought nothing to light. The mystery and meaning of the terrible murder of the previous night were no nearer solution than when he had arrived to take up the case, ten hours before.

The most baffling aspect of the crime to him was the apparent lack of motive and the absence of any clue. In most murders there are generally some presumptive clues to guide those called upon to investigate the crime— such things as finger-prints or footprints, a previous threat or admission, an overheard conversation, a chance word, or a compromising letter. Such clues may not prove much in themselves, but they serve as finger-posts. Even the time, which in some cases of murder offers a valuable help to solution, in this case tended to shield the murderer. It seemed as though the murderer had chosen an unusual time and unusual conditions to shield his identity more thoroughly and make discovery impossible.

The case was full of sinister possibilities and perplexities. It bore the stamp of deep premeditation and calculated skill. As the crime was apparently motiveless, it was certain that the motive was deep and carefully hidden. The only definite conclusion that Merrington had reached was that the murderer would have to be sought further afield, probably in London, where the dead girl had lived all her life. There seemed not the slightest reason to suspect anybody in the neighbourhood, as she was a stranger to the district, and knew nobody in it except Mrs. Weyne, who lived some miles away. It was unfortunate that her husband, who was the only person able to give any information about her earlier life, was too ill to be questioned.

On hearing Captain Stanhill's question, Merrington paused abruptly in his impatient pacing of the carpet, and glanced at him covertly from his deep-set little eyes. If he had consulted his own feelings he would have told the Chief Constable that it was not the time to air theories about the crime. But in his present position it behoved him to walk warily and not make an enemy of his colleague. If there was to be an outburst of public indignation because the murderer in this case had not been immediately discovered and brought to justice, it would be just as well if the county police shared the burden of responsibility. Merrington realized that he could best make Captain Stanhill feel his responsibility by taking him fully into his confidence. He was aware that he had practically ignored the Chief Constable in the course of the day's investigations, and it was desirable to remove any feeling that treatment may have caused. Superintendent Merrington had the greatest contempt for the county police, but there were times when it was judicious to dissemble that feeling. The present moment was one of them.

Captain Stanhill, on his part, cherished no animosity against his companion for his cavalier treatment of him. He realized his own inexperience in crime detection, and had been quite willing that Superintendent Merrington should take the lead in the investigations, which he had assisted to the best of his ability. He thought Merrington rather an unpleasant type, but he was overawed by his great reputation as a detective, and impressed by his energy and massive self-confidence. The Chief Constable had not asserted his own official position, because he was aware that he was unable to give competent help in such a baffling case. He was, above all things, anxious that the murderer of Violet Heredith should be captured and brought to justice as speedily as possible, and he had no thought of his personal dignity so long as that end was achieved.

The abstract ideal of human justice is supposed to be based on the threefold aims of punishment, prevention, and reformation, but the heart of the average man, when confronted by grevious wrong, is swayed by no higher impulse than immediate retribution on the wrongdoer. Captain Stanhill was an average man, and his feelings, harrowed by the spectacle of the bleeding corpse of the young wife, and the pitiful condition to which her murder had reduced her young husband, clamoured for retribution, swift, complete, and implacable, on the being who had committed this horrible crime. And he hoped that the famous detective would be able to assure him that his desire was likely to have a speedy attainment. That was why he asked Merrington whether he had formed any theory about the crime.

"It would be too much to say that I have formed a theory," replied Merrington, in response to Captain Stanhill's question. "It is necessary to have clues for the formation of a theory, and in this case we are faced with a complete absence of clues."

"Do you not think that the trinket found by Detective Caldew in Mrs. Heredith's bedroom has some bearing on the murder?" said Captain Stanhill.

"I attach no importance to it. There were a number of persons in the bedroom after the murder was committed, and any of them might have dropped the ornament. Or it may have been lost there days before by a servant, and escaped notice."

"But it was picked up again during Caldew's absence from the room. Do you not regard that as suspicious? Detective Caldew, when he was relating the incident to us this morning, seemed to think that the trinket belonged to the murderer, who took the risk of returning to the room to recover it for fear it might form a clue leading to discovery."

"Caldew reads too much into his discovery," replied Merrington, with an indulgent smile. "Like all young detectives, he is inclined to attach undue importance to small points. As I told him, I cannot imagine a murderer taking such a desperate risk as to return to the spot where he had killed his victim, in order to search for a trinket he had dropped. Caldew may have concealed the brooch so effectually in the thick folds of the velvet carpet that he could not find it again when he looked for it on his return to the room. That explanation strikes me as probable as his own theory of a mysterious midnight intruder returning to search for it while he was out of the room. The trinket may have some connection with the crime, or it may not, but as I have not seen it I prefer to leave it out of my calculation altogether. This case is going to be difficult enough to solve without chasing chimeras. But to return to your question. Although I have not actually formed a theory, my preliminary investigations of the circumstances have led me to arrive at certain conclusions and to exclude possibilities I was at first inclined to adopt. I will go over the case in detail, and then you will see for yourself the conclusions I have formed, and understand how I have arrived at them.

"In the first place, the greatest problem of this murder is the apparent lack of motive. There seems to be no reason why this young lady should have been killed. She had only recently been married, and, apparently, married happily, to a wealthy young man of good family, who was very much in love with her. It is obvious that money difficulties have nothing to do with the crime. Her husband is the only son of a wealthy father, and he is able to give his wife everything that a woman needs for her happiness and comfort. She is cherished, petted, and loved, and has a beautiful home. Who, therefore, had an object in putting an end to this young woman's life in her own home, in circumstances and conditions attended with the utmost possibility of discovery and capture? The perpetrator of the deed must have acted from some very strong motive or impulse to venture into a country-house full of people, at a time when everybody was indoors, in order to kill his victim.

"In a seemingly purposeless murder like this, a certain amount of suspicion gathers round the other members of the household. Human nature being what it is, one should never take anything for granted, but should always be on the watch for hidden motives. But in this case the members of the household, with the exception of Miss Heredith, were downstairs in the dining-room at the time the murder was committed. Miss Heredith left the room a few minutes before the shot was heard. You will recall that she volunteered that statement to us this morning. It occurred to me at the time that that may have been bluff to put us off the scent. Clever criminals often do that kind of thing. My suspicions against her were strengthened by the additional fact that Miss Heredith did not like her nephew's wife. She masked the fact beneath a well-bred semblance of grief and horror, but it was plain as a pikestaff to me. But, after thinking over all the circumstances, I came to the conclusion that she had nothing whatever to do with it."

"Such a possibility is inconceivable," exclaimed Captain Stanhill. "A lady like Miss Heredith would never commit murder."

"It was not for that reason that I excluded her from suspicion," replied Merrington drily. "The points against her were really very damaging. She was out of the dining-room when the scream was heard, and when the others rushed out of the dining-room on hearing the shot, the first thing they saw was Miss Heredith descending the staircase of the wing in which her nephew's wife had been murdered. Fortunately for Miss Heredith, she was almost at the bottom of the staircase when she was seen. The guests streamed out of the dining-room directly the shot was heard, therefore it is impossible that Miss Heredith could have shot Violet Heredith and then reached the bottom of the stairs so quickly. She is able to establish an alibi of time, by, perhaps, half a minute.

"As all the members of the house party were in the dining-room at the time, it is clear that they had nothing to do with the actual commission of the crime. The next thing is the servants, and they also can be excluded from suspicion. When we examined them this morning they were all able to prove, more or less conclusively, that they were engaged in their various duties at the time the murder was committed. The point is that not one of them was upstairs in the left wing of the house when Mrs. Heredith was shot.

"My original impression that the murder was not committed by a native of the district has been deepened by our afternoon's investigations. Where, then, are we to look for the murderer? To answer that question, in part, let us first consider *how* the murder was committed, and try and reconstruct the circumstances in which the murderer must have entered and left the house.

"Caldew thinks that the murderer entered the house by scaling the bedroom window, and made his exit by the same means. He bases that view on Miss Heredith's belief that the window was closed when she was in the bedroom before dinner. After the murder was committed the window was found open. But Miss Heredith's statement about the closed window does not amount to very much. She does not actually know whether the window was open or shut, because the window curtains were completely drawn at the time she was in the room. Those curtains are so thick and heavy that they would keep out the air whether the window was open or shut, and account for the stuffy atmosphere in a room which had been occupied all day.

"I do not regard the open window as a clue one way or the other. The one thing we must not lose sight of is that nobody can say definitely when it was opened. It may have been opened by Mrs. Heredith herself before Miss

Heredith came into the room, or the murderer may have flung it open and escaped from the room that way after committing the murder. Personally, I do not think that he did, but I am not prepared altogether to exclude the possibility of his having done so. But I am convinced that he did not enter the bedroom by scaling the outside wall and getting in through the window. In the first place, there are no marks of any kind on the window sill or the window catch. There is not very much one way or another in the absence of marks on the sill or even on the catch, supposing the window was locked. The murderer might have opened the catch from outside without leaving a mark–I have known the trick to be done–and he might have got into the room without leaving any marks on the sill, particularly if he wore rubber boots. But, what is far more important, there are no marks on the wall outside, or any disturbance or displacement of the Virginia creeper which covers a portion of the wall, to suggest that the murderer climbed up to the room that way. I think it is certain that if he had done so he would have left his marks on the one or the other. The wall is of a soft old brickwork which would scratch and show marks plainly, and the Virginia creeper would break away. In any case, as I said this morning, it would barely sustain the weight of a boy, or a very slight girl. Finally, there are no marks of footsteps approaching the wall in the garden outside.

"The question of entry is naturally of great importance, and that was why I questioned the butler this morning whether the blinds were drawn in the dining-room last night. At that time, before I had had an opportunity of making my subsequent investigations, I deemed it possible that the murderer might have entered from outside by the window. In that case he would have had to pass the dining-room windows to reach the bedroom window, and might have been seen by one of the guests in the dining-room. It would be dark at the time, but last night was a very clear one, and his form might have been discerned flitting past the dining-room windows. But the absence of footprints in the gravel, and more particularly, in the soft yielding earth beneath the bedroom window, is conclusive proof to me that he did not get into the room that way.

"Did he escape by the window? That question is more difficult to answer. It is quite possible that it might have been done without injury, but it is a desperate feat to leap from an upstairs window in the dark. The murderer was in desperate straits, and for that reason we must not rule out the possibility that he did so. But if the leap was made through the window, my argument about the absence of footprints in the soft garden soil underneath the window comes in with additional force. A person leaping from such a height, even in stocking feet or rubber boots, would be certain to leave the impress of the drop, in footmarks or heelmarks, in the soil where he landed.

"Caldew's principal reason for believing that the murderer escaped by the window was based on the point that there was no other avenue of escape possible. We can only speculate as to what happened in the bedroom immediately before the murder was committed, but Caldew's theory is that Mrs. Heredith saw the murderer approaching her, and screamed for help. That scream hurried the murderer's movements. The scream was sure to arouse the household, and it left the murderer with the smallest possible margin of time in which to shoot Mrs. Heredith and make escape by the window. An attempt to escape down the front staircase meant running into the arms of the inmates of the dining-room rushing upstairs. The only other exit from that wing of the house was the disused back staircase, and that was found locked when it was searched after the murder. Therefore, according to Caldew, the murderer escaped by the window because there was no other way out.

"That theory is plausible enough on the surface, but only on the surface. For the same reason that establishes

Miss Heredith's innocence, the murderer could not have escaped by running down the staircase, because there was not sufficient time to get past the people who had been alarmed by the scream. But if the murderer was a man, it is just possible that he might have darted out of the bedroom and dropped over the balusters, before the dining-room door was opened, getting clear away without being seen by anybody–not even by Miss Heredith. An examination of the staircase of the left wing has convinced me that this feat was possible. The staircase has a very sharp turn in the middle, which has the effect of hiding the top of the staircase from the bottom, and the bottom from the top. The leap is not so dangerous as the one from the window, because it is not so high. It is probably six feet less, allowing for the flooring beneath and the higher window opening above. The spot by the foot of the staircase where the murderer might have dropped is well screened, even from the view of anybody near the bottom of the staircase, by some tall tree shrubs in tubs, and some armour.

"But there is another and likelier way by which the murderer might have escaped. I saw the possibility of it as soon as I examined the upstairs portion of the wing in which the murder had been committed. There are several places where the murderer could have hidden until chance afforded the opportunity of escape. He would avoid seeking shelter in any of the adjoining bedrooms, because he would realize that they would be searched immediately the murder was discovered, but there are excellent temporary places of concealment behind the tapestry hangings, or in the thick folds of the heavy velvet curtains at the entrance to the corridor, or in the small press or wardrobe which is built right over the head of the stairs. Suppose that the murderer, after firing the shot, dashed out into the corridor with the idea of escaping down the stairs. He hears the guests coming upstairs, and realizes that he is too late. He instinctively looks round for some place to hide, sees the curtains, and slips behind them. From their folds he watches the guests troop along the corridor to the murdered woman's bedroom. He could touch them as they passed, but they cannot see him. Then, while they are all congregated round the doorway of Mrs. Heredith's bedroom, he emerges on the other side of the curtains, slips down the staircase, and gets out of the house without meeting anybody."

"But all the guests did not go upstairs," observed Captain Stanhill, who was following his companion's remarks with close attention. "Some stayed in the dining-room. Tufnell, the butler, made that quite clear when you were examining him this morning."

"Yes—a few hysterical females cowering and whimpering with fear as far away from the door as possible," retorted Merrington contemptuously. "The butler made that clear also."

"But the servants would also have heard the scream and the shot," pursued Captain Stanhill earnestly. "Is it not likely that some of them would have been clustered near the foot of the staircase, wondering what had happened?"

"No," replied Merrington. "Servants are even more cowardly than they are curious. They would be too frightened to congregate at the foot of the staircase, for fear the murderer might come leaping downstairs and discharge another shot in their midst. It is possible, however, that the murderer remained hidden upstairs for some time longer—perhaps until the butler left the house to go to the village for the police, and Musard took all the male guests downstairs to make another search of the house. He would then have an exceedingly favourable opportunity of slipping away unobserved. It is true that the upstairs portion of the wing was searched before that time arrived, but the search was conducted by amateurs who knew nothing about such a task, and would probably overlook such hiding-places as I have indicated."

It appeared to Captain Stanhill that Superintendent Merrington, instead of always adopting his theory of fitting the crime to the circumstances, was sometimes in danger of reversing the process.

"From what you say it seems to me that it is very difficult to tell how the murderer escaped," he remarked.

"It is even more difficult to say how the murderer, after entering the moat-house, found his way to Mrs. Heredith's bedroom in order to murder her. The house is a big rambling place, consisting of a main building and two wings. It would be impossible for you or me or any other stranger to find our way about it without previous knowledge of the place, unless we had a plan. How, then, did the murderer accomplish it? How did he know that Mrs. Heredith slept in the left wing? How did he know that he would find her alone in that wing while everybody else was downstairs at the dinner-table?"

Again, it seemed to Captain Stanhill that Merrington's detective methods had a tendency to multiply difficulties rather than clear them up.

"Perhaps he was provided with a plan of the house," he suggested.

"That answers only one of my points. In my consideration of this aspect of the case, two possible solutions occurred to me. It is impossible for any of the guests to have committed the crime, because they were all downstairs at the time, but it is just possible one of them may have instigated it."

"It is incredible to me that a guest staying in a gentleman's house could plot such a crime," said Captain Stanhill.

"Nothing is incredible in crime," replied Merrington. "I've no illusions about human nature. It is capable of much worse things than that. Strange things can happen in a big country-house like this, filled with a large party of young people of both sexes—flirtations, intrigues, and worse still."

"But not murder, as a general rule," commented Captain Stanhill, with a trace of sarcasm in his mild tones.

"You cannot lay down general rules about murder. An unbalanced human being, under the influence of hatred, jealousy, or revenge, is no more amenable to the rules of society than a tiger. But I do not think that this crime was instigated by one of the guests, because in that case it would probably have been arranged to be committed later in the evening, when the members of the house-party were at the house of the Weynes, and the moat-house was occupied only by the servants. Still, I do not intend to lose sight of the hypothesis. Another possibility is that one of the servants was in league with the murderer. A third possibility is that Mrs. Heredith may have brought in the murderer herself."

"What do you mean?"

"She may have had a lover, and the lover may have murdered her."

"Oh, impossible!" Captain Stanhill repelled the idea with an instinctive gesture of disgust. "It is too monstrous to suppose that a happily married young wife would be carrying on an intrigue three months after her marriage."

"More monstrous things happen every day–human nature being what it is," retorted Merrington coolly. "You must remember that we know practically nothing about her. The people who knew her in London left the house before they could be questioned; Miss Heredith and her brother have no knowledge of her past; and her husband is too ill to tell us anything. Her marriage was apparently a hasty love match–a love match so far as young Heredith was concerned. So far, we have only two slender facts to guide us in our estimate of her, which are contained in the two letters in which young Heredith announced his marriage to his people. According to those statements, she was an orphan who was earning her living as a war clerk in the Government department in which young

Heredith held his appointment. That does not carry us very far. During her brief life at the moat-house she seems to have been reticent about her earlier life. Miss Heredith is not the type of woman to have questioned her, and, apparently, she vouchsafed no information. An examination of her boxes and her writing-table has brought to light nothing in the way of writing or correspondence to help us. Such a girl–a bachelor girl in London in war-time–may have had passages in her past life of which her husband knew nothing–passages which may have an important bearing on her murder. Not until we have a thorough knowledge of her antecedents and her past life can we hope to pierce the hidden motives which have led to this murder. It is there, in my opinion, that we must seek for the clue to this strange murder, and it is to that effort I shall devote my energies as soon as I return to London. Until those facts are brought to light we are merely groping in the dark."

10

In accordance with Merrington's instructions, Caldew devoted a considerable portion of the morning seeking information among the moat-house guests. But few of them showed any inclination to talk about the murder. Many of the women were too upset to be seen, and the men had plainly no desire to be mixed up in such a terrible affair by giving interviews to detectives. Everybody was anxious to get away as speedily as possible, and Caldew was compelled to pursue his inquiries amongst groups of hurrying people, flustered servants, and village conveyances laden with luggage. Most of the departing guests replied to his questions as briefly as possible, and gave their London addresses with obvious reluctance; the few who were willing to aid the cause of justice could throw very little light on the London life of the murdered girl. Even those who had been acquainted with her before her marriage seemed to know very little about her.

Caldew finished his inquiries by midday. By that time most of the guests had departed from the moat-house and were on their way to London. Superintendent Merrington and Captain Stanhill were in the library examining the servants. Sergeant Lumbe had gone by train to Tibblestone to sift the story of the suspicious stranger who had descended on that remote village during the previous night.

It wanted an hour to lunch-time, and Caldew decided to spend the time by making a few investigations on his own account before cycling over to Chidelham in the afternoon to see the Weynes.

Caldew had not been impressed with Merrington's handling of the case. Subordinates rarely are impressed with the qualities of those placed over them in authority. They generally imagine they could do better if they had the same opportunities. Caldew was no exception to that rule. It seemed to him that Merrington lacked finesse, and was out of touch with modern methods of criminal investigation. He had been spoilt by too much success, by too much newspaper flattery, by too many jaunts with Royalty. No man could act as sheep-dog for Royalty and retain skill as a detective. That kind of professional work was fatal for the intelligence. Merrington had a great reputation behind him, and his knowledge of European criminals was probably unequalled, but his methods of investigating the moat-house murder suggested that he was no longer one of the world's greatest detectives, if, indeed, he had ever deserved recognition in their ranks. Caldew recalled that his fame rested chiefly on his wide experience rather than on the more subtle deductive methods of modern criminology. It was said in Scotland Yard that when Merrington was at the height of his reputation, twenty years before, his knowledge of London criminals and their methods was so extensive that he could in most cases identify the criminal by merely looking at his handiwork.

As a modern criminologist, Caldew believed that the less a detective intruded his own personality into his investigations the better for his chances of success. He did not think that the loud officialism of Merrington was likely to solve such a deep, subtle crime as the murder of Violet Heredith, and, consequently, he had the chance for which he had waited so long. It now remained for him to prove that he could do better than Merrington. He had sufficient confidence in his own abilities to welcome the opportunity, but at the same time he believed that he was confronted with a crime which would tax all his resources as a detective to unravel.

Like Merrington, he had been struck by the strangeness of the murder. All the circumstances were unusual, and quite outside his previous experience of big crimes. He had also come to the conclusion that the ease with which the murderer had found his way into the moat-house, and afterwards escaped, pointed to an intimate knowledge of the place.

It would be too much to say that Caldew and Merrington reached different conclusions by the same road. Up to a certain point their independent deductions from the more obvious facts of the case were alike, as was inevitable. In every crime there are circumstances and events which are as finger-posts, pointing the one way to the experienced observer. But their subsequent deductions from the outstanding facts branched widely, perhaps because the younger detective did not read so much into circumstances as Merrington. From the same facts they had reached different theories about the murder. Merrington, by a process of minute and careful deductions which he had placed before the Chief Constable, had convinced himself that the key to the murder and the murderer was to be found in London; Caldew believed that the solution of the mystery lay near the scene of the events, and perhaps in the house where the murder was committed.

Caldew was aware that he could have given no satisfactory reason for holding that belief, apart from the point that the murder had been committed by somebody who knew the moat-house sufficiently well to get in and out of the place without being seen. But that point was open to the explanation that the criminal might have provided himself with a plan of the house. Nevertheless, the impression had entered his mind so strongly that he could not have shaken it off if he had tried. But he did not try. He had sufficient imagination to be aware that intuition, in crime detection, is sometimes worth more than the most elaborate deductions.

For the rest, all his speculations about the crime were affected by the trinket he had found in the bedroom on the night of the murder. But the discovery and subsequent disappearance of that clue, as he believed it to be, had not led him very far as yet. He felt himself in the position of a palæontologist who is called upon to reproduce the structure of an extinct prehistoric animal from a footprint in sandstone. The vanished trinket was a starting-point, and no more. It was a possible hypothesis that the person who had dropped the stone and entered the death-chamber in search of it was the murderer, but so far it was incapable of demonstration or proof. As an isolated fact, it was useless, and brought him no nearer the solution of the mystery. But, on the other hand, it was an undoubted fact, and, for that reason, was dependent upon other facts for its existence. It was his task to find out who had dropped the trinket in the bedroom and subsequently returned for it during his own brief absence downstairs. To establish those essential kindred facts was, he believed, to lay hands on the murderer of Violet Heredith.

Caldew walked thoughtfully from the moat-house down to the village, intent on commencing his own independent investigations into the crime. If the solution of the mystery lay near the scene, as he believed, it was possible that some clue might be picked up among the villagers, to whom the daily doings of the folk in "the big house" were events of the first magnitude, and who might, presumably, be supposed to know anything which was likely to throw light on the obscure motive for the crime. It was for that reason he directed his footsteps towards the fountain head of gossip in an English village—the inn. He flattered himself he would be able to extract more local information from the patrons of the place than any other detective could hope to do. To begin with, he was a Sussex man and a native of the village, and since his return, after so many years' absence, he had spent his evenings at the inn renewing old associations and talking to the companions of his boyhood.

A week's renewed village life had taught him the ways of the place and the war-time drinking customs of the inhabitants. Constrained by recent legislation to compress their convivial intercourse into extremely limited periods, the village tradesmen, and a fair proportion of the surrounding farm labourers and shepherds, had fallen into the habit of assembling at the inn at midday, to discuss the hard times and drink the sour weak "war beer" forced on patriotic Britons as an exigent war measure.

Caldew entered a side door which opened into a small snuggery, divided from the tap-room by a wooden partition. It was here that the regular cronies and select patrons of the establishment sat in comfortable seclusion to discuss the crops, the weather, and market prices in the broad Sussex dialect, which Caldew, from the force of old association, unconsciously fell into again when he was with them.

The room was nearly full, but his appearance threw a marked restraint on the group of assembled countrymen. The conversation, which had obviously been about the murder, ceased instantly as he entered and seated himself on one of the forms placed against the partition. The innkeeper, who was standing behind the bar in his shirt sleeves, nodded uneasily in response to his friendly salutation, but the customers awkwardly avoided his glance by staring stolidly in front of them. Caldew attempted to dispel their reserve with a friendly remark, but no reply was forthcoming. It was obvious that the patrons of the inn wanted neither his conversation nor company. One after another, they finished their beer and walked out of the inn with the slow deliberate movements of the Sussex peasant.

Caldew had not allowed for the change the murder had effected on the village mind. His familiar relations with the inn customers had changed overnight. He was no longer the former village lad, returned to his native village, and welcomed from his old association with the place, but a being invested with the dread powers and majesty of the law, from which no man might deem himself safe.

Caldew walked out of the snuggery and opened a door at the side of the house. It opened into a billiard room—a surprising novelty in an English country inn, and the outcome of a piece of enterprise on the part of the landlord, who had picked up a small table cheap at a sale, and installed it in the clubroom, hoping to profit thereby. Again Caldew was conscious of the same distinct air of constraint immediately he entered. Two or three men who were talking and laughing loudly became as mute as though their vocal organs had been suddenly smitten with paralysis. The village butcher, who was at the billiard table in the act of attempting some complicated stroke, stopped abruptly with his cue in mid air, and gazed at the detective with open mouth and a look of apprehension on his florid face, as though he expected instant accusation and arrest for the moat-house murder.

With an irritated appreciation of his changed status in village eyes, Caldew left the inn and walked home for a meal before setting forth to Chidelham to interview Mrs. Weyne.

There was a strong smell of soap suds in his brother-in-law's house, and a vision of his sister's broad back, in vigorous motion over a steaming wash-tub in the kitchen, indicated that she was in the throes of her weekly wash. She ceased her labours at the sound of footsteps, and turned round.

"Oh, it's you, Tom. Come for a bite to eat? Jest sit you down, and I'll have dinner on the table in no time. I got something good for you. Old Upden, the shepherd, brought me a nice rabbit this mornin', and I've stewed it. It's the last one we'll get, I expect. Upden was telling me he ain't going to snare no more, because the boys steal his snares, which ain't no joke, with copper wire at five shillings a pound."

Caldew took a seat at the table, and watched his sister dish up the dinner. As Sergeant Lumbe's income was not sufficient to permit of all the refinements of civilized life, such as a separate room for dining, the family midday dinner was taken in the kitchen, which was the common living room. Mrs. Lumbe's preparations for the meal were prompt and effective. She carried the tub of clothes outside, opened the window to let out the steam, laid knives and forks and plates on the deal table, then put a liberal portion of stewed rabbit into each plate out of the pot which was steaming on the side of the stove. Dinner was then ready, and brother and sister commenced their meal. Caldew ate in silence, and his sister glanced at him wistfully at intervals. She had no children of her own, and she had a feeling of admiration for the brother she had mothered as a boy, who had gone to the great city and become a London detective. From her point of view he had achieved great fame and distinction, and she cherished in her workbox some newspaper clippings of crime cases in which his name had been favourably mentioned by friendly reporters. She hoped he would be successful in finding the moat-house murderer. She would have liked to question him about the case, but she stood a little in awe of him and his London ways.

"What's the best way to Chidelham, Kate?" asked Caldew, as he rose from the table. "There used to be a footpath across by Dormer's farm which cut off a couple of miles. Is it still open?"

"It's still open, Tom. Old Dormer tried to get it closed, and went to law about it, but he lost. Be you going across to Chidelham?"

"Yes, I shall ride over on my bicycle this afternoon. Do you know where the Weynes live?"

"The Weynes? Oh, you mean the writing chap that bought Billing's place. Their house stands by itself a mile out of the village, just afore you come to Green Patch Hill."

"Thanks. I know Billing's place very well, but I wasn't aware that he had sold it. I'd better be getting along. It's a good long ride."

"What be you goin' there for, Tom?" asked Mrs. Lumbe, with keen curiosity. "About this case?"

"Yes," replied Caldew shortly.

"Have you found out anything yet, Tom?" pursued his sister earnestly, her curiosity overcoming her awe of her clever brother. "Jem was telling me before he went to Tibblestone that a ter'ble gre'at detective come down from Lunnon this mornin', and was stirrin' up things proper. Jem says he's a detective what travels about with the King, and 'e's got letters to his name because of that. Is he on the tracks of the murderer yet, Tom?"

"No, and he's not likely to, as far as I can see," said her brother a little bitterly.

"Dear, dear, that's a pity, for it's a ter'ble thing, and an awful end for the young lady. Jem came home all of a tremble like last night with the ghastly sight of her corpse and I had to give him a drop of spirits to help him to sleep. We was a talkin' about it in bed, and wond'ring who could 'ave done it. Nobody hereabouts, for I'm sure there's nobody in the village would hurt a fellow creature. Besides, the folk at the big house is too respected for a living soul to think of harming them."

"They are popular with everybody, are they?" said Caldew, sitting down again with the realization that he was likely to gather as much information about the Heredith family from his sister as he could obtain anywhere else.

"Oh, yes," replied his sister. "It's only nat'ral they should be. Sir Philip is a good landlord, and he and Miss Heredith are very generous to folk."

"Is Philip Heredith well-liked in the district?"

"He's been away so long that folk don't know much about him. But I never heard anybody say anything against him. He's different from Sir Philip, but he seems gentle and kind."

"He used to be a quiet and solitary little chap years ago," remarked Caldew. "I remember climbing a tree in Monk's Hill wood for a bird's nest for him. He couldn't climb himself because of his lameness."

"It doesn't seem like a Heredith to be small and lame," said Mrs. Lumbe thoughtfully. "I've heard those who ought to know declare that Miss Heredith never forgave his mother for bringing him into the world with a lame foot. The servants at the big house say Mr. Phil has always been ter'ble sensitive about his lameness. That's what made him so lonely in his ways, though he was rare fond of animals and birds. We was all taken aback when we heard of his marriage. He always seemed so shy of the young ladies. The only girl I ever knowed him to take any notice of was Hazel Rath. I have met them walking through the woods together."

"Who is Hazel Rath?"

"The daughter of the moat-house housekeeper. She came to the moat-house with her mother nearly ten years agone. She was a pretty little thing. Miss Heredith was very fond of her, and sent her to school. Mr. Philip was fond of her too, in his way, though, of course, there could never a'been anything between them. But nobody hereabouts ever expected him to marry a London young lady."

"Why not?" asked Caldew.

"The Herediths have always married in the county, as far back as can be counted. It was thought Miss Heredith would make a match between Mr. Philip and the daughter of Sir Harry Ravenworth, of the Wilcotes. The Ravenworths are the second family in the county, and well-to-do. 'Twould a'been a most suitable match, as folk here agreed. But 'twas not to be, more's the pity."

Caldew nodded absently. His original interest in his sister's talk was relapsing into boredom because it seemed unlikely to lead to anything of the slightest importance about the murder.

"The young lady he did marry was not a real lady, so I've heard say," continued Mrs. Lumbe, placidly pursuing the train of her reflections. "She didn't come much into the village, but when she did she walked about as though she were bettermost, and everybody else dirt beneath her feet. But I have heard that she had to earn her own living in London before Mr. Philip fell in love with her pretty face. If that's the truth, she gave herself enough airs afterwards, and did all she could to make Miss Heredith feel she'd put her nose out of joint, as the saying is."

"What do you mean by that?" asked Caldew sharply, with all his senses again alert.

"Well, you know, Tom, Miss Heredith has been the mistress of the moat-house and the great lady of the county since Lady Heredith died. But when Mr. Philip brought his young wife down from London that was all changed. The young lady soon let her see that she wasn't going to be ruled by her, and didn't care for her or her ways. They do say it was a great trial to Miss Heredith, though she tried not to let anybody know it."

"Where did you learn this?" Caldew asked abruptly.

"Lord, Tom, how short you pick me up! Milly Saker, who's parlourmaid at the moat-house, told me in the strictest confidence, because she knew I wouldn't tell anybody. And I wouldn't tell anybody but you, Tom. She told me from the very first that she didn't think the two ladies would get on together. They were so different, Milly said, and she was certain Miss Heredith didn't think the young lady good enough to marry into the Heredith family."

"Did she tell you if they had ever quarrelled?"

"I asked her that, and she said no. Miss Heredith is always the lady, and she wouldn't lower herself by quarrelling with anybody, least of all with anybody she did not consider as good a lady as herself. But Milly says she was sorely tried at times. Milly thought it would end up in her leaving the moat-house and marrying her old sweetheart, Mr. Musard, who's just returned from his foreign travels. Perhaps you've seen him."

"Yes, I've seen him," said Caldew. "So he is her old sweetheart, is he?"

"So folk used to say," returned Mrs. Lumbe. "I remember there was some talk of a match between them when I was a girl, but nothing came of it. It's my opinion that Miss Heredith must have refused him then because of his wild days, and he took to his travels to cure his broken heart. But they still think a lot of each other, as is plain for everybody to see, and go out for walks together arm in arm. So perhaps it will all come right in the end."

With this comfortable doctrine of life, based on her perusal of female romances, Mrs. Lumbe got up from her seat to clear the table.

"I trust it will," said her brother, but his remark had nothing to do with the triumph of true love in the last chapter.

He left the room to get his bicycle to ride to Chidelham.

11

On his way to Chidelham, Caldew again pondered over the murder, and for the first time seriously asked himself whether Miss Heredith could have committed the crime. He had glanced at that possibility before, and had practically dismissed it on the score of lack of motive, but his sister's story of the differences between Miss Heredith and her nephew's wife supplied that deficiency in a startling degree. In reviewing the whole of the circumstances by the light of the information his sister had given him, it now seemed to him that Miss Heredith fitted into the crime in a remarkable way.

The most important fact leading to that inference was that she alone, of all the inmates of the moat-house the previous night, was out of the dining-room when the murder was committed. That supposition took no cognizance of the servants, but Caldew had all along eliminated the servants in his consideration of the crime. In the next place, it supplied an explanation for the disappearance of the bar brooch from the bedroom. In all likelihood the butler had first acquainted his mistress with his discovery of the unlocked staircase door, and she, realizing where she had dropped her brooch, had seized upon the opportunity to request Musard to call the detective downstairs and tell him about the door. In his absence she returned to the bedroom for the brooch.

This theory seemed plausible enough at first blush, but as Caldew examined it closely several objections arose in his mind. The hidden motive of the crime, as innocently laid bare by his sister, was strong, but was it strong enough to impel a woman like Miss Heredith, with the rigid principles of her birth, breeding, and caste, and a woman, moreover, who had spent her life in good works, to commit such an atrocious murder? Caldew considered this point long and thoughtfully. With his keener imagination he differed from Merrington by relying to some extent on external impressions, and he could not shake off his first impression of Miss Heredith as a woman of exceptionally good type. He had to admit to himself that her graciousness and dignity were not the qualities usually associated with a murderer. Religion, hypocrisy, smugness, plausibility; these were the commonest counterfeit qualities of criminals; not dignity, worth, and pride.

There was, of course, the possibility that Miss Heredith, grown imperious with her long unquestioned sway at the moat-house, had quarrelled with the young wife, and committed the murder in a sudden gust of passion. The most unlikely murders had been committed under the sway of impulse. Caldew recalled that Miss Heredith had been the last person to see the murdered woman alive, and nobody except herself knew what had occurred at that interview. It might be that the young wife had said something to her which rankled so deeply that she conceived the idea of murdering her.

Caldew, on reaching this stage of his reasoning, shook his head doubtfully. He had to admit to himself that such a theory did not ring true. If Miss Heredith had been maddened by some insult at the afternoon's interview, she was far more likely to have killed Mrs. Heredith immediately than have waited until dinner-time. And, if she had committed the murder, why had she gone about it in the manner likeliest to lead to discovery, openly leaving her guests a few minutes before, and allowing herself to be seen afterwards descending the staircase? Even the veriest neophyte in crime usually displayed some of the caution of self-preservation.

But Caldew was too experienced in criminal investigation to reject a theory merely because it was contrary to experience. There existed presumptions for suspicion of Miss Heredith which at least warranted further inquiry. And, thinking over these presumptions, he arrived at the additional conclusion that the theory of her guilt could also be made to account for the puzzle of the open window in Mrs. Heredith's bedroom. Caldew believed that the open window had some bearing on the crime. His first impression had been that the murderer had entered and escaped by that means. The Virginia creeper to which Weyling had directed attention that morning had strengthened that belief, in spite of Merrington's opinion that the plant would not bear a man's weight. But now it seemed to him that Miss Heredith might have opened the window for the purpose of throwing the revolver into the moat so that it should not be found. He determined to investigate that possibility as soon as he returned to the moat-house.

He reached his destination only to learn that Mr. and Mrs. Weyne had motored over to the moat-house to pay their condolences to the family. He remounted his bicycle and rode back as fast as he could, chagrined to think that he had wasted the best part of an afternoon in a fruitless errand.

It was evening when he reached Heredith again, and rode through the woods towards the moat-house. It looked deserted in the gathering twilight. A fugitive gleam of departing sunshine fell on the bronze and blood-red chrysanthemums in the circular beds, but the shadows were lengthening across the lawn, and the mist from the green waters of the moat was creeping up the stained red walls.

His ring at the front door was answered by the pretty parlourmaid who had been dusting the hall before breakfast. He recognized in Milly Saker a village playmate of nearly twenty years ago, and he recalled that it was she who had told his sister of the difference which had existed between Miss Heredith and her nephew's wife.

Milly greeted the detective with a coquettish smile of recognition.

"How are you?" she said. "You wouldn't look at me this morning. You seemed as if you didn't want to recognize old friends."

Caldew's mind was too preoccupied to meet these rural pleasantries in the same spirit.

"Is Miss Heredith in?" he asked, stepping into the hall.

"I shouldn't be here talking to you if she was," replied the girl pertly. "She's gone to the village in the motorcar to meet Mr. Musard. She's just got a telegram to say he's coming back."

"I thought he was going to France," said Caldew.

"Well, he's not. The telegram says he's not. So Miss Heredith's gone to meet him by the evening train. Tufnell's out too. I don't know where he's poked to, but I shan't cry my eyes out if he never comes back."

"Have Mr. and Mrs. Weyne been here?"

"Yes. They drove over in their car, and saw Miss Heredith and Sir Philip. They weren't here very long."

"Where are Superintendent Merrington and Captain Stanhill?"

"In the library. They come in about an hour ago. The big gentleman has to go back to London to-night–I heard him say so. A good riddance too. He had all the servants in the library this morning, bullying them dreadfully."

"What did he say to you?" asked Caldew, with a smile.

"Nothing," responded the girl promptly, "except what he said early this morning, when he stopped me in the hall here, and put his great ugly hand under my chin, and told me he'd have a talk with me by-and-by. But he didn't get the chance, because I was over in the village all the morning with my mother, who's been ill. But he gave all the other girls such a time that they haven't done talking of it yet. Gwennie Harden, who sleeps with me, says he must have thought one of us murdered Mrs. Heredith, and the cook was so angry with the questions he asked her that she was going to give a month's warning on the spot, but old Tufnell talked her over, saying that it was only done in the way of duty, no personal reflection being intended. Tufnell begged her pardon for what she'd had to put up with, and the cook granted it, and there the matter ended. But they do say that Mrs. Rath–that's the housekeeper–came out of the library looking fit to drop. But Hazel Rath didn't go into the library, although she stayed here last night, and has been with her mother all day. Favouritism, I call it. Why should they put all us servants through our facings, and leave her alone?" The mention of Hazel Rath's name recalled to Caldew's mind the information his sister had given him about the early association between her and Philip Heredith. But the import of that statement, and the significance of the piece of news Milly Saker had just given him, were not made clear to him until later. At the moment his thoughts were fixed on the idea of testing his new theory about the open window while Miss Heredith was absent. As he turned away, he asked the girl where Sir Philip was.

"He's sitting with Mr. Phil," was the reply.

"I suppose there is nobody upstairs in the left wing?" he added.

"Nobody but the corpse," responded Milly, with a slight shiver. "Miss Heredith's had her bedroom shifted. Last night she slept downstairs, but this morning she gave orders for the white bedroom in the right wing to be prepared for her. I reckon she wants to get as far away from it as possible, and I don't blame her."

Caldew proceeded upstairs, and entered the death-chamber in the silent wing. On his way back from Chidelham he had picked up a round stone, which he now took from his pocket, intending to throw it from the window, and mark the spot where it fell into the moat. He opened the window, and looked out across the garden. The distance to the moat was much farther than he had imagined; so great, indeed, that his own shot at the water fell short by several feet. It was impossible that Miss Heredith could have accomplished such a remarkable feat as to hurl a revolver across the intervening space between the window and the moat. No woman could throw so far and so straight.

This unforeseen obstacle rather disconcerted Caldew at first, but on looking out of the window again it seemed to him, by the lay of the house, that the window of Miss Heredith's bedroom was closer to the moat than the window at which he was standing. As Miss Heredith had transferred her bedroom to the other wing, he decided to go into the room and see if he were right. He still clung to his new idea that the revolver had been thrown into the moat, although his altered view that it might have been thrown from Miss Heredith's window meant the abandonment of his other assumption that the disposal of the revolver by that means accounted for the open window in Mrs. Heredith's bedroom. Caldew realized as he left the room that the question of the open window still remained to be solved. What he did not realize was that he was distorting the facts of the case in order to establish the possibility of his own theory.

The door of the room which Miss Heredith had occupied was ajar. He pushed it open and entered. There was within that deserted and desolate air which a room so quickly takes on when the occupant has vacated it. The heavier furniture and the bed remained to demonstrate the ugliness of utility after the accessories and adjuncts of luxury had been carried away.

The blind was down and the room in partial darkness. Caldew went to the window, raised the blind, and looked out. The distance to the moat was appreciably nearer, compared with the window of the room he had just left, but the distance was still considerable.

As Caldew turned from the window, with the reluctant conviction that he had been nursing an untenable theory, a last ray of sunshine shot through the open window, causing the dust he had raised by his entrance to quiver and gyrate like a host of mad bacilli dancing a jig. The shaft of light, falling athwart the dismantled toilet-table, brought something else into view—a tiny fragment of gold chain dangling from the polished satinwood drawer.

Caldew pulled the drawer open. Inside was a lady's thin gold neck chain, with a bundle of charms and trinkets attached to the end, which had evidently been left behind and forgotten. He glanced at the chain carelessly, and was about to replace it in the drawer, when his eye was arrested by one of the trinkets. It was a small image, not much over an inch in length; a squatting heathen god, with crossed arms and a satyr's face—a wonderful example of savage carving in miniature.

It was not the perfection of the carving or the unusual nature of the ornament which attracted Caldew's attention, but the material, of which it was composed, a clear almost transparent stone, with the faintest possible tinge of green. Holding it in the sunlight, Caldew was able to detect one or two minute black flecks in the stone. There was no doubt about it—the image was of the same peculiar material as the trinket he had seen in the murdered woman's room the previous night.

As he stood there examining the charm, the murmur of voices not far away fell on his ears. Looking cautiously out of the window, he saw Musard and Miss Heredith walk round the side of the house to the garden, deep in earnest conversation. Caldew backed away to an angle where he was not visible from beneath, and watched them closely. Musard was talking, occasionally using an impressive gesture, and Miss Heredith was listening attentively, with a downcast face, and eyes which suggested recent tears. As she passed underneath the window at which he was watching, she raised a handkerchief to her face and sobbed aloud. Caldew wondered to see the proud and reserved mistress of the moat-house show her grief so freely in the presence of

Musard, until he remembered what his sister had told him of their supposed early love for each other. And with that thought came another. It must have been Musard, the explorer, the man who had wandered afar in strange lands in search of precious stones, who had brought to the moat-house the peculiar stone of which the missing brooch and the little image had been fashioned.

Acting on the swift impulse to take the image to Miss Heredith and see how she received it, Caldew slipped the chain into his pocket and hurried downstairs. At the bottom of the staircase he was stopped by Tufnell, who had evidently been waiting for him to descend. The usually imperturbable dignity of the butler was for once ruffled, and he looked slightly flushed and dishevelled.

"I have been down to the village looking for you," he said, in a querulous tone. The majesty of the law had not vested Caldew with any dignity in the old butler's eyes. He saw in him only the village urchin of a score of years ago, whose mischievous pranks on the Heredith estate had been a constant source of worry to him.

The detective appreciated the estimation in which the old man held him, and the fact did not tend to lessen his own irritation.

"What did you want me for?" he curtly asked.

"I did not want you, but the gentlemen in the library do. Superintendent Merrington thought you had been a long time away, and he sent me down to the village to look for you. He is anxious to return to London. You will find him in the library."

The butler's cool assumption that it was Merrington's privilege to command, and Caldew's duty to obey, nettled the latter considerably. He felt that Merrington had, in his offensive way, deliberately asserted his official authority in order to humiliate him in his native place. Acting on the impulse of anger he replied:

"I have some things to attend to before I can see him. You can tell him so, if you like."

He walked away towards the hall door, conscious that the butler was standing stationary by the stairs, watching him. When he got outside, he turned his steps towards the garden; but brief as had been the interval since he had seen Musard and Miss Heredith conversing together by the sundial, it had been sufficient to bring the conversation to a conclusion. Miss Heredith was no longer to be seen, and Musard was sauntering along the gravel walk smoking a cigar.

Had they seen him at the window, and broken off their conference in consequence? It looked as if this were so. Miss Heredith must have entered the house by another door, because if she had gone in by the front door he must have encountered her. Caldew would have retraced his steps if Musard had not looked up, and, seeing the detective, waited for him to approach.

Caldew walked towards him, wondering whether Miss Heredith had missed her chain of charms, and had gone upstairs to find it. In that case, he reflected grimly, the position of the previous night was reversed, and this time it was she who was forestalled. It was an ironical situation, truly, but he was to some extent the master of it.

Musard nodded to the detective and proffered his cigarcase. Caldew accepted a cigar and admired the case, which was made of crocodile skin, worked and dressed in a manner altogether new to him. He had never seen anything like it in London tobacconists' shops, and he said so.

"Native manufacture," replied Musard, selecting a fresh cigar. "My Chinese boy shot the crocodile which provided it. It's a rare thing for a Chinese to be a good shot with a modern English rifle, but my boy would carry off anything at Bisley. He never misses. It was lucky for me that he didn't that time, because the brute came along to bag me while I was swimming in a river. Suey, hearing me call, ran out from the tent with my rifle, and shot him

from the bank. He got him through the eye–the eye and
the throat are the only two vulnerable spots in a
crocodile. A bullet will rebound off the head as off a rock."

"Where did this happen?" asked Caldew, in an
interested tone. His own knowledge of crocodiles was
confined to the fact that he had once seen a small one in a
tank at the Zoological Gardens.

"In Zambesi. There are plenty of them there in the
rivers and mango swamps. Some hunters stake a dog
overnight by the river bank, and the animal gives them
warning of the approach of the reptiles by howling with
terror. It is rather cruel–to the dog."

"Undoubtedly," said Caldew.

"How are you getting on with your investigations in
this case?" continued Musard, abruptly changing the
conversation.

Caldew was instantly wary, and stiffened into an
attitude of official reserve, wondering why Musard should
seek to question him about the murder.

"I am an old friend of the Herediths," continued
Musard, as though divining the other's thoughts. "This
murder is a very terrible thing for them. I am afraid it
may mean Sir Philip's death-blow. He is old and feeble,
and the shock, and his son's illness, have had a very bad
effect on him. I should have gone to France to-day for the
War Office, but I arranged for somebody to go in my place
in order to remain with the family in their hour of trial.
Have you found out anything which leads you to suppose
you are on the track of the murdered?"

"I am afraid I cannot tell you anything about the
investigations," replied the detective cautiously. "I am not
in charge of the case, you know."

"I understand," rejoined the other, with a nod.
"Perhaps I should not have asked you. My anxiety must
be my excuse."

He uttered this apology so courteously and pleasantly
that Caldew felt momentarily ashamed of his own rigidly
official attitude. But his instincts of caution quickly

reasserted themselves, and he told himself that in this sinister case it was his business to be on his guard and talk to nobody.

The situation was terminated by the reappearance of Miss Heredith from a door at the side of the house. The detective was a little surprised to see her again, for he had conceived the idea that she had gone indoors to avoid meeting him. She went eagerly to Musard without noticing him.

"Oh, Vincent!" she exclaimed, and the look of relief on her face was unmistakable. "Sir Ralph Horton is just leaving. He says that Phil has passed the crisis, and there is no need for him to stay any longer. Phil still needs great care and attention, but Sir Ralph says it will be quite safe to leave him in Dr. Holmes's hands. There is no fear for his brain, thank God."

"This is good news," said Musard. "Have you told Sir Philip?"

"Not yet. I thought it better to defer it until after dinner. I want you to tell him then."

Miss Heredith turned as though to re-enter the house, but Caldew, who had been hovering a few paces away within earshot of this dialogue, approached her with the gold chain in his hand.

"Excuse me, Miss Heredith," he said. "One of the maids told me that you no longer occupied the room upstairs in the left wing, so I took the liberty of going in there to see if it was possible for the murderer to have escaped by clambering from the window of one room to another, and while I was there I found this chain. It was hanging out of a drawer of the toilet-table near the window, and as it had obviously been forgotten I thought I had better restore it to you."

He held it out to her as he finished speaking, keenly watching her face for some sign of confusion or trepidation. But Miss Heredith received the chain calmly, and thanked him for returning it. Caldew was disappointed at the failure of his test, but he essayed a further shot.

"I noticed a very peculiar little image among the charms on the chain," he said hesitatingly. "I have never seen anything like it before, and I couldn't help wondering where it came from."

It was a clumsy trap, and he realized it, but he was too anxious to achieve his end by more subtle methods. There was nothing in Miss Heredith's calm countenance to suggest that she was alarmed or uneasy at his curiosity. She turned to Musard.

"Mr. Caldew means the strange little image you gave me when you arrived, Vincent. What is it?"

She held out the chain, and the explorer took it in his big brown hand. He separated the image from the other charms with his forefinger, and turned it over carelessly.

"That is a tiki," he said.

The explanation conveyed nothing to Caldew.

"I have never heard the word before," he said. "What is a tiki?"

"It is the Maori word for the creator of man, and is also taken to represent an ancestor," Musard explained. "The Maoris are to some extent ancestor worshippers, and adorn their pahs and temples with large wooden images of immense size, supposed to represent some renowned fighting ancestor. These images are worshipped as gods, and are believed to be visited by the spirits, who ascend to converse with them by the hollow roots of a pohutukawa tree, which descends into the Maori nether regions. The smaller tikis, or, more strictly speaking, hei-tiki, such as this, are carved as representations in miniature of the larger images, and are worn as neck ornaments. They are supposed to render the wearer immune from the wicked designs of evil spirits."

"From what material are they carved?" said Caldew, who had followed this explanation attentively. "I have never seen anything resembling it. It seems as clear and colourless as glass, but it emits a faint greenish lustre, and there are black flecks in it."

"It is nephrite, or Maori greenstone," replied Musard. "London jewellers term it New Zealand jade."

"Surely this stone is not jade?" said Caldew, in some surprise. "I have seen New Zealand jade ornaments in London shops, but they were made from a dull deep greenstone, not a bit like this stone, which is clear as crystal, and has a lustre."

"There are different sorts of jade," replied Musard. "The present craze of Society women is for Chinese pink jade and tourmalin. A good pink jade necklace will readily bring a thousand pounds in Bond Street, and it is going to be the fashionable jewel of the season. New Zealand nephrite has not yet come into popular favour with English ladies, and only the commoner dark green variety, which is frequently spurious, is seen here. This image was made of the rarer kind of pounamu, as the Maoris call it."

"It is very pretty," said Caldew. "Have you any more of it?" He flattered himself that the assumption of carelessness in his tone was not overdone.

"No," replied Musard. "It was the only piece of the rare kind I was ever lucky enough to obtain."

"There was another small piece, Vincent," remarked Miss Heredith. "You brought it about ten years ago. It was the same kind of transparent stone, with black flecks in it."

"I had forgotten. I gave it to Phil, didn't I? What did he do with it?"

"He had it made into a brooch for Hazel Rath, and gave it to her as a birthday gift."

12

As Caldew returned to the house for his interview with Merrington, the one clear impression on his mind was that the discovery of the owner of the missing brooch was the starting point in the elucidation of the murder. In the library he found Superintendent Merrington, Captain Stanhill, Inspector Weyling, and Sergeant Lumbe. The sergeant, who looked tired and dirty, was apologetically explaining that his visit to Tibblestone had been fruitless.

"I had my journey for nothing," he was saying in his thick country voice, as Caldew entered. "I had a wild goose chase all over the place, and then it turned out that this chap Mr. Hawkins telephoned about was only a canvasser for In Memoriam cards for fallen soldiers. I come across him at last sitting by the roadside eating his dinner and reading a London picture paper. He looked a doubtful sort of a customer, sure enough, but he was able to prove that he was playing bagatelle in the inn last night at the time the murder was committed."

Superintendent Merrington dismissed this information with a nod, and turned to Caldew.

"Did you interview Mrs. Weyne?" he asked.

"They were not in," was the reply. "I was told they had motored to the moat-house. Did you see them?"

Superintendent Merrington frowned. He had not seen the Weynes, and he had not been informed of their visit. It was another addition to the sum of untoward incidents which had happened to him since his arrival at the moat-house, and he felt very dissatisfied and wrathful.

"I am returning to London by the next train, Caldew," he said, in his authoritative voice. "Official business of importance demands my immediate presence. I will have some inquiries made at Scotland Yard about the people who have been staying here. In the meantime, you had better remain on the spot and continue your inquiries under the Chief Constable."

"I shall be very glad of Detective Caldew's help in unravelling this terrible mystery," Captain Stanhill remarked courteously.

Caldew drew several conclusions from his chief's speech. Merrington was puzzled about the case, but had no intention of taking him into his counsel. Merrington believed that the murderer had got clear away, and, therefore, further local investigation was useless, but he deemed it advisable to keep a Scotland Yard man on the scene to watch for possible developments, because he placed no reliance on the county police. It was apparent that Merrington thought the murderer had come from a distance, and he was going to seek him in London. But he was leaving nothing to chance. He was retaining control of the investigations at both ends in order to monopolize the glory of the capture. If the murderer escaped, Caldew and the county police could be made the scapegoats for public indignation.

But while paying the involuntary tribute of swift anger towards these astute tactics of his departmental chief, Caldew realized with satisfaction that he was in the possession of a piece of valuable information which might upset his calculations.

"There are several people in the district whom it will be advisable to interview," continued Merrington, hastily consulting his notes. "In the first place, you must make another effort to see the Weynes. Mrs. Weyne may be able to give us some valuable information about Mrs. Heredith's earlier life. And I think you should see the station-master of Weydene Junction. The murderer may have walked across country to the junction rather than face the greater risk of subsequent identification by taking the train at one of the village stations on this side of it. And you had better see the housekeeper's daughter and get a statement from her. I do not suppose she knows anything about the crime, but she was here last night, and she had better be seen. She is employed as a milliner at the market town of Stading."

"Do you mean Hazel Rath?" inquired Caldew, in some surprise.

"Yes. She is the daughter of the housekeeper. She stayed here last night with her mother, but left to go back to her employment by the first train this morning."

"There must be some mistake about that. I understand she is still in the house."

"Who told you so?"

"One of the maidservants."

"We had better have the maid in and question her. What is her name?"

"Milly—Milly Saker." Merrington touched the bell, and told the maidservant who answered it to send in Milly Saker.

The girl came in almost immediately, looking half defiant and half afraid. Merrington glanced at her keenly.

"You're the girl I saw dusting the hall this morning," he said. "Why did you not come in with the other servants to be examined?"

"Because I wasn't here," answered the girl pertly.

"Where were you?"

"Down in the village, at my mother's place."

"Who gave you permission to go?"

"Mrs. Rath, the housekeeper."

"Did you ask her for leave of absence?"

"No. She knew my mother was ill, and she said to me after breakfast, 'Milly, would you like to go and see your mother this morning?' I said, yes, I should, if she could spare me. She told me she could, so I thanked her and went."

Superintendent Merrington and Captain Stanhill exchanged glances. The same thought occurred to both of them. Mrs. Rath, the housekeeper, had assured them that she had sent all the servants to the library to be examined. Merrington turned to the girl again.

"Mrs. Rath's daughter was staying with her last night, wasn't she?"

"Yes."

"Is she still here?"

"Yes."

"Are you quite sure of that?"

"Yes, when I was outside about half an hour ago, I saw her through the window, sitting in her mother's room."

This piece of information conveyed some significance to Merrington's mind which was not apparent to Caldew. He paused for a moment, and then continued abruptly:

"Where were you last night at the time of the murder?"

"Please, sir, I don't know nothing about it," responded the girl with a whimper.

"Control yourself, my good girl," said Captain Stanhill soothingly. "Nobody suggests you had anything to do with it."

For reply, the girl only sobbed loudly. Superintendent Merrington, who had his own methods of soothing frightened females, shook her roughly by the arm.

"Listen to me," he sternly commanded. "Do you want to go to prison?"

"N–o, sir," responded Milly, between a fresh burst of sobs.

"Then you'd better stop that noise and answer my questions, or I'll put you under lock and key till you do. Where were you last night when the murder was committed?"

"I was waiting at table till dessert was served," replied the girl, thoroughly subdued by the overbearing manner of the big man confronting her.

"What did you do when you left the dining-room?"

"I went to the kitchen and was talking to cook for a while."

"And what did you do then?"

"I went up the passage and into the hall to see if dinner was finished. I knew Miss Heredith was anxious to have dinner over early as they were all going out, and I wanted to get dinner cleared away as quickly as I could, because I wanted to go out myself. I saw her leave the room and go towards the front door, but nobody else came out of the dining-room, and I could hear somebody talking. So after waiting a little while, and seeing nobody else come out, I went back towards the kitchen."

"Where were you standing while you were waiting?"

"Just at the corner of the passage leading up from the kitchen."

"You didn't go up stairs at all?"

"No, of course I didn't. 'Tisn't my place to go upstairs."

"Don't be saucy, but answer my questions. Did you hear the scream and the shot?"

"No, I didn't. I was back in the kitchen before then, and the kitchen is right at the back of the house. Cook and me didn't know anything about it till one of the girls came running down and told us about what had happened."

"Did you see anybody except Miss Heredith in the hall or on the staircase of the left wing while you were standing at the end of the passage?"

"Nobody except Miss Rath."

"Do you mean the housekeeper's daughter?"

"Yes."

"When did you see her?"

"As I was standing there waiting for a chance to clear away the dinner things, she come up from the centre passage leading from the housekeeper's rooms, and turned into the hall."

"Where was she going?"

"I don't know. I didn't ask her," replied the girl, who had regained something of her pert assurance.

"Did she see you?"

"No. I was standing at the end of the kitchen passage, which is close to the right wing. The passage she come out of was quite a long way from where I was standing, almost in the centre of the house. She turned the other way."

"She turned to the right, then, as she emerged from the passage, and walked in the direction of the left wing?"

"I don't know where she was going to. All I know is that I saw her turn out of the passage, and walk, as if might be, up the hall in that direction."

"Did you notice her actions?"

"I can't say as I did particular, except that she was walking in the shadow, on the side nearest to the passage she come out of, and seemed to be looking at the dining-room door."

"You are sure it was Hazel Rath?"

"Oh, it was her all right," replied Milly confidently. "I recognized her, as well as the dress she was wearing."

"Was this before or after you saw Miss Heredith leave the dining-room?"

"About ten minutes afterwards."

"Did you mention to anybody that you saw her?"

"I did not," replied the girl, as if the matter were one of supreme indifference to her.

"Why not?"

"I suppose Miss Rath is free to go where she pleases," said the girl airily. "She's privileged. When she used to live here she had the run of the house, just like one of the family. Tain't my business to question her comings and goings."

"Oh, Miss Rath used to live here, did she? How long ago?"

"Till about two years ago, before she went to business."

"And how long did she live here?"

"It must have been a good seven years or more," said Milly, considering. "She come here as a little girl when her mother come as housekeeper. Miss Heredith took a great fancy to her, and she was made quite a pet of the house, and did just what she liked. When she grew up she used to help her mother, and do little things about the house. But she never gave herself airs—I will say that."

"Very well. You may go now."

"Caldew," said Merrington quickly as the door closed behind the girl, "go and find the housekeeper and send her in here. And then keep an eye on her daughter, and do not let her out of your sight, until I send for you. Then bring her in."

When Caldew left the room on his errand, Captain Stanhill turned to Superintendent Merrington with a pained expression on his face. "Do you suspect—" he commenced.

"I suspect nobody—and everybody," was the prompt reply. "My duty is to find out the facts, and my business is now to ascertain why the housekeeper lied to me about her daughter this morning. She was a fool to try and trick me. There's something underneath all this which I'll sift to the bottom before I leave."

There was a timid tap, and the door opened slowly, revealing the frail black figure of the housekeeper standing hesitatingly on the threshold. Her frightened eyes were directed to Merrington's truculent ones as though impelled by a magnet.

"You—you wished to see me?" she stammered.

"Yes. Come in." Merrington curtly commanded. "Close that door, Lumbe. Sit down, Mrs. Rath, I have a few questions to ask you."

The housekeeper took a seat, with her eyes still fixed on Merrington's face. She looked ill and haggard, but the contour of her worn face, and the outline of her slender figure suggested that she had once possessed beauty and attraction. Merrington, staring at her hard, again had the idea that he had seen her long ago in different conditions and circumstances, but he could not recall where.

"Look here, Mrs. Rath," he commenced abruptly. "I want to know why you lied to me this morning."

"I–I don't know what you mean. I didn't come here to be insulted." The housekeeper uttered these words with a weak attempt at dignity, but her lips went suddenly white.

"Don't put on any fine-lady airs with me, for they won't go down," said Merrington, in a fierce, bullying tone. "You know what I mean very well. You told me this morning, when I asked you, that you had sent in all the servants to be examined. I have just discovered that you did not. There was a girl, Milly Saker, whom I did not see. Why was that?"

It seemed to Captain Stanhill that the tension of the housekeeper's face relaxed, and that a look of relief came into her eyes, as though the question were different from the one she had expected.

"I did not tell you a lie," she replied, in a firmer tone. "I sent in all the servants who were in the house at the time. Milly was not at home."

"Where was she?"

"She went across to the village to see her mother, who is ill."

"With your permission, I presume?"

"Yes."

"Why did you permit her to go?"

"The girl's mother was very ill, and needed her daughter."

"You let her go, although I had told you I wanted to question all the servants?"

"No, it was before you told me that I gave Milly permission to have the morning off," responded Mrs. Rath quietly.

"Is that the true explanation?"

"Yes."

"Is it as true as your other statement?"

"What other statement?"

"The statement you made to me this morning when you assured me your daughter had left this house to return to her employment at Stading?" said Merrington, with a cruel smile. "That wasn't true, you know. How do you describe that untruth? As a temporary aberration of memory, or what?"

The housekeeper looked up with swift, startled eyes, and her thin hand involuntarily clutched the edge of the table in front of her, but she did not speak.

"You lied about that, you know," continued Merrington. "I've found out your daughter has been in the house all day. Why did you tell me a lie? Come, out with it!"

"You are too abrupt, Merrington," said Captain Stanhill, interposing with unexpected firmness. "You have frightened her. Come, Mrs. Rath," he said gently, "can you not give us some explanation as to why you misled us this morning?"

"Because I didn't want my daughter to be drawn into this dreadful thing," she exclaimed wildly. "I suppose it was very foolish of me," she added, in a more composed voice, as though reassured by the kindly look in Captain Stanhill's eyes, "but I really didn't think it mattered. My daughter knew nothing about the murder and as she is highly strung I did not want her to be upset."

"Where was your daughter last night when the murder was committed?" asked Merrington.

"In my room."

"Did either of you hear the scream or the shot?"

"No, my rooms are a long way from the left wing, and we were sitting with the door shut."

"Then when did you learn about the murder?"

"Very soon after it happened. One of the maidservants came and told me."

"And you say that your daughter was with you at the time, and had been with you a considerable time before?"

"Yes."

"I think that will do, Mrs. Rath, I have given you every opportunity, but you still persist in telling falsehoods. Your daughter was seen walking up the hall last night in the direction of the left wing shortly before the murder was committed. The person who saw her was the maid Milly Saker. Was that the real reason why you gave Milly leave of absence to visit her mother this morning—so that she should not tell us what she knew?"

"It is not true," gasped the housekeeper. "My daughter was not out of my rooms last night, I assure you that is the truth."

"I wouldn't believe you on your oath," retorted Merrington. "Lumbe, go and tell Caldew to bring in the girl."

13

The girl who entered the room a moment later was tall and graceful, with a yearning expression in her soft dark eyes, as though in search of a happiness which had been denied her by Fate. Her appearance was one of unusual refinement. She had not a trace of the coarsened blowzy look so common in English country girls; there was nothing of rustic lumpishness in her slim figure, and there was more than mere prettiness in her exquisite small features, her thick dark hair, her clear white skin with a tracery of blue veins in the temples. Her high-bridged nose and firm chin suggested some force of character, but that suggestion was counteracted by her wistful tender mouth, with drooping underlip. The face, on the whole, was a paradoxical one, containing elements of strength and weakness, and the eyes were the index to a strange passionate nature.

She advanced into the room quietly, with a swift glance, immediately veiled by drooped lids, at the faces of the police officials who were awaiting her. When she reached the far end of the table at which they were seated she stopped and stood with her hands clasped loosely in front of her, as though waiting to be questioned.

"Please sit down, Miss Rath," said Captain Stanhill politely. "We wish to ask you a few questions."

The girl seated herself in a chair some distance away from her mother, and this time she surveyed the men before her with an air of indifference which was obviously simulated.

But again she quickly dropped her eyes, for Merrington was staring at her with a look of amazement, as though confronted with a familiar presence whose identity he could not recall. He glanced from Hazel to her mother, and his eyes fastened themselves fiercely on the housekeeper with the satisfaction of a man who had solved an elusive puzzle.

"So we *have* met before, Mrs. Rath," he said. "You are–"

"No, no! Please keep silent in front of my daughter," broke in the housekeeper hurriedly.

"I was not mistaken. I remembered this woman's face this morning, but I could not then recall where I had seen her before," pursued Merrington, turning to Captain Stanhill and speaking with a sort of reflective cruelty. "Her daughter's face supplies the clue. She is the image of her mother as I remember her when she stood her trial at Old Bailey fifteen years ago. She was tried for–"

"I beg of you not to say it!" Mrs. Rath started from her seat, and looked wildly around as though seeking some avenue of escape from a threatened disaster.

"Is it necessary to go into this, Merrington?" asked Captain Stanhill in his mild tones, glancing from the excited woman to his colleague with the troubled consciousness that he was assisting in a scene which was distasteful to him.

"Of course it is necessary if we want to get at the truth of this case," retorted Merrington. "You needn't be concerned on Mrs. Rath's account," he went on, with a kind of savage, disdainful irony. "A woman who has been tried as an accessory to murder is not likely to be squeamish. Her name is not Rath. It is Theberton–Mary Theberton. She and her husband were tried at Old Bailey fifteen years ago for the murder of a man named Bridges. The trial made a great stir at the time. It was known as 'The Death Signal Case'."

Caldew looked at the housekeeper with a new interest. He readily recalled the notorious case mentioned by Merrington. Theberton was an Essex miller, who, having discovered that his young wife was in the habit of signalling his absence to Bridges by means of a candle placed in her window, had compelled her to entice him to the cottage by the signal, and was then supposed to have murdered him by throwing him into the mill dam. But though Bridges was seen entering the cottage and was not seen afterwards, the charge of murder failed because the detectives were unable to find his body. Theberton protested his innocence; Mary Theberton said her husband locked her in her room before admitting Bridges, and she knew nothing of what took place between the two men.

There was much popular sympathy with her during the trial as the belief gained ground that the relations between her and Bridges were innocent, though indiscreet; the outcome of a craving for sympathy which had led an unhappy young wife to confide her troubles to a former schoolfellow. She was the daughter of an architect, and had been reared in refinement and educated well, but she had been disowned by her father for marrying beneath her. Her husband ill-used her, and her story was that she had sought the assistance of an old schoolfellow in order to go to London to earn a living for herself and her little daughter. When the trial was over Theberton emigrated, and his wife disappeared, although there was some talk of putting on foot a public subscription for her. This was the end of "The Death Signal Case," for the mystery of the disappearance of Bridges was never solved.

Caldew wondered by what strange turn of Fortune's wheel the woman before him had come to be housekeeper at the moat-house. It was certain that Miss Heredith knew nothing of the black page in her past, because Miss Heredith, in spite of her kind heart and rigid church principles, was the last person to appoint anybody with a tainted name to a position of trust in her household. She was too proud of the family name to do such a thing. The fact that the housekeeper had held the post so long without discovery was proof of the ease with which identity could be safely concealed from everything except chance. Although her nervous demeanour suggested that she had been walking on a razor edge of perpetual suspense in her quiet haven, ever dreading detection, it seemed to Caldew that she might have gone undiscovered to her grave but for a trick of Fate in selecting Superintendent Merrington to investigate the moat-house murder. Fate, after its cruel fashion, had left her on her razor edge for quite a long while before toppling her over, and Caldew reflected that he had been made the instrument of her fall.

But what lay beyond the exposure of the housekeeper's identity? Why had she deceived Merrington about her daughter's presence in the house? Was it only the fear that Merrington would recognize her in her early likeness to her daughter, or were her falsehoods intended to deceive the detectives about Hazel's movements at the time of the murder? What would the girl say? The situation was full of strange possibilities.

While these reflections were passing through Caldew's head there was silence in the room, broken only by the clock on the mantelpiece ticking loudly, with pert indifference to human affairs. Merrington, after dragging the hidden and forgotten tragedy to light, remained quiet, watchfully noting the effect on mother and daughter. The mother stood without a word or gesture, her hand stiffened in arrested protest, like a woman frozen into silence. The girl's look was directed towards her mother with the fixity of gaze of a sleeper awakened in the horror of a bad dream. At least in their stillness they were both in accord. Then Hazel glanced wonderingly at the faces of the others in the room, with the fatigued indifference of a returning consciousness seeking to regain its bearings. This phase passed, and in the sudden wild burst of tears which followed was the belated realization of the meaning of her mother's exposure; the shame, the agony, the disgrace which it implied. With a quick movement she rose from her seat, walked across to her mother, and caught hold of her hand.

"Mother!" she said.

But her mother turned away from her, and, sinking in her chair, covered her face in her hands with a shamed gesture, like a woman cast forth naked in the light of day.

"Never mind your mother just now," said Merrington, as the girl bent over as though to sooth her. "Please return to your seat and answer my questions."

Hazel turned round at the sound of his voice, but stood where she was, regarding him anxiously.

"You stayed here last night with your mother, I understand?" Merrington continued.

"Yes."

"When did you arrive here?"

"Yesterday afternoon."

"Where from?"

"From Stading, by train. I had an afternoon off, and I came to see my mother."

"How long is it since you visited her previously?"

"It must be about three months," said Hazel, after a short reflection.

"Do you always allow three months to elapse between your visits?"

"No." There was a trace of hesitation in the response.

"You used to come oftener?"

"Yes."

"How often?"

"Nearly every week." This time the hesitation before the reply was plainly apparent.

"Why did you allow so long a time to elapse between this visit and the last one when you had previously been in the habit of seeing your mother nearly every week?"

Hazel again hesitated, as though at a loss for a reply.

"I have been so busy," she murmured at length.

"Is this your first visit to the moat-house since Mrs. Heredith came here to live?"

"Yes." The response was so low as to be almost inaudible.

Caldew, who was the only person in the room with the deeper knowledge to divine the drift of these questions, realized with something of a shock that Merrington, with fewer facts to guide him, had reached his absolute conclusion about the events of the last half-hour while he had wandered perplexedly in a cloud of suspicions. The mental jump had been too great for him, but Merrington had not hesitated to take it. Caldew waited eagerly for the next question. It was some time in coming, and when it did come it was not what Caldew expected. As though satisfied with the previous answers he had received, Merrington branched off on another track.

"How did you spend last night?" he asked abruptly.

"I do not understand you." There was the shadow of fear in the girl's dark eyes as she answered.

"I will put it more plainly then. How did you occupy the time between your arrival at the moat-house and bedtime?"

"I spent it with my mother in her rooms."

"Were you there all the time?"

It seemed to Caldew that the elder woman's attitude was that of a listener. Though she still kept her face buried in her hands, her frame slightly moved, as though she were listening to catch the reply.

"Yes." The word was spoken hurriedly, almost defiantly, but the girl's eyes wavered and fell under Merrington's direct glance.

"May I take it, then, that you were in your mother's room at the time Mrs. Heredith was murdered?"

This time Hazel did not reply audibly, but a faint movement of her head indicated an affirmative.

"What would you say if your mother admits that you left her room before the murder was committed, and that she did not see you until afterwards?"

It was a clever trap, Caldew reluctantly conceded, this idea of playing off the mother and daughter against each other, but one that he would have hesitated to use. The effect was instantaneous. Before the girl could frame her frightened lips in reply, her mother lifted her head sharply.

"I didn't say so! Don't answer him, Hazel, don't tell him. Oh!" Too late the wretched woman realized that she had betrayed her daughter, and she sank into a stupefied silence.

"Your mother has let the cat out of the bag," said Merrington to the girl, in a bantering tone. "Come, now," he added, changing swiftly into his most truculent mood. "We may as well have the truth, first as last. You were seen last night going up the hall in the direction of the left wing just before the murder was committed. Do you admit it?"

"I do." The admission was made in a low but calm tone.

"Then your last answer was untrue. What were you doing in the hall at that time?"

Hazel, staring straight in front of her, did not reply, but her quickly moving breast betrayed her agitation.

"Did you hear me? I asked what were you doing in the hall last night."

"I shall not tell you."

"Did you go upstairs?"

"I shall not tell you."

These replies were given with a firm readiness which was in striking contrast to her previous hesitation. She was like a person who had been forced on to a dangerous path she feared to tread, and had summoned fortitude to walk it bravely to the end.

"Of course you realize the position in which you place yourself by your silence?" The quiet gravity with which Merrington put this question was, similarly, in the strangest contrast to his former hectoring style. "It is my duty to warn you that you are placing yourself in a grave situation. Once more, will you answer my questions?"

"I will not." The answer was accompanied by a gesture which contained something of the carelessness of despair.

"Then you must abide the consequences." He turned to Captain Stanhill and Caldew. "It will be necessary to search the housekeeper's rooms. Lumbe, you remain here and take charge of these two women. Do not allow either of them to leave the room on any pretext. You had better keep the door locked until we return."

He strode out of the room followed by Captain Stanhill and Caldew, to the manifest trepidation of two maidservants outside, who had plainly no business there. It was apparent that Milly Saker had been talking, and that strange rumours were agitating the moat-house underworld.

"Where are the housekeeper's rooms?" said Merrington, abruptly accosting one of the fluttered girls. "Come now, don't stand gaping at me like a fool, but take us there directly."

The terrified girl went quickly ahead along a corridor leading from the main hall. Turning down a narrower passage near the end she paused outside a closed door and said:

"This is the housekeeper's room, sir."

"Stop a minute," said Merrington. "Does the housekeeper occupy only one room?"

"No, sir, there are two. A sitting-room, with a bedroom opening off it."

"She has no other room in any other part of the house?"

"Oh, no, sir."

"That will do. You may go."

The maid needed no second bidding, but scuttled back towards the corridor like a scared hen making for cover. Merrington flung open the door in front of him and entered.

The room was well and simply furnished in the style of the house, but the personal belongings and the bindings of some books suggested a mind not out of harmony with the refinement of its surroundings. Merrington, with a swift and comprehensive glance around him, began to upset the neat arrangement and feminine order of the apartment with a thorough and systematic search.

Caldew watched him for a moment, and then walked across to the door of the inner room and entered it. The bedroom was large and airy, and the appointments struck the note of dainty simplicity. Caldew was quick to notice a girl's hat, with a veil attached, cast carelessly on the toilet-table.

He made a circuit round the bed and approached the table to look at the hat. A tight knot and a slight tear in the gossamer indicated that it had been discarded very hastily, and Caldew wondered whether Hazel had it on, waiting for an opportunity to slip away from the moat-house, when he had knocked at the door to summon her to the library.

As he put the hat down his eye fell on a pincushion by the mirror, and he gave a start of surprise. In the midst of hatpins at various angles he saw the little brooch which had disappeared from the death-chamber. The stone with the greenish reflection shone clearly against the blue and gold shot-silk of the pincushion; the portion of the clasp which was visible revealed the beginning of the scratched inscription of "Semper Fidelis." The absence of any attempt to conceal the brooch was proof that its owner was under the delusion that nobody had seen it lying in the death-chamber. Caldew felt a thrill of professional vanity at the success of his ruse.

His own name uttered in a peremptory shout from the next room caused him to pick up the brooch and hasten thither. The first sight that met his eye was the flushed triumphant face of Merrington bending over some articles on the table. Caldew's view of the objects was obscured by Captain Stanhill, who was also examining them, but he guessed by the attitude of both men that a valuable find had been made. He advanced eagerly to the table and saw, lying between them, a small revolver and a handkerchief. The white cambric of the handkerchief was stained crimson with blood.

The room was in great disorder. Superintendent Merrington, in the impetuosity of his search, had reduced the previous order to chaos in the course of a few minutes. Drawers had been opened and their contents strewn about the floor, rugs and cushions had been flung into a corner of the room, and the doors of a cabinet had been forced. Even the pictures on the wall had been disarranged, and some of the chairs were knocked over.

"Where did you find these things?" asked Caldew, picking up the revolver and examining it.

"In that gimcrack thing over there." Merrington pointed to a slight, elegant writing-table standing in a corner of the room. "Isn't it a typical female hiding-place? About as safe as burying your head in the sand. The drawer had been locked and the key taken away, but it was quite easy to open. The lock is a trumpery kind of thing, with the bolt shooting into the soft wood."

"I see that the revolver is still loaded in five chambers," said Caldew, as he put down the weapon.

"Yes, and the sixth has been recently discharged. We don't require much clearer evidence than that. And look at this handkerchief. The blood on it is hardly dry yet."

Caldew took the handkerchief in his hand. As Merrington remarked, the blood on it was hardly dry. It was a small linen square, destitute of feminine adornment except for a dainty "H R" worked in silk in one corner. The letters were barely visible in the blood with which the whole handkerchief was saturated.

"I wonder how she got the blood on the handkerchief?" said Caldew. "Did she try to stop the bleeding after shooting Mrs. Heredith?"

"It would be just like a woman to do so," grunted Merrington. "Women are fond of crying over spilt milk– especially when they have spilt it themselves. However, that's neither here nor there. The point is that this is the girl's handkerchief, and this is the revolver with which she shot Mrs. Heredith."

"But what was her motive for committing such an atrocious crime?" asked Captain Stanhill in bewilderment.

"Jealousy," responded Merrington promptly. "I saw the possibility of that motive as soon as I heard Milly Saker's story, and learnt that Hazel Rath had lived for some years in the moat-house. Young Heredith and she must have been thrown together a lot before the war, and there was doubtless a flirtation between them which probably developed into an intrigue. There are all the materials at hand for it–a well-born idle young man, a girl educated above her station, a lonely country-house, and plenty of opportunity. I know the type of girl well. These half-educated protégées of great ladies grow up with all the whims and caprices of fine females, and their silly little heads are easily turned. Probably this girl imagined that young Heredith was so captivated by her pretty face that he would marry her. When she learnt that she had been dropped for somebody else she brooded in secret until her unbalanced nature led her to commit this terrible crime. Moreover, she is the daughter of a woman with a queer past, who has been living under an assumed name for the past fifteen years."

"Do you think mother and daughter have acted in collusion in this murder?" Caldew asked.

"That is a question I would not care to answer offhand," responded Merrington thoughtfully. "Undoubtedly the mother shielded the daughter and lied to save her, and she obviously knew that the girl was absent from her room at the time the murder was committed. How far this implies guilty knowledge, or the acts of an accomplice, we are not yet in a position to say. We will arrest the daughter, and detain the mother–for the present, at all events. Whether we charge the mother as well as the daughter will depend on our subsequent investigations. It will be no novelty for the mother to be charged as accessory in a murder case," concluded Merrington, with a grim smile.

"We have no direct evidence that the girl went upstairs last night," said Caldew, with a reflective air. "Milly Saker did not see her going upstairs, and apparently nobody saw her coming away."

"No direct evidence, it is true. But the presumptive evidence is so strong that it is hardly needed. In the first place, Milly Saker saw her going down the hall in the direction of the left wing just before the murder was committed. Next day–this morning–the housekeeper sent Milly Saker out of the way before she could be questioned by the police. That act suggests two inferences. First, Mrs. Rath, as she calls herself, had some inkling that Milly Saker saw her daughter in the hall on the previous night, and secondly, that Mrs. Rath feared, in the light of subsequent events, to let it be known that her daughter was seen walking down the hall before the murder was committed. From these inferences we may conclude that, even if the mother had no actual knowledge of the crime, she believed that her daughter was guilty. Her subsequent actions to-day confirm that theory in every respect. And, of course, the recovery of this revolver and the girl's handkerchief in her mother's rooms, where she slept last night, is the strongest possible proof that the girl shot Mrs. Heredith."

"Of course there can be no doubt of that. It would be impossible to find a stronger case of circumstantial evidence," said Caldew earnestly. "But here is a piece of direct evidence. Look here!" He produced the little brooch from his pocket and placed it on the table beside the revolver and the handkerchief. "This is the brooch I told you about. It is the brooch I saw in Mrs. Heredith's room which disappeared while I was downstairs. I found it stuck in a pincushion in the next room, beside the girl's hat. She must have realized that she dropped it in the murdered woman's bedroom, and seized the opportunity to return for it while I was out of the room. That is a piece of direct evidence that she was in Mrs. Heredith's bedroom."

"So you were right about the brooch. I owe you an apology for that, Caldew," said Merrington. He placed the little trinket in his big hand, and turned it over with his finger. The inscription on the back caught his eye, and he held it closer to read it. "Semper Fidelis!" he exclaimed. "The words are typical of the girl. The wishy-washy sentiment would appeal to her, and she's of that partly educated type which thinks a Latin tag imposing. I wonder who gave it to her? Oh, I have it! It was probably a gift from young Heredith, and she added the inscription on her own account so as to enhance the value of the gift and keep her 'Faithful Always.'"

Once more Caldew reluctantly admitted to himself that Merrington's deductions were more swift and vigorous than his own, but he was secretly annoyed to think that the other had gained partly by guesswork the solution of a clue which had caused him so much thought and perplexity.

"The brooch is no more direct evidence than the revolver and handkerchief," continued Merrington. "The girl, unless she is a born fool, is not likely to admit ownership of any one of them. She would be putting the rope round her own neck to do so."

"I realize that," replied Caldew. "But I think that she might be trapped into giving away that she owns the brooch. Women are very impulsive where the loss of ornaments is concerned, and then their actions are instinctive. I have frequently noticed it."

"And how do you propose to find out?" asked Merrington.

"By asking her."

"You'll get nothing out of this girl for the asking," replied Merrington. "She runs deeper than that, or I am very much mistaken.

However, ask your own questions, by all means, after I have questioned her about the revolver and the handkerchief. Let us get back to the library."

They returned to the library. Sergeant Lumbe opened the door in response to their knock, his face furrowed with the responsibilities of office. Mother and daughter were sitting where they had left them, but the elder woman had regained some measure of composure, and was staring drearily in front of her. She did not look at the police officials as they entered, but Hazel glanced towards them, and her eyes fell on the revolver and handkerchief which Merrington carried in his hand. It seemed to Caldew that her face remained unmoved. Merrington walked over to her.

"You must consider yourself under arrest on a charge of murdering Mrs. Heredith," he said, in quiet, almost conversational tones. "This revolver and this handkerchief were found in your mother's sitting-room. If you have any explanation to make you may do so, but it is my duty to warn you that any statement you make now may be used in evidence against you later on."

"I have nothing to say," replied the girl simply.

"You decline to say how this revolver came into your possession, or make any explanation about the bloodstains on this handkerchief?"

"Yes."

"Do you also refuse to tell us what you have done with the brooch you were wearing last night?" added Caldew.

The girl, with an impulsive instinctive gesture, hastily put her hand to the neck of her blouse, then, realizing that she had unconsciously betrayed herself, she let it fall slowly to her side.

14

The popular fallacy which likens circumstantial evidence to a chain naturally found no acceptance in the mind of Superintendent Merrington. If a link in a chain snaps, the captive springs free, but if he is bound by a rope it is necessary for all the strands to be severed before liberty can be regained.

Merrington remained at Heredith to weave additional strands for the rope of circumstantial evidence by which Hazel Rath was held for the murder of Violet Heredith. It was a good strong case as it stood, but Merrington had seen too many strong ropes nibbled through by sharp legal teeth to leave anything to chance. If the circumstances against Hazel Rath remained open to an alternative explanation–if, for example, the defence suggested that the mother was implicated in the crime and the daughter was silent in order to shield her, it might be difficult to obtain a conviction. Merrington knew by wide experience how alternative theories weakened the case of circumstantial evidence, no matter how strong the presumption from the known facts appeared to be.

A useful strand in circumstantial evidence is motive, and it was motive that Merrington sought to prove against Hazel Rath. His own inference about the crime, swiftly and boldly reached shortly before he arrested her, was that the girl was in love with Phil Heredith, and had murdered his young wife through jealousy. Hazel's silence in the face of accusation supported that theory, in his opinion. She was ashamed to confess, not the crime, but the hopeless love which had inspired it. Women were like that, Merrington reflected. A woman who dared to commit murder would blush to admit, even to herself, that she had given her love to a man who was out of her reach. But it is one thing to hold a theory, and another thing to prove it in the eyes of the law. As Hazel Rath was not likely to help the Crown establish motive by confessing her love for Philip Heredith, it was left to Superintendent Merrington to establish his theory, by all the independent facts and inferences he was able to bring to light.

This proved more difficult than he anticipated. He had visualized the situation with excellent insight up to a certain point, and he had imagined that it would not be a difficult matter to obtain proofs of the existence of an early flirtation or intrigue between Phil Heredith and the pretty girl who had occupied an anomalous position in the moat-house. But a further examination of the inmates of the household failed to furnish any proofs in support of that supposition. Merrington could readily understand Miss Heredith and her brother denying such a suggestion; but the fact that none of the servants had seen anything of the kind was fairly convincing proof that no such relation existed.

No class have a keener instinct for scandal than the servants of a country-house. They have opportunities of seeing hidden things which nobody else is likely to suspect. And the moat-house servants asserted, with complete unanimity, that there had been nothing between Phil Heredith and Hazel Rath during the time the girl had lived at the moat-house. Their relations had been friendly, but nothing more. There was no record of secret looks, stolen kisses, or surprised meetings to support the theory of a mutual flirtation or furtive love. It was impossible to doubt that Phil Heredith's attitude to the girl who had occupied a dependent position in his home had been actuated by no warmer feeling than a sort of brotherly regard.

Merrington, versed by long experience in forming an estimate of character from second-hand opinion, was forced to the conclusion that Phil Heredith was not the type of young man to betray the innocence or trifle with the feelings of a young and unsophisticated girl. The servants' testimony revealed him as gentle and courteous, but shy and reserved, not fond of company, and immersed in his natural history pursuits.

Merrington, however, had less difficulty in proving to his own satisfaction that Hazel Rath had been secretly in love with Phil Heredith almost since the days of her childhood. There was, to begin with, the greenstone brooch which Caldew had picked tap in the bedroom after Mrs. Heredith had been murdered. The members of the household were in the custom of making the girl little presents on her birthday anniversary, and Phil had given her the piece of greenstone, set in a brooch, on her birthday six years before. There was no secret about it; the gift had been chosen on the suggestion of Miss Heredith, who told Merrington the facts. What was unknown was the addition of the inscription, "Semper Fidelis," which must have been scratched on the brooch subsequently by the girl herself as a girlish vow of love and fidelity of the giver.

Detective Caldew might have ascertained these facts and shortened the police investigations by the simple process of asking Miss Heredith about the brooch in the first instance. But it is easy to be wise after the event, and Superintendent Merrington was the last man to quarrel with his subordinate for excess of caution in the initial stage of the investigations, when it was his duty to doubt everybody and confide in nobody. Moreover, Merrington could not forget that he himself had completely underestimated the importance of that clue when Caldew had drawn his attention to it.

A search of Hazel's bedroom at Stading brought to light additional testimony of the love which was likely to destroy her. Merrington and Caldew, ruthlessly turning over the feminine appointments of this dainty little nest, had unearthed from the bottom of the girl's box a square parcel tied with ribbon. The packet contained letters and postcards from Phil, principally picture postcards from different Continental places he had visited after leaving Cambridge. There were three letters: two schoolboy epistles, asking the girl to look after the pets he had left at home, and one short note from the University announcing the dispatch of a volume of poems as a birthday gift. There was also a Christmas card, dated some years before, inscribed, "To dear Phil, with love, from Hazel." The girl had kept it, perhaps, because she was too shy to bestow it on the intended recipient, but its chief value in Merrington's eyes was the similarity between the written capital F and the same letter in the scratched inscription on the greenstone brooch.

With these discoveries Merrington was satisfied. In Hazel Rath's secret love for Phil Heredith the Crown was supplied with the motive for the murder of Phil Heredith's wife. In Merrington's opinion, the supposition of motive was strengthened by the fact that the murder was committed during Hazel's first visit to the moat-house since the arrival of the young bride, because until Phil's marriage it had been the girl's custom to visit the moat-house once a week. Miss Heredith informed Merrington that she had questioned the girl on the afternoon of the murder about the sudden cessation of her visits, and Hazel had replied rather evasively. Merrington formed the opinion that she had stayed away because she could not bear to see the woman whom Phil had made his wife. Then, realizing that her prolonged absence was likely to be remarked upon, she went across on the day of the murder to see her mother. Merrington did not think that the murder was premeditated. His belief was that when the girl found herself back in the surroundings where she had spent such a happy girlhood in association with Phil Heredith, she was seized with a mad fit of jealousy against her successful rival, and under its influence had rushed upstairs and murdered her. Merrington had also come to the conclusion that her mother knew nothing about the crime until afterwards, and then she had endeavoured to shield her daughter by lying to the police and sending Milly Saker out of the way.

Merrington was unable to account for Hazel's possession of the revolver with which Mrs. Heredith had been killed. The girl maintained her stubborn silence after her arrest, and refused to answer any questions about the weapon or anything connected with the crime. The police assumption was that she had obtained the revolver from the gun-room of the moat-house shortly before the murder was committed. The gun-room was underground. It had originally been the crypt of the Saxon castle which had once stood on the site where the moat-house was built, and was entered by a short flight of steps not far from the passage which led to the housekeeper's rooms. It was rectangular in shape, and, like the majority of gun-rooms in old English country mansions, contained a large assortment of ancient and modern weapons.

Neither Sir Philip Heredith nor Miss Heredith was able to state whether the revolver found in the housekeeper's room belonged to the moat-house or was the property of one of the guests, and Phil Heredith was too ill to be asked. As expert evidence at the inquest definitely determined that the bullet extracted from the murdered woman had been fired from the revolver, Merrington did not attach very much importance to the question of ownership, but before his departure for London he arranged that Caldew should return to the moat-house later with the revolver for Phil's inspection, in the hope of settling the point before the trial.

Miss Heredith had undertaken to let the detectives know when her nephew was well enough to be seen, but as time went on she doubted whether he would ever recover. Although the delirium which had followed his seizure had passed away, he was slow in regaining health, and remained in bed, listless and indifferent to everything, sometimes reading a little, but oftener lying still, staring at the wall. He was passive and quiet, and obedient as a child. He seemed to have no recollection of the events of the night of the murder, and his aunt did not dare to recall them to his mind.

It was for Phil's sake, and for him only, that she was able to preserve her own courage and calmness through the sordid ordeal of the lengthy inquest and the empty pomp of the funeral of the young wife. Her own heart was bruised and numb within her with the horrors which had been heaped upon her. She was like one who had seen a pit open suddenly at her feet, revealing terrible human obscenities and abominations wallowing nakedly in the depths. It was a poignant shock to her that human nature was capable of such infamy. Her startled virgin eyes saw for the first time in the monstrous passion of sex a force which was stronger than her own most cherished beliefs. If a sweet and gentle girl like Hazel Rath, who had been brought up under her own eye to walk uprightly, could be swept away in the surge of tempestuous passion to commit murder, where did Faith and Religion stand?

Almost as much as the effect of the murder did she fear the result of this second revelation on her nephew. The knowledge that the person accused of killing his wife was a girl who had lived in his own home for years was bound to have an additionally injurious effect on his strange and sensitive temperament. Nobody knew that temperament better than Miss Heredith. It was not the Heredith temperament. It had been the heritage of his mother, a strange, elfin, wayward creature, who had died bringing Phil into the world. Like all sisters, Miss Heredith had wondered what her brother had seen in his wife to marry her. Phil had all along been a disappointment to his father. He had come into the world with a lame foot and a frail frame, and the Herediths had always been noted for masculine strength and grace. Instead of growing up with a scorn for books and an absorbing love of sport, like a true Heredith, Phil had early revealed symptoms of a bookish, studious disposition, reserved and shy, with little liking for other boys or boyish games. His one hobby was an interest in natural history. He devoted his pocket money to the purchase of strange pets, which he kept in cages while they lived and stuffed when they died.

Miss Heredith had disapproved of this hobby, but had suffered it in silence, on the principle that a Heredith could do no wrong, until one winter's morning she had been frightened into her first and only fit of hysterics by discovering a large spotted snake coiled snugly on some flannel garments she was making for the wife of the curate, in anticipation of that unfortunate lady's fifth lying-in. Investigation brought to light the fact that the snake had been surreptitiously purchased by Master Phil from a Covent Garden dealer. He had kept it in a box in the stables, but, finding it torpid with cold one night, he had put it in his aunt's work-basket for the sake of the warmth. When Miss Heredith recovered from her hysterics she had seen to it that Phil was packed off to school almost as quickly as the snake was packed off to the Zoological Gardens.

After Phil's college days his father's influence had obtained for him a Government post which was to be the forerunnner of a diplomatic career, if Phil cared for it. That was before the war, which upset so many plans. In his capacity of assistant departmental secretary, Phil had nothing particular to do, and an ample allowance from his father to spend in his leisure time. Many young men in these circumstances—thrown on their own resources in London with plenty of money to spend—would have lost no time in "going wrong," but Phil's temperament preserved him from those temptations which so many young well-born men find irresistible. He had a disdain for the stage, he did not care for chorus girls, he disliked horse-racing, and he did not drink.

He sought distractions in another way, and rumours of those distractions filtered in due course down to his family home in Sussex. It was whispered that Phil was "queer"–that his old passion for petting reptiles and lower animal forms had merely been diverted into another channel. He had become a Socialist, and had been seen consorting with the lower orders at East End meetings with other people sufficiently respectable to have known better. It was even stated that he had supported an Irish revolutionary countess (who had discovered the first Socialist in Jesus Christ, and wanted to disestablish the Church of England) by "taking the chair" for her when she announced these tenets to the rabble in Hyde Park one fine Sunday afternoon. A Heredith a socialist and nonconformist! These were bitter blows to Miss Heredith, a woman soaked in family and Church tradition, but she bore the shock with uncompromising front, and was able to make the shortcomings of Phil's mother a vicarious sacrifice for the misdeeds of the son.

But the bitterest blow to Miss Heredith's family pride was the news of Phil's marriage. Till then she had pinned her faith, like a wise woman, in the reformative influence of a good marriage. Although a spinster herself, she was aware that there was no better method of reducing the showy nettlesome paces of youth to the sober jog-trot of middle-age than the restraining influence of the right kind of yokefellow. The qualities Phil most needed in a wife were those possessed by a sober-minded, unimaginative, placid girl of conventional mould. Such maidens are not unknown in rural England, and Miss Heredith had not much difficulty in picking upon one in the county sufficiently well-born to mate with the Herediths. Miss Heredith perfected her plan in detail, and had even gone to the length of drafting the letter which was to bring Phil down from London to be matrimonially snared, when the news came that he had snared himself in London without his aunt's assistance. She did not like his wife from the first, and it was equally certain that Phil's wife did not like her. It was a marvellous thing to Miss Heredith that a shallow worldly girl like Violet should have captured the heart of a young man like her nephew so completely as to cause him to alter his ways of life for her. Phil loved Nature, and books, and solitary ways; his wife detested such things. Phil, in his eagerness to please her, and banish her apparent boredom with country life, had suggested asking some people from London with whom, at one time, he would have had very little in common. Perhaps his London life had changed him, but if so, it was a change for the worse for a young man, and a Heredith, to be so much under the thumb of his wife as to give up his own habits of life at her behest. But Phil was so much in love that he had done so, cheerfully and willingly. Violet's lightest wish was his law.

These thoughts, and others like them, passed and repassed through Miss Heredith's mind as she sat, day after day, in her nephew's sick room. It was her custom to take her needlework there of an afternoon, and relieve the nurse for two or three hours. But her sewing frequently lay idle in her lap, and she leaned back in her chair, absorbed in thought, glancing from time to time at Phil's worn face on the pillow, where he lay like one exhausted and weary, reluctant to return to the turmoil of life. He took his food and medicine with the docility of a child, and occasionally smiled at his aunt when she ministered to him. Gradually he mended and increased in bodily strength until he was able to sit up, and smoke an occasional cigarette. Sometimes he talked a little with his aunt, but always on indifferent subjects. He never asked about his wife, or spoke of the murder, as he had done in his delirium. It was apparent to those about him that his recollection of the events which had brought about his illness had not yet returned. Nature had, for the time being, soothed his stricken brain with temporary oblivion.

Then one day the change that Miss Heredith anticipated and feared came on him as swiftly as a dream. She entered the room to find him up and dressed, walking up and down with a quick and hurried stride. One glance from his quick dark eyes conveyed to her that his wandering senses had recrossed the border-line of consciousness, and entered into the horror and agony of remembrance.

"Phil, dear," she said, hastening to his side, "is this wise?"

"How long have I been lying here?" he demanded impatiently, as though he had not heard her speak.

"It is ten days since you were taken ill," she replied, in a low voice. "Ten days!" he repeated in a stupefied tone, as though unable to realize the import of the lapse of time. "It is incredible! It seems to me as though it was only a few hours. What has happened? What has been done by the police? Has the murderer been arrested?"

It came to Miss Heredith with a shock that his dormant brain had awakened to leap back to the thing which had paralysed it, and with that knowledge came the realization that the dreaded moment for the revelation she had to make had arrived. And, like a woman, she sought to postpone it.

"Phil," she said weakly, "do not talk about it—until you are stronger."

"I am strong enough not to be treated as a child," he rejoined fretfully, turning on her a sallow face, with a bright spot in each cheek. "Is the funeral over?"

"Some days ago," she murmured, and there was a thankful feeling in her heart that it was so.

Before he had time to speak again there was a tap at the door, and a maidservant entered.

"Mr. Musard would like to speak to you for a moment, ma'am," she said to Miss Heredith.

Miss Heredith caught eagerly at the respite.

"Tell him I will come at once. Phil," she added, turning to her nephew, "I will send Vincent to you. He can tell you better than I. He has been here all through your illness, and has looked after everything."

She hurried from the room without waiting for his reply. She saw the tall form of Musard standing in the hall, and went rapidly to him.

"Phil has come to his senses, Vincent," she exclaimed, in an agitated voice. "He wants to know everything that has happened since he was taken ill. What shall we do?"

"He must be told, of course," replied Musard, with masculine decision. "It is better that he should know than be kept in suspense. How is he?"

"He seems quite normal and rational. Will you see him and tell him?"

"Yes. As a matter of fact it is advisable that he should know everything without delay. I sent for you to tell you that Detective Caldew has just arrived to ascertain if Phil can identify the revolver. I told him Phil was still ill, but he is persistent, and thinks that he ought to be allowed to see him. It would be better if Phil could see him, and settle the point."

"Oh, Vincent, do you think it is wise?"

"Yes. Phil has had a shock, but it is not going to kill him, and the sooner he takes up his ordinary life again the better it will be for him. Come, now, everything will be all right." He smiled at her anxious face reassuringly. "Leave it to me. I will see that nothing is done to agitate Phil if I do not think him strong enough to bear it. Now, let us go to him."

The bedroom door was open and Phil was standing near it as though awaiting their appearance. He held out his hand to Musard, who was surprised by the strength of his grip. He eyed the young man critically, and thought he looked fairly well considering the ordeal he had passed through.

"I am glad to see you better, Phil," he said. "How do you feel? Not very fit yet?"

"I am all right," responded Phil quickly. "Now, Musard, I want you to tell me all that has happened since I have been lying here. I am completely in the dark. Has anybody been arrested for the murder of my wife?"

He spoke in a dry impersonal tone as though of some occurrence in which he had but a remote interest, but Musard was too keen a judge of men to be deceived by his apparent calmness. He thought that it was better for him to learn the truth at once.

"Yes, Phil," he said quietly, "there has been an arrest. Hazel Rath has been arrested for the murder of Violet."

"Who?" The tone of detachment disappeared. The interrogation was flung at Musard's head with a world of incredulity and amazement.

"Hazel Rath, the housekeeper's daughter."

"In the name of God, why?"

"Gently, laddie. Sit down, and take it quietly. I'll tell you all."

Phil controlled himself with a painful effort, and took a chair near the bedside.

"Go on," he said hoarsely.

Musard seated himself on the edge of the bed at his side, and entered upon a narration of the circumstances which had led to the arrest of Hazel Rath. Phil listened attentively, but the expression of amazement never left his face. When Musard finished he was silent for a moment, and then impetuously broke out:

"I feel sure Hazel Rath did not commit this crime."

Musard was silent. That was a question upon which he did not feel called upon to advance an opinion. Miss Heredith was too moved to speak.

"Why do you not say something?" exclaimed Phil, turning on her angrily. "Surely you do not think Hazel guilty?"

"Oh, Phil," responded his aunt piteously, "it seems hard to believe, but what else can we think? There was the revolver and the handkerchief found in her mother's room, and the little greenstone brooch you gave her was picked up in Violet's bedroom."

"Why do they think she has killed her? Tell me that!"

Musard, in his narration of the facts, had omitted mention of the supposed motive, but he now made a gesture to Miss Heredith to indicate that she had better tell Phil.

"It was because the police believe that Hazel was–was in love with you, Phil," she falteringly said. "They think she murdered Violet in a fit of jealousy."

"Hazel in love with me?" He echoed the phrase in mingled scorn and amazement. "That is preposterous. If the police have nothing better than that to go on–"

"They have," interrupted Musard. "They are going on the clues I have mentioned–the brooch, the handkerchief, and the revolver."

"Where did Hazel get the revolver?"

"It is thought she got it from the gun-room."

"There are no revolvers in the gun-room," rejoined Phil quickly. "We have no revolvers, unless father bought one recently. What make is it?"

"The ownership of the revolver is a point the police have not yet been able to settle," returned Musard. "It is only an assumption on their part that Hazel got it from the gun-room. They thought it either belonged to the house or was left behind by one of the guests. Neither your aunt nor I knew, and Sir Philip was unable to settle the point. The police thought you might know. As a matter of fact, one of the detectives engaged in the investigations has just arrived from London and brought the revolver with him to see if you can identify it."

"I should like to see him. Where is he?"

"In the library. I will bring him in."

Musard left the room and quickly returned with Caldew, who entered with a business-like air.

"This is Mr. Heredith," said Musard.

"I trust you are better, Mr. Heredith," said the detective smoothly. "I am sorry to trouble you so soon after your illness, but there is a point we would like to settle before the trial of the woman who is charged with murdering your wife. We want, if possible, to establish the ownership of the weapon with which the murder was committed." He produced a revolver from the pocket of his light overcoat as he spoke. "In view of the evidence, the identification of the weapon does not matter much one way or another, but it is as well to fix the point, if we can. The girl refuses to say where she obtained the revolver—indeed, she remains stubbornly silent about the crime, and refuses to say anything about it. That doesn't matter very much either, because the evidence against her is so strong that she is bound to be convicted. Can you tell me anything about the revolver, Mr. Heredith? Do you recognize it?"

Phil was turning the revolver over in his hands, examining it closely.

"Yes," he said. "I recognize it. It belongs to Captain Nepcote."

"Captain Nepcote? Who is he?"

"He is a friend of my nephew's who was staying here, but left the afternoon of the day the murder was committed," said Miss Heredith. "He was recalled to the front, I understand. I gave his name to Superintendent Merrington as one of the guests who had been staying here."

"How do you identify the revolver as his property?" asked Caldew, turning to Phil.

"By the bullet mark in the handle. The day before my wife was killed it was raining, and some of the guests were down in the gun-room shooting at a target with Nepcote's revolver. He showed us this mark in the handle, and said that it had saved his life in France. He was leading his men in a night raid on the German lines, and a German officer fired at him at close range, but the bullet glanced off the handle of the revolver."

"Then there can be no doubt Hazel Rath got it from the gun-room," said Caldew, returning the weapon to his pocket. "Captain Nepcote must have left it behind him there, and that is where Hazel Rath found it."

"No, no! That seems impossible," said Phil.

"Well, I think it is quite possible," replied Caldew.

"Is it your opinion, then, that Miss Rath is guilty?" demanded Phil, with a note of sharp anger in his voice.

"Phil!" said Miss Heredith. "You must not excite yourself."

But the young man took no notice of his aunt's gentle remonstrance. His eyes were fixed on the detective.

"I have not the least doubt of it," was the detective's cold response.

"I must say I think you have made a terrible mistake," Phil said, striding about the room in a state of great agitation. "Hazel would not—she could not—have done this thing." He wheeled sharply around, as though struck by a sudden thought. "Are the jewels safe?" he added.

"Yes," said Miss Heredith. "We found Violet's jewel-case locked, so I put it away in the library safe."

"The question of robbery does not enter into the crime," remarked Caldew. "The motive, as we have established it, is quite different."

"I have been told of the motive you allege against this unhappy girl," said Phil indignantly. "That idea is utterly preposterous. Again, I say, I believe that you have made a blunder. I do not think Hazel would handle a revolver. She was always very nervous of fire-arms."

"That is quite true," murmured Miss Heredith.

"A jealous woman forgets her fears," said the detective rather maliciously. "She didn't stop to think of that when she wanted to use the revolver."

"And where did she get it from?" asked Phil quickly.

Caldew shrugged his shoulders, but remained silent.

"You still persist in thinking that she obtained the revolver from the gun-room?" Phil continued.

"Yes, I do."

"Do you not intend to make any further inquiries? You had better see Nepcote about the revolver. I will give you his address."

"Captain Nepcote left here to go to the front, and we have not heard from him since," Miss Heredith explained to the detective.

In a calmer moment Caldew might have realized the expediency of Phil's suggestion, but his professional dignity was affronted at what he considered the young man's attempt to interfere in the case and direct the course of the police investigations. It was the desire to snub what he regarded as a meddlesome interposition in his own business which prompted him to reply:

"It is a matter of small importance, one way or the other. It is sufficient for the Crown case to know the owner of the revolver. The point is that the murder was committed with it, and it was subsequently found in the girl's possession."

"I have nothing more to say to you," said Phil.

"Are you convinced now, Phil?" asked Miss Heredith sadly, when Caldew had taken his departure. "It was hard for me to believe at first, but everything seems so certain."

"I am not at all convinced," was the stern reply. "On the contrary, I feel sure that some terrible mistake has been made. I would stake my life on the innocence of Hazel Rath. How can you, who have known her so long, believe she would do a deed like this? The detective who has just left us is obviously a fool, and I am not satisfied that all the facts about Violet's death have been brought to light. I am going to London at once to bring another detective to inquire into the case. You know more about these things than me, Musard—can you tell me of a good man?"

"If you are determined to bring in another detective, you cannot do better than get Colwyn," replied Musard.

"Colwyn–the famous private detective? He is the very man I should like. Where is he to be found?"

"He has rooms somewhere near Ludgate Circus. I will write down the address. I think he will come, if he is not otherwise engaged."

"Why should he refuse?" demanded Phil haughtily. "I will pay him well."

"It is not a question of money with a man like Colwyn, and I advise you not to use that tone with him if you want his help."

"Very well," said Phil, pocketing the address Musard had written down. "I will catch the 6.30 evening train up. Aunt, you might tell them to give me something to eat in the small breakfast-room. I do not want to be bothered getting dinner in town."

"Phil, dear, you mustn't dream of going to London in your present state of health," expostulated Miss Heredith tearfully. "Why not leave it until you are stronger? Vincent, try and persuade him not to go."

"Phil is the best judge of his own actions in a matter like this," replied Musard gravely.

"At least let Vincent go with you, Phil," urged his aunt. "I want nobody to accompany me," replied Phil, speaking in a tone he had never used to his aunt before. "I will go and get ready. Tell Linton to have the small car ready to drive me to the station."

15

Colwyn had rooms in the upper part of a block of buildings on Ludgate Hill, looking down on the Circus, above the rookery of passages which burrow tortuously under the railway arches to Water Lane, Printing House Square, and Blackfriars. It was a strange locality to live in, but it suited Colwyn. It was in the thick of things. From his windows, high up above the roar of the traffic, he could watch the ceaseless flow of life eastward and westward all day long, and far into the night.

No other part of London offered such variety and scope in the study of humanity. The City was stodgy, the Strand too uniform, Piccadilly too fashionable, and the select areas for bachelor chambers, such as the Temple and Half Moon Street, were backwaters as remote from the roaring turbulent stream of London life as the Sussex Downs or the Yorkshire Moors.

In addition to these things, the spot offered a fine contrast in walks to suit different moods. There was that avenue of wizardry, Fleet Street, whose high-priests and slaves juggled with the news of the world; there was the glitter of plate-glass fronts between the Circus and St. Paul's, the twilight stillness of the archway passages and their little squeezed shops, the isolation of Play House Yard and Printing House Square, the bustle of Bridge Street, and the Embankment. From his window Colwyn could see the City shopgirls feeding the pigeons of St. Paul's around the statue of Queen Anne.

To Colwyn, London was the place of adventures. He had lived in New York and Paris, but neither of these cities had for him the same fascination as the sprawling giant of the Thames. Paris was as stimulating and provocative as a paid mistress, but palled as quickly. In

New York mysteries beckoned at every street corner, but too importunately. Neither city was sufficiently discreet for Colwyn's reticent mind. But London! London was like a woman who hid a secret life beneath an austere face and sober garments. Underneath her air of prim propriety and calm indifference were to be found more enthralling secrets than any other city of the world could reveal. It was emblematic of London that her mysteries, in their strangest aspects and phases, preserved the air of ordinary events.

Colwyn saw nothing extraordinary in this. To him Life seemed so perpetually inconsistent that there could be nothing inconsistent in any of its events. It was to his faith in this axiom, expressed after his own paradoxical fashion, that he partly owed some of those brilliant successes which had stamped him as one of the foremost criminal investigators of his day. He never rejected a story on the score of its improbability. He had seen so many unusual things in his career that he once declared that it was the unforeseen, and not the expected, which occurs most frequently in this strange world of ours. That was, perhaps, partly due to the wide gulf between human ideals and actions, but, whatever the reason, Colwyn never lost sight of the fact that the incredible, once it happened, became as commonplace as the meals we eat or the clothes we wear. It seemed to Colwyn that the unexpected happened too frequently to call forth the astonishment with which it was invariably greeted by most people. In his experience, Life was almost too prodigal of its surprises, so much so, indeed, as to be in danger of reaching the limit of its own resources. But he consoled himself, whimsically enough, with the belief that such an event was too probable ever to happen.

It was nearly eleven o'clock at night, and Colwyn, getting up from a table where he had been busily writing, walked to the window and looked down on the deserted street beneath. It was a nightly custom of his. He lived, as he worked, alone, attended only by a taciturn manservant who had been with him for many years. He accepted with characteristic philosophy the view that a man who spent his time unveiling shameful human secrets had no right to share his life with anybody. Even the articles of furniture of his lonely rooms, if endowed with any sort of entity, might have worn a furtive air in their consciousness of the secrets they had heard whispered in their owner's ears by those who had sought his counsel and assistance in their trouble and despair. There had been many such secrets poured forth in those lonely rooms, perched up high above the roar of the London traffic. It was the Confessional of the incredible.

As Colwyn stood at the window, the electric bell of the front door rang sharply through the empty building. Looking down into the street, he saw the figure of a man in the doorway beneath. He glanced at his watch. It was late for a visitor. He walked to the lift at the end of the passage and descended. As he did so, the bell in his rooms once more pealed forth beneath the pressure of an impatient hand.

The visitor, revealed by the light in the hall, was a young man muffled in a thick overcoat for protection against the sharp autumn wind which was blowing along the rain-splashed street. He stepped inside the door as Colwyn opened it, and, glancing at the detective from a pair of dark eyes just visible beneath the flap of his soft felt hat, said:

"Are you Mr. Colwyn?"

"Yes. What can I do for you?"

"I am afraid it is a very late hour for a visit," said the other, brushing the rain drops off his coat as he spoke, "but I should be very glad if you could spare me a little time, late as it is. I have come from the country to see you."

Colwyn nodded without speaking. Strange adventures had come to him at stranger hours. He showed the way to the lift, switched off the electric light he had turned on in the passage, and ascended with his visitor to his rooms. There his companion, with an impulsiveness which contrasted with the detective's quiet composure, again spoke:

"I want your assistance, Mr. Colwyn."

"Will you not be seated?" said the detective, as with a swift glance he took in the external attributes of his young and well-dressed visitor.

"Thank you. I regret to disturb you at such a late hour, but the train I travelled by was greatly delayed by an accident. I thought at first of postponing my visit till the morning, but it is so urgent—to me, at all events—that I determined to try and see you to-night."

"It was just as well that you did. I may be called out of London in the morning."

"Then I am glad that I came. My name is Heredith—Philip Heredith."

Colwyn looked at his visitor with a keener interest. The London newspapers were full of the particulars of the moat-house crime, and had published intimate accounts of the Heredith family, their wealth, social position, and standing in the county. Colwyn, as he glanced at Philip Heredith, came to the conclusion that the London picture papers had been once more guilty of deceiving their credulous readers. The portraits they had published of him in no wise resembled the young man who was now seated opposite him, regarding him with a sad and troubled look.

"I have heard of your great skill and cleverness in criminal investigation, Mr. Colwyn," continued Phil earnestly, "and wish to avail myself of your help. That is the object of my visit."

Colwyn waited for his visitor to disclose the reasons which had brought him, seeking advice. He had followed the newspaper accounts of the murder and police investigations with keen interest. The special correspondents had done full justice to the arrest of Hazel Rath. There is no room for reticence or delicacy in modern journalism, and no reserves except those dictated by fear of the law for libel. Colwyn was therefore aware that Hazel Rath figured as "the woman in the case," and was supposed to have shot the young wife in a fit of jealousy. The newspapers, in publishing these disclosures, had hinted at the existence of previous tender relations between the young husband and the arrested girl, in order to whet the public appetite for the "remarkable revelations" which it was hoped would be brought forward at the trial.

"I have come to consult you about the murder of my wife," continued Phil, speaking with an evident effort. "I should like you to make some investigations."

Colwyn was sufficiently false to his own philosophy of life to experience a feeling which he would have been the first to admit was surprise.

"The police have already made an arrest in the case," he said.

"I believe they have arrested an innocent girl."

As the young man sat there, he looked so worn and ill that Colwyn felt his sympathy go out to him. He seemed too boyish and frail to bear such a weight of tragedy on his shoulders at the outset of his life. His face wore an aspect of despair.

"If you think that a mistake has been made, you had better go to Scotland Yard," said Colwyn.

"I have already spoken to Detective Caldew, but his attitude convinced me that it was hopeless to expect any assistance from Scotland Yard, so I decided to come to you."

"In that case you had better tell me all that you know, if you wish me to help you," said the detective. "In the first place, I wish to hear all the facts of the murder itself. I have read the newspaper accounts, but they necessarily lack those more intimate details which may mean so much. I should like to hear everything from beginning to end."

In a voice which was still weak from illness, Phil did as he was requested, and related the strange sequence of events which had happened at the moat-house on the night of his wife's murder. Those events, as he described them, took on a new complexion to his listener, suggesting a deeper and more complex mystery than the newspaper accounts of the crime.

From the first the moat-house murder had appealed to Colwyn's imagination and stimulated his intellectual curiosity. There was the pathos of the youth and sex of the victim, murdered in a peaceful country home. The terrible primality of murder accords more easily with the elemental gregariousness of slum existence; its horror is accentuated, by force of contrast, in the tender simplicity of an English sylvan setting. Colwyn's chief interest lay in the fact that, although the case against Hazel Rath was as strong as circumstantial evidence could make it, the supposed motive for the crime was weak. But he reflected that there did not exist in human life any motive sufficiently strong to warrant the commission of a crime like murder. Probably no great murder had ever been justified by motive, in the sense that incitement is vindication, though human nature, ever on the alert in defence of itself, was prone to accept such excuses as passion and revenge as adequate motives for destruction. The point which perplexed Colwyn in this particular case was whether the incitement of jealousy was sufficient to impel a young girl, brought up in good social environment, which is ever a conventional deterrent to violent crime, to murder her rival in a sudden gust of passion.

"Now, let me hear your reasons for thinking that the police have made a mistake in arresting Hazel Rath," the detective said, when Phil had concluded his narration of the events of the night of the murder. "The case against her seems very strong."

"Nevertheless, I feel sure she did not do it," said Phil emphatically. "I understand her nature and disposition too well to believe her guilty.

I have known her since childhood. She has a sweet and gentle nature."

"I am afraid your personal opinion will count for very little against the weight of evidence," replied Colwyn. "It is impossible to generalize in a crime like murder. My experience is that the most unlikely people commit violent crimes under sudden stress. Unless you have something more to go upon than that, your protestations will count for very little at the trial. Criminal judges know too well that human nature is capable of almost anything except sustained goodness."

It was the same point of view, only differently expressed, that Superintendent Merrington had advanced to Captain Stanhill at the moat-house the evening after the murder.

"I have other reasons for thinking Hazel Rath innocent," replied Phil. "If she had murdered my wife we would have seen her as we rushed upstairs after hearing the scream and shot. She hadn't time to escape."

"What about the window of your wife's room?"

"It is nearly twenty feet from the ground, so that would be impossible."

"How do you account for the brooch being found in your wife's bedroom? Is there any doubt that it belongs to Hazel Rath?"

"It is quite true that the brooch is hers. I gave it to her on her birthday, some years ago. The police think that Hazel is in love with me, and murdered my wife through jealousy. But that is not true. I have known her since she was a little girl, and regarded her as a sister."

Phil uttered these words with a ringing sincerity which it was impossible to doubt. But that statement, Colwyn reflected, did not carry them very far. The speaker might honestly believe that the feeling existing between himself and Hazel Rath was like the affection of brother and sister, but he was speaking for himself, and not for the girl. Who could read the secret of a woman's heart? The real question was, did Hazel Rath love Philip Heredith? There lay a motive for the murder, if she did.

"Does Hazel Rath still refuse to explain how her brooch came to be found in Mrs. Heredith's bedroom and subsequently disappeared?" inquired Colwyn after a short pause.

"I understand that she persists in remaining silent," returned the young man. "Oh, I admit the case seems suspicious against her," he continued passionately, as though in answer to a slight shrug of the detective's shoulders. "It is for that reason I have come to you. I believe her innocent, and I want you to try and establish her innocence."

"I am afraid I must decline, Mr. Heredith." A sympathetic glance of Colwyn's eyes softened the firm tone of the refusal. "Apart from your own belief in Miss Rath's innocence, you have very little to go upon."

"There is more than that to go upon," said Phil. "There is the question of the identity of the revolver. Hazel is supposed to have obtained it from the gun-room."

"I know that from the newspaper reports."

"Yes, but you do not know that the detectives have not been able to establish the ownership of the weapon until to-day. They were under the impression that it belonged to the moat-house, but neither my father nor aunt was able to settle the point. Detective Caldew visited the moat-house to-day to see if I could identify it. I immediately recognized it as the property of Captain Nepcote."

"Who is Captain Nepcote?"

"He is a friend of mine. I knew him in London before I was married. He was a friend of my wife's also. He was one of our guests at the moat-house until the day of the murder."

"Did he leave before the murder was committed?"

"Yes; some hours before."

"Then how did Hazel Rath obtain possession of his revolver?"

"That is what I do not know. I must tell you that the day before the murder some of our guests spent a wet afternoon amusing themselves shooting at a target in the gun-room. They were using Captain Nepcote's revolver. When I told Detective Caldew this, he came to the conclusion that Nepcote must have left it there after the shooting, and Hazel Rath found it when she went to look for a weapon."

"I see. And what is your own opinion?"

"I do not believe it for one moment."

"Why not?"

"For one thing, it strikes me as unlikely that Nepcote would forget his revolver when leaving the gun-room. In any case, the police are taking too much for granted in assuming, without inquiry, that he did. Caldew told me that the question of the ownership of the revolver did not affect the case against Hazel Rath in the slightest degree."

"Do you know whether the revolver was seen by anybody between the time of Captain Nepcote's departure and its discovery in Hazel Rath's possession?"

"I understand that it was not."

"Do you know whether Captain Nepcote took it from the gun-room after the target shooting?"

"That I cannot say. I left the gun-room before the shooting was finished."

"Let me see if I thoroughly understand the position," said Colwyn. "In your narrative of the events of the murder you stated that all the members of the household and the guests were in the dining-room when the murder was committed. Nepcote was not there because he had returned to London during the afternoon. Nevertheless, it was with his revolver that your wife was shot."

"That is correct," said Phil.

"If Nepcote did not leave his revolver in the gun-room the police theory would be upset on an important point, and the case would take on a new aspect. Have you any suspicions that you have not confided to me?"

"I cannot say that I have any particular suspicions," the young man replied. "I do not know what to think, but I should like to have this terrible mystery cleared up. I have not seen Nepcote since the day of the murder to ask him about the revolver. He said good-bye to me before he left, and I understood that he had received a wire from the War Office recalling him to the front. After the murder I was taken ill, as I have told you, and it was not until to-day that I was informed of what happened during my illness."

"I am inclined to agree with you that the case wants further investigation," said Colwyn.

"Then will you undertake it?" asked Phil.

The feeling that he was face to face with one of the deepest mysteries of his career acted as an irresistible call to Colwyn's intellect. He consulted the leaves of his engagement book.

"Yes, I will come," he said.

Phil glanced at his watch.

"I am afraid we can hardly catch the last train to Heredith," he said.

"We will drive down in my car," said Colwyn. "Please excuse me for a few moments."

He left the room, and returned in a few moments fully equipped for the journey.

"Let us start," he said.

His tone was decided and imperative, his movements quick and full of energy. That was wholly like him, once he had decided on his course.

16

It was so late that Ludgate Circus was deserted except for a ramshackle cab with a drunken driver pouring forth a hoarse story of a mean fare to a sleepy policeman leaning against a lamp post. The sight of two gentlemen on foot when all 'buses had stopped running for the night raised fleeting hopes in the cabman's pessimistic breast, and changed the flow of his narrative into a strident appeal for hire, based on the plea, which he called on the policeman to support, that he hadn't turned a wheel that night, and amplified with a profanity which only the friendliest understanding with the policeman could have permitted him to pour forth without fear of consequences.

He intimated his readiness to drive them anywhere between the *Angel* on one side of London and the *Elephant* on the other for three bob, or, being a bit of a sport, would toss them to make it five bob or nothing. The boundaries, he explained in a husky parenthesis, were fixed not so much by his own refusal to travel farther afield as by his horse's unwillingness to go into the blasted suburbs. As his importunities passed unregarded he damned them both with the terrible earnestness of his class, and rumbled back into his dislocated story with the languid policeman.

Colwyn kept his car in a garage off the Bridge Street archway. Thither they proceeded, and waited while the car was got ready for the roads by a shock-headed man who broke the stillness of the night with prodigious yawns, and then stood blinking like an owl as he leaned against the yard gates watching the detective backing the car down the declivity of the passage into Bridge Street. Before they had reached it, he banged the gates behind him with another tremendous yawn, and went back to his interrupted slumber in the interior of a limousine.

It was a fine night for motoring. There was a late moon, and the earlier rain had laid the dust and left the roads in good condition. Colwyn cautiously threaded the crooked tangle of narrow streets and sharp corners between Blackfriars and Victoria, but as the narrow streets opened into broader ways he increased the speed of his high-powered car, and by the time London was left behind for the quiet meadows and autumn-scented woods they were racing along the white country roads at a pace which caused the roadside avenues of trees to slide past them like twin files of soldiers on the double.

Mile after mile slipped away in silence. Beyond an occasional direction of route by Phil there was no conversation between the two men in the car. Phil sat back looking straight in front of him, apparently absorbed in thought, and the car occupied Colwyn's attention. When they reached the heights above Heredith, Phil pointed to the green flats beneath and the old house in a shroud of mist.

"That is the moat-house," he said. "The carriage drive is from the village side." And with that brief indication that they were nearing their journey's end he once more settled back into silence.

Colwyn brought the car down from the rise into the sleeping village, and a few minutes later he was driving up the winding carriage way between the rows of drooping trees. On the other side of the woods the moat-house came into view. The moonlight gleamed on the high-pitched red roof, and drenched the garden in whiteness, but the mist which rose from the waters of the moat swathed the walls of the house like a cerement. The moon, crouching behind the umbrageous trees of the park, cast a heavy shadow on the lawn, like a giant's hand menacing the home of murder.

Late as the hour was, Tufnell was up awaiting their arrival, with a light supper and wine set ready in a small room off the library. Phil had telephoned from Colwyn's rooms to say that he was returning with the detective, and the butler, as he helped them off with their coats, said that rumours of a railway accident had reached the moat-house, causing Miss Heredith much anxiety until she received the telephone message.

Colwyn and Phil sat down to supper, with the butler in assiduous attendance. The meal was a slight and silent one. Phil kept a host's courteous eye on his guest's needs, but showed no inclination for conversation, and Colwyn was not the man to talk for talking's sake. When they had finished Phil asked the butler which room Mr. Colwyn was to occupy.

"Miss Heredith has had the room next to Sir Philip's prepared, sir."

"No doubt you are tired, Mr. Colwyn, and would like to retire," Phil said.

"Thank you, I should. I travelled from Scotland last night, and had very little sleep."

"In that case you will be glad to go to bed at once. I will show you to your room," said the young man, rising from the table.

"Please do not bother," replied Colwyn, noting the worn air and white face of the other. "You look done up yourself."

"Miss Heredith was anxious that you should retire as soon as you could, sir, so as to get as much rest as possible after your journey," put in the butler, with the officious solicitude of an old servant.

"Then I shall leave you in Tufnell's care," said Phil, holding out his hand as he said good night.

He went out of the room, and Colwyn was left with the old butler.

"Is it your wish to retire now?" the latter inquired.

"I shall be glad to do so, if you will show me to my bedroom."

The butler bowed gravely, and escorted Colwyn upstairs to his bedroom.

"This is your room, sir. I hope you will be comfortable."

"I feel sure that I shall," replied Colwyn, with a glance round the large handsome apartment.

"Your dressing-room opens off it, sir."

"Thank you. Good night."

"Good night, sir." The butler turned hesitatingly towards the door, as though he wished for some excuse to linger, but could think of nothing to justify such a course. He walked out of the room into the passage, and then turned suddenly, the light through the open doorway falling on his sharpened old features and watchful eyes.

"What is it? Do you wish to speak to me?" said Colwyn, with his pleasant smile.

A look of perplexity and doubt passed over the butler's face as he paused irresolutely in the doorway.

"I merely wished to ask, sir, if there is anything else I can get for you before I go."

His face had resumed its wonted impassivity, and the words came promptly, but Colwyn knew it was not the answer he had intended to make.

"I want nothing further," he said.

The butler bowed, and hurried away. Colwyn stood for a few moments pondering over the incident. Then he went to bed and slept soundly.

He was awakened in the morning by the twittering of birds in the ivy outside his window. The mist from the moat crept up the glasslike steam, but through it he caught glimpses of a dappled autumn sky, and in the distance a bright green hill, with a trail of white clouds floating over the feathery trees on the summit. As he watched the rapid play of light and shade on the hill, he wondered why the moat-house had been built on the damp unwholesome flat lands instead of on the breezy height.

When he descended later, he found Tufnell awaiting him in the hall to conduct him to the breakfast table. In the breakfast-room Sir Philip, Miss Heredith, and Vincent Musard were assembled. The baronet greeted Colwyn with his gentle unfailing courtesy, and Musard shook hands with him heartily. The fact that Phil had brought him to the moat-house was in itself sufficient to ensure a gracious reception from Miss Heredith, but as soon as she saw Colwyn she felt impelled to like him on his own account. It was not the repose and simplicity of his manners, or his freedom from the professional airs of ostentatious notoriety which attracted her, though these things had their weight with a woman like Miss Heredith, by conveying the comforting assurance that her guest was at least a gentleman. There was more than that. She was immediately conscious of that charm of personality which drew the liking of most people who came in contact with Colwyn. In the strong clear-cut face of the great criminologist, there was the abiding quality of sympathy with the sufferings which spring from human passions and the tragedy of life. But, if his serenity of expression suggested that he had not allowed his own disillusionment with life to embitter his outlook or narrow his vision, his glance also suggested a clear penetration of human motives which it would be unwise to try to blind. Miss Heredith instinctively realized that Colwyn was one of those rare human beings who are to be both feared and trusted.

"You will not see my nephew until later," she explained to him as they sat down to breakfast. "He is far from strong yet, and he has had so little sleep since his illness that I am always glad when he is able to rest quietly. I looked in his room a few minutes ago and he was sleeping soundly, so I darkened the room and left him to sleep on."

Colwyn expressed his sympathy. His quick intelligence, gauging his new surroundings and the members of the household, had instantly divined the sterling qualities, the oddities, and class prejudices which made up the strong individuality of the mistress of the moat-house. He saw, for all her dignified front, that she was suffering from a shock which had shaken her to her inmost being, and he respected her for bearing herself so bravely under it.

The breakfast progressed in the leisurely way of the English morning meal. The tragedy which had darkened the peaceful life of the household nearly a fortnight before was not mentioned. Colwyn appreciated the tact of his hostess in keeping the conversation to conventional channels, leaving it for him to introduce the object of his visit in his own time. Only at the conclusion of the meal, as Miss Heredith was leaving the apartment, did she tell him that she hoped he would let her know if there was anything he required or wished her to do. He thanked her, and said there was nothing just then. Later, it would be necessary for him to go over the house, under her guidance, if she could spare the time. She replied that she could do so after lunch if that would be suitable, and went away. Sir Philip followed her, and Colwyn and Musard were left alone.

"Shall we have a cigar in the garden?" said Musard. He wished to know more of the man of whom he had heard so much by repute, and he believed that tobacco promoted sociability. He also desired to find out whether Colwyn's presence at the moat-house meant that Phil had succeeded in impressing him with his own belief in the innocence of Hazel Rath.

Colwyn willingly agreed. He realized the difficulties of the task ahead of him, and he welcomed the opportunity of hearing all he could about the murder from somebody who knew all the circumstances. Phil's personal knowledge of the facts did not extend beyond the point where he had fallen unconscious in the bedroom, and a talk with Musard offered the best available substitute for his own lack of first-hand impressions. The garden basked in the warmth of a mellow autumn sunshine which had dispersed the morning mist. In the air was the scent of late flowers and the murmurs of bees; the bright eyes of blackbirds and robins peeped out from the ornamental yews, and the peacocks trailed their plumes over the sparkling emerald lawns. But Colwyn and Musard had no thought of the beauty of the morning or the charm of the old-world garden as they paced across the lawn. It was Musard who broached the subject which was engrossing their minds.

"It was very good of you to come down here, Mr. Colwyn. Your visit is a great relief to Miss Heredith."

"Does Miss Heredith share her nephew's belief in Miss Rath's innocence?"

"I would not go so far as to say that, though I think his own earnestness has impressed her with the hope that some mistake has been made. But her chief concern is her nephew's health, and she is anxious, above all things, to remove his mental worry and unrest. The mere fact that you have undertaken to make further inquiries into the case will do much to ease his mind."

"I will do what I can. My principal difficulty is to pick up the threads of the case. It is some time since the murder was committed, and the attendant circumstances which might have helped me in the beginning no longer exist. It is like groping for the entrance to a maze which has been covered over by the growths of time."

"Do you yourself believe it possible that Hazel Rath is innocent?"

"I have come here to investigate the case. The police account for the girl's possession of Captain Nepcote's revolver, with which Mrs. Heredith was shot, by the theory that she obtained it from the gun-room of the moat-house shortly before the murder. There is work for me to do both here and in London, in clearing up this point. It is so important that I cannot understand the attitude of Detective Caldew in dismissing it as a matter of no consequence. If Hazel Rath were convicted with that question unsettled, she would be condemned on insufficient evidence. It is for this reason I have taken her interests into my hands. But, apart from this point, I am bound to say that the case against her strikes me as a very strong one."

"Yet it is quite certain that Phil Heredith believes her innocent," remarked Musard thoughtfully.

"Belief is an intangible thing. In any case, his belief is not shared by you."

"How do you know that?"

"You would have said so."

"Well, I will go so far as to say that Hazel Rath is a most unlikely person to commit murder."

"Murder is an unlikely crime. There is no brand of Cain to reveal the modern murderer. Finger-prints are a surer means of identification. This unhappy girl may be the victim of one of those combinations of sinister events which sometimes occur in crime, but I do not intend to form an opinion about that until I know more about the case. For that reason I shall be glad if you will give me your account of everything that happened on the night of the murder. Philip Heredith's story is incomplete, and I wish to hear all the facts."

Musard nodded, and related the particulars with an attention to detail which left little to be desired. His version filled in the gaps of Phil's imperfect narrative, and enabled the detective to visualize the murder with greater mental distinctness. The two stories agreed in their essential particulars, but they varied in some degree in detail. Colwyn, however, was well aware that different witnesses never exactly agree in their impressions of the same event. Phil had made only an incidental reference to the dinner-table conversation about jewels, and Colwyn was not previously aware that the story of the ruby ring had occupied twenty minutes in the telling.

"How did you come to tell the story?" he asked.

"Some of the ladies were admiring my ring, and Phil suggested that they should hear the story of its discovery. I had just finished when the scream rang out from upstairs, followed by the shot."

"How long was the interval between the scream and the shot?"

"Only a few seconds," replied Musard. "Some of us started to go upstairs as soon as we heard it, but the shot followed before we reached the door of the dining-room."

Colwyn reflected that this estimate differed from Phil Heredith's, who had thought that nearly half a minute elapsed between the scream and the shot. But he knew that a correct estimate of the lapse of time is even rarer than an accurate computation of distance.

Musard knew nothing about two aspects of the case on which Colwyn desired to gain light. He had seen nothing of the target shooting in the gun-room the day before the murder, but he thought it quite possible that Captain Nepcote's revolver might have lain there unnoticed until the following night, because the men of the house party were a poor shooting lot who were not likely to use the gun-room much. He had heard the head gamekeeper say that there had been no shooting parties, and Tufnell had told him that only one or two of the men had brought guns with them. Neither was Musard aware whether there existed the motive of wronged virtue or slighted affection to arouse a girl like Hazel Rath to commit such a terrible crime. He had always thought her a sweet and modest girl, but he had seen too much of the world to place much reliance on externals, and he had had very few opportunities of observing whether there had been anything in the nature of a love affair between her and Philip. His own view was that whatever feeling existed was on the girl's side only.

"If there had been love passages between them, Phil's conscience would not have allowed him to be quite so certain of her innocence," added Musard. "I told him of her arrest, and there can be no doubt that he thinks the police have made a hideous mistake in arresting her. Detective Caldew refused to admit the possibility of mistake, but Phil shuts his eyes to everything that tells against the girl, including her mother's unpleasant past."

"Did Miss Heredith know anything of her housekeeper's past?"

"No. Mrs. Rath, as she calls herself, came to Heredith many years ago, took a small cottage, and tried to support her daughter and herself by giving lessons in music and French. She would have starved if it had not been for Miss Heredith, who helped her and her little girl, tried to get the mother some pupils, and finally took her into the moat-house as housekeeper. Mrs. Rath disappeared from the place after her daughter's arrest, when the police had decided that it was not necessary to detain her, leaving a note behind her for Miss Heredith to say that she couldn't face her after all that had happened."

Colwyn did not speak immediately. He was examining the row of upper windows which looked down on the garden in which they were standing.

"Is that the window of the room in which Mrs. Heredith was murdered?" he asked, pointing to the first one.

"Yes. It is high for a first-floor window, but there is a fall in the ground on this side of the house."

Colwyn tested the strength of the Virginia creeper which grew up the wall almost to the window, and then bent down to examine the grass and earth underneath.

"Caldew thought at first that the murderer escaped from the window, but Merrington did not agree with him," said Musard.

If the remark was intended to extract an expression of opinion from Colwyn it failed in effect, for he remained silent. He had regained his feet, and was looking up at the window again.

"Where is the door which opens on the back staircase of this wing?" he said, at length.

"At the extreme end. You cannot see it from here. It opens on the back of the house."

"According to the newspaper reports of the case, the door is always kept locked. Is that correct?"

"As a general rule it is. But it was found unlocked before dinner on the night the murder was committed."

"I was not informed of this before."

"Phil was not aware of it, and Detective Caldew attached so little importance to it when I told him after the murder that I should not have thought it worth mentioning if you had not asked me. Caldew's point of view was that the door had been left unlocked, accidentally, by one of the servants, which is quite possible. I understand both detectives agree that it had nothing to do with the murder, because the door was locked by the butler, who discovered it unlocked, fully an hour before the murder was committed. If Hazel Rath had attempted to escape that way she would have been caught in a *cul-de-sac*, for we rushed upstairs from the dining-room immediately we heard the scream."

"Did you search the back staircase?"

"Almost immediately. It was empty."

"And there is no doubt that the door at the bottom was locked?"

"None whatever—one of the young men tried it."

"What time did the butler make his discovery?"

"Shortly before dinner. I do not know the exact time."

"Thank you. Now, if you will excuse me, I should like to see the room Mrs. Heredith occupied. Is it empty?"

"Yes. The wing has been unoccupied since the night of the murder. Shall I show you the way up?"

"It will not be necessary. I know the way, and I shall be there some time."

"In that case I will leave you till lunch-time," responded Musard, as he walked away.

Colwyn did not go upstairs immediately. He took a solitary walk in the woods, thinking over everything that

Musard had told him. Then he returned to the house and mounted the staircase to the left wing. His first act was to make a thorough examination of the unused back staircase at the end of the corridor. Then he entered the bedroom Mrs. Heredith had occupied.

The room had the forlorn appearance of disuse. The bed had been partly stripped, and the tall-backed chairs, in prim linen covers, looked like seated ghosts with arms a-kimbo. Colwyn's first act was to draw the heavy window curtains and open the window. He then commenced an examination of the room in the morning sunlight. His examination was long and thorough, but it brought nothing to light which added to his knowledge of the events of the murder. The time went on, and he was still engrossed in his scrutiny when the door opened and Phil entered the room.

17

"Lunch is waiting," said the young man. "My aunt thought that you did not hear the gong, so I came up to tell you."

"Miss Heredith was right—I did not hear it. I am sorry if I have kept you waiting. I have been so busy that I forgot the passing of time."

If Phil felt any curiosity as to the matters which had engaged Colwyn's attention in the room where his wife had been murdered, he did not express it in words.

"My aunt will show you over the moat-house after lunch, if you wish," was what he said.

"I should be glad," returned Colwyn. "But I am reluctant to put Miss Heredith to the trouble."

"Do not think of that," responded Phil. "My aunt desires nothing better than to show the old place to anybody she likes. And she has taken a liking to you."

"It is very good of her. I shall be pleased to accept her offer, for I wish to see over the house as soon as possible."

They had started to descend the stairs. Colwyn, happening to glance over the balusters, saw the motionless figure of Tufnell standing at the bottom of the staircase partly concealed by the group of ornamental shrubs in the hall. His face was turned upwards with an aspect of strained curiosity, but it was immediately withdrawn as his eyes encountered Colwyn's downward gaze. A moment later Colwyn saw him enter the dining-room.

When they reached the foot of the staircase, Colwyn, with an explanatory glance at his soiled hands and dusty clothes, promised to join the luncheon party in a few minutes. He went to his own room for a hasty toilet, and when he descended a few minutes later he again saw

Tufnell in the hall. The butler, who was giving a direction to a servant, met his eye calmly, and hastened to open the dining-room door for him.

There was more conversation at luncheon than at the morning meal. The weight of senility relaxed from Sir Philip sufficiently to permit him to talk to his guest with some brightness. He told Colwyn a story of a seagoing ancestor of his who had entertained the Royal Family in his own frigate at Portsmouth in honour of Sir Horatio Nelson's victory of the Nile, and how the occasion had tempted the cupidity of his own fellow to make a nefarious penny by permitting the rabble of the town to take peeps at the guests through one of the port-holes. It happened that one Jack Tar, eager to gaze on his idol Nelson, got his head jammed in the port-hole, and broke up the party with a volley of terrible oaths and roars for assistance. "The servant's name was Egg—Dick Egg, but he was a bad egg," chuckled Sir Philip, as he concluded the narrative. He repeated the poor joke several times in manifest appreciation.

Miss Heredith did not smile at the story. She deprecated anything which had the slightest tendency to cast ridicule on the family name. That was made abundantly clear after the meal, when Sir Philip had retired to his room for his afternoon nap, and the others went over the old house. She took Colwyn under her special charge, and, forgetful of the real object of the detective's visit, discoursed impressively to him on the past glories of the Heredith line. She lingered long in each room, all rich in memories of the past, pointing out the objects of interest with loving pride. It would have been a disappointment to her if she had known that the guest who walked beside her, listening to her stories and legends of each antique relic and ancient picture, had his thoughts fixed on far different matters. Colwyn's reasons for seeing the moat-house had little to do with ancient oak, carved ceilings, panelled walls, and old family portraits.

It was not until they descended to the gun-room that Colwyn's keen professional scrutiny suggested, by force of contrast, that his former air of interest had been largely feigned. There were several underground rooms, entered by a short flight of stone steps, with an oak door at the top and bottom. The two principal rooms were the armoury, full of armour, spears, lances and bows, and the gun-room adjoining. What arrested Colwyn's attention in the latter room was the display of guns on the walls. There were many varieties of them: rifled harquebuses, obsolete carbines, flint-lock muskets, and modern rifles; in fact, the whole evolution of explosive weapons, from the first rude beginnings down to the breech-loader of the present day.

"The Herediths have ever been a family of great warriors, Mr. Colwyn," said Miss Heredith, following his glance along the walls. "Each of those weapons has some story of bravery, I might almost say heroism, attached to it. That sword you are looking at belonged to my grand-uncle, who commanded the British Army in the Peninsula. He was originally a major in the 14th Foot."

"I was under the impression that Wellington commanded in Portugal," said Musard.

"My grand-uncle was Sir Arthur Wellesley's senior officer, Vincent," responded Miss Heredith. "He arrived in Portugal in 1809 to take command, but Sir Arthur most culpably failed to have horses ready to carry him to the field of battle. In consequence of Sir Arthur's neglect my grand-uncle was compelled to take the next boat back to England. There was a question asked in the Commons of the day about Sir Arthur's conduct. I do not know what the question was, but the answer was in the negative, though I am not quite sure what that means. In any case, my grand-uncle was a greater soldier than Wellington. My mother often heard my grand-aunt say so."

"I notice that there are no revolvers or pistols among the weapons on the walls," said Colwyn.

"We never had a revolver," replied Phil.

"There are a pair of horse pistols in that case," said Musard, pointing to an oblong mahogany box with brass corners, resting on a stand in a niche of the wall. He crossed over to the box and fumbled with the brass snibs, but was unable to open it. "The case is locked," he said.

"Perhaps it is only jammed," suggested Phil.

"Oh, no, it is locked fast enough. Do you understand anything about locks, Mr. Colwyn?"

"You will have to break it open if you have lost the key," said Colwyn, after glancing at the box. "It is an obsolete type of lock."

"I should have liked to show you those pistols," said Musard. "They carry as true as a rifle up to fifty yards. Their only drawback is that they are a bit clumsy, and have a heavy recoil."

"I wonder where the key is?" remarked Miss Heredith. "I must ask Tufnell about it."

"Will you tell me where the revolver practice took place that afternoon?" said Colwyn, turning to Phil.

"They were firing from behind the bagatelle board at a target fixed over there," said Phil, pointing to the far wall.

"Who proposed the game?"

"Nepcote. It was a very wet afternoon, and everybody had to stay indoors. He suggested after tea that it would be a good way of killing the time before dinner. Several of the men and two or three of the girls thought it a capital idea, and a sweepstake was arranged. They asked me for a revolver, but I told them we had not one. One of the officers offered his army revolver, but that was objected to as too heavy and dangerous for indoor shooting. Then Nepcote said that he had a light revolver in his bag, and he went upstairs to get it. He came downstairs with it in his hand, and those who were taking part in the sport went downstairs to the gun-room. I went with them for a while, but I did not stay long."

"Captain Nepcote's revolver is not an army weapon?"

"Oh, no. It is a very small and slight weapon, nickel-plated, with six chambers. It is so light as to resemble a toy."

"With a correspondingly light report, I presume. The sound of the target practice would not be heard upstairs?"

"It would be an exceedingly loud report that penetrated to the upper regions through that door," interjected Musard, pointing to the oak door with iron clamps which gave entrance to the gun-room. "Besides, there is another door at the top of the steps. If they were both shut you might fire off every weapon in the place without anybody upstairs hearing a sound."

Colwyn had listened to Phil's account of the target shooting with the closest attention. He remained silent for some moments, as though he were pondering over every point in it. Then he said:

"What makes you feel so sure that Nepcote did not leave his revolver in this room after the shooting?"

"He could only have left it on the bagatelle board or one of the chairs," replied Phil earnestly. "If he had done so it would have been seen by somebody."

"Provided anybody entered the gun-room," put in Musard.

"Of course there must have been somebody here," rejoined Phil with some warmth. "The detectives think that Hazel did not find it until the following evening. Do you suppose nobody visited the gun-room for twenty-four hours?"

"I think it quite likely with such a poor shooting lot—" Musard commenced, but broke off as he caught Miss Heredith's warning glance. "All right, laddie," he added soothingly; "Perhaps you are right, after all."

"I have no doubt I am right," exclaimed Phil excitedly. "Do you not think I am right, Mr. Colwyn?"

"I think that what you have said about the likelihood of the revolver having been seen is quite feasible," responded the detective. "But there is nothing to be gained by discussing that possibility at the present moment. Shall we go upstairs again, Miss Heredith?" he added, turning to her.

She turned on him a grateful glance for his tact and forbearance, and hastened to lead the way from the gun-room. The few words between Phil and Musard had not only brought sharply back to her all the past horror and agony of the murder, but had caused a poignant renewal of her apprehensions about her nephew's health. She realized that he was a changed being, moody and irritable, and liable to sudden fits of excitement on slight provocation. She felt that Musard had been rather inconsiderate to forget Phil's illness and cause him to get excited by differing from him.

Her concern was not lessened by intercepting a strange glance which Phil cast at Musard when they reached the library. Before she had time to reflect on what it meant, Phil turned to her and asked her where she had put Violet's jewel-case.

"I told you yesterday, Phil, that I brought it downstairs and locked it up," replied Miss Heredith, with a glance at the safe in the corner of the room. "I have been keeping the keys until you got better."

"Then you might let me have them now," said the young man. "I should like to see if the jewels are all right."

"Why, Phil, of course they are all right," his aunt replied. "We found the jewel-case locked, and not tampered with in any way."

"Was Mrs. Heredith's jewel-case in her bedroom the night she was murdered?" asked Colwyn.

"Yes," responded Miss Heredith. "We found it on her toilet-table, where she usually kept it."

"Did it contain valuable jewels?"

"It contained a necklace of pearls which was given to poor Violet by Sir Philip," was the reply. "It is an old family necklace."

"Then I agree with Mr. Heredith that the jewel case should be opened."

"Very well. As you think it necessary, I will go to my room for the keys."

Miss Heredith left the library, and returned in a few moments with a small bunch of keys in her hand. She went to the safe, unlocked it, and returned to the table bearing an oblong silver box of quaint design, with the portrait of a stout simpering lady in enamel on the cover. Miss Heredith directed Colwyn's attention to the portrait, remarking that it was a likeness of a princess of the reigning house, who had given it and the box to her great-uncle, Captain Sir Philip Heredith.

"Her Royal Highness held my great-uncle in much esteem, Mr. Colwyn," she added, as she proceeded to fit one of the keys into the box. "He was one of the most famous of Nelson's captains. When he died the residents of his native town erected a memorial to him. It was inscribed with testimony to his worth in a civic, military, and Christian capacity, together with a text stating that he caused the widow's heart to sing for joy. Beneath the text was commemorated his feat in sinking the French frigate *L'Équille*, with every soul on board."

"That hardly seems like causing the widow's heart to sing for joy," commented Musard.

"The reference was to English widows, Vincent," replied Miss Heredith, proceeding to open the box with loving care. "At that period of our history we had not discovered the good qualities of the French people, which have endeared them to—Oh!" Miss Heredith broke off with a startled exclamation as the lid of the silver box fell back, revealing an empty interior.

It is only in moments of complete surprise that the human face fails to keep up some semblance of guard over the inmost feelings. At the discovery that the jewel-case was empty Miss Heredith's dignity dropped from her like a falling garment, and she stared at the velvet interior with half-open mouth and an air of consternation on her face.

"Oh!" she cried again, finding voice after a moment's tense silence. "The necklace is gone."

"By heaven, this is amazing," muttered Musard.

"I thought you said it was safe?" The speaker was Phil. He did not look at his aunt as he uttered this reproach, but gazed at the empty box with glowing eyes under drawn brows.

"Phil, Phil, I thought it was safe—oh, I thought it was safe!" cried Miss Heredith almost hysterically. "Where is it gone? Who could have taken it? The box was locked when we saw it upstairs, and the day after the funeral I found Violet's keys at the back of the drawer where she always kept them."

"The box may have been locked when you found it, but it seems equally certain that it was also empty," said Colwyn. He alone of the excited group was cool enough to estimate the awkward possibilities of this discovery. "How was it that the detectives did not open the jewel-case on the night of the murder, so as to make quite sure that the necklace had not been stolen?"

"I took the necklace downstairs and locked it away before the police arrived," said Miss Heredith tearfully. "When Detective Caldew came he asked me if anything was missing from Violet's bedroom, and I told him no. Of course, I did not dream of anything like this. Oh, how I wish now that I had opened the jewel-case at the time. But I never thought. I tried the case and found it locked, so I thought it had not been touched."

"Really, I am more to blame than Miss Heredith," interposed Musard hurriedly. "I saw the jewel-case first, and I should have thought of having it opened."

"It is a pity you did not inform the detectives about the case," said Colwyn. His face was grave as he realized how completely the police had been led astray in their original investigations by the misunderstanding which had concealed an important fact. "But first let us make sure that the jewel-case was empty when it was brought downstairs. How many people have access to this safe, Miss Heredith? Is there more than one key?"

"There is only one key," she replied. "And that has been in my possession since the night of the murder."

"That disposes of that possibility, then. What about Mrs. Heredith's bunch of keys? Have they also been in your possession since she was killed?"

"Yes; I kept them in an upstairs drawer, which was locked."

"Can you tell me when you last saw the necklace?"

Miss Heredith reflected for a moment.

"Not for some time," she said. "Violet did not care for it, and rarely wore it."

"The necklace was of pink pearls," Musard explained. "Their value was more historical than intrinsic, for they had become tarnished with age, and the setting was old-fashioned. It was for that reason Mrs. Heredith did not like it. I was going to take the pearls to London the following day to arrange to have them skinned and reset."

"When I went into poor Violet's room that night to see if she felt well enough to go to the Weynes' I asked her for the necklace," said Miss Heredith. "She replied that she would give it to me in the morning. If she had only given it to me then, she might have been alive to-day."

"I should like to hear more about this," said Colwyn. "Please tell me everything."

In response Miss Heredith related to the detective all that had passed between the young wife and herself in the bedroom before dinner on the night of the murder. Colwyn listened attentively, with a growing sense of hidden complexities in the crime revealed at the eleventh hour. He saw that the case took on a new and deeper aspect when considered in conjunction with the facts which had been so innocently ignored. When Miss Heredith had finished, he asked her when it was first decided to send the necklace to London for resetting.

"It was the night before the murder," Miss Heredith replied. "Sir Philip suggested that Violet should wear the necklace to the dance on the following night, but Violet said that the pearls were really too dull to be worn. Mr. Musard agreed with her, and offered to take it to London and have it cleaned and reset by an expert of his acquaintance. Mr. Musard had to return to London on the morning after the dance, so that was the reason why I went into Violet's room before dinner on the night of the party to ask her for the necklace."

Colwyn considered this reply in all its bearings before he spoke.

"The best thing I can do is to return to London without delay and bring these additional facts before Scotland Yard," he said. "They have been misled–unwittingly but gravely misled–and it is only right that they should be informed at once. I know Merrington, and I will make a point of seeing him personally and telling him about the discovery of the missing necklace."

The little group heard his decision in a silence which suggested more than words were able to convey. It was Phil who finally uttered the thought which was in all their minds:

"Are you satisfied that Hazel Rath is innocent?"

"I cannot say that," responded the detective quickly. "The loss of the necklace does nothing to lessen the suspicion against her unless it can be proved that she had nothing to do with its disappearance–perhaps not even then. But all the facts must be investigated anew. The necklace must be traced, and the point about the revolver cleared up. But there is nothing more to be done here at present. The field of the investigation now shifts to London. I will get ready for the journey, if you will excuse me."

"I hope you will continue your own investigations, Mr. Colwyn," said Phil earnestly. "I am more than ever convinced of Hazel Rath's innocence, but I have small faith that the police are likely to establish it–even if they attempt to do so. I was not impressed with the skill of Detective Caldew, or his attitude when I told him that I believed Hazel Rath to be innocent."

"I will continue my investigations in conjunction with Scotland Yard, if it is your wish," the detective replied.

18

Colwyn was upstairs in his bedroom preparing for his return journey to London when a meek knock and an apologetic cough reached his ears. He turned and saw Tufnell standing at the half-open door. The face of the old butler wore a look of mingled determination and nervousness–the expression of a timid man who had braced himself to a bold course of action after much irresolute deliberation.

"I beg your pardon, sir," he said, and his trepidation was apparent in his voice. "But might I–that is to say, could you spare me a few minutes' conversation?"

"Certainly," replied the detective. "Come inside, Tufnell. What is it?"

The butler entered the room and carefully closed the door behind him.

"I am sorry to interrupt you, sir," he said. "But I have just heard Miss Heredith give orders for your car to be got ready for your return to London, and I knew there was no time to be lost. It's about the–the murder, sir." He brought out the last words with an effort.

"Go on," said Colwyn, wondering what further surprise was in store for him.

"It's about something that happened on that night. I wanted to tell you before, but I didn't like to. After the murder was discovered I was sent over to the village to fetch the police and the doctor, and while I was hurrying through the woods near the moat-house I thought I saw a man crouching behind one of the trees near the carriage drive. He seemed to be looking towards me. When I looked again he was gone."

"And what did you do?"

"I called out, but received no answer, so I hurried on."

Colwyn scrutinized the butler with a thoughtful penetrating glance. The butler bore the look with the meek air of a domestic animal who knows that he is being appraised.

"Am I the first person to whom you have told this story?" the detective asked after a pause.

"Yes, sir."

"Why did you not inform the police officers when they were investigating the case?"

"For several reasons, sir. It seemed to me, when I came to think it over, that it must have been my fancy, and then it passed out of my mind in the worry and excitement of the house. Then, when I did think of it again, I didn't like to mention it to Superintendent Merrington, because he was such a bullying sort of gentleman that I felt quite nervous of him. Really, for a gentleman who has travelled with Royal Highnesses, as I've heard tell, and might be supposed to know how gentlemen behave, the way he treated the servants while he was here was almost too much for flesh and blood to bear." The butler's withered cheeks flushed faintly at the recollection. "I couldn't bring myself to tell him, sir."

Colwyn smiled slightly. He was not unacquainted with Merrington's methods of cross-examination.

"You could have spoken to Detective Caldew, the other officer engaged in the case," he said.

"Young Tom Caldew!" exclaimed the butler, in manifest surprise.

"You know him then?"

"I know him, but I cannot say I know any good of him," rejoined the butler severely. "Young Tom Caldew was born and bred in this village, and an idle young vagabond he was. Many a time have I dusted his jacket for stealing chestnuts in our park. The place was well rid of him, I take it, when he ran away to London and joined the police force. No, sir, I really couldn't see myself confiding in young Tom Caldew."

"And why have you confided in me now?"

"Well, sir, it was the arrest of the young woman that set me thinking, and caused me to wonder whether I'd done right in keeping this back. What I thought I saw that night may have been merely fancy on my part, but it took on an added importance in my mind when Miss Rath was arrested for murdering Mrs. Heredith. It seemed to me as though I might be doing some sort of injustice to her by not telling about it, and I wouldn't like to have that on my conscience after the way things turned out. But I thought it was too late to say anything after they had arrested Miss Rath and taken her away. Then Mr. Philip got better from his illness and went to London to fetch you. The same evening I heard Miss Heredith and Mr. Musard talking at the dinner table about the murder, and I gathered from what they said that Mr. Philip thought the detectives had made a mistake in arresting Miss Rath. Then I decided to tell you when you arrived, but I couldn't summon up my courage to do so until now," concluded the butler simply. "I hope I have done right, sir."

"You have certainly done right in not keeping the story to yourself any longer," said Colwyn. "Before I leave here you had better show me the place in the woods where you thought you saw this man."

"I shall be happy to do so, sir. I should like to thank you for listening to me. It is a weight off my mind."

"I shall be going almost immediately," continued Colwyn. "I think the best plan will be for you to meet me in the carriage drive, near the spot. Can you manage that?"

"Quite easily, sir."

"Excellent. And now, as you go downstairs, I should be glad if you would tell Mr. Musard that I should like to see him in my room before I go."

"Very well, sir. Afterwards you will find me waiting at the bend of the carriage drive where it winds round the lake."

Colwyn nodded his comprehension, and Tufnell left the room with a relieved countenance. A few moments later there was another knock at the door. In response to Colwyn's invitation the door opened, and Musard appeared.

"Tufnell said you wished to see me," he said, with an inquiring glance from beneath his dark brows.

"Yes. I should be glad if you would give me a description of the missing necklace. It will be useful in tracing it."

"It is not difficult to describe," replied Musard, seating himself on the edge of the bed. "It consisted of a single row of pink pearls, none of them very large. The biggest is about forty grains, and the others between twenty and thirty. It has a diamond clasp, set in antique gold, which is the most valuable part of the necklace. Do you know anything about jewels?"

"A little."

"Then you are aware that blue and red diamonds are the most valuable of stones. This diamond is a blue one— not very large, but a particularly fine stone."

"Of course the necklace is well-known to jewel experts?"

"As well-known as any piece of jewellery in Europe. Some of the pearls in it are hundreds of years old. It would be almost impossible for the thief to dispose of the necklace."

"It might be taken to pieces," suggested Colwyn.

"In order to hide its identity? Well, yes, but the selling value would be greatly reduced. The pearls have been strung."

"What about the diamond? Could not that be sold by the thief without risk of discovery?"

"Only by sending it to Amsterdam to get it cut into two or three smaller stones, so as to lessen the risk of detection. The Heredith blue diamond is known to many connoisseurs. It is cut in an unusual form—a kind of irregular rosette, in order to display its fire and optical properties to the best advantage. If it were cut it would lose a great deal of its value. The money value of one large diamond of first quality is very much greater than the same stone cut into three. But it would be difficult to sell the diamond in its present form. The chances are that it would be recognized in Hatton Garden–if it were offered for sale there."

"But if the diamond fell into the hands of somebody with a knowledge of precious stones he might keep it close for a while and then dispose of it abroad–in America, for instance," returned Colwyn. "That trick has been performed with better-known stones than the Heredith diamond. In fact, it strikes me as possible to sell the whole necklace that way. The disposal of the necklace depends largely upon who stole it–upon whether it has fallen into experienced or inexperienced hands. There are jewel dealers who ask no awkward questions if they can get things at their own price."

"Quite so," assented Musard, casting a quick glance at his companion's face. "It would be a risk, though–the thief might pick the wrong man. I can give you the addresses of two or three men in Hatton Garden who should be able to tell you if the necklace has been offered there. They know everything that is going on in the trade."

"I shall be glad to have them."

Musard scribbled several names and addresses on a leaf of his pocket-book, tore it out, and handed it to the detective.

"There is a curious coincidence about the loss of this, necklace," he remarked casually, as he rose to go. "It is another example of the misfortune which attaches to the possession of a blue diamond."

"Are you thinking of the Hope blue diamond? That certainly has a sinister history."

"That is the most notorious instance. But all blue diamonds are unlucky. I could tell you some gruesome stories connected with them. The previous wearer of the

Heredith necklace–Philip's mother–died in giving birth to him. Incidentally, there is a curious legend attached to the moat-house in the form of a curse laid on it by the original builder, who was burnt alive in the old house. He prophesied that as the house of the Herediths was founded in horror it should end in horror. These old family curses sometimes come home to roost after a long lapse of time, though modern cynicism affects to sneer at such fancies. Of course, there may be nothing in it, but we have had more than enough horror in the moat-house recently, and poor Mrs. Heredith had a blue diamond in her room when she was murdered. But I must not keep you any longer, Mr. Colwyn. If there has been any miscarriage of justice in this terrible case I trust that you will be successful in bringing it to light."

He lingered after shaking hands, as though he would have liked to continue the conversation. Apparently not finding sufficient encouragement in the detective's face to do so, he turned and left the room, and Colwyn resumed his preparations for departure.

When they were completed he, too, went downstairs, carrying his bag. Miss Heredith and Phil were waiting to bid farewell to him. As Miss Heredith said good-bye, she looked into his face with the perplexed expression of a simple soul seeking reassurance from a stronger mind in the deep vortex of extraordinary events into which she had been plunged beyond her depth. Phil looked white and ill, and the hand which he gave into the detective's cool firm grasp was hot and feverish. While his aunt murmured those conventional phrases under which women seek to cover the realities of life as they bedeck corpses with flowers, Phil stood aside with the impatient air of one scornful of the futility of such things. As Miss Heredith ceased speaking he took a step forward, his dark eyes fixed eagerly and searchingly on Colwyn.

"You will lose no time?" he said. "You will find out everything?"

"I have already promised you that I will continue my investigations," replied Colwyn. The quiet sincerity of his words was the indication of a mind which despised the weakness of mere verbal emphasis.

"Lose no time. Spare no money," said Phil rapidly. His words and utterance contrasted forcibly with the stillness and composure of the man he was addressing. "Think what it means! Let me know everything that happens. Send me telegrams. Follow this thing out night and day. I depend on you–"

"Phil, Phil!" remonstrated Miss Heredith. "Mr. Colwyn has already promised to do all he can. You must be patient."

"Patience! My God, don't talk to me of patience," retorted her nephew fiercely. "I shall have no patience nor peace till this thing is settled."

Miss Heredith looked at him sadly. His breach of good manners in uttering an oath in her presence hurt her worse than a blow, but her heart sickened with the realization that it was but another manifestation of the complete change in him which had been brought about by his wife's murder. Colwyn brought the scene to a close.

"Of course I shall communicate with you," he said to Phil, as he took his departure. Phil accompanied him to his car, and stood under the portico watching him as he drove away. Colwyn glanced back as he crossed the moat-house bridge. The young man was still standing in the open doorway, looking after him. The next moment the bend of the carriage way hid him from view.

Colwyn encountered Tufnell at the next bend of the drive, waiting for him on the path under the trees which bordered the edge. The detective pulled up his car and stepped out.

"It was just off here, sir, that I thought I saw the figure that night," said the butler.

He plunged into a leafy avenue which led off the path at right angles, and followed it into the wood until he reached the mossy trunk of a great oak, which flung a gnarled arm horizontally across the narrow walk as though barring further intrusion into its domain. Tufnell stopped, and turned to the detective.

"It seemed to me as though a man was crouching just about here, sir," he said in a whisper, as if he feared that the intruder might still be hiding there and overhear his words.

Colwyn carefully examined the spot. The moss and grass where he stood grew fresh underfoot, with no marks to suggest that they had been trodden on recently. But close by, behind the horizontal branch of the great oak, was a tangled patch of undergrowth and brambles, broken and pressed down in places, as though it had been entered by a human being. As Colwyn was looking at this place, his eye was attracted by a yellow speck in the background of green. It was a tiny fragment of khaki, caught on one of the bramble bushes.

19

Superintendent Merrington sat in his office at Scotland Yard, irascible with the exertions of a trying day which had made heavy inroads upon his temper and patience. He had several big cases on his hands, his time had been broken into by a series of visitors with grievances, and he had been called upon to adjust a vexatious claim of a woman attacked in the street by a police dog, while the animal was supposed to be on duty tracking a sacrilegious thief who had felled a priest in an oratory and bolted with the silver candlesticks from the altar.

The woman had gone mad from the shock and had been placed in a public asylum, where she had imagined herself to be a horse, and in that guise had neighed harmlessly, for some years, until cured by auto-suggestion by a rising young brain doctor who had devoted much time and study to her peculiar case. Her first act of returned reason was to bring a heavy claim for damages against Scotland Yard, and Merrington had fought it out that day with an avaricious lawyer who had taken up the case on the promise of an equal division of the spoils.

Merrington had preferred to pay rather than contest the suit in law, and he was exceedingly wroth in consequence. He was angry with the old woman for presuming to get cured, and angry with the brain doctor for curing her. He considered that the brain doctor had been guilty of a piece of meddlesome interference in restoring the old lady to so-called sanity in a world of fools, without achieving any object except robbery from the public funds by a rascally lawyer. To use Merrington's own words, expressed with intense exasperation to an astonished subordinate, the old woman was quite all right as a horse, comfortable and well-fed, and had probably got more out of life in that guise than she ever had as a human being, compelled to all sorts of shifts and contrivances and mean scrapings before her betters for a scanty living, with nothing but the work-house ahead of her. He concluded in a sort of grumbling epilogue that some people never knew when to leave well alone.

It was in no very amiable frame of mind, therefore, that he received Colwyn's card with a pencilled request for an immediate interview. Merrington disapproved of all private detectives as an unwarrantable usurpation of the functions of Scotland Yard, but he particularly disapproved of a private detective like Colwyn, whose popular renown was far greater than his own. But there were politic reasons for the extension of courtesy to him. The famous private detective was such a powerful rival that it was best to conciliate him with a little politeness, which cost nothing, and he had done Scotland Yard several good turns which at least demanded an outward show of gratitude. He had influence in the right quarter, too, and, altogether, was not a person to be lightly affronted. The consideration of these factors impelled Merrington to inform the waiting janitor that he would see Mr. Colwyn at once, and even caused him to crease his fat red features into a smile of welcome as he awaited his entrance.

When Colwyn appeared in the doorway the big man he had called to see got up from his swing-chair to shake hands with him. When his visitor was seated Merrington leaned back in his own chair and remarked, in his great rolling voice:

"What can I do for you, Mr. Colwyn?"

"Nothing personally. I have called to have a talk with you about the Heredith case."

The veneer of welcome disappeared from Merrington's face at this opening, though a large framed photograph of himself on the wall behind his chair continued to smile down at the private detective with unwonted amiability.

"Ah, yes, the Heredith case," he responded. "A strange affair, that. I investigated it personally. It was a pity you were not in it. There were points about that murder–distinct points. You would have enjoyed it."

Merrington's professional commiseration of Colwyn's ill-luck in missing an enjoyable murder was intended to convey a distinct rebuke to the other's presumption in discussing a case in which he had not been engaged. But Colwyn's next words startled Merrington out of his attitude of censorious dignity.

"I was not in the case at first, but I was called into it subsequently by the husband of the murdered woman. He is dissatisfied with the outcome. He thinks a mistake has been made in arresting the girl Hazel Rath."

The silence with which Merrington received this information was an involuntary tribute to his visitor, implying, as it did, that he knew Colwyn would not have come to see him without weighty reason for the support of what sounded like the repetition of a mere expression of opinion.

"I was reluctant to interfere until Mr. Heredith told me something which suggested that one of your men was in danger of underestimating an important clue," continued Colwyn. "That decided me. I went back with Mr. Heredith in my car the night before last. After my arrival at the moat-house I made an interesting discovery–quite by accident. I discovered that a pearl necklace which had been given to Mrs. Heredith by Sir Philip Heredith was missing from the jewel-case in which it had been locked. That jewel-case was in Mrs. Heredith's bedroom on the night she was murdered."

This piece of news was so unexpected that it caught Merrington off his guard.

"A jewel robbery as well as murder!" he ejaculated, in something like dismay.

"It looks like it. You will be able to form a better judgment when I have told you all the circumstances of the discovery."

Merrington had long ago convinced himself that the case he had worked up against Hazel Rath did not admit of the slightest possibility of doubt; and, like all obstinate men, he adhered to his convictions with additional strength in the face of anything tending to weaken them. As he recovered from his surprise at the private detective's piece of news, he listened to his account of the opening of the jewel-case with the wary air of one seeking a loop-hole in an unexpected obstacle. Before Colwyn had finished he had found it in the belief that Hazel Rath, and nobody else, had stolen the missing jewels.

"This girl is a thief as well as a murderer," was the manner in which he expressed his opinion when Colwyn had ceased speaking. "She has stolen the necklace."

"She may have done so, but it is too great an assumption to make without proof," returned Colwyn. "You must be perfectly well aware, Mr. Merrington, that this belated discovery is of the utmost importance to the Crown case, one way or the other. If you can prove that Hazel Rath stole the necklace, it gives you an unassailable case against her. If the necklace was stolen by somebody else, you are confronted with a new and strange aspect of this murder."

"Not to the extent of lessening the strength of the case against this girl," replied Merrington doggedly. "She was seen going to the staircase leading to Mrs. Heredith's room just before the murder; her brooch was found upstairs in the room; and the revolver and her handkerchief were found concealed in her mother's rooms. Add to that, her silence under accusation, and it is impossible to get away from the belief that she, and nobody else, murdered Mrs. Heredith."

"I am not attempting to controvert your theory or contradict your facts," rejoined Colwyn coldly. "My visit is to bring under your notice a fresh fact in the case which needs investigation. Whether that fact squares with your own theory or not, it is too important to be disregarded or overlooked. That is why I left the moat-house immediately I discovered it. I felt that you had been ignorantly misled, and that it was only right you should be told without delay."

Merrington was conscious of that evanescent feeling which men call gratitude. His impulse of thankfulness towards the man opposite him was all the keener for the realization that he would not have acted so generously if he had been in Colwyn's place. But his gratitude was speedily swallowed up by the knowledge that he had been led astray, and his anger was mingled with the determination to find a scapegoat.

"I am obliged to you for your information, although I do not attach quite so much importance to it as you do," was his careful rejoinder. "But I certainly blame Detective Caldew for not finding it out before you did. He made the original inquiries at the moat-house, and he seems to have made them very carelessly. He said nothing to the Chief Constable of Sussex or myself, when we arrived, about a jewel-case, locked or open."

"He didn't know himself."

"It was his duty to inquire. When he assured us, on the authority of Miss Heredith, that nothing was missing, I naturally assumed that he had made the proper inquiries. But I thank you for letting me know, and I shall, of course, have investigations made. But I should like to know why young Heredith interfered and brought you into the case?"

"For one thing, he has a strong belief in Hazel Rath's innocence."

"Mere sentiment," replied Merrington contemptuously. "Perhaps he's still sweet on the girl."

"There is more than that in it. There's the question of the revolver. Of course you are aware that he identified the revolver with which his wife was shot as the property of Captain Nepcote, a guest at the moat-house who left on the afternoon of the day on which Mrs. Heredith was murdered. Heredith does not accept your theory of the way in which Hazel Rath is supposed to have obtained the revolver. He does not think that Nepcote left the revolver behind him at the moat-house. He told Caldew this, but Caldew said the ownership of the revolver was a matter of no consequence."

"Caldew's a fool if he said that, and I wish I'd never allowed him to meddle in the case," replied Merrington forcibly. "I've had the police court proceedings against the girl put back for a week till the question of the ownership of the revolver could be settled. Now that it is decided I shall have Nepcote interviewed and questioned without delay."

"Before you try to trace the missing necklace?" The faint inflection of surprise in Colwyn's voice might have escaped a quicker ear than Merrington's.

"Scotland Yard will trace the necklace fast enough," he confidently declared. "I like to take things in their proper order. The next thing to do is to ascertain whether Nepcote left his revolver behind him at the moat-house, though I have not the least doubt that he did. The necklace is really a minor consideration. It merely provides another motive for the murder—cupidity as well as jealousy."

"Is that the way you regard it?" A less thick-skinned man than Merrington would this time have caught something more than surprise in the other's tone.

"Is there any other way of looking at it?"

"I would not like to venture an opinion in this case without more knowledge than I have at present," returned Colwyn in sober accents. "But so far as I have gone into it I should say that there are several things which seem to require more explanation. Nepcote's own actions seem to call for some investigation."

"You are surely not suggesting that Nepcote had anything to do with the murder or the robbery of the pearls?" said Merrington in an astonished voice. "That is quite impossible. He left the moat-house in the afternoon before the murder was committed, and went over to France that night."

"He didn't go to France that night. He stayed in London, and did not return to France until the following day."

Merrington was obviously startled at this unexpected information. "This is news to me," he said gravely. "Where did you learn it?"

"From the War Office this morning. There is no possibility of mistake. Nepcote was in London on the night of the murder."

"He probably has an explanation, but what you have just told me is an additional reason for seeing and questioning Nepcote without delay, even if I have to send a man to France for the job."

"It will not be necessary for you to do that. Nepcote returned to London two days ago—sent over on some special mission. I ascertained that fact also from my friend at the War Office."

Merrington glanced at a small clock which stood on the desk in front of him.

"I will go immediately and see him myself," he said.

"I should like to accompany you."

"I shall be delighted to have you," replied Merrington with complete untruth. "I have Nepcote's address included in the list of guests who were at the moat-house at the time of the murder," he added, opening his pocket-book and hastily scanning it. "Ah, here it is—10 Sherryman Street. I'll send for a taxi-cab. Is there anything I can do for you in return for your kindness in bringing me this information?"

"I should be obliged if you would lend me a copy of the coroner's depositions in the Heredith case."

"With pleasure." Merrington touched a bell, and instructed the policeman who answered it to bring a typescript of the Heredith murder depositions and the revolver which figured as an exhibit in the case. "And tell somebody to call a taxi, Johnson," he added.

When Merrington and Colwyn emerged from the swing doors of the entrance a few moments later, a taxi-cab was waiting at the bottom of the stone steps, with a pockmarked driver leaning against the door of the vehicle, gazing moodily over the Thames Embankment. He received Merrington's instructions morosely, cranked his cab wearily, and was soon threading his way through the mazes of Trafalgar Square and Piccadilly Circus with a contemptuous disregard for traffic regulations, due to his prompt recognition of the fact that he was carrying a high official of Scotland Yard who was above rules of the road regulated by mere police constables. He skimmed in a hazardous way along Regent Street, dipped into the network of narrower streets which lay between that haunt of the fox and the geese and Baker Street, and finally stopped abruptly outside a tall house which was one of a row in a quiet street which led into the highly fashionable locality of Sherryman Square.

Sherryman Street, in which the taxi-cab had stopped, was an offshoot and snobbish mean relation of Sherryman Square, which housed a duke, an ex-prime minister, and a fugitive king, to say nothing of several lesser notabilities, such as a High Court Judge or two, several baronets, and a war-time profiteer whose brand-new peerage had descended in the last heavy downpour of kingly honours. Because of their proximity to these great ones of the earth, the inhabitants of Sherryman Street assumed all the airs of exclusiveness which distinguished the residents of the superior neighbourhood, and parasitical house agents spoke of it with great respect because one end opened into the rarefied atmosphere of the Square. It was true that the other end was close to a slum, and there was a mews across the way, but these were small drawbacks compared to the social advantages.

Sherryman Street was full of gaunt, narrow houses, with prim fronts and narrow railed windows, let in segments, flats, and bachelor apartments. Number 10 was as like its fellows as one drab soul resembles another. Superintendent Merrington's ring at the doorbell brought forth an elderly woman with an expressionless face surmounted by a frilled white cap. She informed them in an expressionless voice that Captain Nepcote's apartments were on the second floor. Having said this much, she disappeared into a small lobby room off the entrance hall, leaving them free to enter.

A knock at the entrance door of the second-floor flat brought forth a manservant whose smart bearing and precision of manner suggested military training. He cautiously informed Superintendent Merrington, in reply to his question, that he was not sure if Captain Nepcote was at home, but he would go and see.

"Who shall I say, sir?" he asked, in unconscious contradiction of his statement.

Merrington stopped further parleying by impatiently pushing past the servant into the room.

"Go and tell your master I want to see him," he said, seating himself.

The servant looked angrily at the burly figure on the slender chair, and then, as though realizing his inability to eject him, he left the room without further speech.

The room they had entered was furnished in a style which suggested that its occupier had sufficient means or credit to gratify his tastes, which obviously soared no higher than racehorses and chorus girls. Pictures of the former adorned the wall in oak; the latter smirked at the beholder from silver frames on small tables. The room was handsomely furnished in a masculine way, although there was the suggestion of a feminine touch in the vases on the mantelpiece and some clusters of flowers in a bowl.

The door opened to admit a young man, who advanced towards his visitors with a questioning glance. His appearance, though military, was far from suggesting the sordid warfare of the trenches. He was well-groomed and handsome, and wore his spotless uniform with that touch of distinction which khaki lends to some men.

"Good afternoon," he said, and waited for them to announce the object of their visit.

"Are you Captain Nepcote?" Merrington asked.

"My name is Nepcote," was the response. "May I ask who you are?" His glance included both his visitors.

"My name is Merrington," responded that officer, answering for himself. "Superintendent Merrington, of Scotland Yard. This is Mr. Colwyn, a private detective," he added, as an afterthought. "I wish to ask you a few questions. I understand you were staying at the residence of Sir Philip Heredith when young Mrs. Heredith was murdered."

"That is not quite accurate," replied the young man. "I left the moat-house on the afternoon of the day that the murder was committed, and returned to London. What is it you wish to ask me? I am afraid I cannot enlighten you about the crime in any way, for I know nothing whatever about it. It came as a great shock to me when I heard of it."

"Is this your revolver?" said Merrington, producing the weapon and laying it on the table.

"Why, yes, it is," said the young man, picking it up and looking at it in unmistakable surprise. "Where did you get it?"

"Where did you have it last?" was Merrington's cautious rejoinder.

"Let me think," returned Nepcote thoughtfully. "Oh, I remember. The last time I saw it was at the moat-house on the day before my departure. We were using it for a little target practice in the gun-room downstairs."

"And what did you do with it afterwards?"

"That I cannot tell you," responded Nepcote. "I have no recollection of seeing it since. I have never thought about it."

"Nor missed it?"

"No. It is no use to me—it is not an Army revolver. But it seems to me that I must have left it in the moat-house gun-room after the target shooting. After we finished shooting some of us had a game of bagatelle on a table in the gun-room. I must have put the revolver down and forgotten all about it afterward. I have no recollection of taking it upstairs, and I have certainly never seen it since. Was it found in the gun-room?"

"It was found at the moat-house, at any rate. It was the weapon with which Mrs. Heredith was killed."

"What!" His exclamation rang out in horror and incredulity. "Why, it is impossible. The thing is a mere toy."

"A pretty dangerous toy—as it turned out," was the grim comment of Merrington.

"It seems incredible to me," persisted the young man. "It's very old, and you have to be very strong with the finger and thumb to make it revolve. And the cartridges are very small; only seven millimetres—about a quarter of an inch. I've had the old thing for years, but I never regarded it as a real fire-arm. I'd never have let the girls use it in the gun-room if I'd thought it was a dangerous weapon. Perhaps there is some mistake."

"There is no mistake," replied Merrington. "Mrs. Heredith was killed with that revolver, and no other. We were unable to establish the identity of the weapon until a day or two ago, and that is one of my reasons for calling on you to-day—to make quite sure of the identity and see if you could tell me where you left it."

"I have no doubt now that I must have left it behind me at the moat-house," responded Nepcote. "I was recalled to France and went away in a hurry. God forgive me for my carelessness. To think that it resulted in this terrible murder!" His face had gone suddenly white.

"Did you return to France that night?" asked Merrington carelessly.

"As a matter of fact, I did not. When I returned to London from Sussex I found another telegram here from the War Office extending my leave until the following day. I returned to France the next afternoon."

"Thank you, Captain Nepcote." Merrington, as he rose to go, held out his hand. It was evident that the statement about the telegram had cleared his mind of any suspicions he may have felt about the young man. As Nepcote shook hands he added: "You had better hold yourself in readiness to attend the police court inquiry, which will be held a week from to-day. I will send you a proper notification of time and place. All we need from you is the formal identification of the revolver."

"Is it essential that I should attend?" asked the young man anxiously. "I'd rather not be mixed up in the case at all, you know. Besides, I may have to return to France."

"Perhaps we shall be able to dispense with your evidence now that we have the facts," replied Merrington, after a moment's consideration. "I will see what can be done, and let you know. You had better give me your address in France, in case you have left England. It is necessary for me to know that, because the case has to some extent taken a new turn by the discovery that robbery as well as murder has been committed. A valuable necklace belonging to the murdered woman is missing."

Captain Nepcote had taken out his pocket-book while Merrington was speaking, in order to extract a card. As the other uttered the last sentence, the pocket-book half slipped from his fingers, and several other cards fluttered onto the table. Nepcote picked them up hastily, but not before Colwyn's quick glance had taken in their contents. It seemed to him something more than a coincidence that the name and address displayed in neat black lettering on one of the cards should be identical with one of the Hatton Garden addresses given him by Musard at the moat-house the previous day.

20

Colwyn spent a couple of hours that night reading the depositions he had obtained from Merrington, and next morning he studied them afresh with a concentration which the incessant hum of London traffic outside was powerless to disturb. He was well aware that a report was a poor substitute for original impressions, but in the typewritten document before him lay the facts of the Heredith case so far as they were known. It was a clear and colourless transcription of the narrative of the witnesses, set down with a painstaking regard for the value of departmental records, and chiefly valuable to Colwyn because it contained the expert evidence which sometimes reveals, with the pitiless accuracy of science, what human nature endeavours to hide. In the balance of the scales of justice it is the ascertained truth which weighs heavier than faith, reason, or revealed religion.

When he had finished his study of the depositions, he sat awhile pondering over his own discoveries since he had been called into the case by the husband of the dead woman. These discoveries, due apparently to chance, invested the murder with a complexity which stimulated all the penetrative and analytical powers of his fine mind, because they brought with them the realization that he was face to face with one of those rare crimes where the solution has to be unravelled from a tangle of false circumstances, which, by their seeming plausibility, make the task of reaching the truth one of peculiar difficulty. As Colwyn sat motionless, with his chin resting on his hand, brooding over the sullen secretive surface of this dark mystery, the feeling grew upon him that the murder had been preconceived with the utmost cunning and caution, and that the facts so far brought to light, including his own discoveries, did not penetrate to the real design.

The one conviction in his mind at that moment was that the man he and Merrington had interviewed on the previous afternoon had some connection with the mystery, and that an investigation of Nepcote's actions was the first step towards the solution of the murder. Colwyn based that belief on the apparently detached facts of the revolver, the patch of khaki he had found in the woods near the moat-house, and the accident which disclosed that Nepcote was carrying the address of a Hatton Garden jeweller in his pocket-book. These things, taken apart, had perhaps but slight significance, but, considered as links in a chain of events which started in Philip Heredith's statement that he had first met his wife at a friend's house where Nepcote was also a guest, and finishing with the knowledge that Nepcote had not returned to France on the night of the murder, they assumed a significance which at least warranted the closest investigation.

Colwyn was not affected by the fact that Superintendent Merrington looked at the case from an entirely different point of view. He did not want the help of Scotland Yard in solving the crime. He had too much contempt for the official mind in any capacity to think that assistance from such a source could be of value to him. He always preferred to work alone and unaided. It was the Anglo-Saxon instinct of fair play which had prompted him to tell Merrington about the missing necklace, so that there might be no unfair advantage between them. Merrington had received the information with the imperviable dogmatism of the official mind, strong in the belief in its own infallibility, resentful of advice or suggestion as an attempt to weaken its dignity. It seemed to Colwyn that not only had Merrington's ruffled dignity led his judgment astray in an attempt to fit the discovery of the missing necklace into his own theory of the case, but it had caused him to commit a grave mistake in putting Nepcote on his guard at a moment when the utmost circumspection of investigation was necessary.

To Colwyn, at all events, the discovery of the missing necklace was of the utmost importance because it substituted another motive for the murder, and a motive which carried with it the additional complication that the thief had some motive in trying to keep its disappearance secret as long as possible by locking the jewel-case after the jewels had been abstracted. If Hazel Rath had not stolen the necklace, the whole of the facts took on new values. It was quite true that the mystery of Hazel Rath's actions on the night of the murder, her subsequent silence after the recovery of the brooch and the handkerchief and the revolver in her mother's rooms, remained as suspicious as before, but the changed motive caused these points to assume a different complexion, even to the extent of suggesting that she might be a lesser participant in the crime, perhaps keeping silence in order to shield the greater criminal.

Merrington, stiff-necked in his officialism, had been unable to see this changed aspect of the case, and, strong in his presumption of the girl's guilt, had acted with impulsive indiscretion in going to see Nepcote before attempting to trace the missing necklace.

Colwyn's reflections were interrupted by the appearance of the porter from downstairs to announce a visitor. The visitor, partly obscured behind the burly frame of the porter in the doorway, was Detective Caldew, of Scotland Yard. Colwyn had met him at various times, and invited him to enter. As Colwyn had once said, his feelings towards all the members of the regular detective force were invariably friendly; it was not their fault, but the fault of human nature, that they were sometimes jealous of him. So he made Caldew welcome, and offered him a cigar.

Caldew accepted the cigar and the proffered seat a little nervously. His was the type of temperament which is overawed in the presence of a more successful practitioner in the same line of business. He had long envied Colwyn his dazzling successes, but at the same time he had sufficient intelligence to understand that many of those successes stood in a class which he could never hope to attain.

At the present moment, Caldew's feelings were divided between resentment at Colwyn's action in conveying information to Scotland Yard which had earned him a reprimand from Superintendent Merrington, and the anxious desire to ascertain what the famous private detective thought of the Heredith case.

"Merrington has sent me round for the copy of the depositions he lent you yesterday." It was thus he announced the object of his visit. "Have you finished with it?"

It was apparent from this statement that Superintendent Merrington's gratitude for information received might now be considered as past history. Colwyn, reflecting that it had lasted as long as that feeling usually does, congratulated himself on his forethought in having made a copy of the report. He handed the copy before him to his visitor.

"I am obliged for the loan of it," he said. "It makes interesting reading. You're own share in the original investigations has some excellent touches, if you'll permit me to say so. That trap for the owner of the brooch was a neat idea."

Caldew's resentment waned under this compliment to his professional skill.

"The trick would have worked, too, if I hadn't been called downstairs," he said. "The girl was quick enough to get into the room while I was out of it. Not that it mattered much, as things turned out, but it is a strange thing about this necklace, isn't it?"

"Very. Has Merrington told you all about it?"

"Yes, and he gave me a rare wigging for not discovering the loss. Between ourselves, I do not think that I was treated quite fairly about it. Miss Heredith never said a word to me about a jewel-case being in the room. She took it downstairs before I arrived, and never mentioned it when I asked her if anything had been stolen. If she had told me I should have had the case opened. But that didn't weigh with Merrington. He's beastly unfair, and never loses a chance to put the blame on to somebody else when anything goes wrong."

"I am sorry if you got into trouble through my action in informing him," said Colwyn. "But of course you must realize that a discovery of such importance could not be kept secret."

"That's quite true," replied Caldew, in a softened voice. "Fortunately, it does not affect the issue, one way or another. Mr. Heredith believes that Hazel Rath is innocent, and I suppose that is why he has called you into the case. But she is guilty, right enough. I tried to make that clear to Mr. Heredith, but he appears to be a man of fixed ideas. The question is, what has become of the necklace? My own impression is that she has hidden it somewhere. She had no opportunity to dispose of it before she was arrested."

"That means that you think she has stolen it."

"Why, of course–" Caldew's confident tone died away at the expression of his companion's face. "Don't you?"

"I do not."

"Why not?"

"For one thing, the jewel-case was locked. How did the girl know where the key was kept?"

"She might have got the knowledge from her mother. Mrs. Rath, as the housekeeper, would probably know all about the keys of the household."

"Of the ordinary keys–yes. But that knowledge was hardly likely to extend to Mrs. Heredith's private keys, unless Miss Heredith told her. Even if Hazel Rath did know where the key was kept, it is difficult to believe that she searched for it after committing the murder, and then restored it to the drawer where it was kept. That argues too much cold-blooded deliberation even in a murderer, and more especially when the murderer is supposed to be a young girl."

"I am not so sure of that," responded Caldew, with a shake of the head. "Murder is a cold-blooded crime."

"On the contrary, murders are almost invariably committed under the influence of the strongest excitement, even when the incentive is gain, and the murder has been deeply premeditated. That is a remarkable truth in the psychology of murder. But the important fact about the theft of the necklace is that even if Hazel Rath knew where the key of the jewel-case was kept she had not time to obtain it from the drawer on the other side of the bed, steal the necklace, restore the key to its place, and escape from the room before the guests from downstairs entered the bedroom. If Hazel Rath was indeed the murderess, time was of paramount importance to her. She must have realized that the scream of her victim would alarm the household downstairs, and that some of the men must have started upstairs before the subsequent shot was fired."

Caldew was silent for a space, cogitating over these points with a troubled look which contrasted with his previous confident expressions of opinion about the case. His inward perturbation was made manifest in the question:

"Do you also share Mr. Heredith's view that Hazel Rath is innocent?"

"I cannot say. The facts against her are very strong."

"Of course they are strong!" exclaimed Caldew eagerly, as though clutching this guarded expression of opinion as a buoy for his own sinking conviction. "They are so strong that it is quite certain she committed the murder."

Colwyn remained silent. A statement which was merely an expression of opinion did not call for words.

Caldew, always impressionable, became uneasy under his companion's silence, and that uneasiness was tinctured in his mind with such a dread of the possibility of mistake that it flowed forth in impulsive words:

"I wish you would tell me what you really think of the case, Mr. Colwyn. I have been waiting for years for the chance of handling a big murder like this, and now that it has come my way I should like to pull it off. It means a lot to me," he added simply.

Colwyn reflected that he had already given away more information about the Heredith case than his judgment approved or his conscience dictated. But his kindly nature prompted him to help the anxious young man seated in front of him, who had so much more than he to gain by success.

"I think there is more in this case than you and Merrington have yet brought to light," he said.

"I suppose there is, if it is proved that Hazel Rath did not steal the necklace. But have you found out anything else besides the loss of the necklace?"

Colwyn did not directly reply. He was glancing over the depositions again.

"There are one or two curious points here," he remarked, as he turned over the leaves. "In the first place, the ammunition expert who was called at the inquest to give evidence about the bullet extracted from the body testified that in weight and in length it corresponded with the seven millimetre bullet made for a pinfire revolver. The bullet had undoubtedly been fired from the revolver which you found in Mrs. Rath's rooms. Bullets for English revolvers are not graded in millimetres, but there appears to be sufficient demand for this size to cause British firms to manufacture them. The nearest size in central-fire cartridge to seven millimetres is called the 300, which is .3 of an inch. Seven millimetres is .276 of an inch. The point to which I want to draw your attention is the extreme slightness and smallness of the revolver with which Mrs. Heredith was killed. As Captain Nepcote told Merrington yesterday, it is little more than a toy."

"That struck me as soon as I saw it," said Caldew. "But I do not see what bearing the fact has on the case, one way or another."

"Nevertheless, it is a point not without importance, when it is considered in conjunction with the other circumstances of the case. The evidence of the Government pathologist is also of interest. After stating the cause of death to be heart failure due to hæmorrhage consequent upon the passage of the bullet through the lung, he mentions that there was a large scorched hole through the rest-gown and undergarment which Mrs. Heredith was wearing at the time she was murdered."

"I noticed that when I was examining the body."

"Was the dress-stuff smouldering when you saw the body?"

"No; but there was a smell of a burning fabric in the room."

"The Government pathologist says that the burnt hole was nearly two inches across, but he also states that the punctured wound made by the bullet was about the size of a threepenny piece. The disparity suggests two facts. In the first place, the shot must have been fired at very close range—very close indeed, considering the smallness of the revolver and the largeness of the burnt hole. In the next place, somebody must have extinguished the burning fabric before you arrived, otherwise it would have smouldered in an ever-widening ring until the whole of the dead woman's garments were destroyed."

"Mrs. Heredith may have extinguished it herself in her dying moments," said Caldew, who had been following his companion's deductions with the closest attention.

"That is unlikely, in view of the nature of her injuries. The bullet, after traversing the left lung, lodged in the spinal column. After such a wound Mrs. Heredith was not likely to be conscious of her actions."

"It may have been extinguished by Musard, who tried to stop the flow of blood while Mrs. Heredith was dying."

"He would have mentioned it to you. It is my intention to ask him, but my own opinion is that we are faced with a different explanation."

"What is that?"

"The presence of another person in the room."

"Somebody who escaped through the window!" exclaimed Caldew, placing his own interpretation on the deduction. "Do you suspect anybody?"

"Not exactly. But I intend to investigate Captain Nepcote's actions on the night of the murder."

Caldew, who lacked some of the information possessed by his companion, found this jump too great for his mind to follow.

"For what purpose?" he asked. "Nepcote returned to France before the murder was committed."

"He did not. He stayed in London that night, and did not return to France until the following day. He explained that yesterday by stating that when he reached London after leaving the moat-house he found another telegram from the War Office extending his leave for twenty-four hours."

"Merrington said nothing of this to me. All he told me was that you and he had seen Nepcote, who identified the revolver as his property, and said that he had left it behind at the moat-house by accident."

"Merrington is a man of fixed ideas, to use your phrase. He insisted on trying to fit in the loss of the necklace with his own theory of Hazel Rath's guilt. It was his obstinacy which led him to commit the folly of going to see Captain Nepcote before endeavouring to trace the missing necklace. It is only fair to Nepcote to add that he volunteered the information that he did not return to France on the night of the murder."

"That does not seem like the action of a man with anything to hide," commented Caldew thoughtfully.

"Unless he was facing a dangerous situation. In that case, frankness would be his best course to remove Merrington's suspicions. The fact that the murder was committed with his revolver is in itself a suspicious circumstance, in spite of the apparently plausible explanation. I have realized that all along. I had also previously acquainted Merrington with the fact that Nepcote did not return to France on the night of the murder, as was supposed. Merrington led up to that point skilfully enough, but it struck me that Nepcote saw the trap, and took the boldest course. It gave him time, at all events."

"Time for what?"

"Time to profit by Merrington's folly in putting him on his guard. Time to permit him to make his escape, if he is actually implicated in the crime."

"Surely you are reading too much into this," exclaimed Caldew in a protesting voice. "Nepcote's story seems to me quite consistent with what we know of his movements. Miss Heredith, when giving us the names of the guests who had been staying at the moat-house, mentioned that Captain Nepcote had been recalled to France on the afternoon of the murder by a telegram from the War Office. Nepcote tells you that when he reached London he found another telegram awaiting him extending his leave. Surely that is consistent?"

"Is it consistent that the two telegrams were sent to different addresses? They would have been either both sent to the moat-house, or both sent to his London flat— that is, if they were sent by the War Office. Only a relative or a personal friend would take the trouble to send to different addresses. There lies the weak point of Nepcote's statement."

"By Jove, there is a point in that," said Caldew, in a startled tone. "But these are facts which can be ascertained," he added, as though seeking to reassure himself.

"They can be ascertained too late. I have already set inquiries on foot, but it takes some time to gain any information about official telegrams. Nepcote has plenty of time to take advantage of Merrington's blunder, if there is any occasion for him to do so. No matter what his explanation is, the fact remains that he was in England, and not in France, on the night the murder was committed, and I propose to find out how he spent the time. But it is of the first importance to find out what has become of the missing necklace, which is the really important clue. Is Scotland Yard making any investigations about it?"

"Yes. Merrington has put me on to that because I let you score the point over him of discovering that it was missing. I am sure that he hopes I will fall down over the job of tracing it. I shouldn't be surprised if I did, too. It's no easy thing to get on the track of missing jewellery, especially if it has been hidden. I have not even got a description of the necklace to help me."

"I can give you a description, and perhaps help you in the work of tracing it."

"Can you? That's awfully good of you." Caldew's face showed that he meant his words. "Have you any idea where it is?"

"I have at least something to guide me in commencing the search—something, which, curiously enough, I owe to Merrington's blunder in visiting Nepcote before he looked for the necklace. We will go across to Hatton Garden, and I will put my idea to the test."

21

On reaching the street, they crossed Ludgate Circus, and directed their steps towards Hatton Garden by way of St. Bride Street.

A few minutes later, they emerged in that portion of Holborn which is graced by the mounted statue of a dead German prince acknowledging his lifelong obligations to British hospitality by raising his plumed hat to the London City & Midland Bank on the Viaduct corner. Hatton Garden, as every Londoner knows, begins on the other side of this improving spectacle–a short broad street which disdains to indicate by external opulence the wealth hidden within its walls, though, to an eye practised in London ways, there is a comforting suggestion of prosperity in its wide flagged pavements, comfortable brick buildings, and Jewish names which appear in gilt lettering on plate-glass windows.

Colwyn walked quickly along, glancing at the displayed names. He had almost reached the Clerkenwell end of the Garden when his eye was caught by the name of "Austin Wendover, Dealer in Oriental Stones," gleaming in white letters on the blackboard indicator of a set of offices hived in a building on the corner of a side street. It was the name of the man he was searching for. He turned into the passage, and mounted the stairs. Caldew followed him.

On the landing of the first floor another and smaller board gave the names of those tenants whose offices were at the back of the building. Mr. Wendover's was amongst them, and a pointing hand opposite it revealed that he conducted his business at the end of a long passage with a bend in the middle. When this passage was traversed, Mr. Wendover's name was once more seen, this time on a door, with a notice underneath inviting the visitor to enter without knocking.

Within, a young Jew with a sensual face was busily writing at a desk in the corner, with his back to the door. He ceased and turned around at the sound of the opening door, and, thrusting his fountain pen behind an ear already burdened with a cigarette, waited to be informed what the visitors wanted.

"Is Mr. Wendover in?" Colwyn inquired.

"Yes, he is. What name, please?" The young Jew scrambled down from his stool preparatory to carrying a message.

In answer Colwyn tendered Musard's card of introduction. The young Jew scanned it, shot an appraising glance at the two detectives, and vanished into an inner room. He reappeared swiftly in the doorway, and beckoned them to enter.

The inner room was furnished with leather chairs, a good carpet, and a large walnut table. Mining maps and framed photographs of famous diamonds hung on the walls, but there was nothing about the man seated at the table to suggest association with precious stones except the gleam of his small grey eyes, which were as hard and glistening as the specimen gems in the showcase at his elbow. His face was long, thin and yellow, of a bilious appearance. His gaunt frame was clothed in black, and his low white collar ended in front in two linen tags, fastened with a penny bone stud instead of the diamond which might have been expected. This device, besides dispensing with a necktie, revealed the base of a long scraggy neck, with a tuft of grey hair pushing its way up from below and falling over the interstice of the collar, matching a similar tuft which dangled pendulously from the diamond merchant's nether lip. Altogether, as Mr. Austin Wendover sat at his table with his long yellow hands clasped in front of him waiting for his visitors to announce their business, he looked not unlike a Methodist pastor about to say grace, or a Garden City apostle of culture for the masses preparing to receive a vote of thanks for a lecture on English prose at a workers' mutual improvement society. Even his name suggested, to the serious mind, the compiler of an anthology of British war poets or the writer of a book of Nature studies, rather than the material wealth, female folly, late suppers, greenrooms, frivolity and immorality brought before a vivid imagination by the mere mention of the word diamonds.

"My name is Colwyn; my friend is Detective Caldew, of Scotland Yard," said Colwyn, in response to Mr. Wendover's glance of interrogation. "We are in search of a little information, which we trust you will give us."

"That depends upon what ye want to know." This reply, delivered in an abrupt and uncouth manner, suggested that the diamond merchant's disposition was anything but a cut and polished one.

"Quite so. You have heard of the Heredith murder, I presume."

The diamond merchant nodded his head without speaking, and waited to hear more.

"The Heredith necklace of pink pearls was stolen from Mrs. Heredith's room on the night that she was murdered, and we are endeavouring to trace it."

"And what has that got to do with me?"

"I have reason to think that the necklace may have been offered or sold in Hatton Garden. It may have been submitted to you."

"What d'ye mean by coming to me with such a question? What does Mr. Musard mean by sending ye here? Does he think I've turned receiver of stolen property at my time of life? I'm surprised at him."

"My dear Mr. Wendover, Mr. Musard had no such thought in his mind. We simply come to you for information. Mr. Musard gave me your address as a reputable dealer of stones who would be likely to know if this necklace had been offered for sale in Hatton Garden."

"Well, it has not been offered to me. I've handled no pearls for twelve months."

"Would you know the Heredith necklace if it were offered to you?"

"I would not, and I've already told ye it was not offered to me."

Colwyn was nonplussed and disappointed, but the recollection of Nepcote's furtive glance and hasty concealment of the diamond merchant's card on the previous night prompted him to a further effort.

"It is possible the necklace may have been broken up and the stones offered separately," he said. "The clasp contained a large and valuable blue diamond."

"I tell ye I know nothing about it. I very rarely buy from private persons. It's not my way of doing business."

"We have reason to suspect that the necklace was offered for sale by a young military officer, tall and good looking, with blue eyes and brown hair, slightly tinged with grey at the temples."

"That description would apply to thousands of young officers. They're a harum-scarum lot, and dissipation soon turns a man's hair grey. I have had some of them here, trying to sell family jewels for money to throw away on painted women. There was one who called some days ago in a half-intoxicated condition. He clapped me on the back as impudent as you please, and calling me a thing—a dear old thing, which is one of their slang phrases—asked me what he could screw out of me for a good diamond. I sent him and his diamond off with a flea in the ear." Mr. Wendover's gummy lips curved in a grim smile at the recollection.

"Can you describe him more particularly?" asked Colwyn, with sudden interest.

"I paid no particular attention to him, and I wouldn't know him again if he were to walk in the door. It was almost dark when he came, and my eyes are not young. But he was not the man ye're after. It was days before the murder."

"Did he give you his name?"

"He did not, and I wouldn't tell ye if he did. What's it to do with the object of your visit? Ye're a persistent sort of young fellow, but I'm not going to let ye hold a general fishing inquiry into my business. There are two kinds of foolish folk in this world. Those who babble of their affairs to their womenfolk, and those who babble of them to strangers. I have no womenfolk, thank God! so I cannot talk to the futile creatures."

"Then I shall not ask you to break the other half of your maxim on my account," said Colwyn, rising with a smile.

"It would be no good if ye did," responded Mr. Wendover, with a reciprocatory grin which displayed two yellow fangs like the teeth of a walrus. "My business conscience is already pricking me for having said so much. He that holds his own counsel gives away nothing—except that he holds his counsel. Ye might do worse than lay that to your heart, Mr. Colwyn, in your walk through life. There's fifty years' experience behind it. Good-bye to ye, Mr. Colwyn, and ye, young man. I wish ye both luck in your search, but my advice is, try the pawn-shops." At the pressure of his thumb on the table the young Jew appeared from the next room, as if summoned by a magic wand, to let the visitors out.

"That's a queer old bird," said Caldew, as they walked away. "Do you think he has told us the truth?"

Colwyn did not reply. He was thinking rapidly, and wondering whether by any possibility he had made a mistake. But once more there flashed into his mind, like an image projected on a screen, the little scene which he alone had witnessed at the flat on the previous evening—the fluttering cards, the quick, unconscious gesture of concealment, and the startled glance which so plainly reflected the dread of discovery. No! there was no mistake there, but the explanation lay deeper.

They had reached the angle of the narrow passage which led to the front outlet of the offices. A small window was fixed at the dark turn of the long dark corridor to admit light. Colwyn chanced to glance through this window as he reached it, and his quick eye took in the figure of a man standing motionless in a narrow alley of the side street below. He was almost concealed behind an archway, but it was apparent to the detective that he was watching the corner building. As Colywn looked at him he slightly changed his position and his face came into view. With a quick imperative gesture to his companion, Colwyn ran swiftly along the remainder of the corridor and down the flight of stairs into Hatton Garden.

Caldew followed more slowly, puzzled by the other's strange action. When he reached the doorway Colwyn was nowhere to be seen, so he waited in the entrance. After the lapse of a few minutes he saw Colwyn returning from the direction of Clerkenwell.

"He has got away," he said, as he reached Caldew. His voice was a little breathless, as though with running.

"He? Who?"

Colwyn drew him into the empty entrance hall before he answered:

"Nepcote. He was watching outside. I saw him through the upstairs window. He either followed us here or has been waiting to see if we came. I should have foreseen this."

A flicker of unusual agitation on Colwyn's calm face increased Caldew's mental confusion.

"I don't understand," he stammered. "He—Nepcote—why should he be watching us?"

"Because he penetrated the truth last night. He knew he was in danger."

"But why should he follow us here?"

"He accidentally dropped some cards from his pocketbook when giving Merrington an address at his flat last night, and one of them was Wendover's business card.

Merrington did not see it–it would have conveyed nothing to him if he had–but I did. Nepcote knew that I saw it, and must have realized that I suspected him. He has been watching my rooms and followed us here, or he has been hanging around this place to see if I called on Wendover."

"Even now I do not see the connection. If Wendover told us the truth, Nepcote has not been to him with the necklace. Then what did it matter to Nepcote whether you came here or not?"

"Nepcote may have been the man who offered the diamond to Wendover."

"That is impossible. Wendover says that man called some days before the murder."

"Still, it may have been Nepcote."

"That goes beyond me," said Caldew, with a puzzled look. "What are you implying?"

"Nothing at present. Every step in this case convinces me that we are faced with a very deep mystery. It isn't worth while to hazard a guess, because guessing is always unsatisfactory."

"Perhaps we had better try and get a little more out of Wendover," said Caldew.

"That would be merely waste of time. He has not got the necklace, and he is unable to describe the man who offered him the diamond. I believe now that it was Nepcote, but that doesn't matter, one way or another. It is far more important to know that he came here to-day to watch for us. That implies that he had reason to fear investigations about the necklace. The inference to be drawn is that Nepcote is responsible for the disappearance of the necklace, and is, therefore, deeply implicated in the murder."

"Perhaps it was not Nepcote that you saw?" suggested Caldew. He felt that the remark was a feeble one, but he was bewildered by the sudden turn of events, and in a frame of mind which clutches at straws.

"Put that doubt out of your mind," said Colwyn. "I saw his face distinctly. He had disappeared by the time I got down. The alley where he was standing commanded a view of the entrance of this building. I ascertained that by standing in the same spot. His flight is another proof—though that was not needed—of his guilty knowledge and complicity in this murder. Why should he run away? According to his own story last night he had nothing to fear. But now, by his own actions, he has brought the utmost suspicion on himself."

"I suppose it is no use searching about here for him?" remarked Caldew, glancing gloomily out of the doorway.

"Not in the least. The neighbourhood is a warren of alleys and side streets from here to Grays Inn Road."

"Then I shall go up to his flat at once," said Caldew. "He has not had time to go back."

"He will not return to his flat. We have seen the last of him until we catch him. He has had two warnings, and he is not likely to be guilty of the folly of waiting to see whether lightning strikes thrice in the same spot. He will get away for good, this time, if he can. Nevertheless it is worth while going to the flat. We may pick up some points there." Colwyn uttered these last words in a lower tone at the sight of two office girls descending the staircase with much chatter and laughter.

"Let us go then."

They travelled by 'bus from Grays Inn Road as far as Oxford Circus, and walked along a number of quiet secluded streets—the backwaters of the West End—in order to reach Sherryman Street from the lower end, which, with a true sense of the fitness of things, was called Sherryman Street Approach. If the Approach had not been within a stone's throw of Sherryman Square it might have been called a slum. It had tenement houses with swarms of squalid children playing in the open doorways, its shops offered East End food—mussels and whelks, "two-eyed steaks," reeking fish-and-chips, and horsemeat for the cheap foreign element. There were several public-houses with groups of women outside drinking and gossiping, all wearing the black shawls which are as emblematic of the lower class London woman as a chasuble to a priest, or a blue tattooed upper lip to a high-caste Maori beauty. A costermonger hawked frozen rabbits from a donkey-cart, with a pallid woman following behind to drive away the mangy cats which quarrelled in the road for the oozing blood which dripped from the cart's tail. An Italian woman, swarthy, squat, and intolerably dirty, ground out the "Marseillaise" from a barrel-organ with a shivering monkey capering atop, waving a small Union Jack, and impatiently rattling a tin can for coppers.

To turn from this squalid quarter into Sherryman Street was to pass from the east to the west end of London at a step. It was as though an invisible line of demarcation had been drawn between the lower and upper portion of the street, and held inviolate by the residents of each portion. There were no public houses or fish-shops in Sherryman Street; no organ-grinders, costermongers, unclean children, or women in black shawls. It had quiet, seclusion, clean pavements, polished doorknockers, and white curtains at the windows of its well-kept houses, which grew in dignity to the semblance of town mansions at the Square end.

Number 10 showed a blank closed stone exterior to the passer-by, like an old grey secretive face. As they approached it Colwyn, with a slight movement of his head, drew his companion's attention to the upper windows which belonged to Nepcote's flat. The blinds were down.

"It looks as if Nepcote left last night," he said.

The sight of the drawn blinds, like yellow eyelids in the grey face, awakened some secret irritation in Caldew's breast, and with it the realization of his powers as an officer of Scotland Yard.

"I shall force a way in and see," he angrily declared.

"Better get a key from the housekeeper," suggested Colwyn. "The women who look after these bachelor flats always have duplicate keys. But the front door is ajar. Let us go upstairs first."

They ascended the stairs to the flat, and the first thing they noticed was a Yale key in the keyhole of the door.

"A sign of mental upset," commented Colwyn. "At such moments people forget the little things."

They opened the door and entered. The front room was much as Colwyn had seen it the previous night. The flowers drooped in their bowl; the chorus girls smirked in their silver settings; the framed racehorses and their stolid trainers looked woodenly down from the pink walls.

"Nepcote does not seem to have taken anything away with him," remarked Caldew, looking into the bedroom. "The wardrobe is full of his uniforms, but the bed has not been occupied."

"Here is the proof that he has fled," said Colwyn, flinging back the lid of a desk which stood in the sitting-room. It was filled to the brim with a mass of torn papers.

"Anything compromising?" asked Caldew, eagerly approaching to look at the litter.

"No; only bills and invitations. Any dangerous letters have been burnt there." He pointed to the grate, which was heaped with blackened fragments. "He's made a good job of it too," he added, as he went to the fireplace and bent over it. "There's not the slightest chance of deciphering a line. But it would be as well to search his clothes. He may have forgotten some letters in the pockets."

Caldew took the hint, and disappeared into the inner room, leaving Colwyn examining the contents of the grate. He returned in a few minutes to say that he had found nothing in the clothes except a few Treasury notes and some loose silver in a trousers' pocket.

"That looks as if he had bolted in such a hurry that he forgot to take his change with him," said Colwyn. "It is another interesting revelation of his state of mind, because there is very little doubt that he returned to the flat this morning after leaving it last night."

"How do you arrive at that conclusion?"

"By the burnt letters in the grate. They are still warm. He was in such a state of fear that he dared not sleep in the flat last night, but he returned this morning to burn his letters and change into civilian clothes. Then he rushed away again in such a hurry that he forgot his money. There is nothing more to be seen here. We had better make a few inquiries of the housekeeper as we go downstairs."

They walked out, and Caldew locked the door behind him and placed the key in his pocket. When they reached the entrance hall Colwyn paused outside the door of the recess where the housekeeper lurked, like an octopus in a pool. At Colwyn's knock a white face, topped by a white cap, came into view through the narrow slit in the curtained glass half of the door, and swam towards them in the interior gloom after the manner of the head of a materialized ghost in a spirit medium's parlour. The door opened, and the apparition appeared in the flesh, looking at them with stony eyes. Caldew undertook the conversation:

"Did Captain Nepcote sleep here last night?" he curtly asked.

"I don't know."

"Well, has he been here this morning?"

"I don't know." The tone of the second reply was even more expressionless than the first, if that were possible.

"It's your business to know," said Caldew angrily.

"It is not my business to discuss Captain Nepcote's private affairs with strangers." The woman turned back into her room without another word, closing the door behind her.

"D—n her!" muttered Caldew, in intense exasperation.

"These ancient females learn the wisdom of controlling their natural garrulity when placed in charge of bachelors' flats," said Colwyn with a laugh. "We will get nothing out of her if we stay here all day, so we had better go."

"I am going straight back to Scotland Yard," Caldew announced with sudden decision when they reached the pavement. "I must tell Merrington all about this morning's work, and the sooner the better. We must have the flat watched. Perhaps Nepcote may return."

"He will not return," said Colwyn. "He knows that we are after him, and that the flat will be watched. But it is a good idea not to let him have too long a start. Come, let us see if we can find a taxi, and I will drop you at Scotland Yard."

They walked along to Sherryman Square, and esteemed themselves fortunate in picking up a cruising taxi-cab with a driver sufficiently complaisant to drive them in the direction they wished to go.

22

It was to Merrington's credit as an official that he suppressed his feelings as a man on hearing Caldew's story, and did everything possible to retrieve the situation once he was convinced that Nepcote had fled. Any lingering doubts he may have had were scattered on learning, after confidential inquiry at Whitehall, that Captain Nepcote had not put in an appearance at the War Office that day, and had neither requested nor been granted leave of absence from his duties.

On receipt of this information Merrington turned to his office telephone, and, receiver in hand, bellowed forth peremptory instructions which set in motion the far-reaching organization of Scotland Yard for the capture of a fugitive from justice. Nepcote's description was circulated to police stations, detectives were told off to keep an eye on outgoing trains and the docks, and the entrances to the tubes and underground railways were watched. After enclosing London, Merrington made a wider cast, and long before nightfall he had flung around England a net of fine meshes through which no man could wriggle.

But it is difficult even for Scotland Yard to lay quick hands on a fugitive in the vast city of London, as Merrington well knew. While waiting for the net to close over his destined captive, he decided in the new strange turn of the case to investigate the whole of the circumstances afresh. Inquiries set afoot in London, with the object of discovering all that could be learnt of Nepcote's career and Violet Heredith's single life, occupied an important share in Scotland Yard's renewed investigations into the Heredith murder.

Caldew was sent to Heredith to look for new facts. He returned after a day's absence with information which might have been obtained before if chance had not directed suspicion to Hazel Rath: with a story of an unknown young man who had left the London train to Heredith at Weydene Junction on the night of the murder. The story, as extracted from an unintelligent ticket collector, threw no light on the identity of the stranger beyond a statement that he had worn a long light trench-coat, beneath which the collector had caught a glimpse of khaki uniform as the gentleman felt for his ticket at the barrier.

On that slight information Caldew had pursued inquiries across a long two miles of country between Weydene and the moat-house, and had deemed himself fortunate in finding a farm labourer who, on his homeward walk that night, had been passed by a young man in a long coat making rapidly across the fields in the direction of Heredith. The labourer had stared after the retreating figure until it disappeared in the darkness, and had then gone home without thinking any more of the incident. Caldew was so impressed by the significance of the second appearance of the man in the trench-coat that he had timed himself in a fast walk over the same ground from Weydene to the moat-house, and was able to cover the distance in half an hour. On the basis of these facts, he pointed out to Merrington that, if Nepcote was the man who left the train at Weydene at seven o'clock, he had time to walk across the fields and reach the moat-house by half-past seven, which was ten minutes before the murder was committed.

Merrington admitted the possibility, but refused to accept the inference. He was forced by recent events to accept the theory of Nepcote's implication in the mystery, but he was not prepared to believe without much more definite proof that he was the murderer. He was still strong in his belief that Hazel Rath was the person who had killed Mrs. Heredith, whatever the young man's share in the crime might be. The discovery about the man in the trench-coat was all very well as far as it went, and perhaps formed another clue in the puzzling set of circumstances of the case, but it did not carry them very far, and certainly did nothing to lessen the weight of evidence against the girl who was charged with the murder.

Merrington was forced back on the conclusion that the most important step towards the solution of the mystery was to lay hold of Nepcote, and to that end he directed his own efforts and that of the service of the great organization at his command. As the days went on, he supplemented his original arrangements for Nepcote's arrest with guileful traps. The female dragon who guarded masculine reputations at 10, Sherryman Street, was badgered into cold anger by pretty girls, who sought with tips and blandishments to glean scraps of information about the missing tenant. Scented letters in female handwriting, marked "Important," appeared in the letter racks of Nepcote's West End clubs. Merrington even inserted an advertisement in the "Personal" column of the *Times,* setting forth a touching female appeal to Nepcote for a meeting in a sequestered spot.

At the end of three days, with no sign of Nepcote in that period, Merrington was compelled to make application to the Sussex magistrates for another adjournment of the police court proceedings, on the ground that fresh information needed investigation before Scotland Yard could proceed with the charge against Hazel Rath. An additional week was granted with reluctance by the chairman of the bench, a Nonconformist draper with political ambitions, who seized the opportunity to impress the electors of a constituency he was nursing for the next general election by making some spirited remarks on the sanctity of British liberty, which he coupled with a scathing reference to the dilatory methods of Scotland Yard. He let it be understood that the police must be prepared at the next hearing to go on with the charge against the prisoner or withdraw it altogether.

In the face of these awkward alternatives, Merrington pursued the quest for Nepcote with vigour. The men working immediately under his instructions were spurred into an excess of energy which brought about the detention of several young men who could not adequately explain themselves or their right to liberty in the great city of London. But none of these captures turned out to be Nepcote. Merrington believed he was hiding in London, but at the end of five days he still remained mysteriously at liberty in spite of the constant search for him. He seemed to have disappeared as completely as though he had passed out of the world and merged his identity into a chiselled name and a banal aspiration on a tombstone.

In the angry consciousness of failure, Merrington was not blind to the fact that he had only his own impetuosity to blame for allowing Nepcote to slip through his fingers. His mistake was due to his dislike of private detectives and his unbelief in modern deductive methods of crime solution. His own system, which is the system of Scotland Yard, was based on motive and knowledge. If he found a strong motive for a crime he searched for the person to whom it pointed. If there was no apparent motive he fell back on his great knowledge of the underworld and its denizens to fit a criminal to the crime. The system has its measure of success, as the records of Scotland Yard attest.

Merrington had brought both methods to bear in his handling of the Heredith case. When his original investigations failed to reveal a motive for the murder, he determined to return to London to ascertain what dangerous criminals were at liberty who might have committed the murder. His own view then was that the murder was the work of an old hand who had entered the moat-house to commit burglary, and had murdered Mrs.

Heredith to escape identification. The isolation of the moat-house, the presence of guests with valuable jewels, the time chosen for the crime, and the scream of the victim, tended to confirm him in this belief. Caldew's chance discovery about Hazel Rath, and the subsequent events which arrayed such strong circumstantial evidence against her, brought the other side of the system uppermost and set Merrington seeking for a motive which would accord with the presumption of the girl's guilt. Having found that motive, he was satisfied that he had done his duty, and he thought very little more about the case.

It was his tenacious adhesion to conservative methods which caused him to blunder in his treatment of Colwyn's information about the missing necklace. He rarely acted on impulse. His habitual distrust of humanity was deep, and to it was wedded a wariness which was the heritage of long experience. But his obstinate conviction of Hazel Rath's guilt led him to make a false move in his effort to square the loss of the necklace with the evidence against the girl. His own poor opinion of human nature hindered him from seeing, as Colwyn had seen, any inconsequence between such widely different motives as maddened love and theft; that was one of those subtle differentiations of human psychology in which his coarse-grained temperament was at fault. It is probable that Merrington's dislike of private detectives contributed to obscure his judgment at a critical moment. He was unable to see that Colwyn, by reason of his intellect and practical capacity, stood in a class apart and alone.

In his contemplation of the case Merrington's thoughts turned to Colwyn, and he wondered in what direction the private detective's investigations into the case had progressed–if they had progressed at all–since he had seen him last. In a chastened mood, he reflected that Colwyn had not only given him a warning which was annoyingly different from other advice in being well worth following, but had acted generously in informing him of the missing necklace when he might have kept the discovery to himself, in order to score a point over Scotland Yard and place one of the Yard's most distinguished officials in an awkward position.

With a belated but unconscious recognition of an intelligence which far surpassed his own, Merrington felt that it would be worth while to have another talk with Colwyn, in the hope of finding some way out of the perplexities in which he had plunged himself by permitting Nepcote to escape.

The next interview, which was of his seeking, took place at Colwyn's rooms in the evening, after Merrington had previously arranged for it by telephone. The face of the private detective revealed neither surprise nor resentment at the sight of Merrington. He invited his guest to sit down, and then seated himself a little distance from the table, on which whisky and cigars were set out.

"Well, Mr. Colwyn, you were right and I was wrong about that fellow Nepcote," Merrington commenced, realizing that it was best to come to the point at once. "I wish now that I had followed your advice."

"If you hadn't gone to see him perhaps you wouldn't know as much as you know now," said Colwyn drily.

"That's one way of looking at it," responded Merrington with his great laugh. "Unfortunately, that interview caused Nepcote to bolt, and so far he has shown us a clean pair of heels."

"You've had no news of him?"

"Only a lot of false reports. I am convinced that he is still hiding in London, but the trouble is to get hold of him. These infernal darkened streets make it more difficult. A wanted man can walk along them at night right under the nose of the police without fear of being seen."

"Have you made any fresh discoveries about the case?"

"We have ascertained that a man who may have been Nepcote was seen near the moat-house on the night of the murder."

Colwyn nodded indifferently. The tracing of Nepcote's movements on the night of the murder was to him one of the minor points of the problem, like the first pawn move in chess—essential, but without real significance, in view of the inevitable inference of the flight.

"I have been working on the case from this end," he said.

"In what direction?"

"Trying to arrive at the beginning of the mystery. I have been endeavouring to find out something about Mrs. Heredith's earlier life. It struck me that it might throw some light on the subsequent events."

"I have been investigating along similar lines. Shall we compare notes?"

"With pleasure, but I should think that you have been able to find out more than I have been able to discover single-handed. For one thing, I have seen Lady Vaughan, the wife of Sir William Vaughan, of the War Office. She is a kind and gracious woman, taking a great interest in the hundreds of girl clerks employed at her husband's department in Whitehall. Last winter she gave a series of dances at her house in Knightsbridge, and the girls were invited in turns. Mr. Heredith was present at one of these functions."

"So much I know," said Merrington.

"Then you are probably aware that Captain Nepcote was also present that evening, and brought several other young officers with him. It was he who introduced Philip Heredith to the girl whom he afterwards married."

"I knew Nepcote was a guest at one of the dances, but it is news to me that he introduced the girl to young Heredith. Lady Vaughan did not tell us this."

"Lady Vaughan did not know. I ascertained the fact later from one of the guests who witnessed the introduction. I attach some importance to the point. Last winter Philip Heredith and Nepcote were on fairly intimate terms, working together in the same room at the War Office, and sometimes going together to the houses of mutual friends. It was evidently a case of the attraction of opposites."

"It must have been," replied Merrington emphatically. "I have had inquiries made about Nepcote, and I should not have thought he would have appealed to Mr. Heredith. There is nothing actually wrong so far as we can learn, but he had the reputation, before the war, of a fast and idle young man about town, with a weakness for women and gambling. He came into a few thousands some years ago, but soon spent it. I imagine that he has subsisted principally on credit and gambling since he squandered his money, for he is certainly not the type of man to live on his pay as an officer. As a matter of fact, he was in serious trouble with the Army authorities recently for not paying his mess bills in France. He was not brought up to the Army, and he has seen very little active service. He got his captain's commission about twelve months after the war commenced, when the War Office was handing out commissions like boxes of matches, but he managed to keep under the Whitehall umbrella until quite recently. He seems to have a bit of a pull somewhere, though I cannot find out where. Perhaps it is his charm of manner—everybody who knows him says he has a charming manner, though it wasn't apparent to me that night I interviewed him at his flat."

"Perhaps he was too afraid to exercise it on that occasion," suggested Colwyn, with a smile. "He must have thought that it was all up with him."

"Have you discovered anything about Mrs. Heredith's antecedents?" asked Merrington with an abruptness which suggested that he had little relish for the last remark.

"Very little, apart from the fact that she lived in rooms, and had no real girl friends, so far as I can ascertain. Apparently she was a girl who played a lone hand, as they say in America. The type is not uncommon in large cities. My information, such as it is, is not of the least importance one way or the other."

"I have learnt very little more than you, except that she changed her rooms pretty frequently, but always kept within an easy radius of the West End, living in dull but respectable neighbourhoods like Russell Square and Woburn Place. It was precious little time she spent there, though. The people of these places know nothing about her except that she used to go out in the morning and did not return till late at night—generally in a taxi, and alone, so far as is known. She was, apparently, one of those bachelor girls who have sprung into existence in thousands during the war—one of that distinct species who trade on their good looks and are out for a good time, but keep sufficiently on the safe side of the fence to be careful of their reputations. It's part of their stock in trade.

"Such girls contrive to go everywhere and see everything at the expense of young men with more money than brains, who have been caught by their looks. It's the Savoy for lunch, a West End restaurant for dinner, revue, late supper, and home in a taxi—with perhaps, a kiss for the lot by way of payment. The War Office was a godsend to this type of girl. It gives them jobs with nothing to do, with a kind of official standing thrown in, and the chance of meeting plenty of young officers over on leave from the front, with money to burn and hungry for pretty English faces. It is difficult to find out anything about these bachelor girls. They have no homes—only a place to sleep in—they confide in nobody, and their men friends will never give them away. Almost any woman will give away a man, but I have never yet known a man give away a woman."

"If Mrs. Heredith was that type of girl, it is possible that some early episode or forgotten flirtation in her past life is mixed up with the mystery of her death."

"You think that, do you?" asked Merrington regarding his companion attentively.

"How else can we explain Nepcote's appearance in the mystery, except on the ground that he may have murdered her for the necklace? It is important to bear in mind that Nepcote knew her in her single days. If she had a secret she has taken it to the grave with her. There remains Nepcote, who is deeply implicated in the case in some way. You may learn something from him if you can catch him and induce him to speak, though I must confess I find it difficult to reconcile the supposition that he committed the murder with the known circumstances of the case."

"There I agree with you," exclaimed Merrington. "What is Hazel Rath's position if we admit any such supposition? Nothing has yet come to light to shake the evidence which points to her as the person who murdered Mrs. Heredith."

"Does she still refuse to speak?"

"Yes. She is as obstinate as a mule and as mute as a fish. I sent a very clever woman detective down to the gaol at Lewes to try and coax her to say something, but she could get nothing out of her. She said she had no statement to make, and nothing whatever to say. She refused to go beyond that."

"She may have some strong reason for keeping silence," remarked Colwyn thoughtfully. "Arrested persons sometimes remain silent under a grave charge because they are anxious to keep certain knowledge in their possession from the police. Nepcote's implication in the case lends colour to the theory that Hazel Rath may be keeping silent for some such purpose."

"In order to shield Nepcote?"

"It is possible, though I do not think we are in a position to infer that much without further knowledge.

But now that we know that Nepcote is connected with the case I certainly think that a strong effort should be made to induce Hazel Rath to speak."

"It is not to be done," replied Merrington, with an emphatic shake of the head. "The girl is not to be drawn."

"Have you told her about the recent developments of the case?"

"About Nepcote, do you mean?"

"Yes."

"Certainly not," replied Merrington, in a tone of outraged officialism. "To give the girl that piece of information before I know what it means would place such a powerful weapon in the hands of the lawyer for the defence that I should have to withdraw the charge against Hazel Rath at the next police court proceedings if I did not arrest Nepcote in the meantime. I do not want any dramatic developments—as the idiotic newspapers call it-in my cases. There is a certain amount of public sympathy with this girl already."

"I think you stand to gain more than you lose by telling her that Nepcote is suspected."

"I prefer to arrest Nepcote first. We may get him at any moment, and then, I hope, we shall find out where we stand in this case. But what do you mean by saying that I have more to gain than lose by telling the girl about him?"

"If she is keeping silent to shield Nepcote, she is likely to reveal the truth when she knows that there is nothing more to be gained by silence. She will then begin to think of herself. In my opinion, you have now an excellent weapon in your hand to force her to speak."

"Can we go so far as to assume that she is keeping silence to shield him? Let us assume that they went to Mrs. Heredith's room together for the purpose of murder and robbery. The girl, we will suppose, fired the shot and Nepcote escaped from the window with the necklace. Is

Hazel Rath likely to reveal such a story when she knows it will not save herself?"

"Your assumptions carry you too far," returned Colwyn. "Our presumptive knowledge does not take us that distance. Till Nepcote's share in the case is explained it is useless indulging in speculations outside our premises. Let us defer inferences until we have marshalled more facts. We do not know whether more than one pair of eyes witnessed the murder of Mrs. Heredith; the theory that Hazel Rath fired the shot is merely a presumption of fact, and not an actual certainty. Much is still hidden in this case, and the question is, can Hazel Rath enlighten us? As she and Nepcote are now both implicated, it seems to me that the best inducement to get her to speak is by letting her know that you have arrested Nepcote. In my opinion, the experiment is well worth trying."

Merrington rose to his feet and paced across the room, pondering over the proposal.

"I am inclined to believe you are right," he said. "At any rate, I shall go down to Lewes to-morrow and put it to the test. I would ask you to accompany me, but it would be a little irregular."

"I shall be content to learn the result," Colwyn answered.

23

There are moments when the human brain refuses to receive communication from its peripheries, and the rapidity of thought becomes so slow that it can be measured by minutes. The stage of consciousness on which life's drama is solitarily played for every human being is too circumscribed to expand all at once for the reception of a strange and unexpected image. Such moments follow in, the wake of a great shock, like a black curtain descending on a lighted scene. When the curtain begins to rise again it is on a darkened stage, on which the objects are seen dimly at first, then clearer as returning intelligence, working slowly for the accommodation of the new setting, places the fresh impression in order with the throng of previously existing ideas.

Such a moment seemed to have come to Hazel Rath as she stood looking at Merrington, who sat in an easy chair on the other side of the table confronting her with the tangible perception of his massive presence, reinforced by the weight of an authority which, if not so perceptible, was sufficiently apparent in the stolid blue back of a policeman on duty outside the glass door, and in the barred windows of the little room to which she had been brought to receive the news which had just been conveyed to her. But she gave no sign of having heard, or, at least, understood the import of Merrington's relation. Her dark eyes wandered around the little office, and slowly returned to the face of the big man who was watching her so closely. Her look, which at first had been one of utter bewilderment, now revealed a trace of incredulity which suggested a returning power for the assimilation of ideas. But she did not speak.

"Have you nothing to say?" Merrington demanded. He had been a silent listener to many criminal confessions in his time, but in the unusual reversion of roles he was becoming unreasonably angry with the girl for not repaying his confidence with her own story.

His loud hectoring voice startled her, and seemed to accelerate the mechanism of her mind into the association of her surroundings with her position.

"Why did you bring me here to torture me?" she cried, with a sudden rush of shrill utterance which was, in its way, almost as pitiful and surprising as her previous silence. "Oh, why cannot you leave me alone?"

She threw her arms out wildly, then, as if realizing the futility of gesture, dropped them helplessly to her sides. There was something in the action which suggested a bird trying to stretch its wings in a cramped cage. Her quivering lips, tense facial muscles, and strained yet restless bearing plainly revealed an unbalanced temperament, bending beneath the weight of a burden too heavy and sustained. As an experienced police official, Merrington was well versed in the little signs which indicate the breaking point of imprisonment in those unused to it. He saw that Hazel Rath had reached a state in which kindness and consideration, but no other means, might induce her to tell all she knew.

"Come now, my good girl," he said in a gentle pleasant voice which would have astonished Caldew beyond measure if he had heard it, "nobody wants to torture you. On the contrary, I have come down from London purposely to help you."

He paused for a moment in order to allow this remark to sink into her mind and then went on:

"I do not think that you quite understood what I have been trying to tell you. I will tell you again, and I wish you to listen to me for your own sake."

He glanced at her again, and satisfied that he had now gained her attention, repeated the news he had endeavoured to tell her previously. The story, which he embellished with additional details as he went on, was a practical demonstration of the trick of conveying a false impression without telling an actual untruth. Merrington's sole aim was to convince Hazel that further silence on her part was useless, so, to that end, he used the incident of his visit to Nepcote's flat in a way to suggest that Nepcote's admission of the ownership of the revolver amounted to an admission of his own complicity in the murder.

It was an adroit narration—Merrington conceded that much to himself, not without some pride in his own creation—but he was not prepared for its immediate and overmastering effect on the girl. She listened to him with an intensity of interest which was in the strangest contrast with her former inattention and indifference. When Merrington reached the point of his revelations by telling her about the missing necklace in order to assure her that the police were aware that Nepcote had gained more from the commission of the crime than she had, she surprised him by springing to her feet, her eyes blazing with excitement.

"I knew it would be proved that I am innocent," she exclaimed. "Now I can tell you all I know."

"It is the very best course you can pursue," responded Merrington with emphasis.

"I know it—I see it now! Oh, I have been very foolish. But I—" A burst of hysterical tears choked further utterance.

Merrington waited patiently until she recovered herself. He was troubled by no qualms of gentlemanly etiquette at watching the distress of the distraught girl sobbing wildly at the little table between them. There is a wide difference between pampered beauty in distress and a female prisoner in self-abasement. So he waited composedly enough until she lifted her head and regarded him with dark wistful eyes through a glitter of tears.

"You had better tell me all," he said.

"Yes, I will tell you everything now," she quickly replied.

"Before you do so it is my duty to warn you that any statement you make may be used in evidence against you at your trial," Merrington said, with a swift resumption of his official manner. "At the same time, I think you will be acting in your own interest by keeping nothing back."

"I quite understand. But it is such a strange story that I hardly know how to begin."

"Tell me everything from the first. That will be the best way."

"That night I went up to Mrs. Heredith's room just to see her," she commenced, almost in a whisper. "My mother had told me earlier in the evening that she was alone in her room suffering from a headache. I thought I would take the opportunity while the others were at dinner to go up to her room and ask her if she wanted anything. So I left my mother's room and walked quietly down the hall to the left wing. There was nobody about. All the guests were at dinner, and the servants were busy in the kitchen and the dining-room.

"When I got upstairs I noticed that Mrs. Heredith's door was open a little, and I saw that there was no light in the room. I thought that strange until I remembered she had been suffering from a bad headache, and probably had turned off the light to rest her head. I did not knock because I thought she might be asleep. I was just going to turn away when I heard a sound like a sob within the room. I listened, and heard it again. I hardly knew what to do at first, but the thought came to me that perhaps Mrs. Heredith was worse, and needed someone. So I pushed open the door and went in.

"I know the moat-house well, so I was aware that the switch of the electric light was by the side of the fireplace, near the head of the bed, and not close to the door, as in the other rooms. To turn on the light I had to walk across the room. It was very dark, and I walked cautiously for fear of stumbling and alarming Mrs. Heredith. Twice I stopped to listen, and once I heard a sound like somebody whispering. I was dreadfully nervous because I didn't know whether I was doing right or wrong by going into Mrs. Heredith's room like that, but something seemed to urge me on.

"I must have mistaken my direction in the dark, for I couldn't find the electric switch. I kept running my hand along the wall in search of it, and while I was doing this, somebody caught me suddenly by the throat.

"All the blood in my veins seemed to turn to ice, and I screamed loudly. Immediately I screamed the hand let go, but I was too frightened to move. It was so silent in the room then, that I could hear my own heart beating, but as I stood there by the wall not daring to move I thought I heard a rustling sound by the window. My hands kept wandering over the wall behind me, trying to find the switch of the light. Then, suddenly, there was a dreadful sound–the report of a gun. It seemed to fill the room with echoes, which rolled to the window and back again. As the sound of the report died away, my fingers touched the switch and I turned on the light.

"I was standing close to the head of the bed, and the first thing I noticed was something glittering on the carpet at my feet. I stooped and picked it up. It was a revolver. Then my eyes turned to the bed, and I saw poor Mrs. Heredith. She was lying quite still with blood on her mouth. I could see that she was still alive, because her eyes looked at me. At that terrible sight I forgot everything except that she was in agony. I was bending over her wiping her mouth when I caught the sound of footsteps running up the stairs. It flashed across my mind that I must not be found there, in a room where I had no right to be, holding in my hand a revolver which had just been discharged. I switched off the light and ran out of the room. The light from the landing outside guided me to the door. I had just time to get outside and slip behind

the velvet curtains when some of the gentlemen appeared
on the landing.

"I stayed there hidden for some time, too frightened to
move, and expecting every moment to be discovered. I
could hear them moving about searching, and I thought
that somebody would draw aside the curtains and see me
hiding underneath. But nobody came near me. I heard
them go into Mrs. Heredith's room, and Mr. Musard
started talking. The corridor was silent, and it seemed to
me that I had a chance of escaping downstairs if the
staircase was clear. I crept across to the balusters, still
keeping under the cover of the curtains, and looked over.
I could see nobody in the hall downstairs. I slipped the
revolver into my dress and ran downstairs as quickly as I
could. I got to the hall without meeting anyone, and then
I knew that I was safe. But just as I turned into the
passage leading to my mother's rooms I heard the dining-
room door open. I looked back and saw Tufnell come out
and go upstairs, but he did not see me. Then I reached my
mother's rooms."

She was silent so long that Merrington thought she
had finished her story. "And what about your brooch—the
brooch which you dropped in the room. When did you get
that again?"

"I did not miss it until some time after I had returned
downstairs. I wondered at first where I had dropped it. I
then remembered the hand on my throat, which must
have unloosened the brooch and caused it to fall. I knew
it was necessary for me to recover it so it would not be
known that I had been in the room. The house was very
quiet then, and the hall was empty, though I could hear
the murmur of voices in the library, so I walked along the
hall and ran upstairs. The door of the bedroom was partly
open, and by the light within I could see that the room
was empty—except for *her*. I went into the room. The first
thing I saw was my little brooch shining on the carpet,
close by the bedside, near where I had been standing

when the hand clutched at my throat. I picked it up and ran downstairs."

"Is that the whole of your story?"

She considered for a moment. "Yes, I think that I have told you everything."

"What took you to Mrs. Heredith's room in the first place?"

"I–I wanted to see her."

"For what purpose? If you want me to help you, you had better be frank."

"I wished to see the girl whom Mr. Phil had married." She brought out the answer hesitatingly, but the colour which flooded her thin white cheeks showed that she was aware of the implication of the admission.

But Merrington was impervious to the finer feelings of the heart. He disbelieved her story from beginning to end, and was of the opinion that she was trying to hoax him with a concoction as crude as the vain imaginings of melodrama or the cinema. It was more with the intention of trapping her into a contradiction than of eliciting anything of importance that he continued his questions.

"You say that you heard a noise at the window after the shot was fired. What did you imagine it to be?"

"I was too nervous at the time to think anything about it, but since I have thought that it must have been someone getting out of the window."

"Did you hear the window being opened?"

"No; I heard nothing but the rustle, as I told you. But it may have been the wind, or my fear."

"Did you catch a glimpse of the person in the room— whoever it was–when you were caught by the throat?"

"No. I only felt the hand. It was quite dark, and I could see nothing."

"You are quite sure this happened to you? You are sure it is not imagination?"

"Oh, no, it was too terribly real."

"Did you observe anything about the revolver when you picked it up?" said Merrington after a pause.

"No, except that it was bright and shining."

"Nor when you placed it in your dress to carry it downstairs?"

"I do not know anything about fire-arms. When I got downstairs I locked it away as quickly as I could."

"So you picked up a revolver which had just been fired, without noticing whether the barrel was hot or cold. Is that what you wish me to believe?"

"I picked it up by the handle. I seem to remember now that it was warm, but I cannot be sure. I hardly knew what I was doing at the time."

Her confusion was so evident that Merrington did not think it worthwhile to pursue the point.

"If your story is true, why have you not told it before?" he said. "If you are merely the unfortunate victim of circumstances that you claim to be, why did you not announce your innocence when I was questioning you at the moat-house on the day after the murder?"

The girl hesitated perceptibly before answering the question.

"Perhaps I might have done so but for your recognition of my mother," she said at length, in a low tone.

"I fail to see how that affected your own position."

"It seemed to me then that it did," she responded in a firmer tone. "I knew that my story sounded improbable, but after learning what you knew about my mother it seemed to me that you would be even less likely to believe me, so I thought the best thing I could do was to keep silence, and trust to the truth coming to light in some other way."

The recollection of the incidents of his visit to the moat-house came thronging into Merrington's mind at this reply.

"Did you see your mother when you got downstairs on the night of the murder?" he asked.

"Not at first. She came in afterwards."

"How long afterwards?"

The girl, struck by a new note in his voice, looked at him with horror in her widened eyes.

"I understand what you mean," she replied, "but you are wrong–quite wrong. My mother knows nothing whatever about it. She did not even know that I had been upstairs. She is as innocent as I am."

"That does not carry us very far," said Merrington coldly, rising to his feet and touching a bell in front of him. "I do not believe you have told all."

24

Strong in his conviction that the story of Hazel Rath was largely the product of an hysterical imagination, Merrington dismissed it from his mind and devoted all his energies to the search for Nepcote. The task looked a difficult one, but Merrington did not despair of accomplishing it before the day came round for the adjourned hearing of the charge against the girl. He knew that it was a difficult matter for a wanted man to remain uncaptured in a civilized community for any length of time if the pursuit was determined enough, and in this instance the military police were assisting the criminal authorities.

Merrington's own plans for Nepcote's capture were based on the belief that he had not the means to get away from London unless the Heredith necklace was still in his possession. As that seemed likely enough, Nepcote's description was circulated among the pawn-brokers and jewellers, with a request that anyone offering the necklace should be detained until a policeman could be called in. He also had Nepcote's former haunts watched in case the young man endeavoured to approach any of his friends or acquaintances for a loan. Having taken these steps in the hope of starving Nepcote into surrender if he was not caught in the meantime, Merrington next directed the resources at his command to putting London through a fine-tooth comb, as he expressed it, in the effort to get hold of his man.

But it was to chance that he owed his first indication of Nepcote's movements since his disappearance. He was dictating official correspondence in his private room at Scotland Yard three days after his visit to Lewes, when a subordinate officer entered to say that a man had called who wished to see somebody in authority. It was Merrington's custom to interview callers who visited Scotland Yard on mysterious errands which they refused to disclose in the outer office. The information he received from such sources more than compensated for the occasional intrusion of criminals with grudges or bores with public grievances.

The man who followed the janitor into the room was neither the one nor the other, but a weazened white-faced Londoner, with a shrewd eye and the false, cringing smile of a small shopkeeper. He explained in the strident vernacular of the Cockney that his name was Henry Hobbs—"Enery Obbs" was his own version of it—and he kept a pawnbroker's shop in the Caledonian Road. It was his intention to have called at Scotland Yard earlier, he explained, but his arrangements had been upset by a domestic event in his own household.

"They've kep' me runnin' about ever since it happened," he added, bestowing a wink of subtle meaning upon the pretty typist who had been taking Merrington's correspondence. "The ladies—bless their 'earts—always make a fuss over a little one."

"When it is legitimate," Merrington gruffly corrected. "Miss Benson," he said, turning to the typist, who sat in a state of suspended animation over the typewriter at the word where he had left off dictating, "you can leave me for a little while and come back later. Now my man," he went on, as the door closed behind her, "I've no time to waste discussing babies. Tell me the object of your visit."

The little man stood his ground with the imperturbable assurance of the Cockney.

"We thought of calling it Victory 'Aig. Victory, because our London lads seem likely to finish off the war in double-quick time, and 'Aig after our commander, good old Duggie 'Aig, whose name is every bit good enough for *my* baby. What do *you* think? Don't get your 'air off, guv'nor," Mr. Hobbs hastily protested, in some alarm at the expression of Merrington's face, "I'm coming to it fast enough, but my head is so full of this here kiddy that I hardly know whether I'm standing on my 'ead or my 'eels. It's like this 'ere: a few days ago there was a young man come into my shop to pawn his weskit. I lent him arf-a-crown on it and he goes away. But, yesterday afternoon he comes back to pawn, a little pencil-case, on which I lends him a shilling. Now, I shouldn't be surprised if this young man wasn't the young man we was warned to look out for as likely to offer a pearl necklace."

"What makes you think so?"

"By the description. I didn't notice him much at first, but I did the second time, perhaps because I'd just been reading over the 'andbill before he come in. He looks a bit the worse for wear since it was drawn up–hadn't been shaved and seemed down on his luck–but I should say it was the same man, even to the bits of grey on the temples. Bin a bit of a dandy and a gentleman before he run to seed, I should say."

"What makes you think that?" asked Merrington, who had scant belief in the theory that gentility has a hallmark of its own.

"Not his white hands–they're nothing to go by. It was his clothes. I was a tailor in Windmill Street before I went in for pawnbroking, and I *know*. This chap's suit hadn't been 'acked out in the City or in one of those places in Cheapside where they put notices in the window to say that the foreman cutter is the only man in the street who gets twelve quid a week. They hadn't come from Crouch End, neither. They was first-class West End garments. It's the same with clothes as it is with thoroughbred hosses and women–you can always tell them, no matter how they've come down in the world. And it's like that with boots too. This chap's boots hadn't been cleaned for days, but they were *boots*, and not holes to put your feet into, like most people wear."

"You made no effort to detain him?"

"How could I? He didn't offer the necklace, or say anything about jewels, so I had no reason for stopping him. I could see 'e was as nervous as a lady the whole time he was in the shop, so before I gave him a shilling for his pencil I marked it with a cross as something to 'elp the police get on his tracks in case he is the man you're after. When he left I went to my door to see if there was a policeman in sight, but of course there wasn't. I doubt if he'd have got him, though. He was off like a shot as soon as he got the shilling—down a side street and then up another, going towards King's Cross. Here's the pencil-case he pawned. I didn't bring the weskit, but you can 'ave it if it's any good to you."

Merrington glanced carelessly at the little silver pencil-case, and after asking the pawnbroker a few questions he permitted him to depart. Then he touched his bell and sent for Detective Caldew.

Half an hour later Caldew emerged from his chief's room in possession of the pawnbroker's story, with the addition of as much authoritative counsel as the mind of Merrington could suggest for its investigation. Caldew did not relish the task of following up the slender clue. He had not been impressed by the relation of Mr. Hobbs' supposed recognition of Nepcote, although as a detective he was aware that unlikely statements were sometimes followed by important results. But the element of luck entered largely into the elucidation of chance testimony. There were some men in Scotland Yard who could turn a seeming fairy tale into a startling fact, but there were others who failed when the probabilities were stronger. Caldew accounted himself one of these unlucky ones.

But luck was with him that day. At least, it seemed so to him that evening, as he returned to Holborn after a long and trying afternoon spent in the squalid streets and slums of St Pancras and Islington. The goddess of Chance, bestowing her favours with true feminine caprice, had taken it into her wanton head, at the last moment, to accomplish for him the seemingly impossible feat of tracing the pawnbroker's marked shilling, through various dirty hands, to the pocket of the man who had pawned the pencil-case. Whether she would grant him the last favour of all, by enabling him to prove whether this man and Nepcote were identical, was a point Caldew intended to put to the proof that night.

Caldew was in high good humour with himself at such a successful day's work, and he alighted from the tram with the intention of passing a couple of hours pleasantly by treating himself to a little dinner in town before returning to Islington to complete his investigations. He wandered along from New Oxford Street to Charing Cross by way of Soho, scanning the restaurant menus as he passed with the indecisive air of a poor man unused to the privilege of paying high rates for bad food in strange surroundings.

The foreign smells and greasy messes of Old Compton Street repelled his English appetite, and he did not care to mingle with the herds of suburban dwellers who were celebrating the fact that they were alive by making uncouth merriment over three-and-sixpenny tables d'hôtes and crude Burgundy and Chianti in the cheap glitter of Wardour Street. As a disciplined husband and father, Caldew's purse did not permit of his going further West for his refection, so when he reached Charing Cross he turned his face in the direction of Fleet Street. He had almost made up his mind in favour of a small English eating-house half-way down the Strand, when he encountered Colwyn.

The private detective was wearing a worn tweed-suit and soft hat, which had the effect of making a considerable alteration in his appearance. He was about to enter the eating-house, but stopped at the sight of Caldew looking in the window, and advanced to shake hands with him.

"Thinking of dining here, Caldew?" he asked.

"Yes," replied Caldew. "It seems a quiet place."

"It certainly has that merit," responded Colwyn, glancing into the empty interior of the little restaurant. "You had better dine with me if you have nothing better to do. I should like to have a talk with you."

Caldew expressed a pleased acquiescence. He had not seen the private detective since he had taken him a copy of Merrington's notes of his interview with Hazel Rath, and he wished to know whether Colwyn had made any fresh discoveries in the Heredith case.

At their entrance, a waiter reclining against the cash desk sprang into supple life, and with a smile of prospective gratitude sped ahead up the staircase, casting backward glances of invitation like a gustatory siren enticing them to a place of bliss. He led them into a room overlooking the Thames Embankment, hung up their hats, took the wine card from the frame of the mirror over the mantelpiece, wrote down the order for the dinner, and disappeared downstairs to get the dishes.

"It seems to me that you've been here before," said Caldew.

"I always come here when I have an expedition in hand," was the response.

Caldew wondered whether his companion's expedition was connected with the Heredith mystery, but before he could frame the question the waiter returned with a bottle of wine, and shortly afterwards the dinner appeared. It was not until the meal was concluded that Colwyn broached the subject which was uppermost in his guest's thoughts by asking him if he had met with any success in his search for Nepcote.

"We are still looking for him," was Caldew's guarded reply, as he accepted a cigar from his companion's case.

"In Islington, for instance?" The light Colwyn held to his own cigar revealed the smile on his lips.

Caldew was so surprised at this shrewd guess that his match slipped from his fingers.

"What makes you think we are looking for Nepcote in Islington?" he demanded.

"I am not unacquainted with the ingenious methods of Scotland Yard," was the reply. "I can see Merrington working it out with a scale map of London to help him. He is convinced that Nepcote is still in London without a penny in his pockets. Merrington asks himself what Nepcote is likely to do in such circumstances? Borrow from his friends or attempt to cash a cheque? We will guard against that by watching his clubs and his bank. Raise funds on the necklace–if he has it? Merrington knows how to stop that by warning the pawn-brokers and jewellers. When he has done so he has the satisfaction of feeling that his man is cut off from supplies, wandering penniless in stony-hearted London, as helpless as a babe in the wood. Where will he hide? He is a West End man, knowing little of London outside of Piccadilly, so the chances are that he will not get very far, and that his wanderings will end in surrender or starvation. But Scotland Yard cannot wait for him to surrender, and Merrington, with an imagination stimulated by the necessity of finding him, decides in favour of Islington– the so-called Merry Islington of obsequious London chroniclers, though, so far as my personal observation goes, its inhabitants are merry only when in liquor. Islington is congested, Islington contains criminals, and Islington is an ideal hiding-place. Therefore, says Merrington, let us seek our man there."

"Oh, come, Mr. Colwyn, you don't put me off like that. Somebody must have told you that I was out there to-day."

"I saw you myself. As a matter of fact, I have been looking for Nepcote in that part of London–in an area between Farringdon Street and Euston."

"Why there in particular? London is a wide field."

"I have endeavoured to narrow it by considering the possibilities. The suburbs are unsafe, and so is the West End; the City affords no shelter for a fugitive. There remain the poorer congested areas, the docks, and the

East End. But that does not help us very much, because
there is still a vast field left. What narrowed it
considerably for me is my strong belief, taking all the
circumstances into consideration, that Nepcote has not
got very far from where we last saw him. What finally
determined me to select Islington as a starting point for
my search was that strange law of human gravitation
which impels a fugitive to seek a criminal quarter for
shelter. A hunted man seems to develop a keen scent for
those who, like himself, are outside the law. Islington, as
you are aware, has a large percentage of criminals in its
population. At any rate, I am looking for Nepcote in
Islington."

"Although I could pick flaws in your theory, I am
bound to say that you are right," said Caldew. "Nepcote is
hiding in Islington. At least, we think so," he cautiously
added.

"Good! How did you find out?"

Caldew gave his companion particulars of the
pawnbroker's visit to Scotland Yard that morning.

"I have been looking for Mr. Hobbs' marked shilling in
the small shops between King's Cross and Upper Street
all the afternoon," he said. "I traced it quite by accident
after I had decided to give up the attempt. One of the
uniformed men at the *Angel* happened to tell me, as a
joke, about a coffeestall keeper who had gone to him in a
fury that morning about a chance customer, who, in his
own words, had diddled him for a bob overnight. He
showed the policeman a shilling he had taken from the
man, and was under the impression that it was a bad one
because it was marked with a cross. The policeman put
the coin in his pocket and gave the man another one to
get rid of him. I obtained the shilling from him, and went
to see the coffeestall keeper. His description of the man
who passed it resembled Nepcote, and he added the
information that the customer, after changing the shilling
for a cup of coffee, had asked him where he could get a
bed. The coffeestall keeper directed him to a cheap

lodging-house near the *Angel*. I went to his lodging-house, and ascertained that a man answering to the description had slept there last night, and on leaving this morning said that he would return there for a bed to-night. I have a policeman watching the place, and I am going out there shortly to see this chap–if he comes back. Do you care to go with me?"

"I'll go with pleasure," said Colwyn, who had listened to this story with close attention.

"Then we'd better be getting along. But, I say, don't mention this to Merrington if anything goes wrong and I don't pull it off. The old man has his knife into me over this case, and my life wouldn't be worth living if Nepcote slipped through our fingers again. I want to try and surprise him, and let him see that there are other men at Scotland Yard besides himself."

"I don't think you have much to fear from Merrington," said Colwyn, laughing outright. "He is in a chastened mood at present. But you can rely on my discretion, and I hope you will get your man."

"I believe I shall," returned Caldew in a confident tone. "Shall we make a start?"

Colwyn paid the bill, and they set out through the darkened streets, upon which a light autumn fog was descending. The Kingsway underground tramway carried them to the *Angel*, where they got off. Caldew threaded his way through the unwashed population of that centre, and turned into a side street where a swarm of draggle-tailed women were chaffering for decaying greens heaped on costers' stalls in the middle of the road. He turned again into a narrower street running off this street market, and stopped when he got to the end of it. He nudged his companion, and pointed to a sign of "Good Beds," visible beneath a flare in a doorway opposite.

"That's the place," he said.

A policeman came up to them, looming out of the fog as suddenly as a spectre, and nodded to Caldew.

"Nothing doing," he briefly announced. "I've watched the place ever since, but he hasn't been in."

"All right," said Caldew. "You can leave it to me now. I shan't need you any longer. Good night!"

"Good night, and good night to you, Mr. Colwyn," the policeman responded, turning with a smile to the private detective. "I didn't recognize you at first because of the fog. I didn't know you were in this job."

"And I hope that you won't mention it, now that you do know," interposed Caldew hastily.

"Not me. I'm not one of the talking sort." The policeman nodded again in a friendly fashion, and disappeared down the side street.

The two detectives stood there, watching, screened from passing observation in the deep doorway of an empty shop. The flare which swung in the doorway opposite permitted them to take stock of everybody who entered the lodging-house in quest of a bed. By its light they could even decipher beneath the large sign of "Good Beds, Eightpence," a smaller sign which added, "Or Two Persons, a Shilling," which, by its careful wording, seemed to hint that those entranced in Love's young dream might seek the seclusion of the bowers within unhindered by awkward questions of conventional morality, and, by its triumphant vindication of the time-worn sentiment that love conquers all, tended to reassure democracy that the difference between West End hotels and Islington lodging-houses was one of price only.

But the visitors to the lodging-house that night suggested thraldom to less romantic tyrants than Cupid. Drink, disease and want were the masters of the ill-favoured men who shambled within at intervals, thrusting the price of a bed through a pigeon-hole at the entrance, receiving a dirty ticket in exchange. These transactions, and the faces of the frowzy lodgers were clearly visible to the watchers across the road, but none of the men resembled Nepcote. Shortly after ten o'clock raindrops began to fall sluggishly through the fog, and, as if that were the signal for closing, the figure of a man appeared in the lodging-house doorway and proceeded to extinguish the flare.

"We had better go over," Caldew said.

They walked across the oozing road, and he accosted the man in the doorway.

"You're closing early to-night," he observed.

The man desisted from his occupation to stare at them. He was an ill-favoured specimen of an immortal soul, with a bloated face, a pendulous stomach, and a week's growth of beard on his dirty chin. A short black pipe was thrust upside down in his mouth, and his attire consisted of a shirt open at the neck, a pair of trousers upheld by no visible support, and a pair of old slippers. Apparently satisfied from his prolonged inspection of the two visitors that they were not in search of lodgings, he replied in a surly tone:

"What the hell's that to do with you? If you let us know when you're coming we'll keep open all night–I don't think."

Caldew pushed past him without deigning to parley, and opened a door adjoining the entrance pigeon-hole. A man was seated at the table within, reckoning the night's takings by the light of a candle. It was strange to see one so near the grave counting coppers with such avid greed. His withered old face was long and yellow, and the prominent cheekbones and fallen cheeks gave it a coffinlike shape. His sunken little eyes were almost lost to view beneath bushy overhanging eyebrows, and from his shrunken mouth a single black tusk protruded upward, as though bent on reaching the tip of a long sharp nose. He started up from his accounts in fright as the door was flung open, and thrust a hand in a drawer near him, perhaps in quest of a weapon. Then he recognized Caldew, and smiled the propitiatory smile of one who had reason to fear the forces of authority.

"That chap you're after didn't turn up to-night," he mumbled.

"You're closing very early. He may come yet."

"Tain't no use if 'e do. 'E won't get in. All my reg'lars is in, and I ain't going to waste light waiting for a chance eightpence. P'r'aps you'd like to see the room where he slep' last night?"

Caldew nodded, and the lodging-house keeper, calling in the man they had seen closing the door, directed him to show the gentlemen the single room. The man lit a candle, and took the detectives upstairs to the top of the house. He opened the door of a very small and filthy room, with sloping ceiling and a broken window. A piece of dirty rag which had been hung across the window flapped noisily as the rain beat through the hole. The man held up the candle to enable the visitors to see the apartment to the greatest advantage.

"We charge tuppence more for this bedroom because it's a single doss," he said, not without a touch of pride in his tone.

"And well worth the money," remarked Caldew.

"Look here, Mr. — Funnysides, I didn't bring you up here to listen to no sarcastical remarks," retorted the man, with the sudden fury of a heavy drinker. "If you've seen enough, you'd better clear out. I want to get to bed."

"You had better behave yourself if you don't want to get into trouble," counselled Caldew.

"So you're a rozzer, are you? D–d if I didn't think so soon as I clapped eyes on you. But you've got nothing against me, so I don't care a snap of my fingers for you. You'd better hurry up."

Caldew took no further notice of him, but joined Colwyn in examining the room. They found nothing giving any indication of its last tenant. The only articles in the room were a bed, a broken chair, and a beam of wood shoved diagonally against one of the walls, which threatened to fall in on the first windy night and bury the wretched bed and its occupant. After a brief search they turned away and went downstairs. The door was immediately slammed behind them, and the turning of the lock and the rattling of a chain told them that the place was closed for the night.

Pulling up his coat collar in an effort to shield himself from the persistence of the rain, Caldew expressed his disappointment at the failure of the night's expedition in a bitter jibe at his bad luck. At first he thought he would wait a little longer on the watch, then he changed his mind as he glanced at the unpromising night, and decided that it wasn't worth while. He lived in Edgeware Road, so he shook hands with Colwyn and set out for the Underground at King's Cross.

Colwyn returned to the *Angel* to look for a taxi-cab. The fog was lifting, and crowds were emerging from the cinemas and a music-hall with the fatigued look of people who have paid in vain to be entertained. Outside the music-hall some taxi-cabs were waiting for the more opulent patrons of refined vaudeville who had been drawn within by the rare promise of an intellectual baboon, reputed to have the brains of a statesman, which shared the honours of "the top of the bill" with two charming sisters from a West End show. The drivers of the taxi-cabs said they were engaged, and uncivilly refused to drive the detective to Ludgate Circus.

A Bermondsey omnibus came plunging through the fog, scattering the filth of the road on the hurrying pleasure-goers, and stopped at the corner to add to its grievous load of damp humanity. Those already in the darkened interior sat stiffly motionless, like corpses in a mortuary wagon, as the new-comers scrambled in, scattering mud and water over them, feeling for the overhead straps. Colwyn did not attempt to enter. Even a Smithfield tram-car would be better than the interior of a 'bus on a wet night.

An ancient four-wheeler went past, crawling dejectedly homeward. The driver checked his gaunt horse at the sight of Colwyn standing on the kerb-stone, and raised an interrogative whip. He added a vocal appeal for hire based on the incredible assumption that a man must live, which he proclaimed with a whip elevated to the sodden heavens, calling on a God, invisible in the fog, to bear witness that he hadn't turned a wheel that night. The phrasing of the appeal helped Colwyn to recall that it was the same cabman who had accosted Philip Heredith and himself on the night they had motored to the moat-house.

He engaged the cab and entered the dark interior. The whip which had been uplifted in pious aspiration fell in benedictory thanks on the bare ribs of the horse. The equipage jolted over the *Angel* crossing into the squalid precincts of St. John's Street. In a short time the overpowering smell of slaughtered beasts announced the proximity of Smithfield. The cab turned down Charterhouse Street towards Farringdon Market, and a little later pulled up under the archway at Ludgate Circus.

"I leaves it to you, sir," said the cabman, in a husky whisper. His expectant palm closed rigidly on the silver coins, and his whip fell on the lean sides of his horse with a crack like a pistol shot as he wheeled round, leaving the detective standing in the road.

The fog had almost cleared away, but the unlighted streets were plunged in deep gloom, through which groups of late wayfarers passed dimly and melted vaguely, like ghosts in the darkness of eternity. As Colwyn was about to enter the corridor leading to his chambers, a man brushed past him in the doorway. There was something about the figure which struck the detective as familiar, and he walked quickly after him. By the light of the departing cab he saw his face. It was Nepcote.

25

In that swift unexpected recognition Colwyn observed that the man for whom they had been searching looked pale and worn. He stood quite still in the doorway, his breath coming and going in quick gasps.

"We have been looking for you, Captain Nepcote," Colwyn said.

"I am aware of that. I have been waiting to see you, but I could get nobody to answer my ring."

"My man is out. You had better come upstairs to my rooms."

He led the way to the lift at the end of the corridor. When they reached the rooms Colwyn switched on the electric light. Nepcote dropped wearily into a chair, and for the first time Colwyn was able to see his face clearly.

He looked very ill: there could be no doubt of that. His face was haggard and unshaven, his clothing was soiled, his attitude one of utter dejection. He crouched in the chair breathing hurriedly, with one hand pressed to his right side, as though in pain. Occasionally he coughed: a short, high-pitched cough, which made him wince.

"You had better drink this before you talk," Colwyn said.

He handed him a glass of brandy and water. Nepcote seized it eagerly and gulped it down.

"I've caught a bad chill," he said in a hoarse unnatural voice. "I couldn't carry on any longer. That's why I came to see you to-night. But I'd given up hopes. I was ringing for some time."

"You came to surrender yourself?"

"Yes; I am fed up—absolutely. I was a fool to bolt. I've had a horrible time, sleeping out of doors and in verminous lodging-houses, with the police after me at every turn. I stuck it as long as I could, but to-day I was ill, and when I saw a policeman watching the lodging-house where I meant to sleep to-night I felt that I had to give in."

"Why have you come to me instead of going to the police?"

"I thought I would get more consideration from you. I know you are searching for Mrs. Heredith's necklace. Here it is."

He drew from his pocket a small parcel wrapped in dirty tissue paper, and put it on the table. The untidy folds fell apart, exposing the missing necklace, but the diamond was missing from the antique clasp.

"The diamond is in that," he said, placing a small cardboard box beside the pearls. "I wish I had never seen the cursed thing."

"How do you come to have Mrs. Heredith's necklace?"

Nepcote hesitated before replying.

"I was terribly upset by Mrs. Heredith's death," he said at length. "I knew her before she married Phil Heredith. We were old friends."

The inconsequence of this statement convinced Colwyn that he was seeking time to frame an evasive answer.

"If that is all you have to say it is useless to prolong this interview," he coldly remarked.

"I–I am going to tell you where I got the necklace," Nepcote said, with downcast eyes. "Mrs. Heredith gave it to me."

"Why did Mrs. Heredith give you her necklace?"

"She asked me to raise some money on it for her."

"For what purpose?"

"I cannot say. Pretty women always need money. It may have been for dress, or bridge, or old debts. She brought me the necklace one day, and asked me to get some money on it. I suggested that she should apply to her husband, but she said she needed some extra money, and she did not wish him to know."

"And you complied with her request?"

"I did, after she had pressed me several times. I am always a fool where women are concerned. I promised to raise money on the necklace in London for her. That was the beginning of my troubles. But who could have foreseen? How was I to know what was going to happen?"

He sat brooding for a space with gloomy eyes, like a man repelled by the menace of events, then burst out wildly:

"I'm in a horrible position. Who will believe me? My God, what a fool I've been!"

"You are doing yourself no good by going on like this," Colwyn said. "You are keeping something back. My advice to you is to be quite frank with me and tell me everything."

"You must give me a few minutes first to think it over," responded Nepcote. He cast a doubtful glance at the detective, and relapsed into another brooding silence.

"Before you say anything more it is my duty to inform you of my own connection with the case," said Colwyn. "There has been an arrest for the murder, as no doubt you are aware, but the family are not satisfied that the right person has been arrested. You are suspected."

"Do they think that I murdered Violet? Oh, I never dreamt of this," he added, as Colwyn remained silent. "I thought that you and the police were searching for me because of the necklace. It is even worse than I thought. I will now tell you all. Perhaps you will then help me, for I am innocent."

Until that moment he had flung out his protestations with an excited impetuosity which told of a mind suffering under a grievous burden, though it was impossible to determine whether that state of feeling arose from anxiety or conscious guilt. His quietness now was in the oddest contrast. It was as though he had been sobered by his realization of the difficulty of convincing an outsider of his innocence of a foul crime in which he was deeply entangled by an appalling web of circumstance.

He began by explaining, vaguely enough, his past friendship with the murdered girl. He had first met her in London two years before. Their relations, as he depicted them, conveyed a common story of a casual acquaintance developed in the familiar atmosphere of secluded restaurants, with dances and theatres later on. His story of this phase had all the familiar elements which make up the setting of a modern sophisticated love episode, into which a man and a girl enter with their eyes open. In the masculine way, Nepcote refrained from saying anything which could hurt the dead girl's reputation, but it was his reticence and reservations which completed the story for his listener. He said that their flirtation ceased when Violet became engaged to Philip Heredith. On his own showing he then acted sensibly enough in a delicate situation, and was afterwards reluctant to accept the invitation to the moat-house. With one of his reticent evasions he slurred over his reason for changing his mind, but Colwyn guessed that it was due to the feminine disinclination to bury an old romance. Violet had probably written and asked him to come.

He conveyed to Colwyn a picture of the state of things existing at the moat-house when he arrived. It was an unconscious revelation on his part of a giddy shallow girl hastily marrying a wealthy young man for his money, quickly bored by the dull decorum of English country life, sighing for her former existence—for the gay distractions of her irresponsible London days. It seemed that in this frame of mind she welcomed Nepcote as a dear link with the past, and sought his society with a frequency which had its embarrassments. Of course there was nothing in it—Nepcote was fiercely insistent on that—she was bored, poor girl, and liked to talk about old times with her old friend, but it was awkward, devilish awkward, in a country house full of idle people and curious servants with nothing to do but use their eyes.

She had taken him aside to tell him of her little troubles. Miss Heredith did not think her good enough for Phil–she was sure she thought that. They had the vicar and old frumps in to tea, and she had to listen to their piffle. They all went to bed soon after ten–just when people were beginning to wake up in London and go out for the night. And she had to go to church on Sunday because it was expected of her, did he ever hear of such rot–and so on. It seemed that everything in her life bored her. Of course Phil worshipped her, but that didn't help her much. How could it, Nepcote asked, fixing his burning glance on his listener, when she had only married him for his coin? It appeared he had given her such counsel as his worldly experience suggested. He told her to get Phil to take her up to London now and again for a change. He advised her to stand no nonsense from anybody, pointing out to her that she was the future Lady Heredith, and, within limits, could do practically what she liked.

These intimate details of the confidences between them brought Nepcote to the vital point of his possession of the necklace. He now admitted that his former story was untrue. The actual truth was that he had needed some money badly for his gambling debts. He told Violet of his position, and asked her had she any money to lend him. She had not, and rather than ask Phil, she had, for old friendship's sake, offered him her necklace to raise money on, or to sell outright the diamond in the clasp. He accepted her offer, and went up to London on the following day to try and sell the diamond. Wendover's card had been given to him by a brother officer in France as that of a man who gave a good price for jewels without asking too many questions. But the diamond merchant had not lived up to his reputation. He had refused to look at the diamond. He had been horribly rude, treating him as though he was a pickpocket, and had practically ordered him out of his office. In fact, his whole attitude was so suspicious that Nepcote decided it would be better to leave his gambling debts owing than run the risk of trying to raise money on a married woman's jewels. He returned to the moat-house, leaving the necklace locked in his desk at his flat.

At this point Nepcote ceased speaking again, interrupted by a paroxysm of coughing, and when it passed his eyes turned towards the window, as though he were listening to the gentle patter of rain on the panes. For a space the two men sat with no sound in the room except Nepcote's laboured breathing. When he did resume he spoke with a quickened emphasis, like a man aware that he was entering upon the part of his narrative most incredible of belief.

"It happened three nights later," he said. "I was in my room writing some letters before retiring, when I heard a light and hurried tap at my door. When I opened it Violet was standing there. She stepped quickly inside. Before I could express my opinion of her reckless foolishness she burst into passionate sobs and reproaches. It was all my fault–that was the burden of her reproach between her sobs. It was some time before I could get out of her what was wrong. Then she told me that Sir Philip had asked her to wear the necklace at some dance we were to attend on the next night. It was then that I learnt that the necklace had been given to Violet by Sir Philip as a wedding present. Violet attached such little value to the gift that she had given the necklace to me, thinking it would not be missed, but she had found out her mistake that night. It was in the presence of Phil and Miss Heredith that Sir Philip had asked her to wear it. Violet tried to get out of it by saying that the pearls were dull and the necklace wanted resetting. On hearing this Miss Heredith had gone out of the room and returned with Mr. Musard, an old family friend who had arrived that day on a short visit. He is a connoisseur in jewels, and Miss Heredith asked his advice about the necklace. Musard told her that the pearls had long needed some treatment technically known as "skinning," and he offered to take the necklace to London two days later and get it done by an expert. Violet accepted the offer, and then promised Sir Philip that she would wear the necklace at the party.

"She slipped upstairs to see me as soon as she dared. She was greatly relieved when she learnt that I had not parted with the necklace, and she wanted me to go up to London and bring it back so that she could wear it to the party. I was willing to do so, but I doubted whether I would be able to get back in time. The local train service had been restricted on account of the war, and the only train I could catch back did not reach Heredith until half-past seven.

"It was Violet who hit on the plan. The big thing—the vital thing for her, she pointed out, was to have the necklace in time to give to Musard before he went to London. She said she could easily get out of going to the dance by pretending to have one of her bad headaches, and she did not wish to meet Mrs. Weyne again. Her idea was that I should pretend I had been recalled to France, delay my departure until the afternoon train to prevent suspicion, and return secretly with the necklace. She said that the afternoon train reached London at twenty-five minutes past five, which would give me thirty-five minutes to take a taxi to my flat, get the necklace, and catch the return express at six o'clock. I was to leave the train at Weydene Junction, where nobody was likely to recognize me, and walk across country to the moat-house. She expected that by the time I reached the house the others would have left for the Weynes, so the coast would be clear. I was to enter the house by a little unused door at the back of the left wing which she would leave unlocked for me, and wait at the foot of the staircase until she came down.

"I did not like this plan because of the risk, but Violet grew almost hysterical when I objected to it. She said there was no danger, and it was her only chance of safety. She believed that Phil suspected something, because he had looked at her strangely when they were talking about the necklace downstairs. I put that down to nervousness on her part, but I realized she must have the necklace, so I gave in, and said I would do as she wished. I have since bitterly regretted that I did not go openly to London and back, even at the risk of a little idle curiosity.

"I announced my recall and departure next morning at the breakfast table, and returned to London by the afternoon train. I drove to Sherryman Street, got the necklace, and returned to Victoria just in time to catch the six o'clock express. I left the train at Weydene, and walked across the fields to the moat-house. It was quite dark when I reached there. I crossed the back bridge over the moat and went to the door in the left wing, as we had arranged. To my surprise it was locked.

"I waited outside the door expecting Violet to come down. Everything was silent, so I thought the others must have started for the dance. But the time went on, and nobody came. Then I decided to creep round the, side of the wing and see if there was a light in Violet's bedroom. At that moment I heard a loud scream from somewhere upstairs, followed by a deafening report.

"I had no idea what had happened, but I knew that I must not be found there, so I slipped back the way I had come. I ran along the outside of the moat wall, making for the wood in front of the house. As I passed Violet's window I looked up, and it was in darkness. I suppose that was why I did not connect the shot or the scream with her.

"I plunged through the woods till I came to the carriage drive. From there the front of the moat-house was visible to me. I could see lights flashing, and people moving hurriedly about. After I had stood there for some time I saw a man hurrying across the moat-house bridge in my direction, so I went back into the wood and hid behind a tree. The man stopped as he walked along the carriage drive, and looked towards the tree where I was crouching. He called out 'Who is there?' I recognized his voice. It was Tufnell, the butler. I thought I was discovered, and crept into some undergrowth, but in a moment he walked on.

"I remained hidden in the undergrowth for some time—an hour or more. Once I heard footsteps crunching on the gravel-path, then all was silent again. After waiting for some time longer I decided to walk back to Weydene and return to London. But I made such a wide detour for fear of being seen that I lost my way, and it was nearly midnight when I found myself at Rainchester, on the main line, just in time to catch the last train to London.

"It was a terrible shock to me when I opened my paper the next morning and read about poor Violet's murder. I had never thought of anything like that. At first I could think of nothing but her terrible end, but then it occurred to me that my own position would be awkward if the loss of the necklace was discovered. As the papers said nothing about the necklace I concluded that it had not been missed. But I knew the police would be searching for clues, and might discover the loss at any moment. I knew it was dangerous for me to keep it in my possession, so I decided to get rid of it without delay.

"I thought at first of returning it anonymously, but I immediately abandoned that idea as too dangerous. Then I thought of dropping it into the river. It occurred to me, however, that if by any chance the police discovered that the necklace had been given to me, and I couldn't produce it if I were questioned, I should be in a worse fix still. So I tried to think of a safe hiding-place where I could lay my hands on it in case of necessity. I could think of none. Time went on, and before I had decided what to do with the thing my man came along and said it was time to catch the boat train. So in the end I put the necklace into my pocket and took it to France with me. It seemed as safe there as anywhere else for the time being.

"I was only going to the base, so I saw the London papers every day. I was very relieved when I read of the arrest of Hazel Rath for the murder. I returned to London feeling reasonably safe, though it seemed strange to me that the loss of the necklace had not been discovered.

"I thought everything was found out when you and that Scotland Yard detectives visited my flat. But Merrington seemed to have no suspicions of me, and I was just beginning to think I was finally safe when he remarked that the police knew of the missing necklace. I started, and that gave me away to you, at all events. I saw you glance at Wendover's card as it fell on the table, and I knew that you suspected me.

"After you had both left I had a bad half-hour. I could see I was in a dangerous fix. You were aware of the address of the diamond merchant to whom I had gone, and who, no doubt, would be able to identify me. I had made my own position worse by lying about the War Office telegram, as could easily be proved. There was also the possibility that the police might find out about my return to Heredith on the night of the murder. I did not then see what all these facts portended for me, though I do now. But I feared arrest for the theft of the necklace, with the alternatives of imprisonment if I kept silent, or facing a horrible scandal if I told the truth. I was not prepared for either.

"I slept at an hotel that night because I feared arrest, but next morning, early, I returned to the flat to exchange my khaki for a civilian suit. After thinking over things during the night I had come to the conclusion that I had most to fear from you, and I decided to watch you. If you did not visit Wendover's place during the day it seemed to me that I might be alarming myself needlessly. You know what happened. I bolted when I saw you emerge from the buildings, and wandered about for hours, not knowing what was best to do. When I discovered that I had no money—nothing in my pockets except that cursed necklace, which I had taken with me because I knew the flat would be searched–I decided to return to the flat for the money I had left behind in my other clothes. I was too late. When I reached Sherryman Street I saw two men watching the flat from the garden of the square opposite, and I knew I would be arrested if I went inside.

"What's the use of talking about what followed? I hadn't the ghost of a show from the start. Do you think you know anything about London? Believe me, you don't until you have been cast adrift in it with empty pockets. It's a city of vampires and stony hearts, a seething inhuman hell where you can wander till you drop and die without anyone giving a pitying glance–much less a helping hand. Even a man's guardian angel deserts him. It doesn't take a man very long to get to the gutter, to fall lower and lower until there's nothing but the Thames Embankment or the mortuary in front of him. I've had my eyes opened–I've talked to some of these poor devils in this Christian city. But what's the good of telling you this? I've been down to the gutter myself the last few days, falling each day to lower depths, tramping hungry and footsore in the midst of herds of respectable human brutes, slinking away from the eye of every policeman, pawning clothes for the price of a verminous bed, to lie awake all night knowing that I would be murdered by the vulture-faced degenerates sleeping in the same hovel, if they had caught a glimpse of the necklace.

"How many wild schemes have I planned in the night for raising money on the necklace in the morning! Once I went into a pawnshop, but the pawnbroker's eyes glittered when I spoke of pearls, and I got away as quickly as I could. I suppose there was a reward, and he was on the look out for me. One way and another I have been through hell. I feel like a man in a fever. I was drenched through yesterday, and I've had no food for twenty-four hours."

He ceased, and sat staring into vacancy as though he were again passing through the horror of his wanderings.

Then another fit of coughing seized him, prolonged and violent. When it had subsided he looked at Colwyn with bloodshot eyes.

"I feel pretty bad," he said weakly.

That fact had been apparent to the detective for some time past. Nepcote's frequent fits of coughing and a peculiar nasal intensity of utterance suggested symptoms of pneumonia. As Colwyn lifted the telephone receiver to summon a doctor, the thought occurred to him that, if the immediate problem of the disposal of Nepcote had been settled by his illness, his inability to answer questions necessitated his own return to the moat-house without delay. In any case, that course was inevitable after what he had just heard. It was only at the place where the murder had been committed that he could hope to judge between the probabilities of Nepcote's strange story and Hazel Rath's confession. It was there, unless he was very much mistaken, that the final solution of the Heredith mystery must be sought.

26

It was late afternoon when Colwyn reached Heredith the following day. The brief English summer, dying under the intolerable doom of evanescence for all things beautiful, presented the spectacle of creeping decay in a hectic flare of russet and crimson, like a withered woman striving to stave off the inevitable with pitiful dyes and rouge.

In this scene the moat-house was in perfect harmony, attuned by its own decrepitude to the general dissolution of its surroundings. Its aspect was a shuttered front of sightlessness, a brick and stone blindness to the changes of the seasons and the futility of existence. The terraced gardens had put on the death tints of autumn, but the house showed an aged indifference to the tricks of enslaved nature at the bidding of creation.

Colwyn's ring at the door was answered by Milly Saker, whose rustic stare at the sight of him was followed by an equally broad grin of recognition. She ushered him into the hall, and went in search of Miss Heredith. In a moment or two Miss Heredith appeared. She looked worn and ill, but she greeted Colwyn with a gracious smile and a firm handshake, and took him to the library. Refreshments were brought in, and while Colwyn sipped a glass of wine his hostess uttered the opening conversational commonplaces of an English lady. Had he a pleasant journey down? The roads were very good for motoring at that time of year, and the country was looking beautiful. Many people thought it was the best time for seeing the country. It was a fine autumn, but the local farmers thought the signs pointed to a hard winter. Thus she chatted, until the glass of sherry was finished. Then she lapsed into silence, with a certain expectancy in her mild glance, as though waiting for Colwyn to announce the object of his visit.

"I presume you have come down to see Phil?" she said, as Colwyn did not speak. "Unfortunately he is not at home," she went on, answering her own question in the feminine manner. "He has gone to Devon with Mr. Musard for a few days. It was my idea. I wanted him taken out of himself. He is moping terribly, and of course that is bad for him. I hope to persuade him to go with Vincent for a complete change when this—this terrible business is finished." Again her eye sought his.

"When do you expect them to return?"

"To-morrow night. Phil would not stay away longer. He has been expecting to hear from you. Can you stay till then?"

"Quite easily. In fact, I came down prepared to stop for a day or so. I have some further inquiries to make which will occupy me during that time."

"Then of course you will stay with us, Mr. Colwyn."

"You are very kind, but I do not wish to trouble you. I have engaged a room at the inn."

"It is no trouble. I will send down a man for your things. Phil would not like you to stay at the inn—neither should I." Miss Heredith rose as she spoke. "Please do whatever you wish, Mr. Colwyn. I quite understand that you have work to do, and wish to be alone."

"Thank you. Then I shall stay."

Colwyn sat for a while after she had left him, forming his plans. He was grateful to her for a tact which had not transgressed beyond the limits of unspoken thought during their brief interview, but he was more pleased with the fortuitous absence of Phil and Musard at that period of his investigations. He welcomed the opportunity of working unquestioned, because he was not prepared to disclose the statements of Nepcote and Hazel Rath to any of the inmates of the moat-house until he had tested the feasibility of both stories in the setting of the crime.

"It has all turned out very fortunately, so far," was the thought which arose in his mind. "And now—to work."

He glanced at his watch. It was nearly four o'clock. His immediate plans were a walk to Weydene, and another observation of the bedroom which Mrs. Heredith had occupied in the left wing. He decided to leave his investigation of the room until later so as to have the advantage of the waning daylight in his walk across the fields.

When he returned to the moat-house it was dark, and on the stroke of the dinner hour. That meal he took with Sir Philip and Miss Heredith in the faded state of the big dining-room—three decorous figures at a brightly lit oasis of snowy linen and silver, with the sober black of Tufnell in the background. Sir Philip greeted Colwyn with his tired smile of welcome. He seemed somewhat frailer, but quite animated as he pressed a special claret on his guest and told him, like a child telling of a promised treat, that he was dining out the following night. He insisted on giving the wonderful news in detail. He had yielded to the solicitations of an old friend—Lord Granger, the ambassador, who had just returned to Granger Park after five years' absence from England, and would take no denial. But it was Alethea's doing—she had arranged it all.

"I'm going to put back the clock of Time," he said, with a feeble chuckle. "Put the hands right back."

"I think it will do him good, don't you, Mr. Colwyn?" said Miss Heredith with a wistful smile.

"I have no doubt of it," said Colwyn with an answering smile. "A meeting with an old friend is always a good thing. Are you going with Sir Philip?"

"Oh, yes. I wouldn't go without her," said the baronet, with the helpless look of senility. "You're going, aren't you, Alethea?"

"Of course, Philip," was the gentle response.

This conversation, slight and desultory as it was, gave sufficient indication to the detective of the heavy burden Miss Heredith was bearing. The baronet could talk of nothing else during the remainder of the dinner, and when the meal was finished he begged his guest to excuse him as he wished to obtain a good night's rest to fortify him against the excitement of the coming outing. With an apologetic smile at Colwyn his sister followed him from the room.

The old butler busied himself at the sideboard as Colwyn remained seated at the table sipping his wine. His movements were so deliberate as to convey a suspicion that he was in no hurry to leave the room, and the glances he shot at Colwyn whenever he moved out of the range of his vision carried with them the additional suggestion that the detective was the unconscious cause of his slowness. More than once, after these backward glances, he opened his lips as though to speak, but did not do so. It was Colwyn who broke the silence.

"Tufnell!" he said.

"Yes, sir?" The butler deposited a dish on the sideboard and stepped quickly to the detective's chair.

"I want to ask you a question or two. It was you who found the back door of the left wing unlocked on the night of the murder, was it not?"

The butler gravely bowed, but did not speak.

"What made you try the door? Did you suspect that it was unlocked?"

"No; it was just chance that caused me to turn the handle. I'm so used to locking up the house at nights that I did it without thinking. I certainly never expected to find it unlocked, and the key in the inside of the door. That was quite a surprise to me. I have often wondered since who could have unlocked it and left the key in the door."

"You told me last time I was here that this door is usually locked and the key kept in the housekeeper's apartments. I suppose there is no doubt about that?"

"Not the least, sir. The key is hanging there now with a lot of others. Nobody ever thinks of using the door. That is why I was so astonished to find it open that night."

"If the key was hanging with a number of others it might have been taken some time before and not be missed?"

"That's just it, sir. It might not have been missed by now if I had not discovered it that night."

"What time was it when you found it?"

"Shortly before six o'clock—getting dusk, but not dark."

"You are quite sure you locked the door after finding it open?"

"There can be no doubt of that, sir. The lock was stiff to turn, and I tried the handle of the door to make sure that I had locked it properly."

"Did you return the key to the housekeeper's apartments immediately?"

"I intended to return it after dinner, but I forgot all about it in the excitement and confusion. It was still in my pocket when I informed Mr. Musard about it."

"Here is another question, Tufnell, and I want you to think well before answering it. Do you think it would have been possible for anybody to enter the house and gain the left wing unobserved while the household was at dinner that night?"

"I have asked myself that question several times since, sir—feeling a certain amount of responsibility. It would have been difficult, because the windows of the downstairs bedrooms of the left wing were all locked. There was always the chance of some of the servants seeing anybody crossing the hall on the way to the staircase, unless the—person watched and waited for an opportunity."

Colwyn nodded as though dismissing the subject, but the butler lingered. Perhaps it was his realization of the implication of his last words which gave him the courage to broach the matter which had been occupying his mind.

"Might I ask you a question, sir?" he hesitatingly commenced.

"What is it?"

"It's about the young woman who has been arrested, sir. Is there any likelihood that she will be proved innocent?"

"You must have some particular reason for asking me that question, Tufnell."

"Well, sir, I am aware that Mr. Philip thinks her innocent."

"So you told me when I was down here before, but that is not the reason for your question. You had better be frank."

"I wish to be frank, sir, but I am in a difficulty. I have learnt something which seems to have a bearing on this young woman's position, which I think you ought to know, but I have to consider my duty to the family. It was something–something I overheard."

"If it throws the slightest light on this crime it is your duty to reveal it," the detective responded gravely. "You are aware that I have been called into the case by Mr. Heredith because he is not convinced of Hazel Rath's guilt."

"Quite so, sir. For that reason I have been trying to make up my mind to confide in you. When you have heard what I have to say you will understand how hard it is. It relates to Mr. Philip, sir. Since his illness I have been worried about his health, because he is so changed that I feared he might go mad with grief. He hardly speaks a word to anybody, but sometimes I have seen him muttering to himself. The night before he went away with Mr. Musard he did not come down to dinner. Miss Heredith was going to send a servant to his room in case he had not heard the gong, but I offered to go myself. When I reached his bedroom, I heard the most awful sobbing possible to imagine. Then, through the partly open door, I heard Mr. Philip call on God Almighty to make somebody suffer as he had suffered. He mentioned a name–"

"Whose name?"

The butler looked fearfully towards the closed door, as though he suspected eavesdroppers, and then brought it out with an effort:

"Captain Nepcote, sir."

Colwyn had expected that name. Nepcote's statement on the previous night had led him to believe that Philip Heredith had suspected Nepcote's relations with his wife, but could not bring himself to disclose that when he sought assistance. It was Colwyn's experience that nothing was so rare as complete frankness from people who came to him for help. It was part of the ingrained reserve of the English mind, the sensitive dread of gossip or scandal, to keep something back at such moments. The average person was so swaddled by limitations of intelligence as to be incapable of understanding that suppressed facts were bound to come to light sooner or later if they affected the matter of the partial confidence. Of course, there was sometimes the alternative of a reticence which was intended to mislead. If that entered into the present case it was an additional complication.

"What interpretation did you place on these overheard words?" he asked the butler. "Did you suppose that they referred to the murder?"

"Well, sir–" the butler hesitated, as if at a loss to express himself. "It was not for me to draw conclusions, sir, but I could not help thinking over what I had heard. I know Mr. Philip believed the young woman to be innocent, and–Mrs. Heredith was shot with Captain Nepcote's revolver."

"I see. You had no other thought in your mind?"

"No, sir. What else could I think?"

The butler's meek tones conveyed such an inflection of surprise that Colwyn was convinced that he, at all events, had no suspicion of the secret between Mrs. Heredith and Nepcote.

"Your confidence is quite safe with me, Tufnell," the detective added after a pause. "But I cannot answer your question at present."

"Very well, sir." The butler turned to the sideboard again without further remark, and left the dining-room a few minutes later.

Colwyn went to his room shortly afterwards, and occupied himself for a couple of hours in going through his notes of the case. It was his intention to defer his visit to the bedroom in the left wing until the household had retired, so as to be free from the curious speculations and tittle-tattle of the servants.

The moat-house kept country hours, and when he had finished his writing and descended from his room he found the ground floor in darkness. A clock somewhere in the stillness chimed solemnly as he walked swiftly across the hall. Its strokes finished proclaiming the hour of eleven as he mounted the staircase of the left wing.

The loneliness of the deserted wing was like a moving shuddering thing in the desolation of the silence and the darkness. It was as though the echoing corridor and the empty rooms were whispering, with the appeal of the forgotten, for friendly human companionship and light to disperse the horror of sinister shapes and brooding shadows which lurked in the abode of murder. Colwyn entered the bedroom where Mrs. Heredith had been murdered, and by the ray of his electric torch crossed to the bedside and switched on the light.

He stood there motionless for a while, trying to picture the manner and the method of the murder. If Hazel Rath had spoken the truth, the murderer had stood where he was now standing when the girl entered the room in the darkness. Had the light from the corridor, streaming through the open door, revealed her approaching figure to him? How long had he been there in the darkness, waiting for the moment to kill the woman on the bed?

If Nepcote was the murderer he must have entered almost immediately before, because he could not have reached the moat-house until nearly half-past seven, and the shot was fired at twenty minutes to eight. How had he known that Mrs. Heredith was there alone, in the darkness? A secret assignation might have been the explanation if the time had been after, instead of before the household's departure for the evening. But even the most wanton pair of lovers would hesitate to indulge their passion while the risk of chance discovery and exposure was so great.

As he pondered over the two stories Colwyn did not attempt to shut his eyes to the fact that Hazel, on her own showing, fitted into the crime more completely than Nepcote. She had ample opportunities to slip into the room and murder the woman who had supplanted her. She had really strengthened the case against herself by the damaging admission that she had sought Mrs. Heredith's room in secret just before the crime was committed. Her explanation of the scream and the shot was so improbable as to sound incredible. It was not to be wondered that Scotland Yard preferred to believe that it was the apparition of the frantic girl, revolver in hand, which had caused her affrighted victim to utter one wild scream before the shot was fired which ended her life.

But Colwyn had never allowed himself to be swayed too much by circumstance. Appearances were not always a safe guide in the complicated tangle of human affairs. Things were forever happening which left experience wide-eyed with astonishment. The contradictions of human nature persisted in all human acts. In this moat-house mystery, the grimmest paradox of his brilliant career, Colwyn was determined not to accept the presumption of the facts until he had satisfied himself that no other interpretation was possible. His subtle mind had been challenged by a finger-post of doubt in the written evidence; a finger-post so faint as to be passed unnoticed by other eyes, but sufficiently warning to his clearer vision to cause him to pause midway in the broad track of circumstantial evidence and look around him for a concealed path.

It was the point he had mentioned to Caldew at his chambers after reading the copy of the coroner's depositions which Merrington had lent him. While perusing them he had been struck by a curious fact. The medical evidence stated that the cause of death was a small punctured wound not larger than a threepenny piece, but added the information that the hole in the gown of the dead woman was much larger, about the diameter of a half-crown. The Government pathologist had formed the opinion that the revolver must have been held very close to the body to account for the larger scorched hole. That inference was obvious, but Colwyn saw more in the two holes than that. It seemed to him that the live ring of flame caused by the close-range shot must have been extinguished by the murderer, or it would have continued to smoulder and expand in an ever-widening circle. And that thought led to another of much greater significance. The shot had been fired at close range to ensure accuracy of aim or deaden the sound of the report. But, whichever the murderer's intention, the second purpose had been achieved, intentionally or unintentionally. How had it happened, then, that the sound of the report had penetrated so loudly downstairs?

As Colwyn moved about the room, examining everything with his quick appraising eye, he noticed that the position of the bed had been changed since he last saw it. The head was a trifle askew, and nearer to the side of the wall than the foot. The difference was slight, but Colwyn could see a portion of the fireplace which had not been visible before. The bed stood almost in the centre of the room, the foot in line with the door, and the head about three or four feet from the chimney-piece. In noting this rather unusual position during his last visit, Colwyn had formed the conclusion that it had been chosen for the benefit of fresh air and light during the summer months, as the window, which looked over the terraced gardens, was nearer that end of the room.

Colwyn approached the head of the bed and bent down to examine the bedposts. A slight groove in the deep pile carpet showed clearly enough that the bed had been pushed back a few inches. The change in position was so trifling that it might have been attributed to the act of a servant in sweeping the room if a closer examination had not revealed the continuance of the groove under the bed. The inference was unmistakable: the bed, in the first instance, had been pushed much farther back on its castors, and then almost, but not quite, restored to its original position.

Had the bed been moved to gain access to the fireplace? He could see no reason for such a proceeding. It was too early in the autumn to need fires, and the room had not been occupied since the murder. In any case, the appearance of the grate showed that no fire had been lit. There was ample space to pass between the head of the bed and the fireplace, though perhaps not much room for movement. On his last visit Colwyn had looked into this space to test its possibilities of concealment. In the quickened interest of his new discovery he pushed the bed out of the way and examined it again.

The first thing that caught his eye was a scratch on the polished surface of the register grate. It looked to be of recent origin, and for that reason suggested to Colwyn's mind that the bed had been moved by somebody who wanted more room in front of the grate. For what purpose? He turned his attention to the grate itself in the hope of obtaining an answer to that question.

The grate was empty, and in the housewifely way a sheet of white paper had been laid on the bottom bars to catch occasional flakes of soot from the chimney. But there were no burnt papers or charred fragments to suggest that the grate had recently been used. Dissatisfied and perplexed, Colwyn was about to rise to his feet when it chanced that his eyes, glancing into a corner, lighted on something tiny and metallic in the crevice between the white paper and the side bars of the grate. Wondering what it was, he succeeded in getting it out with his finger and thumb. It was a percussion cap.

This discovery, strange as it was, seemed at first sight far enough removed from the circumstances of the murder, except so far as it brought the thought of lethal weapons to the imagination. But a weapon which required a percussion cap for its discharge had nothing to do with Violet Heredith's death. She had been killed by a bullet which fitted Nepcote's revolver, which was a pinfire weapon. The medical evidence had established that fact beyond the shadow of a doubt. Moreover, the percussion cap was unexploded, which seemed to make its presence in the grate even more difficult of explanation. It looked as though it had been dropped accidentally, but how came it to be there at all? The strangeness of the discovery was intensified by the knowledge that percussion caps and muzzle-loading weapons had become antiquated with the advent of the breech-loader. Who used such things nowadays?

By the prompting of that mysterious association of ideas which is called memory, Colwyn was reminded of his earlier visit to the gun-room downstairs, and Musard's statement about the famous pair of pistols in the brass-bound mahogany box, which "carried as true as a rifle up to fifty yards, but had a heavy recoil." They belonged to the period between breech-loaders and the ancient flint-locks, and were probably muzzle-loaders. With that sudden recollection, Colwyn also recalled that Musard had been unable to show him the pistols because the key of the case had been mislaid or lost.

This incident, insignificant as it had appeared at the time, seemed hardly to gain in importance when considered in conjunction with the discovery of the cap in the grate. Apart from the stimulus to memory the percussion cap had produced, there was no visible co-ordination between the two facts, because it was, apparently, quite certain that Mrs. Heredith had been shot by Nepcote's revolver, and by no other weapon. But the balance of probabilities in crime are sometimes turned by apparently irrelevant trifles which assume importance on investigation. Was it possible that the key of the pistol-case had been deliberately concealed because the box had something to hide which formed a connection between the pistols and the presence of the cap in the grate? That inference could only be tested by an examination of the case of pistols. The experiment was undoubtedly worth trying. Colwyn left the room and descended the stairs.

27

The gun-room was dark and silent as a vault. In the deep recesses the armoured phantoms of dead and gone Herediths seemed to be watching the intruder with hidden eyes behind the bars of their tilting helmets and visored salades. The light of Colwyn's electric torch fell on the shell of a mighty warrior who stood with one steel gauntlet raised as though in readiness to defend the honour of his house. His initials, "P.H.," were engraved on his giant steel breast, and his steel heels flourished a pair of fearful spurs, with rowels like daggers. Standing by this giant was a tiny suit of armour, not more than three feet in height, which might have been worn by a child.

"A strange pair," murmured Colwyn, pausing a moment to glance at them. As he turned his light in their direction his eye was caught by an inscription cut in the stone above their heads, and he drew nearer and read that the large suit had been worn by the former Philip Heredith, "A True Knight of God." The smaller suit had been made for a dwarf attached to his house, who had followed his master through the Crusades, and fought gallantly by his side.

Colwyn turned away and flashed his light along the walls in search of the case of pistols. His torch glanced over the numerous trophies adorning the walls, lances, swords, daggers, steel head-pieces, bascinets, peaked morions–relics of a departed age of chivalry, when knights quarrelled prettily for ladies, and fighting was fair and open, before civilization had enriched warfare with the Christian attributes of gas-shells, liquid fire, and high explosives. Then the light fell on that which he was seeking–a dark oblong box, with brass corners, and a brass handle closing into the lid.

Colwyn lifted the case down from the embrasure in which it was placed, and carried it to the bagatelle table. A brief examination of the lock satisfied him that it was too complicated and strong to be picked or broken. It was curiously wrought in brass, of an intricate antique pattern which would have puzzled a modern locksmith. He turned the case over, and saw that the bottom had been mortised and screwed. The screws had been deeply countersunk, and were embedded in rust, but a few were loose with age. Colwyn unscrewed these loose ones with his pocket-knife, and then set about unloosening the others.

It was a tedious task, but Colwyn lightened it with the aid of a bottle of gun oil which he found in one of the presses. Some of the screws yielded immediately to that bland influence, and came out easily. Others remained fast in the intractable way of rusty screws, but Colwyn persevered, and by dint of oiling, coaxing, and unscrewing, finally had the satisfaction of seeing all the screws lying in a little greasy brown heap on the faded green cloth of the bagatelle table. The next thing was to lever off the bottom of the lid. That was not difficult, because the glue in the mortises had long since perished. Soon the bottom was lying on the table beside the screws, and the interior of the case revealed.

The pair of weapons which Colwyn lifted from the case were horse pistols of a period when countryfolk feared to ride abroad without some such protection against highwaymen. They were superior specimens of their type. They were beautifully made, rich in design and solid in form, with ebony stocks and chased silver mountings. The long barrels were damascened, and the carved handles terminated in flat steel butts which would have cracked the pate of any highwayman if the shot missed fire. As Colwyn anticipated, the pistols were muzzle-loaders. The cock, which laid over considerably, was in the curious form of a twisted snake. When the trigger was pulled the head of the snake fell on the nipple.

Colwyn examined them carefully. He first ascertained that they were unloaded by probing them with the ramrod which was attached to each by a steel hinge. Then he ran his finger round the inside of the muzzles to ascertain whether either pistol had been recently fired. One was clean, but from the muzzle of the other he withdrew a finger grimed with gunpowder. While he was doing this his other hand came in contact with something slightly uneven in the smooth metal surface of the butt. He turned the pistol over, and noticed a small inner circle in the flat steel. It was a small hinged lid, which hid a pocket in the handle. He raised the little lid with his finger-nail, and a shower of percussion caps fell on the bagatelle table. This contrivance for holding caps was not new to Colwyn. He had seen it in other old-fashioned muzzle-loaders.

Colwyn compared the caps which had dropped on the table with the one he had found upstairs. They were the same size. He tried the solitary cap on the nipple, and found that it fitted perfectly. As he did so, he saw something resembling a thread of yellow wool caught in the twisted steel of the hammer. It was a minute fragment, so small as to be hardly noticeable. Colwyn was quite unable to determine what it was, but its presence there puzzled him considerably, and he was at a loss to understand how it had got caught in the hammer of the pistol. It struck him that the thread might be khaki, and his mind reverted to his earlier discovery of the patch of khaki in the wood outside the moat-house.

It was with the hope of finding out whether this pistol had been lately used that Colwyn turned his attention to the velvet-lined interior of the case. The inside was divided into a large compartment for the pistols and several small lidded spaces. In one of these he found some shot, a box of percussion caps, and a powder-flask half-full of common gunpowder. Another space contained implements for cleaning the pistols. The contents of the next compartment puzzled him. There were some odd lengths of knotted string, and a coil of yellow tubular fabric, about the thickness of his little finger, some inches in length. Colwyn recognized it at once. It was the wick of a tinder-lighter, then being sold by thousands by English tobacconists to replace a war-time scarcity of matches, and greatly used by cigarette smokers.

The mystery of the presence of the wick in the pistol-case was not lessened because it enabled Colwyn to identify the tiny yellow fragment adhering to the cock of the pistol. He picked up the wick and observed that one end was cut clean, but the other end was blackened and burnt. At that discovery there entered his mind the first prescient warning of the possibility of some deep plan in which the pistol and the wick played important parts. With his brain seeking for a solution of that possibility, he proceeded to examine the pieces of string.

They were odd lengths of ordinary thick twine, but they all seemed to consist of loose ends which had been knotted together. It was not until Colwyn took them out of the compartment that he noticed an amazing peculiarity about them. Each piece of knotted string was burnt at both ends.

There are some discoveries which spring into the mind with shattering swiftness. This was one of them. A revelation seemed to come to Colwyn as light from the sky at midnight, which, lays everything bare in one frightful flash.

"Is it possible?"

He felt as though these words rushed from him like a thunder-roll reverberating through the empty space around him. But his set lips had not uttered a single sound. With tingling nerves he proceeded to carry out an experiment. He first laid the wick of the tinder-lighter along the stock of the pistol, just behind the hammer. He next took up one of the lengths of string, and pulling back the hammer and the trigger of the pistol, proceeded to bind them both firmly back with the string, which he passed twice round the wick. When he had tied the string tight he lit a match and applied it to the end of the wick which was farthest from the string. His idea was to see whether this extemporized fuse would creep along the stock of the pistol, burn the string, and release the bound cock and trigger.

The wick smouldered and glowed, and began to creep towards the string, which crossed the stock of the pistol about three inches from the burning end. Colwyn took out his watch and timed its progress. In four minutes the first inch of the wick was consumed, and the spark at the end continued to creep sullenly forward in a dull red glow. In another eight minutes it reached the string, and Colwyn eagerly watched the process of the burning of the binding. The string singed, smouldered, and when nearly severed, sprang apart under the pressure of the hammer and trigger it had been holding back. The released hammer fell with full force on the cap on the nipple, and exploded it.

There, then, seemed the explanation. Mrs. Heredith had been shot with Nepcote's revolver, but it was not the deliberately deadened sound of that slight weapon which had startled the guests in the dining-room on the night of the murder. The report they had heard was made by the heavier pistol in front of him. It was a ruse of terrifying simplicity but diabolical ingenuity. The wick of the tinder-lighter was an admirable slow match, obtainable in any tobacconist's shop for a few pence, which, by means of this trick, had established a false alibi for the actual murderer by causing the report which had reached the dining-room, and sent the inmates hastening upstairs to ascertain the cause. The shot which had mortally wounded Mrs. Heredith must have been fired before.

How long before? Obviously not very long. That would have been dangerous to the murderer's plans. He had to

consider two things. There was the chance of somebody
entering the room before the false charge exploded, and
the possibility that the coldness of the body of his victim
might arouse medical suspicions. Colwyn did not think
that the criminal had avoided killing Mrs. Heredith so as
to ensure against that risk of discovery. The infliction of a
mortal wound which failed to cause immediate death not
only required a high degree of anatomical knowledge, but
left the door open to a dying confession which might have
upset the whole plan. Fate had helped the murderer to
that extent.

But the murderer owed more than that to Fate. It was
to that grim goddess he was indebted for the last
wonderful touch of actuality which lifted the whole
contrivance so superbly above the realm of artifice.
Suspicion was in the last degree unlikely in any case, but
Hazel Rath's entry and loud scream, just before the
moment fixed for the explosion, ensured complete success
by adding a natural verisimilitude which might have
deceived the very Spirit of Truth. Colwyn esteemed
himself fortunate indeed in lighting on what he believed
to be the facts. Who could have imagined a situation in
which whimsical Destiny had ironically stooped down
from her high place to dabble ignobly in a murderer's
ghastly plot?

The one point which perplexed Colwyn was the
successful concealment of the pistol on the night of the
murder. That part of the plan was as essential to the
murderer as the false report, but it seemed strange that
the pistol had not been discovered when the room was
searched. An examination of the grate upstairs might
reveal the reason.

Before leaving the gun-room Colwyn replaced one of
the pistols and restored the case as he had found it to its
original position. He carried away with him the pistol
which had been used.

When he reached the upstairs bedroom he locked the
door before proceeding to examine the fireplace. It was

immediately apparent to him that the pistol had not been placed in the grate or beneath it. Either place would have meant discovery when the room was searched. It was a careful examination of the upper portion of the grate which suggested the hiding-place. The weapon could have been safely hidden within the broad iron flange running round the open damper of the grate.

The complete revelation of this portion of the murderer's design came to Colwyn as he was passing his hand over the inner surface of this ledge. It was a register grate, and the space at the back had not been filled in. The murderer, when concealing the pistol at the top of the grate, had only to balance it carefully on the flange, with the muzzle pointing into the room, to ensure that the recoil from the report would cause the weapon to fall into the deep hole between the back of the grate and the chimney.

This additional proof of the murderer's perverted intelligence impressed Colwyn as much as the mechanism for the false report. The pistol, blindly recoiling and jumping behind the grate after the explosion of the blank charge, was almost as effectually concealed as at the bottom of the sea, and might have remained there for years without discovery. Colwyn plunged his arm into the hole, but could not reach the bottom.

But the murderer had more in his mind than the effectual concealment of the pistol, important though that was to him. The grate was an excellent choice for two other reasons. It carried the slight vapour from the tinder wick up the chimney, and the convex iron interior formed an excellent sounding board which would enhance the sound of the report. Truly the dark being who had planned it all had left nothing to chance. He had foreseen everything. His handiwork bore the stamp of unholy genius.

Who had done this thing? Who had sought, with such patient cunning, to upset those evidential principles by which blind Justice gropes her hesitating way to Truth? In concocting his masterpiece of malignant ingenuity the murderer had worked alone. His only accomplice—apart from the after-hand of Fate—was a piece of automatic mechanism which had done his bidding secretly, and would never have betrayed him. It was this ability to work alone, scheming and brooding in solitary concentration until the whole of the horrible conception had been perfected in every degree, which stamped the designer as a ferocious criminal of unusual mould, remorseless as a tiger, with a neurasthenic mind swayed by the unbridled savagery of natural impulse.

As Colwyn meditated over the murder, his original impression of the guests assembled in the dining-room downstairs in a premeditated scene set for its production came back to him with renewed force. The murderer had taken his part in that scene as one of the unconscious audience, dining and taking his share in the conversation, while his secret consciousness was strained to an intense anticipation of the false signal from his mechanical accomplice upstairs. Colwyn could picture him joining in the mockery of meaningless phrases with dry lips, his ears listening for every sound, his eyes covertly watching the crawling hands of the clock. Then, when the crack had pealed forth, he had been able to exchange suspense for action, and rush upstairs with the others, confident in the feeling that, let suspicion point where it would, it could not fall on him.

But the murderer had not foreseen the scream which preceded the shot. How had he comported himself under the shock of that cry, which was outside the region of his calculations? He had not time to reflect upon its origin, to investigate its source. He had to steel his nerves to face it because he dared not do otherwise. But its sudden effect on the nerve centres of his brain, previously strained almost to the breaking point, must have brought him to the verge of a subsequent collapse.

Colwyn believed he saw the end in sight. The presumptions, the facts, and the motive all pointed to one figure as the murderer of Violet Heredith. She had been killed from the dual motive of punishment in her own case and vengeance on a greater offender than herself. The alibi had been devised to ensure a tremendous revenge on the man by bringing him to the gallows as her supposed murderer. That part of the plan had gone astray, so the murderer, in the fanatical resolve of his latent fixed idea, had recourse to a further expedient as daring and original as the scheme which failed. The second instrument had been the means of his own undoing.

But as he reached this final stage of his reasoning, Colwyn stopped short in something like dismay. He had left a point of vital importance out of his calculations. If the murderer was the man he thought, he was downstairs in the dining-room at the time the false shot was fired. Then whose hand had clutched Hazel Rath's throat in the murdered woman's bedroom upstairs, just before the shot was fired?

Colwyn slowly paced up and down the room in the midnight silence, conning all the facts over again in the light of this overlooked incident.

28

The three dined together in the big dining-room almost in silence. Musard and Philip Heredith had not returned until after six, and their first knowledge of Colwyn's presence was by some oversight deferred until they met at the dinner table. In the awkwardness of that surprise they sat down to dine, and Musard's half-hearted efforts to start a conversation met with little response from his companions. Colwyn was preoccupied with his own thoughts, which apparently affected his appetite, for he sent away dish after dish untouched. Phil hastened the service of the meal considerably, as though he were anxious to get it over as speedily as possible in order to hear what the detective had to say. As soon as the dessert was on the table he turned to Colwyn eagerly and asked him if he had any news.

"I have many things to say," was the response.

"In that case, shall we take our coffee into the smoking-room?" suggested Musard with a slight glance at the hovering figure of the butler.

"I prefer to remain here, if you do not mind," said Colwyn.

Musard shot a puzzled look at him, which the detective met with a clear cold gaze which revealed nothing. There was another silent pause while they waited for the butler to leave the room. But Tufnell was pouring out coffee and handing cigars with the slow deliberation of a man sufficiently old to have outlived any illusions about the value of time. Philip Heredith lit a cigarette. Musard waved away the cigar-box and produced a strong black cheroot from the crocodile-skin case. Colwyn declined a cigar, and his coffee remained untasted in front of him.

"You can leave the room now, Tufnell," said Phil impatiently. "Do not return until I ring. We do not wish to be disturbed."

Tufnell bowed and left the room. As he did so Colwyn pushed back his chair and walked across to the window, where he stood for a few moments looking out. A wan young moon gleamed through the black tapestry of the avenue of trees, pointing white fingers at the house and plunging the old garden into deep pools of shadow. The trees huddled in their rows, whispering menacingly, and stretching half-stripped branches to the silent sky.

Colwyn returned to the table and confronted the two men who were awaiting him. He glanced from one to the other of their attentive faces, and said abruptly:

"Hazel Rath is innocent."

"I was certain of it." Philip Heredith's hand came down emphatically on the table in front of him as he made this declaration. "I knew it all along," he added in additional emphasis.

"This is an amazing piece of news, Mr. Colwyn," said Musard, turning earnestly to the detective. "Who, then–"

Colwyn made a detaining gesture.

"Wait," he said. "I cannot tell you that just yet." He turned to Phil, whose dark eyes were fixed on his face. "It was you who asked me to try and solve the mystery of your wife's death. It is to you that my explanation is due. Shall I speak freely in Mr. Musard's presence, or would you rather hear me alone?"

"I can go to the smoking-room," said Musard, rising as he spoke.

But Phil waved him to his seat again.

"No, no, Musard, stay where you are. There is no reason why you should not hear what Mr. Colwyn has to say. Your advice may be needed," he added as an afterthought.

"So be it," said Colwyn. "Then I had better commence by informing you that Hazel Rath has broken her silence. She has made a statement to the police, which, whilst affirming her innocence, does very little to clear up the murder. Her story, briefly, is that she went up to the left wing about half-past seven, noticed that Mrs. Heredith's room was in darkness, and went in under the impression that she might be ill and in need of assistance. She groped her way across the room to turn on the light, and she had reached the head of the bed and was feeling for the switch when a hand clutched her throat. She screamed wildly, and the hand fell away. A moment afterwards the report of a shot filled the room. She found the electric switch, and turned on the light. The first thing she saw was a revolver—Nepcote's revolver—lying at her feet near the head of the bed. Then her eyes turned to the bed, and she saw Mrs. Heredith, bleeding from the mouth and nose. While she was attempting to render her some assistance she heard footsteps on the stairs, and thought of her own safety. She switched off the light and ran out, carrying the revolver and the handkerchief with which she had been wiping the blood from the dying woman's lips. She was just in time to conceal herself behind the curtains in the corridor and escape the observation of those who were rushing upstairs. There she stayed while the rooms were searched, and was afterwards able to steal downstairs unobserved and gain the safety of her mother's apartments, where the revolver and the handkerchief were subsequently found."

"This is a remarkable story," said Musard slowly. "Do the police believe it?"

"They do not, but I have my reasons for thinking it true," responded Colwyn. "The next step in the story of how this unhappy girl became the victim of an apparently irrebuttable set of circumstances through her own silence, has to do with another person's secret visit to the moat-house on the night of the murder. That person was a man, who came to return to Mrs. Heredith the necklace which we subsequently discovered to be missing from her locked jewel-case. It is not necessary to relate how the necklace came to be in his hands. He had undertaken to return the necklace from London to enable Mrs. Heredith to produce it on the following day, and it was arranged between them that when he reached the moat-house that night he was to enter the unused door in the left wing, which was to be previously unlocked for him, and was to wait on the staircase until Mrs. Heredith was able to steal down to him and obtain the jewels. That plan was upset by Tufnell finding the door unlocked, and locking it again before his arrival. When he did arrive he found himself unable to get in."

"Stop a moment," exclaimed Musard hoarsely. "This story goes too deep for me. Who is this man? Do you know him? Has he anything to do with the murder?"

"Yes, I know him, and he has much to do with the murder," said the detective. "Shall I mention his name, Mr. Heredith?"

Phil nodded, as though he were unable to speak.

"The man is Captain Nepcote."

"Nepcote!" A swift flash of wrath came into Musard's heavy dark eyes as he uttered the name. Then, in a wider understanding of the sordid interpretation of Colwyn's story, he hesitatingly added: "I think I see. It was Nepcote's revolver. Was it he who shot Violet?"

"Before answering that question it is necessary to give Nepcote's explanation of his actions on that night. His own story is that he did not enter the house. He says that while he was waiting outside he heard a scream followed by a shot, and he then hid in the woods in front of the house until he thought it safe to return to London. He declares he is innocent of the murder."

"That is a lie!" Phil burst forth. "Who will believe him?" He stopped abruptly, and turned fiercely to Colwyn. "How do you know Nepcote said this?" he demanded.

"Because I saw him the night before I left London. He told me everything, and gave me the necklace."

"And you let him go again? Are you mad?" Phil was on his feet, shaking with excitement.

"What makes you think I let him go?" retorted Colwyn coldly. "You need not be afraid that your wife's murderer will escape justice. Nepcote is lying ill of pneumonia in a private hospital in London. He can only escape by death. But the manner in which you have received this information suggests to my mind that you have had your own suspicions of Nepcote all along, but have kept them to yourself."

"I cannot conceive that to be any business of yours," replied the young man, with a touch of hauteur.

"It seems to me that it is, in the circumstances. You came to me seeking my assistance because you believed in the innocence of Hazel Rath, but—as I am now convinced—you suppressed information which pointed to Captain Nepcote."

"I told you all that I thought necessary."

"You told me that your wife had been shot with Nepcote's revolver. Is that what you mean?"

"Yes. That was sufficient to put you on the track without taking you into my confidence about ... something which affected my honour and the honour of my family." Phil turned very pale as he uttered the last words.

"Perhaps Phil should have told you, but you must make allow—" commenced Musard. But Colwyn silenced him with an imperative glance.

"At the time you came to see me, you believed that Captain Nepcote had murdered your wife?" he said, facing Phil.

"I did."

"Do you mind telling me now on what ground you based that belief?"

"I fail to recognize your right to cross-question me," replied the young man haughtily, "but I will answer your question. It was for the reason that you have supposed. I suspected his relations with my wife. There was his revolver to prove that he had been in her room. I do not know why Hazel Rath carried it away."

"Perhaps I could enlighten you on that point. As you knew so much, it is equally certain that you knew about your wife's missing necklace, though you did not tell me of that, either. But I will not go into that now—I wish to hurry on to my conclusion. I have at least done all that you asked me to do; I have proved Hazel Rath's innocence. But I have proved more than that. Captain Nepcote is also innocent."

"I should like to hear how you arrive at that conclusion." Phil strove to utter the words calmly, but his trembling lips revealed his inward agitation.

"His story, as told to me, fits in with facts of which he could have had no knowledge. He says he found the door of the left wing locked, and we know it was locked by Tufnell more than an hour before. He states that after the shot he hid in the woods in front of the house. It was there Tufnell thought he saw somebody hiding; it was there I found a scrap of khaki adhering to a bramble at the spot indicated by Nepcote as his hiding-place. Tufnell admits that he called out in alarm when his eye fell on the crouching figure. Nepcote says that he saw Tufnell, heard his cry, and plunged deeper into the bushes for safety. Tufnell returned along the carriage drive twenty minutes afterwards with Detective Caldew and Sergeant Lumbe. Nepcote heard the crunch of their feet on the gravel as they passed. His accuracy in these details which he could not possibly have known helped me to the conclusion that the whole of his story was true."

"He had plenty of time to commit the murder, nevertheless," said Phil.

"It is useless for you to try and cling to that theory—now."

There was something in the tone in which these words were uttered which caused the young man to look swiftly at the detective from beneath furrowed brows.

"You seem to have constituted yourself the champion of this scoundrel," he said, in a changed harsh voice.

Musard glanced from one to the other with troubled eyes. There was a growing hint of menace in their conversation which his mind, deeply agitated by the strange disclosures of the evening, could only fear without fathoming.

"I do not understand you," he said simply, addressing himself to Colwyn. "If this man Nepcote did not commit the murder, who did? Was it not he who was in the bedroom when Hazel Rath went there in the dark?"

"No," said Colwyn; "it was not he."

"Who was the man, then, who clutched Hazel Rath, by the throat?" persisted Musard.

"It was no man," responded Colwyn, in a gloomy voice. "*That* was the point which baffled me for hours when I thought the whole truth was within my grasp. Again and again I sought vainly for the answer, until, in mental weariness and utter despair, I was tempted to believe that the powers of evil had combined to shield the perpetrator of this atrocious murder from justice. Then it came to me—the last horrible revelation in this hellish plot. It was the hand of the dying woman, spasmodically clutching at the empty air in her death agonies, which accidentally came in contact with Hazel Rath's throat, and loosened her brooch."

"Oh, this is too terrible," murmured Musard. His swarthy face showed an ashen tint. "What do you mean? What are you keeping back? Where does all this lead to?"

"It leads to the exposure of the trick—the trick of a false report by which the murderer sought to procure an alibi and revenge."

"What do you mean? What have you found out?" cried Phil, leaping to his feet and facing Colwyn.

As he uttered the words, a loud shot in the room overhead rang out with startling distinctness.

"I mean—that," said Colwyn quietly.

Even up to the moment of his experiment he was not quite certain. But in the one swift glance they exchanged, everything was revealed to each of them.

Before Musard could frame the question which trembled on his amazed lips, Phil spoke. His face was very white, and his dark eyes blazing:

"Yes. That is it. You have found me out." His voice, deepened to a bitter intensity, had a deliberate intonation which was almost solemn. "What did they do to me? Shall I ever forget my feelings when, unobserved by them, I caught them in the house one day, whispering and kissing? I walked straight out into the woods to be alone with my shame. My brain was on fire. When I recalled his lecherous looks and her wanton meaning glances I was tempted to destroy myself in misery and despair. Human nature–ah, God, what a beastly thing it is. I had trusted them both so utterly–I loved her so deeply. How had they repaid my trust and love? By deceiving me, under my eyes, in my own home, before my marriage was three months old.

"That night I dreamt of obscene things. I awoke with their images hovering by my bedside, looking at me with sneering eyes, mocking me with lewd gestures. 'Your honour and the honour of the Herediths–Where is it?' they kept repeating: 'Sold by the wanton you have made your wife. What is honour to the lust of the flesh? There is nothing so strong in the world.' But as I watched them the ceiling rolled away, and in the darkness of the sky a stern and implacable face appeared. And it said, 'There is one thing stronger than honour, stronger even that the lust of the flesh, and that is–Death.'

"It was the answer to a question I had been asking myself ever since I knew. I got up, and sat by the open window, to plan how I should kill them both. But I wanted the man to feel more than a swift thunderstroke of mortal agony. I wished to make him suffer as I had suffered, but at first I could see no way.

"Then it came to me in the strangest way–a light, a direction, a guide. I had been smoking as I sat there thinking–smoking cigarettes which I lit with a little automatic lighter I always used. I must have laid it down carelessly, for I was interrupted in my meditations by the sight of a thin trail of vapour ascending from the window ledge. I had failed to put the extinguisher on the lighter, and the wick had gone on burning. As I watched the red spark crawling almost imperceptibly along the yellow wick, there dawned in my mind the first glimmering of the idea of a slow match and a delayed report. Bit by bit it took form, and the means of my revenge was made clear to me. I went back to bed and slept soundly.

"I was in no hurry to act. There was much to think over, much to do, before the plan was finally perfected. I carried out experiments in the gun-room when everybody was in bed, secure in the knowledge that no report, however loud, could penetrate from those thick walls upstairs. While I was making ready I watched them both. Not a furtive glance or caress passed between them which I did not see.

"The night my aunt asked Violet about the necklace I suspected that it was no longer in her possession. I guessed that by her evasive answers and telltale face. When she left the room and went upstairs I crept after her in the shadows and followed her to the door of Nepcote's room. I listened to their conversation; I heard him promise her to return secretly to the moat-house on the following night with the necklace. My heart leapt as I listened. I believed that I had him.

"I stole away quietly without waiting to learn any more, but I stayed up till far into the night preparing my final plans. My intention was to shoot her just before dinner, and arrange for the false report to explode after he had arrived and hidden himself in the old staircase, waiting for her to go to him. Then, when the report startled everybody in the dining-room, I intended to be the first to rush upstairs, and lead the search in the direction of the old staircase. I would have had him by the throat, before he had time to get away. How would he have been able to account for his secret presence in the house when her jewels were in his pocket and her dead body upstairs, close to where he was hiding?

"I had intended to kill Violet with a small revolver which I had bought in a second-hand place at London last winter, but Nepcote's carelessness in leaving his own revolver in the gun-room gave the last finishing touch to my plan. I could scarcely believe my luck when I found it. It seemed as though he himself were playing into my hands. I hid it away, expecting that there would be inquiries, but there were none. He had forgotten all about it. It was strange, too, that Violet herself helped by telling my aunt before dinner on the night of her pretended illness that she did not wish to be disturbed by anybody. That removed a defect in my arrangements which had caused me much anxious thought. I had feared that somebody, probably a servant, might enter the room in the period between the first and second reports. It was a chance I could not afford to overlook, and I could see no way of guarding against it except by locking the door, which I did not want to do. I wanted to leave the door partly open so as to make sure of the second report penetrating to the dining-room downstairs.

"When my aunt gave me Violet's message in the library shortly before dinner I knew that the moment had arrived. The altered arrangements for an earlier dinner cost me a moment's perplexity, but no more. One cannot hurry one's own guests, and I knew it would be impossible to get dinner over as quickly as my aunt anticipated. If it were ending too quickly for my purpose it would be an easy matter to introduce a subject which would set somebody talking. That, as you know, is what actually happened.

"After my aunt left me I waited until the last possible moment before slipping upstairs. The revolver and the pistol were locked away in my own bedroom in readiness. I got them out. The pistol was completely prepared except for the cap. I had bound a twelve inch tinder-wick to the stock in order to allow for a delay of nearly fifty minutes between the lighting and the report. I knew that Nepcote expected to arrive at the moat-house by half-past seven at the latest, but I gave him a margin of a few minutes for unexpected delays. I put the pistol in my pocket, and wrapping the revolver in a silk muffler to deaden the report, went swiftly to my wife's room. I closed the door behind me as I entered.

"She was lying on the bed with her eyes closed, and did not hear me approach. That helped me. Can you understand my feelings. I was about to destroy something I loved better than life itself, but it was not she who was lying on the bed. *She* had died before–died by her own act–leaving behind her another woman whose life was a living lie, who was so corrupt and worthless as to be unfit to live. It was *that* I was going to destroy. I felt no compunction–no remorse. As I placed the muzzle of the revolver against her breast, she opened her eyes in terror, and saw me. I pulled the trigger quickly.... As I did so I heard the dinner gong sound downstairs.

"The muffled report made less noise than the clapping of a pair of hands. I knew that faint sound would not be heard downstairs. She never moved, and I thought she was dead. I bent over the fireplace, shook some caps out of the butt of the pistol, and placed one on the nipple. Then I lit a match and started my prepared fuse. It was an easy matter to place the pistol in position at the top of the grate; the difficulty of recovering it subsequently was not made manifest to me until after my illness, although my previous secret examination of the grate had convinced me that the recoil of the explosion would cause the pistol to fall to the bottom of the chimney behind the grate. When I had placed the pistol in position I turned off the electric light, and opened the window to allow the

fumes of the burning wick to escape. Then I hurried
downstairs. I was not in the room three minutes
altogether. I saw nobody on my way down; nearly
everybody had gone in to dinner, but I was in time to sit
down with the others.

"I felt quite cold and collected as I sat at the dinner
table waiting for the moment of my vengeance. I felt as
though I was under the control of some force immensely
stronger than myself which held me firm with giant
hands while the minutes slowly ebbed away. I am sure
there was nothing unusual in my behaviour. I pretended
to eat, and joined in the conversation around me.

"The report did not come at the moment I anticipated,
but I was not perturbed at the delay. My experiments had
taught me the difficulty of fixing an explosion for an exact
period. The time was in general approximately the same,
but there were reasons which caused a slight difference.
The wick always burnt at a uniform rate; the trouble was
with the string. Sometimes it was slow in catching.
Sometimes the pressure of the string partly extinguished
the wick and made combustion slower as it neared the
point of contact. Once I tied the string so tight that the
wick went out altogether just before reaching the string.
But I had taken measures to overcome these little
irregularities, and to make sure of the string catching
readily I had rubbed a little petrol on it where it crossed
the wick.

"But it was the scream before the report which upset
my calculations and almost caused me to collapse. When
that terrible cry rang out my false strength fled from me,
leaving me weak and trembling. I think I should have
betrayed myself if the report had not followed so quickly,
throwing everybody into the same state of confusion as
myself. I do not know how I managed to make my limbs
carry me upstairs with the others. I did not know what
had happened. My brain refused to act. I was conscious of
nothing except that a great wheel seemed turning inside

my head, tightening all my nerves to such taut agony that I could hardly refrain from crying aloud.

"What I said or did when I found myself in the bedroom I do not know. When I saw that everything was as I had arranged my mind began swinging like a pendulum towards my revenge, and I struggled to lead the search towards the staircase. But I was unable to move. I was like a man in a dream, encompassed by invisible obstacles. Then the wheel in my head suddenly relaxed, I felt the room and its objects slipping from me, and everything went black.

"You know about my illness. It was not until I was supposed to be recovering that the power of clear thought came back to me. There were days when my brain was numb and powerless, like that of one newly awakened from a terrible nightmare, striving to recall what had happened. Then one day the veil was drawn, and I remembered everything. My aunt was in the room, and I questioned her. She brought Musard to me, and from him I learnt the truth.

"Intuitively I realized what had happened. Hazel Rath had gone to the room for some unknown reason, had seen my wife lying there, and screamed. Then, hardly conscious of what she was doing, she picked up the revolver I had left lying by the bedside, and ran out of the room in fright. I was even able to divine a reason for her silence under the accusation of murder. She felt that nobody would believe her story, especially after the history of her mother's past was brought to light.

"As I turned over what they had told me and realized that my own secret was safe, I thought I saw the way to accomplish my revenge and save Hazel Rath. Up till then the revolver had not been identified as Nepcote's. It seemed to me that the mere disclosure of that fact was sufficient to direct attention to Nepcote and bring to light his movements on that night. But the detective who came to see me about the revolver was too foolish and obstinate to grasp the importance of my information. It was then I decided to go to you. It was daring, perhaps, but it seemed safe enough to me. I was determined to entangle Nepcote, and to free Hazel Rath.

"I told you no more than I had told to the other detective. I had powerful motives for reticence. If I had told you more you would have seen that I had an ulterior reason for directing attention to Nepcote. I had not the least fear that you would discover my secret, but the knowledge, if imparted to you, would have weakened the impression I wanted to convey by suggesting to your mind that I was actuated by hatred of Nepcote. Besides, I did not wish any living being to know of my shame. I believed that I could accomplish my revenge without its ever being known. I thought Nepcote would prefer to perish as the victim of circumstances rather than incur public opprobrium by a defence which he knew would never be believed. The actual facts against him were too strong. He could neither extenuate nor deny them. He could not explain his lying telegrams, his secret return, his presence in the moat-house, his possession of the necklace, the revolver in the bedroom where the body was. Therefore, it was only necessary to give you a starting point, because discovery was inevitable where so much was hidden. I saw to it that the loss of the necklace was discovered after your arrival. That was all you needed to know.

"I do not know what oversight of mine put you on the track of the truth. There was one, but I do not see how that could have helped you. It was not until the following afternoon in the gun-room, when Musard drew your attention to the pistol-case, that I remembered that the pistol I had used was still at the back of the fireplace upstairs, where apparently it had lain undiscovered during my illness. I had taken the precaution of concealing the key of the case, but I decided to restore the pistol that night after you left. It was more difficult to recover than I anticipated, owing to the depth of the space behind the grate. I had to push back the bedstead and use the tongs before I could reach it. I believe it would have lain there undiscovered for years. There was nothing else that I can recall, except that when I restored the pistol I saw I had left the end of one of my experimental tinder-lighter wicks lying in the case.

"But I do not wish to know how you found out, now that Nepcote has escaped. I have nothing left to live for. The doctor thinks I am recovering, but I knew that it was only the hope of revenge which kept me going. Now that is gone I have not long to live. I rejoice that it is so. But whatever had happened, I would have saved that poor girl, Hazel Rath.... I ask you to believe that ... Violet...."

He ceased, and with a weary gesture, let his head fall on his outstretched arms, as though the strength which bore him up while he told his tale deserted him when he had made manifest the truth.

His two listeners sat for some minutes in silence, each engrossed in his own thoughts. Musard stared gloomily at Phil with unseeing eyes. He was as one who had passed through unimagined horrors in a space not to be measured by time, to emerge with a fatigued sense of the black malignity of unknown gods who create the passions of humanity for their own brutal sport. His moving lips betrayed a consciousness loosened from its moorings, tossed in a turbulent sea of disaster. Then they formed the whispered words:

"The house was founded in horror and it ends in horror. So the old tradition comes true."

The next moment he turned his eyes on Colwyn with a look askance, as though he saw in him the instrument of this misery.

"Why did Hazel Rath keep silence?" he asked.

"Women have made greater sacrifices for love," Colwyn gently replied. "Hazel Rath loved him, and kept silence to shield him. She would not have spoken at all if suspicion had not fastened on Nepcote, and even when she did speak she kept something back. We may now learn later what actually passed between Hazel and Mrs. Heredith in the bedroom that night. My own opinion is that, while Hazel was bending over her, the dying woman whispered the name of her murderer."

"What are you going to do now?" Musard abruptly demanded, in sudden change of mood, speaking as though there were nobody present but their two selves.

"There is only one thing to do."

"Do you mean to let the world know the truth—to give him up to justice?"

"What other course is there open for me to pursue?" said Colwyn sadly.

"I cannot see what earthly purpose will be gained by making this horrible story public. Consider, I beg of you, all the circumstances before you inflict this dreadful sorrow and scandal on an honoured family."

"It is because I have to consider all the circumstances that I have no option."

"Is there no other way?" persisted Musard. "He is mad. He must have been possessed. You heard his story; his hallucinations were those of an insane person. He had some justification. He would never have committed this terrible deed of his own free will."

Colwyn did not reply. It was useless to point out that there is no such thing as free will in human affairs, and that if Philip Heredith had been impelled to his crime by the evil force of passions which were stronger than the restraining power of human reason, he must pay the full price demanded by humanity for the only safeguard of its supremacy.

There was the sound of an opening door and footsteps outside, and a voice called:

"Phil! Vincent! Where are you?"

"They have returned!" Musard excitedly exclaimed. "What are they to be told?"

"I cannot say," replied Colwyn, casting a sombre glance at Phil's drooping and motionless figure.

There was something new in his posture—a stark stillness which arrested his eye. He stepped quickly to his side and bent over him.

"He is dead," he said.

"Dead? My God! Impossible!"

"It is quite true. It is better so."

"Vincent!" Miss Heredith's voice sounded not far away. "She is coming here. Quick, what am I to say to her?"

"I cannot tell you," responded Colwyn, with another glance at the still form. "It was he who called me in to solve this mystery, and I have done what he asked. I will leave you to tell her what you will, but I cannot keep silence afterwards where the liberty of innocent people is involved. Justice is as impersonal as Truth herself."

"Vincent!" This time the voice sounded just outside the door.

"I must stop her—she must not come in here," said Musard, starting up.

But he was too late. The door opened, and Miss Heredith stood in the doorway.

Her startled eyes took in the agitated face of Musard, and then travelled to the drooping attitude of the figure at the table. She went quickly past the two men, and bent over her nephew. As she did so, she sobbed aloud. All the pity and pathos of a woman, all the misery and mystery of a broken heart, welled forth in her faint mournful cry.

"This will kill her," said Musard savagely.

But Colwyn felt that it would not be so. As he turned from the room, leaving the living and the dead together, he knew that when the first bitterness of the shock was over, and she was faced again with the consciousness of duty, she would call on her abiding faith to help her to wear, without flinching, the heavy grey garment of life.

THE END

Now from the Resurrected Press

The Hampstead Mystery

High Court Justice Sir Horace Fewbanks found shot dead in his Hampstead home, a butler with a criminal past, a scorned lover and a hint of scandal. These are the elements of the *Hampstead Mystery* that Detective Inspector Chippenfield of Scotland Yard must unravel with the assistance of the ambitious Detective Rolfe. But will he be able to sort out the tangled threads of this case and arrest the culprit before he is upstaged by the celebrated gentleman detective Crewe. Follow the details of this amazing case at it plays out across Hampstead, London and Scotland until it reaches a stunning conclusion in the courts of the Old Bailey.

The Hampstead Mystery
by John R. Watson & Arthur J. Rees
RPM -101

Visit www.resurrectedpress.com to order now.

Other Resurrected Press Mysteries

From the pen of R. Austin Freeman

Dr. John Thorndyke - Lecturer on Medical Jurisprudence and Forensic Medicine. Before Bones, before CSI, before Quincy, M.E – there was Dr. John Thorndyke solving the most baffling cases of Edwardian London using the latest tools of medical science. Read about his cases in:

The Eye of Osiris
John Bellingham, noted Egyptologist has vanished not once but twice in the same day. Now Dr, Thorndyke must unravel the tangled claims on his estate, solve the riddle of the missing man and find the "Eye of Osiris".

The Mystery of 31 New Inn
When Dr. Jervis is whisked away in a coach with no windows to an unknown location to treat a man in a coma from undivulged causes it is Dr. Thorndyke who must come up with the solution.

The Red Thumb Mark
The first of Dr. Thorndyke's cases finds him trying to prove the innocence of a young man accused of being a diamond thief despite the fact that his finger print was found at the scene of the crime.

John Thorndyke's Cases
More cases of medical mysteries as told by his trusted assistant Jervis, M.D. Eight stories of crime and deduction in Edwardian London.

Visit www.resurrectedpress.com

Other Resurrected Press Mysteries

Mysteries on a Train

Before the Orient Express there was:

The Rome Express by Arthur Griffiths
A man is found dead in his first class sleeping compartment on the express from Rome to Paris. Who was his murderer? The Countess? The English General? His brother the clergy man? The maid who has disappeared? Is the French justice system up to solving the crime? Read about it in The Rome Express.

The Passenger from Calais by Arthur Griffiths
Colonel Basil Annesley finds he is the only passenger on the train from Calais to Lucerne. That is until a mysterious woman shows up at the last minute to book a compartment. Who is after her? What is her secret? Is she a criminal or a victim? Read about it in The Passenger from Calais

Visit us at www.resurrectedpress.com

The Fictional Detective
by Greg Fowlkes

Who killed Ezekial O. Handler?

A beautiful dame, a hard-boiled private eye – and a dead body.

It started like any other case. When a famous writer dies in a mysterious car crash, private detective Frank Slade is called in to find answers, but all he finds is more questions. Who killed Ezekial Handler? Who is Janet Nielsen and why is she so interested in finding out? Who is leaving the neatly typed clues? And as Slade tries to find answers to these questions he starts to wonder if the ultimate answer will threaten his very existence.

Read about it in
The Fictional Detective

Visit www.thefictionaldetective.com

About Resurrected Press

A division of Intrepid Ink, LLC, Resurrected Press is dedicated to bringing high quality, vintage books back into publication. See our entire catalogue and find out more at www.ResurrectedPress.com.

About Intrepid Ink, LLC

Intrepid Ink, LLC provides full publishing services to authors of fiction and non-fiction books, eBooks and websites. From editing to formatting, from publishing to marketing, Intrepid Ink gets your creative works into the hands of the people who want to read them. Find out more at www.IntrepidInk.com.